THE CURSE OF
SOTKARI TA

MARIA A. PEREZ

This is a work of fiction. Names, characters, places, and incidents either are the product of the author's imagination or are used fictitiously. Any resemblance to actual persons, living or dead, events, or locales is entirely coincidental.

Published by: Maria A. Perez

Editor: Stephanie Hoogstad

Cover Design: Christian Bentulan

ISBN: 978-1-7351133-1-9

Ebook ISBN: 978-1-7351133-0-2

Disclosure: Sexual Content, Violence, Attempted Rape

DEDICATION

To Ms. Whelan, my ninth grade English teacher
You were so sure that you would see my stories published.
I don't know where you are these days, and it's been a while,
but this first one is for you.

BOOKS BY THIS AUTHOR

The Curse of Sotkari Ta: Book One

Broken Bonds, The Curse of Sotkari Ta: Book Two

Rising From The Curse, The Curse of Sotkari Ta: Book Three

Song of the Caged Warrior, The Curse of Sotkari Ta: Prequel

Montor's Secret Stash of Poems (A companion book to The Curse of
Sotkari Ta series)

FARTHEST LIGHT

Drawn by the gleam
Of ancient azure woods
We gather...
Sotkari skies above
Rendering lavender shadows
From our blood-red moon

Reminding us of
The age of Discipline lost
Struggles & confusion
Before the New Light
Shined upon us
From deep within

We are the keepers
Of this New Light
Sotkari Ta!
In full beam
From Path to Path
Connected forever

The past recedes
Our future unfurls
We claim our place
In destiny's bosom
Our bright New Age
As we begin, renewed

We share with you
This Wheel of the Spirit
This Perfect Circle
Of our essence
The true forever Ta
Enlightened fire

We harness the Flame
From the Power of
Our minds
The Center of it All
Sharpened by
Trancelike meditation

Our focus inverted
A luminescent prism
Shining within us
We practice this High Art
From now until always
In Continuous Evolution

Recall the names
Of our greatest Talents
Our purest Faith
Translated to achievement
Through exercise of mind & body
With rigorous self-control...

*Telepathy... **Ta!***
*Telekinesis... **Ta!***
*Healing... Blocking... **Ta!***
*Memory command... **Ta!***
*Mind control... **Ta!***
Spokes of the Wheel!

Assemble here together
In this Great Circle
Unbounded by time
Looking deep within
Seeking our best selves
Our Farthest Light

The Wheel
An unbroken ring
A Continuous Path
Never ending
A guiding ember
To a lifetime of Ta

Now, gentle breezes
Of Sotkari shores
Rustle the glowing leaves
Into a phosphorescence
Ushering us forward
To the brightest distant stars

<u>Meditation taken from the Sacred Sotkari Ta archives</u>

1

The Lostai abducted me on a typical winter evening when South Floridians complain about wearing sweaters with their flip-flops. I remember only bits and pieces of the trip from Earth to the Lostai science station. Horror—what you feel once it becomes clear. You truly are a hostage, and there's no way back home.

Muddled memories. Strapped to a bed. Medical equipment like nothing I had seen before. Strange alien beings. Paralyzing beams of light. Sleep-inducing mists.

I woke up one day alone, disconnected from any restraints, wearing a long-sleeve shirt and pants made of a lightweight material. Both had various flaps that opened, allowing access to my skin. These were nothing like the hospital gowns I was accustomed to. All my jewelry, including my wedding band, had been removed, and no personal items were in sight. A strange vinegary smell permeated the air.

Of course, my first reaction was to get out of there. Scanning the room, I saw no windows, but a doorway caught my attention. I got up from the bed to investigate. My head rattled like it was filled with marbles. Even though my brain ordered my legs to move fast, I took slow and labored steps. The doorway led to a small bathroom and shower. Back in the main room, a sliding door with no doorknobs, handles, or controls offered the only possible exit.

Why am I not more agitated?

I wanted to scream, but I only whimpered. I banged on the door maybe once or twice before the room filled again with that mist that made me sleepy.

The kidnappers found me huddled by the door when they came to escort me out of the room. One addressed me in English, and noticing the breasts, I assumed it was a female. Other than that, she looked like the other two, shorter than me with prominent brow bones disturbing an almost perfectly round, bald head.

"Mina, my name is Exzer. You may wonder how I have a knowledge of your language. We Lostai have been visiting your planet for decades, transporting people like you to our facilities, and I am a specialist in several Earth languages."

Still under the effect of the mist, my brows furrowed as I concentrated to understand her words.

"This is the science station Xixsted, which is located on the third moon of the Lostai home world. We will leave this spacecraft, traverse the docking station, and take you to the dormitory section. No breathable atmosphere exists on this moon, so all the structures here are enclosed by domes. Do not try to venture outside."

Everything spun around me. She and another alien held me by the arms as I tripped over my feet walking down the long corridor. We arrived at an area with several doors on both sides of the hallway. A sliding door opened to what looked like a small hotel room.

"These are your living quarters. Make yourself comfortable and let me know of anything you need."

It took so long to formulate even one question. My eyes blinked in slow motion.

"How long will I remain here?" I asked in a small voice.

"There is no exact predetermined timeframe. All will depend on how quickly you integrate into your new military functions."

Military functions? What the hell is she talking about?

"Tonight, you should rest. Your training will commence tomorrow. In the morning, you will hear an alarm. Soon after, I will come back here to inform you of your daily routine and familiarize you with these facilities. Do not leave these quarters without permission. It is dangerous for you, and doing so will result in punishment."

Punishment?

Without another word, she turned around and left. The door closed behind her, and I was at a loss of what to do next.

Should I accept what Exzer told me as fact and continue to follow the instructions given to me? Am I really in another galaxy? If so, what is my family going through? Am I now just another unsolved missing person case? My picture might already be displayed by the bathrooms at the Florida Turnpike rest stations.

I wept at the thought.

Should I leave the room and try to investigate? Should I fight back somehow? Could this just be a bad dream?

The sedative soon wore off, but I remained disoriented. I might have slept for only an hour or so. Hard to be sure with no clock or watch available to track time. I should have been exhausted, but nervous energy fueled my pacing the room long before the alarm buzzed. The door opened, and Exzer walked in unannounced.

"I am glad to see you are ready."

I hadn't bathed or touched the three sets of dark-colored tops and pants folded on the desk. I'm sure I didn't look "ready."

"Did you rest well?" she said, her voice monotone.

Exzer's deep-set, expressionless eyes revealed that she couldn't care less how I had slept. I dug my fingernails into the palms of my hands, attempting once again to wake up from this nightmare. Clearly, this was no dream because everything around me remained unchanged. Emboldened by her short stature, I crossed my arms and tried to look as fierce as possible.

"How can you expect me to sleep? You've brought me to this place against my will, talking crazy shit about integrating me into your military. I can barely wrap my mind around the fact that I am no longer on Earth, much less joining some alien army."

"Crazy shit? Wrap your mind?" The figures of speech confused her for a moment until she consulted her tablet-looking device. She ignored my posturing.

"Mina, it is a shame you wasted your resting hours. You have a long day ahead of you."

"Guess what? I don't intend to follow any of your instructions."

"That would be unwise and would result in punishment. Here, take this. It is your personal tablet."

Punishment...the second time she used that word.

My heartbeat accelerated, and I decided to pay attention when Exzer scrolled through the screens on the device. Surprised, I viewed information in English, including a map of the areas I could access without escort, a daily schedule, and several reference documents I was expected to study. She motioned for me to step out into the corridor. As we walked down the hall, I thought perhaps I should try a different approach.

"Exzer, I have a husband and children who need me. My youngest is only nine years old. I miss them. I need to get back. Do you have family? You must understand what I'm feeling."

No response. My palms were sweaty.

"Seriously, I'm the last person you'd want as a soldier...I'm not strong. I've never fired a weapon, and I'm too old...thirty-seven years old. I'm in no shape for military boot camp."

"While you were sedated during your trip from Earth, we injected rejuvenation hormones and steroids to address this. I have planned a physical evaluation for you this morning, but I am sure that as long as you focus on your duties, you will be fine."

Her indifference reignited my anger. I grabbed her by the shoulders, attempting to make her stop and turn to face me. Stronger than what I expected for someone only about four feet tall, she shrugged off my hold and whipped around, her thin lips pressed together. Once she spoke, her voice was an octave lower than before.

"Do not touch me."

I finally incited some emotion, but not the compassion I was hoping for. More like disgust, but it lasted only for a moment.

"You need to embrace your mission. We are battling against the Sotkari, a ruthless and warlike race who traveled to your planet long before we Lostai did. The Sotkari embedded some of your people with their Sotkari Ta genes. We believe this was their first step in a plan to take over your planet. You have a complete set of these genes. They provide you with extraordinary dormant telepathic and telekinetic abilities. We will guide you in unleashing these skills. With the help of people like you, we can stop the Sotkari from continuing their rampage. We need to keep them in check. If not, they may return to enslave your people."

My God, she's serious.

My heart beat even faster.

Could it be true?

"Listen, Exzer, you need to understand me. I'm not qualified for what you're describing. I need to find a way out of here and return to my family!"

I intended to run back to the docking station through the same corridor we had walked the night before. What was I even going to do if I made it back to the spacecraft? I had no plan and was running on pure adrenaline.

I sped the wrong way, instead heading to a large open area the size of a football field buzzing with busy people similar in appearance to Exzer. They were all dressed in military garb, some working individually at various workstations or in group discussions around conference tables. Others were studying gigantic screens and holographic images displaying star charts, maps, and documents with symbols that I couldn't comprehend. No one noticed me at first as I looked around, trying to find my way back to the docking station.

I turned around at the sounds of heavy boots. Lostai in military uniform were coming after me. I bolted across the room but soon found myself surrounded by more soldiers. Two grabbed each of my arms while the others pointed their weapons at me. My brain didn't even register their weapons. I tried to muscle my way out of the grip the two had on me but was no match for them. Exzer arrived minutes later with the same tight-lipped expression as before. She spoke in her language, and one of the soldiers held out my arm while she placed a band on my wrist. A sudden burning sensation caused me to cry out in pain. The smell of scorched skin made me nauseous.

"I am disappointed, Mina," she said. "I understand this is disconcerting, but you must accept your new mission. I was hoping we would not need to use the wristband on you. This band not only tracks your location but also can impart severe pain as punishment. Now, let us go through your first day of duty and introductions to your various stations."

I tried to rip the band off, but it adhered to my skin, so I only made the pain worse. I doubled over, holding my injured arm up with the other hand. It was shaking now, and I couldn't think of anything other than the pain searing my wrist.

"Mina, I can stop the pain, but no more outbursts and trying to run away. Agreed?" Exzer said.

My wrist was already a bloody mess. If I was going to find a way back home, the pain needed to stop. I answered, "Yes," between gritted teeth. Exzer tapped her tablet, and I let out a deep breath of relief as the burning sensation subsided.

"Follow me," she said while motioning to the two soldiers to stay with us. I trudged behind, wiping the tears away. We arrived at an office that, based on the medical beds and equipment, I guessed was the infirmary.

"The doctor will check your vitals and perform a detailed physical examination. Take your tablet. You will need it to communicate with him. I will remain in the waiting area until it is completed. Please do not cause any trouble."

I followed the doctor into the examination room and expected they would draw blood. Instead, he placed round metallic chips on my body everywhere a flap in my outfit allowed access to skin. I heard a buzz on my tablet and saw words come across the screen.

"Follow me."

We walked into another room, and immediately, it appeared as if I were outside under a greyish sky facing a running track.

"This is a holographic room. Walk to the end and return. No need to rush."

In spite of his instructions, I started off on a quick pace. Along the way, the temperature changed, slowing me down, triggering bouts of profuse sweating to violent shivering. Amazingly, at some point, the track turned into a mountainous trail. The change in altitude made me dizzy, and I struggled to breath. The trail led back down the mountain through damp caves, where it ended. I turned around and walked through it all again to return to my starting point. My guess is that the whole route took me about an hour to complete. When I was done, the doctor took me back to the examination room, where he showed me globes of different sizes made of a dark, heavy, metallic material. The first five that he gave me were impossible to lift. I was able to pick up one I estimated was close to thirty pounds. When we were done, he walked to a console and studied the data on the screen before taking me back to the waiting room.

Hopefully, I failed the test.

While Exzer and the doctor spoke, I stared at the wristband and the dry blood around it.

When she was done talking to the doctor, Exzer turned to me and said, "The doctor says that although in excellent health, you are well below the strength and stamina possessed by a typical female Lostai soldier. Regardless, you are still physically capable of reaching that fitness level through proper training. This is a science station, but we do have military squadrons here to help protect against enemy incursions. It is not appropriate for us to send you to our regular military training camps since you will need specialized Sotkari Ta training. Instead, you will integrate into one of the squadrons here and join them in their daily workout routines. You will need to work hard to reach their level. I will explain your situation to the squadron leader. I will take you to meet them now."

A part of my mind still had not accepted my surroundings and what I was hearing. I just drifted behind her. We arrived at a large room resembling a gymnasium where a group of female Lostai soldiers was working out. Exzer introduced me to the female lieutenant, who seemed bored with her explanations.

"The lieutenant does not speak your language either, but like the doctor, she can communicate using the tablet. She will take you through their workout routine, and I will be back later to escort you to your next station."

I watched as the squadron went through exercises comparable to what I would have expected for boot camp. I did my best to calm down and try to memorize their drills. They moved to another room for weapons training. Lack of sleep was catching up to me, and I struggled to stay alert.

At the end of the drill session, Exzer arrived as promised and took me through the rest of my daily schedule. In addition to military drills, I was assigned to the maintenance crew in charge of cleaning the dormitories and would need to take classes to learn Lostai language, history, and civics. Exzer explained that learning to use dormant Sotkari Ta abilities would also soon be a part of my schedule.

After the last station on my schedule, Exzer escorted me to the Commander's office. Sitting at his desk, he looked up and greeted me with a smile that didn't reach his eyes. I remained as far from him as possible, hardly any space between my back and the door closing behind me. He looked like Exzer and the others. Same round bald head, deep-set eyes, small mouth, but his brow bones protruded much more than hers. I couldn't figure out the color of his dark eyes. Two soldiers stood by his desk. My muscles tensed as they moved closer to me while Exzer stepped forward.

Still sitting, he spoke using Exzer as a translator. I hung on her every word.

"My name is Zorla, and I am in charge of this science station. We are pleased to have acquired such an invaluable specimen. You do not have full understanding of this yet, but your complete set of Sotkari Ta genes makes you quite the prize. We acquired you at a lot of risk and expense."

He stood and walked towards me with slow, deliberate steps. I shifted my weight as my heartbeat accelerated. For some reason, he gave me the creeps. A few inches taller than

Exzer but still shorter than me, he tilted his head up to meet my eyes while speaking in slow, drawn-out syllables. Contempt crept into his expression as he looked me over. I tried to inch back, but there was no space. Our eyes locked again for a moment before mine shifted towards the soldiers now on either side of me.

"However, let me be clear. I have no tolerance for any disobedience. I hear you tried to escape this morning. Therefore, you must be punished."

I glanced at my arm, preparing myself for the wristband to be activated as Exzer had done before. He barked an order in their language. My eyes darted around the room, trying to anticipate what he meant. One of the soldiers turned towards me, grabbing the ends of my shirt. I tried to get away from him, but the other pointed a weapon at me.

I whimpered as the first soldier gestured for me to lift my arms so that he could remove my shirt. My heart pounded with fear and shame for having my breasts exposed. I quickly lowered my arms to cover them. No one stopped me or was interested in ogling at them. Instead, the two soldiers immediately turned me to face away from Zorla, holding me in place.

A moment of deadly silence.

What are they going to do to me?

Three quick breaths and I had my answer. He poked me with some sort of rod that delivered an electric burn. A searing, scraping sensation on my upper back caused me to gape a silent scream of shock. I struggled trying to free myself, but the soldiers were strong and the pain was debilitating. After the first jab, he did it again, this time dragging the end down the length of my back. He increased the intensity. Now, in addition to feeling the damage on my skin, spasms of pain shook my entire body. This was far worse than the earlier wristband burn. I wailed and screamed, shaking my head.

"Stop it!" I uttered those words only once as the rest of the time, my breath came only in ragged gasps.

My body went limp, and the soldiers exerted extra effort to keep me standing. I looked over my shoulder to search for Exzer. Her eyes met mine without any sign of compassion. Zorla used the rod on me three more times, hovering it by my ear first so that I could hear the buzz and sense the vibration. He was slow about it. Each time I hoped it was over, he prodded me at a higher setting. At the end, I fell to my knees and became dizzy, surely about to pass out, but the soldiers pulled me to my feet, and someone threw my shirt back to me. Exzer continued to translate for Zorla.

"Put on your shirt. I do not want to look at your awful body any more than I have to."

My whole body trembled, and Exzer needed to help me get my shirt on as I didn't even have the strength to lift my arms. She wasn't gentle. The fabric coming in contact with the wounds on my back provided a new torment. Once I was dressed, she turned me to face Zorla. His lips curled in disgust, and he tapped the rod as he spoke his final words. Exzer translated again.

"Let this serve you as a lesson. If you do not meet expectations, I will have you punished even more severely."

My legs were jelly, so the soldiers held me up and Exzer led us to the medical office.

"The doctor will apply an ointment to avoid infection but will not attend to the pain or repair the damage. We will leave your skin scarred so that you are reminded to follow instructions going forward," said Exzer.

After my brief visit with the medic, Exzer escorted me to my dormitory and showed me how to use the equipment in the room, including the food reproducer. Still in shock, I had no words for her.

Before leaving, she said, "I suggest you make better use of

your resting hours tonight. Tomorrow, your squadron leader is expecting you to join their military drills at the appointed morning hour. Do not be late."

My dormitory included a communication system with a large video screen that could be programmed to selfie mode. Before getting into bed, I checked my back and sobbed again as the broken skin and grotesque welts came into view.

2

My second day on Xixsted was just as bad as the first. I woke up late, dressed, and ran to the gymnasium, wincing with each stride due to the wounds on my back. The lieutenant didn't even introduce me to the other eleven young female Lostai soldiers in my squadron. I received an audio message on my tablet in English that simply said, "Follow what the rest do."

No one acknowledged me as they all started to jog around the gymnasium. It was a slow, steady pace and I was grateful that I used to jog a few times a week. My body let me know when a half hour had gone by. They were just warming up. I was already winded when they increased to a full-on run. Soon, the entire squadron was way ahead of me, halfway across the gym. The lieutenant pressed her lips together and, shaking her head, activated my wristband. Although not as strong as the previous day, the shock was enough to bring tears to my eyes. I stumbled, and another, stronger shock made me nauseous. The run lasted about an hour, and the squadron never slowed their pace until the last few minutes of cool down. Not being used to this much continuous cardio, my legs cramped up, and I gasped for air.

The squadron moved on to a kind of plyometric workout including jumping squats and a type of push up that involved clapping behind the back. Of course, I couldn't do even one of those. They also did heavy weight training and planks lasting for much longer than the two-minute ones I used to do. The squadron leader continued to deliver punishment via the wristband. Blood smudges reappeared around my wrist, and I couldn't stop crying. Some of the soldiers snickered, and I glared at them, a slow rage seething throughout my body. I grabbed my tablet, walked over to the lieutenant, and spoke words in English that were translated into Lostai. The other soldiers froze in expectation while the lieutenant eyed me with suspicion. The arm with the wristband trembled as I spoke.

"As leader of this squadron, you are responsible for our training, correct?"

She spoke into her tablet and tapped the screen. Audio emitted on mine in English.

"Yes, of course."

"Am I a part of this squadron?"

"Unfortunately, yes."

"Is that any of our fault?" I gestured, pointing to her, myself, and the rest of the group.

"No."

"So, regardless of whether we like it or not, you are responsible to make me into a Lostai soldier, yes?"

"Yes."

"I have never done this before. Give me a chance, or we will both fail miserably."

"Exzer said you need plenty of physical training to catch up to our military standards."

"Yes, but I'm not a soldier. I won't be able to do any training at all if you keep hurting me. I promise to do my best, but it's going to take some time before I reach that level."

She rolled her eyes. "I will take this into consideration, but if I think you are slacking, I will inform Zorla that you need an attitude adjustment."

I walked back to my spot, and the workout continued. I tried to execute every single exercise, even if only one or two repetitions. She didn't activate the wristband again.

Hand-to-hand combat drills followed the workouts. I was even more ill-prepared for those. I had taken a few months of martial arts training with my younger son, so I knew how to parry, block, and basic front kick, but these Lostai females were already full-contact sparring at an advanced level. There was no safety gear, and I was paired with a particularly aggressive partner. The lieutenant barked some instructions in Lostai that I didn't have a chance to translate. My partner wasted no time kicking me on my left side, and I doubled over in pain. She conceded me no recovery time and landed another blow to my head. I went down, and when I opened my eyes, I was on an infirmary cot with my tablet on my stomach. A notification tone let me know I had a message.

I tapped the screen and heard in English, "You were treated for a broken rib and concussion. The injuries have been repaired. You should proceed to your Academics session."

I walked out of the infirmary still disoriented and checked the schematics on my tablet to figure out how to get to my classes. I remembered it was a lab room with consoles where people took courses through individualized video sessions, but I had forgotten how to get there. My vision was a little blurry, and it was hard to concentrate. I walked around slowly trying to gather my bearings but soon found myself in an unfamiliar area. An alarm went off, and the wristband activated, causing me to shout out in pain. I turned to see several Lostai soldiers coming for me.

OK, I'm not going to run because they'll think I did something wrong.

I began speaking an explanation into my tablet when they grabbed me and started dragging me off. My tablet fell to the floor, and one of them picked it up without looking at it. I screamed, asking for Exzer the whole way to Zorla's office. She was not there when I arrived. Zorla greeted me with the same hypocritical smile, sending shivers down my spine. I knew what was coming next. Without Exzer there for translation, he didn't even try to communicate to me before he used the rod on my back again. I later learned the word for the rod in Lostai is *zirem*.

At the end of that day, I was sure that I wouldn't survive the week. Until then, I never had a stitch on my body, never had any broken bones. My only prior hospital stays had been for giving birth and one time in the ER for a bad urinary tract infection. In the weeks and months that followed, I became a zombie to survive. Prayer and a certain stubbornness helped me deal with the pain and fear. For many weeks, I was a punching bag for my sparring partners, but at least the lieutenant minimized the use of the wristband.

Zorla continued to be my nemesis, punishing me for anything he construed as insubordination, such as failing an exam or missing a step in the dorm cleaning protocol. Within the first few weeks on the Lostai station, my back was completely scarred, my wrist badly burned. I suffered more cracked ribs and concussions, black eyes, a broken arm, but finally I became familiar with the station and my schedule. Their medical technology quickly repaired the fractures and injuries, so there was no downtime for recovery.

Exzer was right about the hormones and steroids they had

pumped into me. In a matter of days, I built up my stamina, and once I learned the routine, I was able to keep up with the other soldiers with sprints, longer runs, and workouts. Using my tablet, I kept track of Earth time. After three months or so, my leg and arm muscles were defined. I never imagined I would ever have such a flat belly and hard abs.

One Lostai day equated about twenty-one Earth hours. A normal workday consisted of the equivalent of fifteen Earth hours. Every four hours, we were allowed a one-hour break to either nap or eat, and at the end of each workday, six hours were allotted for sleep time. At least the grueling daily routine left me exhausted, so at night, I usually passed out into deep sleep. After twelve Lostai days, everyone on the station took a full day of rest. During this time, everyone was allowed to mingle informally, meet with friends, and take advantage of various entertainment and relaxation options.

On rest days, I kept to myself. I had no friends, the rest of the squadron wanted nothing to do with me, and I had no desire to hang out with my kidnappers, either. Although I had submitted to my duties, I was not resigned to my fate. In my prayers, I asked for strength and guile, using my free time to gain knowledge that could improve any opportunities for escape.

I viewed on my tablet local telecasts from the Lostai home world, and this helped me improve my Lostai language skills and understand the structure of their government. These people were currently governing several planets, many with natives of other species subjugated to Lostai rule. According to the news, everyone was living in harmony. I wondered if it was true.

A variety of instructional courses were available via the tablet and academics lab. I focused on subjects related to astronautics and piloting spacecraft. One of the recreation options available on the station were simulated flights on shuttles and other spacecraft where I could practice take off, landing, and other piloting basics. When I was not in my room, at the academics lab, or practicing piloting spacecraft, I walked around the areas I had access to, trying to memorize every corridor, every station, and every possible exit. These activities occupied my mind, but sometimes it was hard not to feel hopeless knowing the wristband was programmed to alert security any time I ventured to an unauthorized area.

My heart ached as I thought about my family. I was alone the evening the Lostai took me. What was the last thing I said to my husband and younger son, Bobby, as they left to their martial arts training that night? I'm sure it was a quick "I love you" and kisses. To my older son, I typically would say "God bless" whenever he went off on his own to meet with his friends. I last saw my daughter when I dropped her off at school in the morning. Her friend's mom had given her a ride to their after-school science club meeting. My last words to her were "See you later." Now all these quick phrases held much more significance. Thankfully, that day had been an easy one with no disagreements or arguments or harsh words. That would have been tough to live with now.

When I needed a break from trying to absorb information, I composed short letters to my husband. It helped me feel like I was still in touch with my family. After completing the letters, I promptly deleted them for fear that Lostai security might intercept them.

Dear Josh,

How are you and the kids doing? How's Coco? I miss you all so much. I'm ok...actually, physically, in the best shape of my life. Unfortunately, it has taken blood, sweat, and tears...literally. I'm so scared and sad. I can't believe what has happened to me. I was kidnapped because supposedly I have alien DNA. Don't roll your eyes! It's true. Remember how you hated all the Star Trek reruns I used to watch? They certainly didn't prepare me for this. I've been praying that I would wake up one day and realize this was all a nightmare, but unfortunately, that's not the case. I have the scars to prove it.

It's been several months now. What is the theory regarding my disappearance? Perhaps that I was murdered and dumped somewhere? Are the police looking for me? I hope these kidnappers left some evidence behind. Please don't give up on me. I'm devoting all my free time to figuring out how I can get out of here. Believe it or not, I'm learning on my own how to pilot a spacecraft. I hope I will soon have a chance to escape this place and return home. It's the only thing that keeps me going.

I miss you all so much, and I think if I focus hard enough, you'll sense that I'm writing this message. Take care of yourself and the kids.

Love you, Mina

Afterwards, I cried myself to sleep.

One morning, I received a message on my tablet that I should skip my normal boot camp session because someone would be meeting with me in my room. By then, I possessed a good understanding of the Lostai language, although some words were still difficult for me to enunciate properly. At the scheduled time, my door buzzed. I approved, and in walked my visitor. Quite a contrast from the short and bald Lostai, she stood a majestic six feet tall. Creases in her slate-colored skin reflected her old age, but she showed no signs of feebleness. The short-sleeved garment that grazed her knees displayed strong, toned arms and legs. The whites of her eyes were barely visible, and I couldn't discern pupils within the vivid blue irises. Thick, wavy, cornflower-blue hair crowned her head. Other than the appearance of her eyes and skin, she could have passed for human.

"Greetings. My name is Kaya. I am here for your training."

Her lips didn't move. I didn't hear her voice out loud. Instead, I sensed the words in Lostai, her voice and tone in my mind. She communicated using perfect Lostai grammar, but there was definitely an accent, including a strong inflection on words starting with vowel sounds. Clearly, Lostai was not her native language.

The word "training" worried me. By then, I had mastered my schedule and duties. My squadron leader and Zorla were not bothering me much anymore.

Will this be the beginning of another round of punishments for not meeting expectations?

She extended her arm in greeting, grasping my wrist instead of my hand, and pressed down with her thumb. The minute we made physical contact, a slight electric shock vibrated through my body, followed by an overwhelming feeling of well-being. She cocked her head in surprise, followed by a brief smile.

"Hello, my name is Mina. What kind of training?" I replied out loud in Lostai, since that was the language she had used.

"I am a Sotkari Ta, meaning one of the few remaining fully evolved Sotkari. I have been tasked with helping you learn how to use your dormant evolved Sotkari capabilities."

My chest tightened. Hadn't Exzer described the Sotkari as a warlike and ruthless people?

"Really?" I said, trying to sound curious and mask my concern. "I have heard the Lostai consider your people a menace to their society...and yet they have you working with them?"

Her expression was a mixture of annoyance and sarcasm, but only for a second.

"You have been grossly misinformed. We pose no threat to the Lostai, but let us focus on your training. I see why they are so excited with having acquired you. Evolved Sotkari can recognize each other by the touch of our hands. You are extremely receptive to telepathic communication and connection. This signals your high potential for other abilities."

Her reply put me at ease again. My curiosity about these supposed abilities took over.

"I had no idea I had these abilities. Can I communicate telepathically in any language?"

"Yes, of course...obviously a language that both parties are familiar with. Whatever language you are using as you formulate the words in your mind is what the other person perceives."

"Up until now, the only knowledge I have had about telepathy is from fictional stories," I said, amazed. "Tell me, how physically close to each other do people need to be?"

"If you are at a distance where it would be possible to recognize the other person with the naked eye, you are close enough for telepathic connection. They do not necessarily need to be in your visual range. For example, you can connect telepathically with someone who is behind you, hiding from plain sight, or in the next room."

"Impressive," I said, wondering where we would go from here.

"We should start with some meditation, which is how we strengthen our minds to tap into our abilities."

I marveled at how easy it was for her to transfer her thoughts to mine. Since I had no idea how to reciprocate, I continued to speak as usual.

"Back on Earth, the planet I am from, we have a discipline called *Yoga*. It includes meditation."

I was trying to establish some type of rapport while trying to figure her out.

"Interesting, and what is the purpose of this meditation?"

"Basically, it helps clear our minds to avoid focusing on problems or pain."

"I understand. However, the meditation we will work on has a different purpose. It will assist you to have faith in the extraordinary capabilities that you have been given."

She placed a small rock on my desk.

"Let us sit, please."

We both sat at the desk. She showed me an image on her tablet that looked like a bicycle wheel.

"Our elders used a model like this one to teach the children. Each spoke represents a talent: Telepathy, Telekinesis, Healing, Blocking, Memory Command, and Mind Control. The hub in the center represents the mental energy from which our power emanates, which we strengthen through meditation, and the outside circle, our continuous evolution. I think we should start with a bit of Telekinesis. See how I can move this rock without touching it."

She didn't use any extreme gestures. I only noticed a brief knitting of her brows before the rock levitated, floating in front of us for about a minute before it landed back on the desk.

"Now, your turn."

She smiled as she stood and positioned herself behind me, rolling up my sleeves and placing her hands on my bare shoulders. A sort of vibration generated where her fingers touched my skin.

"Focus on this rock. You have the capability of moving this rock without touching it or moving this desk. Think about the rock. Without touching it, think about its appearance and color, how might it feel in your hands...its weight. Now, imagine yourself picking it up and placing it somewhere else but without reaching for it. Keep your eyes focused on it. Repeat this thought in your mind: I have been given total control of myself and my surroundings."

I tried my best to focus on making the rock move. I mean, she seemed convinced I could do it. I worried that Zorla would punish me if I wasn't successful. An hour went by. Stiff from sitting in the same position, I figured she was also uncomfortable and ready for a break, but she did not waiver.

"Do not stop focusing on the rock. Do not think about how you are feeling physically. Only concentrate on believing you can move the rock."

Well, another hour went by. I closed my eyes and kept repeating the mantra she had taught me. I opened them and stared at the rock. Kaya never shifted in her position while standing behind me. Nothing changed, and finally, I let her know it was time for me to go to my Academics session.

"Very well. May I see your daily schedule?" she replied as she snatched my tablet and perused the contents. "I will explain to your squadron leader that we need to replace your Academics session with our training. This will allow us to devote the equivalent of four of your Earth hours to Sotkari Ta training. I will return tomorrow at this same time."

On her way out, she glanced at the rock. It flew off the desk through the air and smashed into pieces against the wall. Stunned, my body jerked, and I covered my face to avoid being pelted by any pieces. I rolled my shoulders back, embarrassed and angry at myself for not moving that damn rock.

She makes it look so easy. I'll do better next time.

Kaya did not look back again when she walked out. Talk about a dramatic exit.

The next seven days proved to be frustrating after following the same routine every day for four hours without any visible progress.

"Is there anything else I should be doing other than repeating this phrase? Should I focus on any other part of my body?"

"Nothing other than believing you are capable of doing this."

"Kaya, maybe I do not really have these powers that you all think I have."

"Keep in mind that unleashing these abilities can take a long time. It varies with each person."

I pressed my fists against my face and continued, "I think a big problem for me is that I am a person of faith."

"Please clarify. Faith is exactly what you require."

"I mean I have faith in *God*."

I didn't know the Lostai translation for the word God, so I pronounced it in English.

"I am not a super religious person, but I do believe...I do not know if you can understand," I explained.

"I understand. You have faith in a higher power...as do I. Does that surprise you?"

"Well, yes, it does. You have me here repeating that I have total control, yet I believe there are some things beyond my..."

She didn't let me finish.

"Incorrect! I said you have been GIVEN total control. This *God* you believe in has allowed you to possess these capabilities. It is up to you to have faith in this and then decide how to use these gifts."

She paused for a long while, as if carefully considering her next words.

"Mina, honestly, what is the thing you want the most right now?"

I answered on impulse, forgetting about possible repercussions.

"I want to be back home with my family!"

At best, I expected to hear a speech about how I needed to embrace my new mission of helping defend the Lostai against their enemies and forget about my previous life on Earth. On the other hand, it could have been much worse. She could have reported what I said to Zorla. Instead, she surprised me.

"Mina, what has happened to you is terrible. For a mother to be taken from her spouse and children is unspeakable. Believe me when I say this. Any small chance you have of ever seeing your family again will depend on you taking full control of your capabilities. I have no doubt that you can move that rock through only the use of your mental strength."

I thought it odd Kaya would say that, considering she was working for the Lostai, but was glad to hear she was sympathetic to my situation. She made a good point. Developing these abilities might be the edge I needed to figure out a way to escape Xixsted.

"OK, but I need to do this my way."

"No problem. I am here to support you in this journey. Do you wish me to do anything in particular?"

I remembered how I was taught to believe God was present where two or more people gathered together in prayer.

"Maybe...please mimic what I do."

For some reason she smiled and nodded.

I dimmed the lights and, clasping my hands, knelt on the floor. She did the same, after which I shut my eyes and prayed out loud.

"God, I am not sure why I find myself in this situation, but I believe there must be a reason for all of this. Please help me to learn to use the powers you have gifted me so that I may achieve your will. Thank you for always listening. Amen."

I repeated the phrase several times and, with deep concentration, imagined the rock floating off the desk and landing like a feather on the floor in the space between Kaya and me. A vibration in my brain caused my eyelids to flutter ever so faintly, and my fingertips tingled. I can't recall how long I spent praying, but a feeling of otherworldly conviction took over. Pure unadulterated joy replaced my doubts. Confident the rock would be exactly where I imagined it, I opened my eyes. Kaya opened hers and, noticing the rock on the floor, smiled again.

"I am impressed. Some of my prior pupils have required the equivalent of many of your Earth lunar cycles—*months*, I think you call them—to achieve telekinesis. It might be one of your stronger Sotkari Ta traits."

Now out of the trance, my faith faltered.

"Seriously, did you do it?" I asked.

"No, Mina. I did no such thing. This was all you."

3

With Zorla's approval, Kaya rearranged my schedule to accommodate what she called the Sotkari Ta regimen, which included different types of physical and mental exercises, skills practice, and meditation. I was grateful to no longer have to clean dorms. We progressed from small rocks to levitating other items in my room.

"Mina, telekinesis can be used not only to move items from one place to another but to manipulate them as well."

Kaya showed me how to fold linen and place them into drawers without touching them.

"Is it possible for me to learn how to do this while I am sleeping?" I said with a laugh. "That would be a great way not to waste time tidying up, right?"

"No, that is not possible," she replied simply.

So much for acknowledging my joke.

I shouldn't have expected anything different. Kaya always treated me with respect and fairness but didn't tend to deviate from the task at hand. Being so isolated, I longed for friendship. Sometimes I tried to lighten things up between us, but other than the one time she expressed sympathy for my situation, she kept our interaction professional and to the point.

As our lessons advanced, my initial enthusiasm was marred with a certain uneasiness. She showed me how to move various items at the same time. Causing the drawers to open and close and objects to fly around all at the same time spooked me.

"Oh!" I shouted, placing my hands on my head. All the objects fell to the ground with a thud.

"What is wrong, Mina? You were doing just fine."

"I do not know. Sometimes this feels unnatural to me," I said with a deep sigh.

"We have been through this before. You need to put these feelings aside. I know you did not ask for these abilities, but they are a part of who you are. Remember that your genetic makeup is equal to a fully evolved Sotkari. Moving things around is a minor representation of what you can learn to do."

I nodded and started my practice again, chewing my lip the whole time. At the end of our session, Kaya said it was time to move our training outside of the room to deal with larger items. She coordinated everything with my squadron leader and secured permission for me to practice moving heavy weights in the gym.

Three days after, I received a notice on my tablet that going forward, security would escort me everywhere. Up until then, I walked unaccompanied to my scheduled duties, training sessions, and the recreational and entertainment areas on the station. I hadn't yet identified any opportunity for escape, but having a security officer as a constant companion would only make it even more difficult. Although this upset me, I had no choice but to resign myself to the new requirement. Zorla's severe punishments had taught me not to question rules.

During the next lesson with Kaya, while we were still in my dorm, I wasted no time asking her about the additional security.

"Do you have any idea why I am no longer allowed to walk around on my own? I have not done anything wrong."

"Something significant has occurred on another station located on the other side of this moon. There has been an escape."

"An escape? Who escaped?"

"Mina, I do not know if you were aware, but there were three others who were also taken from Earth. They arrived some time before you were transported."

"Transported? Really? You must mean before I was kidnapped. Yes, I remember Exzer mentioned to me about other hostages from Earth."

Kaya always acted oblivious to my sarcasm.

"They have escaped. Zorla invested significant resources into transporting and training these people. Now, they are gone. This is why he is taking every precaution with you."

"How did they escape?" I dared to ask.

Her brow furrowed, and she scanned the room before simply replying, "I do not know any other details."

That same day, before Kaya and I headed to the gym for telekinesis practice, the security detail arrived at my dorm. He introduced himself as Dimlet. After looking over my schedule, he confirmed that going forward, he would accompany me everywhere any time I left my room.

I soon got used to him following me everywhere. No different than most of the Lostai I had interacted with, he didn't engage much in small talk. The only time I got a visible reaction from him was when he accompanied Kaya and me to our telekinesis practice. He fidgeted, his wide eyes darting, while weights and equipment moved across the floor and in the air. During these sessions, I could swear that Kaya encouraged me to be as disruptive as possible at his expense. I was surprised to see her lip twitching ever so slightly in amusement as she communicated telepathically to me.

"This one would rather clean the common restrooms than be here with us."

His discomfort became even more obvious when he asked me, "Why do you require repeating this training so often and for such long periods of time?"

"Kaya has explained to me that like any other skill set, we need to practice to remain agile and continuously improve."

"I would like to hear this from Kaya directly," he said.

Kaya had explained to me that the most fully evolved original Sotkari Ta such as herself possessed perfect hearing but were born mute; their vocal cords nonexistent.

"Come on, Dimlet. You know that is not possible, but I can have her send a message to your personal tablet."

He turned away, but not before I noticed the annoyed expression on his face. I sensed more amusement from Kaya, and I couldn't help smiling myself.

With Dimlet following me everywhere, other than sleeping and personal grooming, my only private time was when I ate. Kaya took to sharing meals with me in my room and had me explain to Dimlet that this allowed us more time to practice telepathic communication. He was more than happy to have time away from us. At first, we only talked about my training, but over time, our conversations became more casual. I soon looked forward to our private time together.

The idea that these other hostages from Earth had escaped excited and fueled my imagination. Several months had passed since Dimlet started escorting me, and it was about a year since the Lostai had kidnapped me. Sometimes, I tried to avoid certain thoughts as I was not sure if Kaya's ability to communicate with me telepathically also gave her a window to my soul. Was she aware of my emotions and inner thoughts? She claimed she would not do so without my permission, but how could I be sure? I thought a sort of friendship was growing between us, but I also assumed she was loyal to Lostai interests. After all, she was working for them.

One day during dinner, I dared to try and better understand her motivations.

"Kaya, I find it curious that you are friendlier towards me than with most Lostai on this station."

"It serves your training well that we have a good rapport."

"I suppose, but sometimes it seems that you do not even like them. Also, I do not mean any offense, but the Lostai have described your people to me as a dangerous and unscrupulous race focused on conquest and pillage. Yet, here they have you doing their bidding."

She looked me in the eyes and turned away as if considering what to say next. I shifted in my chair, waiting for her response.

"Mina, because I perform certain tasks for the Lostai does not signify that I agree with all they do and say. For example, they have informed you incorrectly about my race."

"Then I would like to know the truth."

She leaned back and briefly closed her eyes before answering.

"My people come from a beautiful planet with many natural resources. They are accomplished in the sciences and arts. By the time we came across the Lostai, we already had a long experience in space exploration and had embraced a philosophy of peace and respect towards all species we encountered. We did not disturb them in any way other than exchange of information where it made sense."

She went on to tell me how, over a period of about ten

generations, there was a development on her planet that changed their history forever. The Sotkari race entered what probably was the next step in their natural evolution. Some were being born with extraordinary abilities. In the beginning, these individuals were honored and revered.

"Mina, remember when I explained to you the different skills an evolved Sotkari can exhibit? My siblings and I are considered pure blood evolved Sotkari because both pairs of our grandparents were among the first Sotkari to be born with all these capabilities. My grandparents' generation was the first to understand what was happening to our people and to see the benefits of creating a regimen around honing these abilities. They are considered the elders of our culture."

"OK, so if I understood correctly, not everyone was born with all the abilities. What about those who did not have any of these evolved traits?"

Her gestures became more animated.

"Over time, intermarriage between those born with these abilities and lesser-evolved Sotkari was inevitable. Some of the offspring of these hybrid unions exhibited no desire to communicate or establish relationships. They appeared enclosed in their own world and displayed what was inferred to be mental distress or disability."

"So, you mean some sort of genetic defect."

Kaya frowned, and I hoped that I hadn't offended her since she was finally sharing more about her background.

"No! I do not believe these were genetic defects but a normal part of our evolution towards telepathic behavior."

"Oh, I see," I said, nodding. I wanted it to be clear that I was not questioning her opinion. She continued her explanation.

"Unfortunately, over time, this situation created a major shift on how the rest of the population viewed the Sotkari Ta, as we fully evolved Sotkari called ourselves. 'Ta' is our word for 'enlightened'. The Sotkari who only had partial capabilities were designated 'Pasi', which means 'partial light'. Fear and mistrust began to divide the people. Eventually, Sotkari Ta were requested and then forced by law to remain segregated from the rest of the population. Some Sotkari Ta became resentful. Others insisted they were superior and were happy to be separate and keep their Sotkari Ta gene pool pure. Many people from either side adopted extreme opinions, viewing children and spouses of mixed unions as outcasts and not belonging with one group or the other."

Kaya had never communicated so much to me at one time, and it began to tax me mentally. She suggested I lay down, close my eyes, and relax a bit before she continued.

"While this crisis was developing on our planet, the Lostai, who were from a neighboring star system, had adopted an expansion policy. They, not the Sotkari, were the ones who focused on the development of weapons and military strength to invade other planets. It was easy for them to take advantage of the strife occurring on Sotkar to successfully gain control of our government and subjugate us to Lostai rule. Some of the Sotkari Ta wanted revenge against their own governments for the rejection they had suffered and assisted the Lostai. Others used their resources and abilities to escape to remote areas of the galaxy and even to other galaxies. The Lostai hunted down as many of them as possible to force them into servitude and take advantage of their abilities for their own selfish purposes."

Kaya stood and started pacing around and gesticulating as she continued her narrative.

"No other species in this galaxy had displayed these characteristics. Some Sotkari Ta elders feared extinction or that our evolution would be forever thwarted. Scientists who were in hiding were asked to develop a solution. They found a way to transfer their genetic material to other species in the hope of preserving their gene pool. The planets chosen were technologically inferior to ensure the transfer was achieved undetected. Apparently, this is what happened to you."

I had a slight headache and dizziness when she concluded. She suggested some relaxation and stretch exercises, which helped.

This sounds nothing like how Exzer described the Sotkari to me. Should I trust Kaya? It's conceivable that she's deceiving me, but why?

Kaya had shown me respect and compassion. The Lostai, on the other hand, had been ruthless and cruel. Kaya's description of the Lostai and the Sotkari matched up to my own personal experience, and so I decided to believe her. Still, I had unanswered questions on my mind.

"Kaya, I understood everything you said, and I believe it to be true, but it leaves me even more confused about why you would work for the Lostai."

She looked up to the ceiling and around the room, tightlipped and hesitating before communicating her next words.

"Mina, I am not sure if we have complete privacy here. There might be devices in this room that we have not detected that allow the Lostai to view or hear our interactions..."

My heart skipped a beat.

"Pretend I have rebuked you for asking so many questions and that I have told you that I am one of those resentful Sotkari Ta who have turned against their own people. The truth is that I work for the Lostai to secure the safety of my granddaughter. The Lostai killed my brave son because he refused to work with them. They have threatened to harm his daughter and her mother if I don't comply with their requests. My son's widow is Sotkari with no evolved capabilities, and their hybrid daughter was born with some of the issues I mentioned earlier. She needs special care. They have no way to defend themselves. What I do here secures them safety and a dignified life."

Yessss! She was not one of them. In some way, she was as much a hostage as I was. I made sure to continue with the pretense she suggested, raising my arms in surrender mode.

"OK...OK. I am sorry. I was just curious! I get it. Your own people rejected you, and that is what motivates you to help the Lostai."

"Good job, Mina. I should leave now, and we will continue our training tomorrow as usual."

That evening, I lay in bed pondering everything Kaya had explained and her behavior since we first met. Could I count on her as an ally if I tried to escape? I assumed not. She wouldn't take a chance of jeopardizing her granddaughter's wellbeing. Still, at least she had advised me on the Lostai's true nature and kept me out of trouble. Perhaps I wasn't all alone after all.

A few weeks after, Zorla ordered me to his office. As I walked in, I tried my best to control my nerves. In the past, coming before Zorla meant a severe beating or having my back scored with electric burns. Now, Dimlet was there with two other security guards and my squadron leader. Exzer was there also. I had not seen her for a long time. They ordered me to sit, and Exzer started a line of questioning. The Lostai always cut to the chase.

"Dimlet has told us that you are progressing well with your mind-matter interactions. Has Kaya begun any new training?"

The others stared at me.

"We continue to practice with more challenging objects and movements," I answered.

"Yes, but has she helped you become aware of other capabilities? For example, we notice that she uses telepathic communication with you, but you continue to speak to her verbally. Has she started to show you how to initiate telepathic communication? Have you practiced mind-control tactics?"

I was incredulous, a tremor in my voice.

"Mind control? No, we have not done anything like that."

"Has Kaya given you any input on what her role is here with us?" Exzer continued.

Now I began to worry. I reminded myself to tread carefully with my responses.

"Exactly what do you mean?" I asked.

"Do you know why Kaya works with us?"

"Kaya doesn't talk much about herself, but one time, I did ask her how she came to be employed by the Lostai. She mentioned that her family, being Sotkari Ta, was harassed and shunned by the Sotkari government. Apparently, it suits her fine that the Lostai have taken control over the Sotkari home world and is glad to assist you to that end."

Exzer leaned into my personal space and cocked her head, a steely glint in her eyes.

"She has lied to you. We force her to help us. We have her loved ones within our reach and can take them into custody whenever we want," she explained plainly.

"I am not sure why you are sharing this with me."

But I knew her purpose. She was striking fear in my heart.

"Are you aware that some time ago, three others who were transported from Earth escaped the other station on this moon?"

"Yes, I am aware. I asked Kaya about the added security because Dimlet barely speaks to me." Dimlet rolled his deep-set eyes. "Without giving me many details, she explained this was the reason he was now accompanying me everywhere."

"Well, let me expand on that then. Your fellow Earthians were able to transmit a message from this station that was intercepted by rebels. These criminals took over a Lostai supply ship, landed on our station posing as merchants, moved the Earthians onto their ship, and took off again, right under the noses of our security guards!" shouted Exzer, finally showing some emotion.

Her tone was accusatory. Did she think Kaya or I had anything to do with the escape? Having just lied about what Kaya had explained to me, I hoped to conceal any trace of deceit by speaking with bravado.

"I never met those people. I still do not understand what this has to do with me!" I answered, matching her tone.

They began a lengthy discussion amongst themselves. As I suspected, they were trying to ascertain if Kaya or I had anything to do with the escape of the other hostages from Earth. There was also discussion regarding an assignment they were planning for me. To send me on this mission, they would have to authorize Kaya to take my training to a higher level. Finally, Zorla said he would discuss this with his commanding officer, and the conversation abruptly stopped with everyone's eyes back on me.

"Dimlet, walk Mina back to her quarters," Zorla ordered.

No one addressed me any further or clarified any next steps. I didn't bother to ask Dimlet any questions. The next day was a rest day. I stayed in my room, worried about the mission they were discussing. To calm myself down, I composed a letter to my daughter. I had written several of these pretend letters to my husband, but this was the first one addressed to one of my children. The tone was of someone who was off on a long trip. I pretended she could really see the letter, and I wanted to reassure her that things were not so bad. As usual, I promptly deleted it when I was done.

My daughter's eyes are like mine. According to her, we have one of the rarest of eye colors. Unlike hazel, our eyes have a solid coppery tint with no hints of other colors. Her eyes are lighter and more striking than mine are and have not changed since she was a baby. By the time she was one year old, we had nicknamed her and then officially added the name to her birth certificate.

Dear Amber,

Honey, how are you doing? I guess you've started your freshman year now in high school. Under other circumstances, I'd love for you to be able to experience this with me. My being here confirms everything we always discussed at the dinner table. Yes, there are several worlds within and outside of our galaxy with people that don't necessarily look like us but represent civilizations that have been around for a long time and who have the ability to travel across star systems. This convinces me that one day, if we don't destroy our Earth beforehand, we will be doing the same.

I pray to God that you are doing well. I can imagine my being away for so long has been so tough on you all. I hope this hasn't affected your studies. You have a gift for science. Stay focused on your goals. We need more female scientists.

This will sound crazy, but I've learned to move things with my mind. Yes! Mind-Matter Interaction! I'm thinking if I've learned to do it, perhaps one of you kids might have the capability of doing the same. Someone here is showing me how to unleash all these abilities I never could have imagined that I possessed.

Don't worry about me. Other people from Earth who were here recently left this place, so I'm sure that I will soon figure out a way to leave as well. Once I make it back to Earth, trust me, I'll have a hell of a story to tell. I miss you so very much.

God bless, Mom

4

A few days later, Exzer met with me to communicate Zorla's plans. She didn't even bother to sit. This was going to be quick.

"We have an insurgency problem in a nearby star system. A small group of people on a planet called Renna One is trying to stir up a rebellion against Lostai rule. Your first mission will be to identify and kill those responsible."

I shook my head in disbelief. There was no way I was killing anyone. She ignored my reaction and continued as if going through a basic to-do list.

"Once you help us get rid of the problem on Renna One, you will return here and mate with another soldier who also has a full set of Sotkari Ta genes. Our hope is that your offspring will inherit your evolved Sotkari genes and learn to use them."

She stuck out her chin and straightened her posture.

"Be proud. You will procreate children who will be molded into fine Lostai soldiers."

I guess Zorla was into long-term planning.

My eyes must have been the size of saucers by then. I

wanted to grab Exzer by the shoulders and shake some sense into her. How could she expect me to make babies for Zorla? I bit my tongue and controlled my outrage. Protesting would only earn me a beating, but at that precise moment, I resolved to no longer be paralyzed by fear. I would escape Xixsted at all costs.

To prepare me for this mission, Zorla authorized Kaya to move on to the next phase of our training. This suited me just fine, the one time that Zorla and I would ever be on the same page. I wanted more than anything to learn to communicate telepathically with Kaya. Keeping our conversations secret was an important step in planning my escape. I hoped I'd be able to convince her to help me.

I learned from Kaya that evolved Sotkari telepathy worked on different levels. The first level was mere communication. A deeper telepathic probe discovered a person's true intentions, emotions, and inner thoughts. The strongest connection initiated a change of behavior or control over the actions of another. On the other hand, a properly trained Sotkari Ta could block any type of telepathic connection.

During our next shared meal, I brought up the subject.

"Kaya, I understand that Zorla has asked you to start training me on something new."

"Yes, he wants me to help you unleash mind control abilities. This is something that goes against all my core beliefs. I am not sure if it is even possible. Even some Sotkari Ta are not able to execute this properly."

"I assume that to be able to do the mind control thing, you first need to teach me how to communicate telepathically, right?"

Her eyes were like daggers. She was not happy with this suggestion. I assumed there was still a level of distrust between us.

"Mina, the different ways in which evolved Sotkari can

connect with others telepathically require extreme finesse and trust and honor. I promise that during our time together, I have limited myself to transmitting information to you. The reason that you are not able to reply to me telepathically is because I have purposely blocked my mind from receiving any such connection from you."

It was time to bare my soul and for Kaya to become aware of my anxiety and desperation. I couldn't imagine myself killing anyone, having sex with a stranger, procreating a child, and handing that child over to the Lostai military for their evil purposes. I had no one else to turn to and needed to be able to communicate with her telepathically. I needed to trust Kaya to gain her confidence.

"Kaya, I feel it is important that you see my thoughts and emotions. Please do so now. I give you permission."

I made a conscious effort to focus on my anguish at being forced to execute Zorla's despicable plans. I thought of how I much wanted to escape Xixsted and reunite with my family.

I fidgeted and avoided looking at her. What does probing someone's mind look like? Yet, she made no obvious gestures other than taking deep breaths and communicated nothing for a while. My heart pounded while I waited for her reaction. It could mean the difference between escaping Xixsted and being forced to do unspeakable things.

"Mina, I have connected to your emotions and am sympathetic to your situation. I understand your anxiety, but my main concern is the safety of my family. Allowing you to access me telepathically represents a risk of you betraying me to the Lostai, intentionally or not. First, you must give me permission to continue to monitor your emotions and thoughts. If so, I will also open my mind when we are together so you can communicate with me telepathically. You must make sure you limit yourself to exchange of information. I will explain to you how to stay within these limits. If you try to probe me further, I promise you will get no second chances. I will also give some thought to an escape plan for you, but I cannot assure you anything. In the meantime, we can practice mind control with small animals in the lab so that Zorla will assume we are working on your training according to his plans."

I was so thankful, I almost hugged her, but of course, that would have been unacceptable since I had no idea if the Lostai were watching us. A quick smile made it clear that she understood I agreed with her conditions.

"Mina, close your eyes and tell me what you see."

"Just darkness."

"I will allow you in this time. Try again."

A light appeared like a shimmering doorway at the end of a tunnel.

"To communicate telepathically, imagine walking towards the light, but remember, I forbid you to go beyond that point."

I wondered what secrets she was hiding, but just being able to communicate with her privately was a big step forward. She said at first, I would feel the need to close my eyes, but with practice, it would become more fluid.

My very first telepathic words to her were, "Thank you for this, Kaya."

Long telepathic conversations with Kaya during our mealtimes helped me practice. I had countless questions about why the Lostai needed a simple individual such as myself to help them carry out their plans. They were a mighty military machine with enough technology to travel across galaxies, subdue other races, and amass a large empire consisting of several planets across more than one star system. Why didn't they send an army to Renna One to squash the rebellion? Why couldn't they embed the Sotkari Ta genes into themselves?

Kaya explained that Lostai military and government officials were under a lot of pressure to convince the constituents on their home world that everything was running smoothly in the vast Lostai Empire. On their home planet, expansion policies were growing unpopular. Citizens were complaining of all the resources focused on maintaining order on these foreign territories, as they referred to them. Any significant show of military force would make this fact even more evident.

On the other hand, someone with telepathic, telekinetic, and mind control abilities had an advantage in rooting out leaders of any rebellious activities and covertly eliminating these threats without calling attention to themselves.

She also clarified that the Lostai would have loved nothing more than to either figure out how to download Sotkari Ta DNA into themselves, somehow clone Sotkari Ta individuals, or use surrogates for bearing in vitro-created Sotkari Ta offspring. Several expensive attempts had been unsuccessful. The elder Sotkari Ta scientists who had developed the process of embedding their genes into other species were long dead and purposely had not left any record of their work. They had foreseen the possibility of governments wanting to weaponize these evolved Sotkari abilities and ensured the embedded genes could only be inherited through natural conception and birth. The Lostai constantly searched for any remnants of that biotechnology without success. That was why they had turned their efforts to identifying and kidnapping people with embedded evolved Sotkari genes. Understanding all of this made me even more determined; I wouldn't allow them to use me for their evil plots.

As we had other conversations, it became clear that Kaya did not want to share much about her personal life. I guessed that, despite our growing friendship, there was too much at stake for her to divulge personal details. Instead, she asked about my family and what life was like back home. It was cathartic for me to share with her some of my life stories.

I told her how my parents divorced when I first started high school. I was the oldest of three sisters. My parents tried to make their separation amicable, agreeing on financial issues and how we would spend equal time living with both of them. Then my mother passed away unexpectedly a year later. We remained with my dad, who had occasional relationships but never remarried. I became the de facto mother figure and was especially protective of my youngest sister, who was only eight at the time. I had always been mature and independent, and having to assume this role only accentuated this trait.

Kaya found especially interesting the story of my relation-ship with my husband, Josh.

"How did you meet him?" Kaya asked.

I launched into an explanation of the typical education system in the United States and how I met Josh in my junior year of college.

Once we got through that, Kaya asked, "Was he your first suitor?"

"Not my first, but certainly my only serious one. The first time I saw him, I told my best friend I thought he was the hand-somest male I had ever seen."

She must have noticed that I had momentarily transported myself back to that time because a rare full smile graced her face. The way she nodded made me think she also knew what it was to feel the excitement of first love.

"He was never overly romantic or expressive of his feelings, but he kept me close to him," I added.

I also needed to explain to Kaya aspects of Earth life so that she could understand what I meant when I said he was a bit of a spoiled, rich, bad boy. Josh's family was in a higher income bracket than mine. They gifted him toys like a sports car, a motorcycle, and a beachside condo. Kaya was curious about how he finally became my husband.

"Many of my female friends had been sexually active for some time, but I had not. Some months into our relationship, I decided he would be my first one. He brought out a reckless-ness in me that I had never exhibited before, and suddenly, I found myself pregnant."

"I see. How was your wedding ceremony? I imagine your family was pleased."

"Oh, we did not have a wedding ceremony. We could not spend money on one. My father was not happy to hear I was expecting, especially considering I was unmarried and not even done with my studies. Still, he said he would support me in whatever decision I made regarding my future."

"And Josh's family?"

"They were upset and, from then on, wanted nothing to do with us."

Kaya offered a rare glimpse into her family history.

"That must have been very difficult for you. My daughter-in-law's family did not want their daughter marrying my son because he was Sotkari Ta. When it became clear that their child was exhibiting some problems communicating, they turned against him even more. That type of family division is hard on a young couple."

"Yes, we had a quick civil marriage without any formal cele-bration but were overjoyed when Chris was born. I interrupted my studies for six lunar cycles to care for my baby. Later, with my sisters helping to care for Chris, I was able to complete my degree, and my father's friend offered me a job. Josh wanted to get a higher-level degree, so he remained studying while working part-time. His family kicked him out of the apartment they had gifted him. My father had to quietly help us financially."

"Well, even though you had a rocky start, things eventually worked out for you and Josh."

Memories of the early years of my marriage were like a dark cloud.

"It was not so easy at first," I admitted. "Josh was restless and not ready for married life. Without warning, he quit his studies and announced he was joining the military. I thought it was a joke. Next thing I knew, he was overseas in an area of open combat. Over the next six—how do you say *years*?—revolutions, that is it! Over the next six revolutions, I saw him only a few times."

Kaya's brow furrowed.

"I can only imagine how difficult that was for you...a young mother alone for so long and worried for your husband's safety."

"Yes, and it was even more difficult when, during one of those visits, we conceived our second child, a girl. I love her with all my heart, but it's even harder to raise two young children when your husband is deployed for so long. I was lonely and frustrated that although married on paper, and except for Josh's military paycheck, I was, for all practical purposes, a single mother."

Biting my lip, I recalled how, during those six long years, I remained faithful to Josh, in spite of my doubts that he was corresponding in kind. When he returned, he was a different man. Much stronger physically, more mature and determined to make our marriage work. He completed his master's degree and secured a well-paying job in a global manufacturing firm. We welcomed the birth of our youngest son, but life as a soldier left a mark on Josh. He had lost friends, seen gruesome things. He could be moody and distant at times. The years alone had further accentuated my independent and self-reliant personality. He tried his best to be a good husband and father, and we became a good team, but we never regained the

carefree joy and closeness of the early stages of our relationship.

I cried while communicating some of these stories to Kaya.
She made a point not to show any physical signs of affection
but told me she understood how it felt to be separated from
family. She pointed out that my family seemed to have strong
ties—my husband and children, my father and sisters, my best
friend—and I should focus on the fact that they were most
likely all helping each other deal with my absence. Her input
was comforting.

Seeing Kaya alter animal behavior in the lab was mind-
boggling. She was able to direct them to drink, eat, fight, or
mate only using the power of her mind. Dimlet was always
uncomfortable and irritated during these sessions. Kaya
explained I first needed to exercise my "mind muscle," as she
described it, and identify telepathically the light in my mind
that represented the subject whose behavior I wanted to
manipulate. She clarified that if there were several beings in the
rooms, it could be tricky, but each subject's light appeared
differently in our minds. I already knew how to recognize
Kaya's "light," but then there was Dimlet and more than one lab
animal in the room. She said the "light" of less evolved crea-
tures would appear dull and near, while more evolved beings
appeared bright and distant. For example, Dimlet's "light"
appeared dimmer and closer than Kaya's ("Ridiculous," he
exclaimed when I pointed this out) but shinier and farther
away than those of the animals. It was fascinating but, at the
same time, unnerving. She also explained that manipulating
behavior became harder, the more evolved the subject was.

Weeks went by, and I was still not successful in working
mind control with the lab animals. Trying to exercise a "mus-

cle" I never even knew existed proved to be challenging. I was surprised to find that moving objects with my mind was easier than communicating telepathically, and for sure mind control, at the time, was out of my reach. The whole process made me uncomfortable and impatient. Kaya explained that although I eventually should be able to perform most, if not all, Sotkari Ta abilities, it was normal to be more adept to certain skills. We pressed on to ensure Zorla believed I was preparing as best as possible for my mission.

One evening while Kaya and I were having dinner alone in my room, she told me something I had wanted to hear since my abduction.

"Mina, I cannot help you escape this place, but I know of someone who is in a better position to assist you. His name is Montor, and I think he is the one they plan to have you mate with. He is from a planet called Aranda and also has a complete set of embedded Sotkari Ta genes. The Lostai have complete trust in him because, although he was once a hostage such as yourself, he embraced his new lifestyle and position in the Lostai military. He now enjoys the same freedoms and benefits as any Lostai soldier."

"Uhhh, I am confused. Why would this person help me? It sounds more likely that he would turn me in rather than help me escape."

Kaya walked around without immediately replying. Finally, she clarified, "He also secretly cooperates with rebel factions to help them cause many problems for the Lostai military. Luckily, neither side has ever suspected the truth. He is loyal to no one..."

"Oh, I see, what we call a *double agent* on Earth."

Abruptly, her pacing came to a stop, and she swung around to face me, looking me straight in the eyes.

"...except to me. He is loyal to me. I successfully trained him in all facets of Sotkari Ta abilities. He has become an extremely powerful being and is a complicated person with a complicated history. He lost his whole family during famine and wars that ravaged his planet. Similar to what occurred on Sotkar, the Lostai came in and took advantage of the situation. He was a child when they identified him as having Sotkari Ta genes and brought him to this station. I was the closest thing to a mother he had growing up here."

"Kaya, I do not get how you can be OK with the work he does for the Lostai. I am grateful for your friendship, but sometimes I am not clear on your moral compass."

"Mina, do not try to pass judgement on me. I have already explained my situation. My job here is to train people as per Lostai requests. To not comply would put my granddaughter in grave danger. How my trainees choose to live their lives, how they use these abilities, whether they become part of Lostai society or rebel against them, is out of my control."

I disagreed with her position, but it was a discussion for another time.

"OK, Kaya, so do you think I can trust this person?"

She pressed her lips together and sighed.

"He agreed I reveal to you the fact that he is involved with covert activities against the Lostai so that you could trust him. We have both taken this tremendous risk on your behalf. Please do not make me regret it. If he suspects that you might in any way divulge this secret, he will kill you without a second thought. I will not be able to intervene."

I gulped as Montor sounded more and more frightening by the minute.

"I am going to inform Zorla we have not progressed much in your next phase of training and we need Montor's help. I will explain that because he too was once dormant, he might have good advice for you. This will allow the three of us time together to discuss your next steps."

I hardly slept that night as I tried to anticipate what kind of person this Montor was and how he might help me escape. I didn't have to wait too long.

The next day while Kaya and I were having dinner, there was a buzz at my door. I pressed the button on my console that opened the door, and he strolled in with great swagger and a long gait. Built like a heavyweight boxer, he was more than a foot taller than my five-foot, four-inch frame. His face had a leonine appearance with wide, high cheekbones and yellow eyes that slanted upwards. The nose was broad and flat, and he had a strong jaw. Thin lips, when parted, revealed perfectly aligned, shiny white teeth except for the large beastly canines. Long, wild hair hung from his head in thick, twisted locks. A dark skintight suit made of a stretchy material covered all of his body except his hands, outlining every muscle and contour. Let's just say, everything was in perfect proportion to his height. With not much left to the imagination, I felt the need to avert my eyes. His face and hands were a tawny color and covered by soft fuzz.

He walked up to Kaya and nodded in deference. Taking his time to look me over, a smirk appeared on his face. He spoke out loud with a deep voice in perfect Lostai.

"Kaya, is this insignificant, tiny creature what they expect me to procreate with?"

My face was hot and I'm sure red as a tomato. He walked up into my personal space and glared down at me.

"These orange eyes remind me of my canine pet. Revolting," he said.

Kaya's expression was apologetic while he continued.

"Frankly, I do not even think it is physically possible without causing her some injury, but I suppose it will be entertaining to find out."

He reached out to rub my cheek with the back of his hand. Evenly filed, short, dark fingernails grazed my skin. For some reason, I was surprised by his well-manicured hands. His touch first felt like peach fuzz and something else I couldn't pinpoint but left me uncomfortable. I'd had enough. With a sudden outward block, I aggressively pushed his hand away, but he was quicker. He grabbed my hand twisted it and with his other hand pulled me up against him, the smirk replaced with a cruel snarl. Now that we were up close, I noticed he wore two dark leather-like cords around his neck, each with a silver-tone amulet. In a matter of seconds, Kaya reached up to place her hand on his shoulder, a stern expression on her face. He let me go while stumbling back several feet, rubbing his hands and cracking his knuckles. He lowered his head and spoke again in a quiet voice.

"Forgive me, Kaya. I was only having some fun. She is a feisty one. We might be able to copulate after all."

The whole situation upset me. Was I supposed to put my trust in this unpleasant, aggressive person? I turned around so they wouldn't notice my tears.

I sensed Kaya communicating telepathically to the both of us.

"Mina, I apologize for Montor's behavior. He has a misplaced need to intimidate everyone he meets, but you will need to learn to deal with him, as I believe he is the one person who can get you out of here," said Kaya.

I turned back around to face them, chewing my lip and concentrating to reply telepathically to both of them at the same time. I offered my forearm to Montor in the typical Sotkari handshake.

"Hello, Montor, my name is Mina. Trust me, I find the idea of having sexual relations with you pretty disgusting too."

He chuckled and accepted my outstretched forearm with a tight wrist squeeze but quickly let go. In that brief moment of skin contact, the weird sensation came over me again, like I'd been touched intimately. My heartbeat raced, but I brushed it out of my mind. Kaya and I sat down to continue eating. He replicated food to join us. We continued to communicate tele-pathically in conference mode. At first, Kaya and Montor exchanged pleasantries as he updated her on his latest missions and female conquests. Apparently, he was considered quite the ladies' man in his circles.

"Really?" I rolled my eyes, thinking to myself in English, "He doesn't seem so suave to me."

He cocked an eyebrow, a quizzical look on his face. I suppose I wasn't that skilled yet at separating my own thoughts and communicating telepathically. Too bad he didn't under-stand English.

Once we finished eating, the conversation grew more serious.

"Mina," Montor addressed me, "the only escape option I see for you is to convince Zorla that we should go together on the mission he has outlined for you. We will tell him that you are not ready to execute this assignment on your own and need the mentoring of someone who is both an experienced soldier and Sotkari Ta."

He side-glanced, arrogance in his eyes.

"There will be no deception there. I do not know what Zorla is thinking. You have no chance of accomplishing this mission by yourself."

"I have no desire to accomplish it at all," I said, injecting some attitude of my own.

We locked eyes for a moment, and he took a deep breath before he continued, as if summoning patience.

"Since Zorla's latest fixation is on breeding Sotkari Ta offspring, I will also tell him that we will take advantage of our time together to begin our mating process. Once on the planet, I will coordinate with my contacts to set you up with an autopilot shuttlecraft that will take you to another planet where I am sure you will find friendly people and, with luck, will be able to evade any Lostai search teams. We will have to make it look like I have been ambushed. Perhaps have me incapacitated with a drug. I am not sure yet, but I can sort out those details later."

It was a viable plan, but it did put him at considerable risk.

"Montor, why are you willing to put yourself and your good standing with the Lostai in danger to help me escape?"

"I suppose I have been bored lately and always welcome a good challenge. Quite honestly, I am not pleased with the idea of making babies with you. Then there is the fact that, for some odd reason, Kaya has taken a liking to you."

He shook his head with a smile. I was happy to know that at least we had one thing in common.

"OK...so, what is my next step?"

"You, my dear, from now on, only need follow my instructions. Once I discuss with Zorla and he agrees, things will move fast. The Lostai are anxious to solve their little problem on Renna One before it grows out of control," he said.

I looked at Kaya. She nodded in agreement and stood.

"It is time for my private meditation. I will see you tomorrow," she said as she walked out.

Montor and I also got up from our seats. His lips curved into a sly smile.

"Mina, if you like, I can sleep here with you tonight. That will show Zorla we are committed to his mission. It will be a... tight fit," he said, looking me over and then glancing at my cot, "but I think we can manage."

I hated that his insinuations made my face flush.

"No, I do not think that is necessary."

He chuckled.

"True. We have plenty of time on our trip to Renna One. Good night, Mina."

The minute he stepped out, I exhaled slowly.

Patience.

This obnoxious creature is my ticket out of here.

5

Things did move fast. In a matter of days, Zorla called me to his office and notified me that the next day, Montor and I would be traveling together to Renna One. Our mission was to quietly eliminate the rebellion brewing there. I would be under Montor's command and should follow any of his orders, including allowing him into my bed when he so advised me. Zorla's tone was impatient.

"I am getting a lot of pressure from my commanders. We incur significant expense and risk to capture specimens from Earth. Now, under my supervision, three are lost and you have rendered minimal profit so far for all our trouble. At least we can use you for breeding until you begin earning your keep. I realize that, even with the hormones we injected in you, your childbearing potential is limited, so we cannot waste time. I will demand proof from Montor that he is thoroughly engaged in impregnating you. He is not looking forward to this activity, but we need to start the process as soon as possible. It will take many revolutions before we see any payback from our investment!"

He was shouting by the time he was done with his speech. It

took all my self-control not to spit in his face. By the time Zorla dismissed me, I was damn close to demonstrating the return on his investment by tossing him around his office.

That evening, Kaya and I were both pensive and quiet during dinner. Finally, halfway through our meal, she initiated conversation.

"Montor has told me you will both be leaving tomorrow early to Renna One. I am focusing positive energy towards the Farthest Light so that your escape is successful."

In other words, she was praying for me.

"Thank you, Kaya. To be honest, I am so nervous. I do not know what to expect from Montor. He does not seem to like me at all. You have said he can be unpredictable. Also, I am concerned if somehow this puts you in danger."

"Do not worry about me, Mina. They have no reason to connect me to your escape. All I have done since you have arrived is follow their instructions. The one who will be at significant risk is Montor, but he knows how to take care of himself. I am sure he will be difficult at times, but he is aware that I have put you in his care, and I am sure he will help you get away from the Lostai."

"I am going to miss you, Kaya. You have been my only friend throughout this whole time. I will never forget you."

I wanted to hug her, but I couldn't risk anyone spying anything that would reveal our close relationship. She moved her hand slightly, and one of her fingers touched mine. Instantly, I was relaxed and calm.

"Mina, I will remember you always as well. Perhaps we should not say farewell. We may meet again under happier circumstances."

❄

Montor was punctual the next morning. I carried a small travel bag with only my few pieces of clothing, toiletries, and my tablet. He greeted me speaking out loud in a condescending tone.

"Hello, my dear. I am glad you are ready. As Zorla keeps reminding me, there is no time to waste," he said, followed by a wink and a sardonic smile.

Apparently, Zorla had given Montor the same speech as he had given me. We hadn't yet started out on our trip and already he was annoying me. We rushed to the docking station to find Dimlet standing at the entrance. The smile left Montor's face but reappeared after a few seconds.

"Dimlet, how are you doing, sir? There was no need for you to get up so early to see us off." The condescending tone continued.

"Zorla has asked I accompany you as an observer on your mission to Renna One," replied Dimlet with a hint of arrogance.

Montor's eyes narrowed ever so slightly before he said, "Dimlet, you are much too busy for that. I am sure you must realize that it would be an unnecessary waste of your time. Zorla needs to be made aware of all the other priorities you have responsibility for."

A look of confusion swept over Dimlet's face.

"Yes, that is correct, that is correct, correct, correct. I do need to clarify this with Zorla. I have evaluations to complete, and I need to hire new security personnel for this station...that is correct...that is correct...I need to speak to Zorla."

He continued rambling as he walked away.

I'd never seen Dimlet act like that before, so as Montor and I continued into the spaceship, I communicated to Montor telepathically, "Dimlet's behavior was strange. He is not the type to be questioning orders."

Montor's expression turned mischievous.

"Well, you never know when someone is going to have a change of heart."

As I realized what had happened, I covered my wide-open mouth with my hand, stunned.

"Oh. It was you. Kaya has told me she is against mind control."

Montor looked at me like a parent to an ignorant child.

"Kaya is a pure soul. I cannot say the same for myself. I would not likely do such a thing to a fellow Sotkari Ta, but Dimlet, he is a fool. Besides, what would you have me do? Allow our plan to be ruined?"

I couldn't argue with that, but it was clear to me what Kaya had meant when she said Montor had become extremely powerful and unpredictable. Once we were in the spaceship, he showed me around and then to my quarters. The ship accommodated a few separate living quarters, a common kitchen area, an exercise room, an observation deck, a small lounge area, and a conference room in addition to the normal engineering, weapon, and flight stations. Montor told me telepathically to get settled in my room while he handled take off and that we should meet later to iron out the details of our strategy.

We met in the early evening to share a meal in the kitchen, continuing to communicate telepathically.

"Hello, my dear. Are your quarters comfortable? Is everything in order?"

"Yes, Montor, everything is fine."

"Good. The first thing I need you to know is that I would not be surprised if Zorla has installed spying devices all over this spaceship to monitor our activities. We need to be careful of how we conduct ourselves and what we say aloud. I told him we would be communicating telepathically most of the time so that you can get continued practice. But occasionally I may speak aloud purposely. Make sure you follow my lead. I also expect he will be checking in with me often to get updates on our progress. We need to discuss how we will trick Zorla into believing we are busy making a Sotkari Ta baby. Any suggestions?"

I shifted uncomfortably in my seat with my fist covering my mouth. I had avoided thinking about this part of the mission and hated the fact that we needed to have this discussion.

"Suggestions, what do you mean?"

"Well, my dear, we must put on a show of sorts for Zorla. There are different options on how we do it. I have my suggestion, but obviously, we need to be in sync."

The whole conversation was making me sick to my stomach, but I understood that Montor was right. We needed to agree on a plan.

"OK, what do you recommend? By the way, I am tired of you calling me 'my dear'. Call me by my name, please."

He raised his eyebrows.

"Yes, my de...uhhh, Mina. I informed Zorla that the idea of taking a female by force is distasteful to me."

"Distasteful?" Outrage took over. "No, it is not distasteful. It is plain wrong. How would you like it if someone raped you? Or perhaps your sister or mother?"

His face crumpled for only a moment.

"Yes, it is wrong," I heard his voice soften in my mind.

Did I just hit a nerve?

His recovery was quick as he adopted a sardonic tone. "I have never had the need to do such a thing, as I am known to be quite the seducer. Some of my female companions have admitted they do not know why they find me so irresistible."

After seeing what had happened with Dimlet, the implication of what he was saying wasn't lost on me.

"That is disgusting!"

He laughed for a beat. Then his demeanor changed, and he became serious.

"Mina, let me get to the point. Either I play the part of

violent rapist or, on the other hand, we pretend that I am slowly winning you over. I think the latter is something we can better stage. If we put on an act like I am trying to take you by force and you are fighting me off, it will be hard at the same time to strategically cover or position ourselves in such a way as to conceal that we are not really..."

"OK, OK. I get the picture."

"Picture? Excuse me?"

I counted to ten in my mind. He enjoyed highlighting my Lostai language blunder and my frustration in general.

"I mean, I understand."

"It will take us thirty-one days to reach Renna One. That is plenty of time for us to become acquainted and for you to pretend that you are succumbing to my charms. When the time comes, we can stage consummating our love affair."

His words dripped with sarcasm. By this time, I was so red-faced I couldn't look him in the eyes. He, on the other hand, found the conversation entertaining.

"So, Mina, as we spend time together alone on this trip, I will eventually start making some overtures, and I will give you time and space to decide when you want to act like you are attracted to me. Eventually, the time will come for us to pretend that nature is taking its course, but remember, Zorla is under much pressure. We cannot keep him waiting too long."

I covered my face with my hands for a moment and then folded them tightly in my lap. I had hoped that by escaping the Lostai, I'd be avoiding this whole situation, but clearly, I wouldn't be able to get away from it entirely.

"Montor, this is not going to be easy for me, even if it is pretend. I am married and have never been unfaithful."

With a wave of his hand, he dismissed this as irrelevant.

"That is touching, but the fact is, you will never see your husband again. Do you realize how far away you are from your home planet? Galaxies away. You need to pull yourself together if you want to be successful in this escape attempt. How long has it been since you were first taken?"

The harsh reality of his statement was a slap to the face. My heart broke under the crush of his words.

"More than a full revolution," I said.

Now, tears began to flow down my cheeks.

"That is a long time sleeping alone. Your body must clamor for some male companionship."

He leaned forward, smiled, and, same as he did the first time we met, rubbed my cheek with the back of his hand. Again, a certain sensation came over me. Last time, I didn't have much time to think about it. I had responded with an immediate defensive move. This time, it was clear. My toes curled. It was in my hips and between my legs. I pressed my thighs together. There was no doubt; I was sexually aroused, very much so. I looked at him, and he was relaxed with his eyes almost shut. Confused that I should have this reaction from only a simple touch, I became infuriated and lost control.

"Stop. It. Right. Now!" I shouted out loud.

He sat back and pulled his hand away, lips pressed together. His eyes opened, and they bore into mine.

"Be very careful, Mina, on what you say out loud."

Hearing his words in my mind helped me regain composure, and I returned to telepathic communication.

"How dare you! I cannot believe I have to spell this out for you, but you have no permission whatsoever to get into my head. You said you would not do that to a Sotkari Ta. Well, I am as much a Sotkari Ta as you are. In case it was not clear, you will only use telepathy to communicate with me. Nothing else, do you understand? Do. You?"

I trembled with rage and pointed my finger at his face.

He crossed his arms, sitting up straight with his legs wide and eyes narrowed.

"Mina, you are overreacting. I am not, as you say, getting in your head. I suppose Kaya did not explain to you that, over time and as part of their evolutionary process, Sotkari Ta became genetically predisposed to seek out and prefer other Sotkari Ta as mates. They have a heightened sense of touch and certain types of energy can be exchanged this way. The truth is that this is a new experience for me as well. Other than Kaya, who is like my...uhhh, who is very old, I have never met another Sotkari Ta female. I suppose this would explain our reaction."

"Our reaction? You felt it too?"

"Yes. Unfortunately, I must admit, I sensed the physical attraction as well," he said, rolling his eyes.

"How so very sad for you that you should be attracted to an insignificant creature like me."

He couldn't help but smile at my sarcasm. It helped diffuse the tension a bit.

"Anyway, Mina, I assure you that I have not and will not go beyond simple telepathic communication without your permission. So, let us be clear: any of these sensations that you might be feeling are out of my control."

I shook my head, thinking of the predicament I had found myself in.

"Wonderful."

"To show my good faith, I will try to train you how to block out any unwanted telepathic incursions. It is not an easy thing to master and requires much practice, but it will serve you well in case you encounter other telepathic beings in the future. We should set up a daily schedule for training in Sotkari Ta enhanced capabilities, self-defense, and weapons practice. I suggest we get some rest and start our routine early tomorrow."

I wasn't sure if he would keep his word, but I had no other choice than to trust him.

6

W e met the next morning in the kitchen. I reproduced the same thick warm cereal that had been my breakfast for the past year. Montor walked in and cocked an eyebrow after taking one look at my bowl.

"Do you actually like that disgusting mud the Lostai call a morning meal?"

"I do not know of food options other than what the Lostai offer on Xixsted."

"Reproduced food is bad enough. Lostai reproduced food, even worse. Here, let me introduce you to something different from my planet, Aranda."

I pressed my lips together, preparing myself for whatever it was he planned to give me. He was right. The Lostai cereal was an unappetizing brown color and flavorless with the consistency of oatmeal that had sat out for far too long. Even worse, it smelled like cooked cauliflower mixed with rotten eggs, but at least by now I was used to it. On the other hand, I didn't know what to expect from Montor...in general.

What if he wants to mess with me?

After all, not one Lostai soldier had ever shown me an ounce of kindness.

Skepticism must have been written all over my face because he quickly clarified, "Do not worry. It is made with the eggs of a domesticated bird and mixed with cured meat and vegetables."

He walked over to the food reproducer, spoke instructions in an unrecognizable language, and came back with a plate in each hand. His height allowed him to easily swing his leg over the back of the chair to sit. I smiled to myself.

Just like how Riker does it on Star Trek: TNG.

I was pleasantly surprised by the aroma, reminiscent of onions, potatoes, and bacon, even before he pushed the plate in front of me. What I saw looked like a quiche without the crust. He watched me intently as I tasted it.

"Mmmm...this is actually very good."

The flavor and texture reminded me of eggs, but it also contained pieces of what looked like vegetables and salty meat. Savory, like a mix of Thai and Spanish cuisine, and yes, a bit spicy, but delicious.

"A pale reproduction of the real thing but better than that Lostai slop," he said, after which he scarfed down his portion.

"Thank you. It is kind of you to share it with me. There has been some unpleasantness between us, but I think we can agree to get along better," I said, trying to be gracious.

He rolled his eyes.

"OK, finish up. Let us agree on a daily routine. I think you would benefit from some additional training."

Maybe he prefers it when we are being sarcastic with each other.

"Let me give you a more detailed tour of the ship's flight, weapons, and engineering systems."

As we walked through the different stations, I let him know about the astronautics knowledge I had acquired on my own.

"That is good, but I think you have more to learn. Once you define the destination coordinates, it is true the ship runs itself, but it is important that you are prepared for any emergency or malfunction. Most likely, the shuttle craft you will escape in will have similar controls. Teaching you more about manual control of the flights systems will be the first activity on our schedule."

Next, we worked out in the exercise room and practiced telekinesis. He chose the heaviest weights to lift both with his arms and his mind, showing off his impressive strength. I pretended not to notice and launched several lighter weights in the air in all directions at the same time. I chuckled as he backed against a wall with a thud. He crossed his arms and glared at me.

"Very funny...I am hungry. Let us take a break for the midday meal."

While we ate, he went into more detail on what would happen once we arrived at Renna One. We would have to spend a few days there searching for the leaders of the rebel factions before executing the escape plan. Together we cleaned up the kitchen after our meal. He suggested we take a short rest and meet up again at the exercise room for self-defense and weapons practice. As members of Lostai military, it was perfectly normal for us to be engaging in all of these activities, but Montor said his goal was to get me in the best combat shape possible in case something related to my escape didn't go according to plan.

"One would think you truly care about my safety," I said with a smirk.

I knew how to dish out sarcasm, too.

He gave me that impatient look that was becoming all too familiar.

"As I have mentioned before, it is also in my best interest

that you do not end up back on Xixsted, or I will be forced to make those babies for Zorla after all."

We began the self-defense practice. Physically in much better shape than when I first arrived on Xixsted, I now held my own against even the most experienced members of my female squadron. Of course, Montor was in a different league in terms of strength and skill. We started with basic sparring using a variety of kicks, blocks, feints, and strikes. At first, I worried he would take advantage of my smaller size, maybe make a point to hurt me, like my squadron partners did in the beginning. I was relieved that he kept his strikes restrained. Impressed with my quick moves, he nodded, pursing his lips.

"You are strong for your size, and you counter and move well. However, we should practice on how you would escape different types of holds if you should face a larger, stronger opponent."

He applied a headlock. I knew what my next steps should be. First, protect my face by turning into his torso. He was wearing that stretchy, skintight suit again. I tried to ignore the wall of hard muscle underneath the fabric. Next, grab his arm and pull down to release the pressure from my neck. The minute I made skin-to-skin contact, a pleasurable sensation coursed through my body. I became distracted. He sighed deeply, his hold loosening and then tightening again. He shook his head, annoyance in his eyes.

"Mina, by now, I could have completely cut off your air supply. What next?"

I gritted my teeth, shook off the agitation, punched his upper thigh, and grabbed a fistful of hair to pull his head backward.

"That took much too long," he said, irritated.

"Do not worry. We are just starting," I snapped.

We practiced some more. As much as I tried to focus, any

time his hands were on me, I became flustered and self-conscious. I didn't mention anything but was relieved when we were done. We returned to our rooms to shower up and change clothes. Next on our schedule, meet in the observation deck for meditation, mental strength exercises, and learning how to block unwanted telepathic connections.

I arrived to find him staring out the observation deck window. He turned to look down at me. For the first time, I studied his eyes: Yellow, not golden, with hardly any of the sclera visible. Similar to cat eyes, the pupils were slits instead of tiny circles.

Is he examining mine as well?

Our eyes told a story of two beings from different worlds. Yet portions of our DNA were identical. As I mused on this, a thought took me by surprise.

What if we had met under different circumstances?

His voice in my mind brought me back to our present place and time.

"I am sure Kaya has explained that meditation is the fuel for our mental energy. Each person can choose their own way. The important thing is that we renew the faith in our abilities. I focus on one star out of the many to help me concentrate. Do you have any preference?"

"Yes, I like to kneel and close my eyes."

He tilted his head and nodded, as if making a mental note of it.

"Feel free to proceed as you usually do," he said, turning back to look out to the darkness.

I knelt and clasped my hands. We remained that way for about half an hour. I came out of meditation first, standing and rolling back my shoulders. He remained in a trance for a few minutes longer.

I waited in silence until he turned back to me and said,

"Tomorrow, I will start training you on how to block telepathic incursions."

Afterwards, we had dinner and a final drink in the lounge area. He explained that the alcoholic beverage—called *vormey* in his language—was made of a fermented fruit. I decided it looked and tasted close enough to wine to have a glass. It relaxed me, and we settled into conversation.

"Montor, what is so special about the planet I will be escaping to?"

"Yes, good question. Did Kaya explain to you what happened when the Lostai invaded Sotkar?"

"She said some evolved Sotkari sided with the Lostai, others escaped, and many were hunted down and imprisoned by the Lostai."

"Exactly. The Lostai were able to hunt them down because an evolved Sotkari emits certain types of brainwaves. It is also how they find people with embedded Sotkari genes like you and me."

"I see."

"The planet is called Fronidia by its people. The atmosphere around the planet and certain of its mountainous areas have electro-magnetic properties that impede the Lostai sensors from detecting these Sotkari brainwaves. For this reason, some evolved Sotkari chose to take refuge there. Fronidians are a friendly, peaceful, but technologically advanced race. Their government preemptively warned the Lostai that they wanted to remain neutral in any wars among different races and planets but demonstrated that they had a devastating biological weapon that could wipe out the Lostai if they attempted to invade Fronidia. The Lostai have a peace treaty with Fronidians and can visit the planet, but they are not allowed to openly search for or kidnap anyone who lives there. I think whoever you meet there will be sympathetic once you explain your situation."

"Are you sure they will they let me land on their planet?"

"As a matter of protocol, they will establish contact with you once you approach their atmosphere. They have a long history of accepting refugees, especially those fleeing the Lostai. I am sure they will let you in."

This made me hopeful and helped end the second day of our trip on a high note. I returned to my room and decided to compose a short letter to my oldest son before I went to sleep. He had a great personality, always looking at things optimistically and with a can-do attitude.

Dear Chris,

Hi there! Sweetie, I hope you and the rest of the family are doing well. How do you like junior year? I guess you must be starting to think about which colleges you will want to apply to. Obviously, not being there to help you think through your options makes me sad. I'm sure you're attacking this new challenge as you do everything, grabbing the bull by the horns and pushing ahead without any fear. I pray that my absence hasn't sidetracked you from achieving your goals.

I'm so excited to let you know that I have started off on a trip that I am very hopeful will get me away from the people who kidnapped me. I won't lie, I'm fearful of what lies ahead, but I'm sure it's better than remaining a prisoner. I'm heading to a technologically advanced planet. I'm hoping I meet people there who can help me find a way back home.

I miss you all very much. Take care of yourself. Maybe when you look up at the night sky you might be able to feel how much I'm thinking of you.

Love, mom

The third day of our trip went well until we started practicing with choke holds. I willed myself to ignore the sensations provoked by his hands on my neck. I huffed at the thought that our shared Sotkari Ta genes were at the root of this extreme arousal. Instead of getting easier, the more we practiced, the harder it became for me to focus and execute the escape moves.

Is he feeling this too?

His pupils grew from slits to almond-shaped.

"Mina, I suggest you increase your meditation time to improve your lack of focus. We are regressing, not improving."

I bit my lip, trying to control the frustration at his rebuke, and wasted no time at the end of our session to retreat to my room for a cold shower.

Later, at the observation lounge he insisted that we meditate for an hour. During dinner, he was in a better mood. He had reproduced for us a favorite meal from his planet's cuisine.

"Which foods do you miss from your planet?" he asked.

"Oh, so many different things. I think I miss *pizza* the most."

"*Pee...xa*," he repeated.

"Yes, a dough is created and rolled into a large flat circle. Sauce and toppings are added." I had not seen anything similar to cheese on Xixsted and had no idea of a Lostai word to describe it. "Then you bake it in a hot oven until the dough is crispy and the toppings are melded."

"It sounds tasty. Maybe we can figure out how to reproduce something similar."

Is he serious?

His smile appeared genuine and a certain enthusiasm lit his expression. He tilted his head a bit and stared at my face.

"I have never seen eyes that color."

His voice in my mind sounded mellow. No sarcasm now, but my memory was not so short.

"You said they remind you of your pet."

He chuckled under his breath.

I didn't think it was funny.

"May I touch your cheek, Mina?"

What is wrong with him?

Annoyed by the memory of his previous insult, I stood up.

"I think not. I am ready to go to bed."

He chuckled again.

"Rest well, Mina."

7

I woke up the next day determined not to lose control for any reason. Montor's morning lesson revolved around possible problems that could occur during the landing sequence. I kept our conversation centered on his explanations and any questions that I had. Later, I was proud of how well I sparred. When we met midday at the kitchen, he greeted me with "Let us try to make *pee xa*."

I blinked.

"Umm, I'm not sure..."

"From what you described, I think I know what instructions to give the food reproducer for the dough and sauce. My only question is what kind of toppings."

The meals provided on Xixsted were mainly warm cereals, vegetable soups, and protein bars. I didn't know what my options were.

"It could be cured meat similar to what was in the egg dish you shared with me yesterday morning. Also vegetables, but we need something that melts when heated to kind of meld everything together."

I had learned the names of mammal-like animals in the

Lostai language, so it would seem possible for dairy products to exist, but I had not seen any.

"We have something called *cheese* that is made from the curdled milk of domesticated cattle," I explained.

He wagged his finger at me and nodded.

"Yes, I think I know what you are referring to. The Lostai do not like it, but we have several varieties in Aranda."

He spoke his order in Arandan. Within minutes, he brought to the table a piping hot concoction resembling a rustic pizza-like dish that a Turkish friend had once prepared for me back in my college days. He made vertical slices and served himself a piece first. After he swallowed his first bite, an exuberant smile brightened his face.

"I like my version of *pee xa*."

I tried it and was impressed.

"Not bad for a first try."

He laughed with a boyish joy that didn't match his large body.

We finished eating and cleaning up. On my way out of the kitchen, he stopped me, placing one hand on my shoulder. Shortening the space between us to a proximity that we only used when sparring, he said, "Mina, I enjoyed making *pee xa* for you."

I had to admit, it was a kind gesture on his part.

"It was thoughtful of you. I appreciate it." I looked down because my heart swelled with a feeling of bonding that was absurd considering our overall circumstances.

His hand slid from my shoulder to my hand. He lifted my hand to his mouth, and before I knew it, he licked my palm and the back of my hand and began nipping and sucking in between my fingers. Shock morphed into disbelief and then amusement once I realized this was meant to be a romantic gesture.

What the hell?

I pulled my hand away.

"Ewww...What are you doing?" I said, wiping my hand on my shirt.

"I, errr...I just thought..." He stepped away from me, his hands in the air.

I could not believe my eyes. He was truly flustered, but within moments, the familiar acerbic tone returned.

"Oh, nothing. Zorla has been asking when we are going to start the mating process. I wanted him to see that we were working on it. Come now, stop pretending. I am sure you found it pleasant."

The mention of Zorla's name erased any of the earlier warm and fuzzy feelings.

"So, I guess that was one of your umm...overtures? No, I would not call that...pleasant."

"Oh...I see. Well, let us move on then. I will see you later for our self-defense drills."

I left to my quarters and rested while pondering on his behavior and our situation in general. Per our schedule, we met up again at the exercise room. I drew in a deep breath and said to myself, "OK, Mina, stay focused no matter what."

By now, he was all back to business.

"I am assuming that you have practiced with your squadron on how to deal with an opponent who has you pinned on the ground and may be punching or choking you."

"Yes."

"OK, let's see how good you are at it. Go ahead, lie on the ground."

I did, and he got on his knees positioning himself over me with his hands around my neck. I was so angry with myself the minute my heartbeat accelerated. I steadied my breath, but the arousal was immediate. Willing myself to ignore it, I executed the escape moves, using my arms to bring his down, thrusting my hips up, and curling my ankle around his to flip him on his back. Now I was over him. My next move should have been to strike him and run away. Instead, we just stared at each other. He broke the silence.

"Well, what are you waiting for?" he shouted out loud in a cranky tone, forgoing telepathic communication.

He made a quick move to flip me on my back again. This time, instead of choking me, he pinned each of my hands against the floor.

"Now what, Mina? I can head butt you or..." Our eyes locked again. His voice became quiet and smooth in my mind. "Tell me, Mina, what next?" It was only for a few seconds until he regained his normal tone.

"By now, you would be dead."

I gathered my bearings and kneed him on his butt, causing him to fall forward, giving me a chance to pull away my hands and flip him.

"That is better, but you need plenty of practice."

By the sixth day of our trip, Montor was back to the unpleasant attitude he exhibited when we first met. Potent sexual tension built up every time we had close physical contact. It irritated him to no end. During our self-defense practices, he berated me, shouting that he was not going to be my babysitter. He became more aggressive when we sparred. I knew his training could mean the difference between life and death for me in the future, so I sucked up his bad temper. Needing a break from his crankiness, I told him that I preferred to have dinner, perform meditation, and practice mental exercises alone in my quarters.

He replied, "Fine. That is your loss."

I wasn't sleeping well at night. I fantasized that my husband was in bed with me.

The tenth day started off with a bit of a turnaround. Montor told me that he wanted us to take a break from self-defense drills and to have the evening meal together. I wanted a break from him, period. Alternating between constant arguing and infuriating horniness was taking a toll on me, but I grudgingly accepted. When I arrived, he had already set the table. Our place settings were across from each other, but our eyes did not meet.

I thanked him for preparing the meal. Even though he cleared his throat a few times, he didn't speak, and we ate without any conversation. We finished our meal and picked up in silence.

This is bizarre.

I had already planned a quick getaway when he surprised me with an apology.

"Mina, I am sorry if I have been extra tough on you. I am only concerned for your ability to defend yourself."

I took a moment to check his face and expression. He seemed sincere and didn't look well rested either. Certain things were out of our control.

"I understand. This whole situation is stressful, and I am grateful for what you are doing for me."

"Would you like to join me for a glass of *vormey*?"

"Yes, that sounds nice."

We went to the lounge and sat on a sofa. He got a bottle of the Arandan wine and poured two glasses. We chatted a bit, making fun of Dimlet, Zorla, and other Xixsted station personnel. Soon, his lips curled into a more mischievous smile.

"You know, Mina, I am supposed to seduce you before this trip is over, and I realize that I have no idea what the mating rituals of your people are. I mean, for example, does the male pursue the female, and if so, how does he show his affection for her?"

I tried to behave as if he was asking a basic question, like what type of animals we have on Earth.

"Well, in most of our traditional societies, the male pursues the female, but for more modern-minded people, it can go either way. Romantic love can also happen between people of the same sex. We have ways we show affection that are used between parents and children, or friends and family, and also these can also be used between couples, but as the relationship becomes more serious, things get more intimate."

I sounded like a nutty professor giving a lecture. Either I had his undivided attention or he was mocking me. I wasn't sure.

"Really? Clarify, please."

Without thinking, I was wringing my hands.

"Well, for example, a mother will hold her children's hands to keep them close and safe. However, one of the first signs that a male and a female are a couple is if they walk hand-in-hand. Or he might hold her hand while they talk."

"Like this?"

He took my hand, softly rubbing and squeezing it. My heartbeat raced like it did during our self-defense sessions.

"Yes."

His eyes were almost shut and his voice down to a whisper.

"Tell me more."

"Well, another important sign of affection for us is *kissing*."

I didn't know any Lostai word that might mean kissing, so I said it in English. He was alert again and shook his head.

"I have no idea what that is."

"There can be a friendly *kiss* on the cheek or forehead, but between a couple, the *kiss* will be on the mouth and can get more intimate."

"Mina, I think you should show me," he said in a deep voice.

I no longer heard the humming of the spaceship engine, and everything was quiet in my mind. I leaned over and kissed him gently on the cheek and then on the forehead. The soft fuzz covering his skin tickled my lips and had an odd bitter-sweet taste. I straightened up again. He didn't move an inch, and I thought my heart would explode from the palpitations. He continued to hold my hand in his, and for some reason, I became a bit flirty. I smiled, leaned over again, and kissed his lips. Being so thin, there was not much to them, but they were soft, and I lingered.

"That is nice. I like it," he said.

"And couples take it a bit further as they get more passionate."

He licked his lips.

"And how would that be, Mina?"

I leaned over yet again and this time kissed him with my lips slightly parted.

"You should open your mouth slightly," I said.

I slid my tongue in and rolled it around his. He was a quick learner and slowly pushed me down on the sofa, one hand behind my neck, his thumb stroking my cheek. His tongue was large and with a slightly rough texture. I found myself sucking and imagining how it would feel on my skin. He enjoyed more nipping and tasting my lips.

"My people use the tongue also, but not in the mouth," he said in a husky tone.

After that, things progressed fast. His hands were under my clothing, and mine were in his hair.

"Mina, I think it is time we take this lesson to my quarters."

Before I replied, in one swift motion he picked me up in his arms and walked to his room. He carefully laid me on his bed and dimmed the lights. Speaking words in his language, he patted his shoulders and collar area. The skintight suit inflated and slit open from the neck to the groin area. I looked away as he stepped out of it. He got in the bed and covered us with the blanket. Quickly disposing of my shirt, he licked my skin slowly, savoring the taste, starting on my neck and traveling down over my breasts. The sensation of his rough tongue on my nipples was everything I had imagined and more.

Up until that moment, I had only been this intimate with Josh. This was truly different. Overwhelmed with desire in just a matter of seconds, I forgot who and where I was. I caressed his back and shoulders and didn't want him to stop. Our bodies pressed together, and there was no doubt how aroused he was. His hands slipped under my shorts. My hips encouraged him.

He stopped. His glowing yellow eyes, wild and urgent, met mine.

"Mina, I do not want any confusion. Are we pretending, or do you really want this?"

The reality of what was happening left me breathless. I couldn't blame him, but suddenly, I was terrified.

"I am scared to death, Montor!"

"Do not worry, Mina. I will be gentle. If you give me permission to go further in your mind, I will know exactly how to please you," he said in a hurry.

He thought I was afraid he might physically hurt me, but my fear was more on an emotional level.

Will I regret this in the morning?

It was too late. All the past long, lonely months were coming to a head.

"Yes, Montor. Tonight, I give you permission for everything."

He growled softly.

I pulled up my knees to help him get rid of my shorts. I had given him free reign of my mind, so I decided to make the most of it, focusing on everything I wanted him to do to me. Now that nothing separated us, he began a slow discovery of my body, his large fingers probing, massaging, pleasuring.

We rolled back and forth, over and under each other until, out of breath, I gasped, "Do it already, please."

Tentative, he pushed in only a bit.

"You're tiny."

Frustration took over. My body needed him.

"I've given birth three times. I can handle you."

Eyebrows raised first, followed by a sly smile.

"OK, sweetness," he whispered.

I should have thought twice before spurring him on. It took only two or three deep thrusts for orgasms to rock my body, but he continued to slam into me with the full force of his desire. With my body already so sensitive, the pleasure was agonizing. He groaned when he pulled out at the end, and warm fluid sprayed over my belly.

8
———————

When I woke up, it was already midday and he was spooning me. I slowly turned my head. Still fast asleep with a look of contentment on his face, he reminded me of someone taking a long nap after a heavy meal.

I ran my hands over my pelvic area and between my legs. The soreness didn't surprise me. The night had turned into a marathon, and my body felt as if I had slept with twenty men. It was worth it. I had experienced the weirdest, most pleasurable orgasms, feeling the release in areas of my body that I never had thought possible: behind my eyes, my eardrums, belly button, between my toes. I had always categorized my sex life with Josh as satisfying. Now, it paled in comparison to what I shared with Montor.

Have I been missing out all along, or is this something specific to Montor and me?

After a few minutes, his sparkling eyes and sly smile greeted me. I turned my body towards him and pressed my face to his chest, running my fingers over the amulets he wore around his neck.

Before I was able to comment on them, Montor said, "Mina,

I never expected to say this, but you are by far the most delicious female I have ever had. We should thank those Sotkari Ta scientists for their genes."

I suppose it was meant as a compliment, but it was hard to be sure when so much of what Montor said was tinged with sarcasm. He stretched out his arms.

"I guess we should get up. Come shower with me, Mina."

I don't know why I was bashful considering the night we had just shared, but I grabbed the blanket and draped it around myself.

"Umm, maybe that is not such a good idea. I need to rest," I said.

He guffawed.

"Do not worry, Mina. It will take at least until this evening for me to get my energy back."

He led me into the shower. In the light, we had full view of each other's bodies. I saw bruises on my thighs and arms, the marks of his relentless onslaught. I was sure there were probably a few on my butt as well. His body looked like a chiseled statue—so tall with hard, defined muscles in perfect masculine proportion. In general, his body features and shape were similar to a human man, except for the six fingers and six toes on each hand and foot, the soft fuzz covering his skin, and, of course, the third testicle.

"I like your hair, Mina, so full of curls. Let me help lather it."

When I turned around, he shouted out loud, "What is this?"

He caught himself and continued telepathically, "Mina, what are all these scars on your back?"

I quickly turned around, embarrassed, and avoided looking up at his face.

"When I first arrived on Xixsted, Zorla ordered that I be punished severely for different reasons. Sometimes, it was because I could not keep up with the physical training, or if he assumed I was being disrespectful, or if I got lost on the station and he suspected I was trying to escape, or other times, it was for no reason at all. I try not to think about those days."

"That idiot! How dare he damage such soft, smooth skin." His nostrils flared with anger, and he punched a fist in his other open hand. "At least they should have erased the scars. I will make him pay for that." He took a deep breath. "Anyway, do not worry. I still find you very attractive."

Confused and surprised at his emotional reaction, I said nothing, trying to gather my thoughts.

He put his hand under my chin and tilted my head up.

"I was untruthful about your eyes, the day I met you. I thought they were the most gorgeous I had ever seen."

What the hell is this? A new and improved Montor? Tender and romantic but still sarcastic and annoyingly full of himself.

I still was at a loss of how to react or what to say. He didn't expect a response, simply turning me around and continuing to wash my hair. After he was done rinsing, while I was still facing away from him, he gently tilted my head back so that I was looking up. He towered over me and bent down to kiss me on the lips.

"I really do like this *kix-ing* thing," he said, pronouncing it carefully but still with an accent.

I liked it too.

When we finished showering, we went to the kitchen for a meal. It was already early afternoon, and we both had developed a ravenous appetite.

"Montor, about Zorla, I do not want you to cause trouble for yourself over something that happened to me a long time ago. Once I got accustomed to the routine on Xixsted, he no longer bothered me."

"I will punish him, and he will not even realize it. I—how did you say?—get into his head every now and then to amuse myself. I make him include errors in his reports to his commander and forget where he has placed important items. I will think of something. He is such an idiot. I should make him go outside the station without an air mask."

"Montor, honestly, I am so confused about your relationship with the Lostai. Kaya's behavior confuses me as well. You are both powerful beings. You could overcome them easily, leave to somewhere safe, and not have to deal with them at all. In fact, I do not know why any trained Sotkari Ta would remain a prisoner considering the abilities they possess."

"Well, Sotkari Ta are not omnipotent. Also, be aware, the Lostai tend to use loved ones as ransom. Many Sotkari Ta have family members or loved ones who do not possess evolved abilities and are vulnerable. The Lostai investigate and identify these connections. Then they find these people and threaten to harm them. Therein lies the Lostai strength. Kaya works for the Lostai to protect her granddaughter. The Lostai can be ruthless. She will not take any risk."

"And you, do you have family? Children? What do they hold against you?"

He masked any emotion. If he had such a weakness, he wasn't about to reveal it to me.

"No, my family died when I was very young. The Lostai brought me to Xixsted as an orphan once they identified that I had Sotkari Ta genes."

He smiled but hid something behind those eyes that tried so hard to appear aloof.

"As I grew into adulthood, I purposely avoided any personal entanglements so that I am not bound by anything. They hold nothing against me. Do not misunderstand my situation, Mina. I am not a Lostai soldier against my will. The Lostai have built up an impressive empire in this area of the galaxy. I enjoy being a part of their influential and powerful military, the freedom and luxuries that come with being a decorated Lostai soldier...but I do not agree with all of their policies, so I also secretly sometimes work with rebel factions, which also has its rewards. What can I say? I live an interesting and full life."

"You seem to have a close bond with Kaya—"

He cut me off.

"Mina, I think we have discussed enough regarding this topic. I prefer we change the subject."

After that, he remained in a pensive mood and suggested we skip the normally scheduled activities for the rest of the day except for some quiet meditation at the observation deck. He asked me to join him at the lounge to relax. Instead of wine, Montor mixed up some alcoholic cocktails that were ridiculously strong. I had one, and he had a few. He stood in front of the window and stared in silence at the star-studded darkness. I was about to excuse myself and retire to my room when he turned around and straddled a lounge chair, motioning for me to come sit there in between his legs.

"Come here, Mina. Relax."

This is awkward. I should go to my room.

There had been no time yet to process what had happened between us. In spite of it all, something made me decide to sit with him as he suggested. I leaned my back into his torso, my head against his chest and my legs stretched out on the lounge chair. He placed his hands on my shoulders and softly slid them up and down my arms, stroking me with his fingertips. I sighed with pleasure.

"Mina, last night was a revelation. I never expected us to have so much, how should I say, affinity. It is a shame we did not meet under other circumstances. We would have made a great team, going off on missions together and relieving any stress in the evenings," he said with a sly smile.

I understood what he meant. This thing with Montor was on steroids.

Of course, this can't compete with the trust, friendship, and shared values that come with almost twenty years of marriage, right?

I was guilt-ridden for even making the comparison in my head.

"No offense, but I probably would not agree with many of the things you do when you are off and about on your missions."

"Yes, but imagine for a moment if we were both fighting for a common cause. I would train you until you were almost as powerful as I am. Then together we would be unstoppable."

"Montor, that is a big pivot from how you treated me the first time we met not too long ago."

Putting one arm around my waist, he tilted my head forward with the other hand and, gathering my hair to one side, licked my ear lobe, followed by kisses down the side of my neck. I tingled all over.

"Yes, I know, Mina. That was before we became... acquainted. I did not want you to get too cocky. You know, I had to give one of your fellow Earthians a similar lesson. One of the other three who were brought to Xixsted from your planet. I was tougher on him than I was with you. He did not have Kaya there to defend him."

The memory of whatever he did to the poor prisoner made him chuckle to himself. I woke up from my daze and turned to face him.

"You mean the three who escaped from the other station on Xixsted. You knew them?"

Maybe it was the cocktails because he replied without hesitation.

"Knew them? Mina, I helped them escape."

I barraged Montor with questions. We got up from the lounge chair, and he prepared himself another cocktail. He explained that the three other hostages from Earth were an elderly male, a little girl, and a young adult male.

"The younger male confronted me and challenged my authority. I wasted no time teaching him a lesson and getting him in line," Montor said, puffing his chest out and strutting around like a peacock.

I think the cocktails were beginning to have an effect as his speech and gestures became more animated.

"I must admit, Mina, I felt no concern about the fate of the two males, but I admired how they protected the little girl. I learned that Zorla had come up with a plan to accelerate her growth and the onset of puberty and force her and the young male to have intercourse."

I shook my head in disgust.

"What is wrong with Zorla? Does he not have any morals at all? Not even a young child is safe from his ruthless plans."

Montor stopped his pacing, and his expression turned grave.

"You know, Mina, I had a twin sister..." his voice lowered. "She died right before my eyes, sometime before I was brought to Xixsted as a child."

He crossed his arms and turned away from me before continuing.

"I do not know why, but this young girl from Earth reminded me of her. It was bad enough to see her cry for her mother every day. I could not allow Zorla to ruin that little child's life any further."

He turned back to face me, his hand covering his mouth. Kaya was right when she described him as complicated. He could appear cold and calculating one minute, then emotional and vulnerable, the next.

"I was the one who arranged for the rebel forces to come rescue them, and I manipulated the minds of the security guards so that they would drink themselves to a drunken stupor that evening. The hostages were able to easily slip away from the station and be transported safely off Xixsted."

"So, these rebels do not know that you are in the Lostai military?"

"No, they have no idea. I use a different name when I work with them, and I do not deal with them in person. While they were helping the hostages get off the station, I was on another area of Xixsted in full Lostai uniform. The Earthians themselves have no idea who coordinated the escape."

"Amazing. Where were the Earthians taken?"

"To Fronidia, the same place I am sending you. It is the only place in this sector where the Lostai are kept somewhat in check."

"Montor, what if Zorla accuses you of having something to do with these escapes?"

"I do not worry about that," he said with a smug expression. "As I said before, I hide my identity well. Even if he were to come to that conclusion, I am able to manipulate his thoughts, but most probably, he would not bring it up for discussion, anyway.

"And why is that?"

"Mina, I am an indispensable asset for Zorla. For example, I have attended diplomatic meetings with Lostai high government officials and representatives of other planets posing as Zorla's bodyguard and have manipulated the other parties into signing agreements that he proposes. Zorla and I go into these meetings already with a plan for me to sway the decisions of others to the benefit of the Lostai while he takes the credit for being influential and persuasive. The fact that I have pledged loyalty to Zorla reflects favorably on him, and he is growing in the ranks of Lostai military. He would much rather keep me by his side than accuse me of anything."

The extent of Montor's power and influence was becoming clear to me.

"Now, do not think I have free rein to do as I please. There are limits even to my abilities. It takes an extreme amount of concentration and mental strength to manipulate the actions of others. I need to choose wisely when and how I use it. Also, I must keep a delicate balance and not appear to outright disobey Zorla's orders. It serves my interests that his commanders see him as a strong leader and not suspect that he might be under my influence."

"I do not like at all the idea of controlling people's behavior, but on behalf of that little girl, I thank you for helping her escape. It was a noble thing for you to do."

"Let us not forget that I am helping you escape too."

"Of course. I guess I have Kaya to thank for that."

"She did ask that I help you, but to be honest, I also had a vested interest. I do not want to father children destined to be used by the Lostai military any more than you do."

"Yes, I am thankful we agree on that."

That brought to my mind how, to my relief and as best as I could remember, Montor had been careful to avoid ejaculating inside of me.

"Montor, things got a bit crazy last night. We did not remain under the covers. Do you think Zorla was spying on us and maybe noticed that you avoided—"

Thankfully, he cut me off. I would have preferred avoiding the subject but felt it needed to be addressed. Our deception in that matter was as bad as if Zorla would have caught us not really having sex, since his goal was for us to procreate.

"Mina, the Lostai are not comfortable with sexuality at all. I am sure that once he saw us engaged, he did not remain watching, but you bring up a good point. I need to be more careful to conceal what is happening...or should I say, not happening."

"You know, Montor there is something I have not mentioned."

"Yes?"

"I have three children..." I hesitated. The mention of them

brought on a wave of sadness, and I swallowed hard. Montor placed his hands on my shoulders as in support.

"Yes," he said again. "Kaya told me."

It took me a few minutes to regain composure.

"After my third child, I decided to have a procedure that prevents pregnancy. However, the procedure is reversible. During the trip from Earth to Xixsted, I believe the Lostai scientists spent a lot of time studying my physiology. I have no idea if they discovered this and figured out how to reverse it. Of course, I could not ask them."

I was curious if he had heard anything from Zorla on the topic. His reaction surprised me. He shook his head and came up close.

"Too bad we do not know for sure, as I would love to be able to just...let...go."

His hands traveled from my shoulders down to my wrists. Holding my hands, he bent down to kiss me on the lips. Skin contact of any kind with him made me want only one thing, to have more. The chemistry between us was addicting. I stood on my toes and kissed him back with abandon. Squatting, he placed his hands on the back of my thighs, lifting me up easily while I wrapped my legs around his waist. He glanced at the sofa.

"What do you think, Mina, here or back in our room?"

"I do not care."

So, we made love on the floor.

9

The days that followed were rays of bright light shining through what had been more than a year of dark loneliness, sadness, and pain. Montor treated me with kindness and was committed to training me in all aspects of military and Sotkari Ta skills. Self-defense practice became foreplay for the synchrony and cadence we shared in bed. I moved into his room since we slept together each night. He made a habit, first thing each morning, to caress my cheek with the back of his hand, a sign of affection in his culture.

Montor soon tired of the pull-out method of birth control. One evening, he came to bed naked, ready to go, with a vial in his hand.

"What is that?"

He flashed that sly smile.

"Always so inquisitive."

He opened the vial and showed me a transparent liquid.

"The liquid is applied on the male's member, immediately creating an invisible, microscopic barrier. Once it evaporates, neither of us will feel anything other than each other. Later, it disintegrates all the Sotkari Ta baby-making sperm."

"Are you sure it works?" I said, shaking my head.

First, he seemed offended that I should question him.

"Of course, it works. What do you mean? Trust me. I have used it many times." His expression changed. "Oh, I understand. You do not have contraception methods on your planet."

I huffed, irritated at his smugness.

"Of course, we do. Do you not remember about the operation I told you I had?"

"Yes, but so barbaric to make the female go through a surgical procedure."

"We have birth control for the males, too," I said, feeling a little defensive. "It is a rubber that is placed over the male's penis."

He nodded his head, pursing his lips.

"I suppose that could be fun. The partner can put it on and take it off as part of foreplay."

"No, it stays on until the couple is done."

"What—you must be joking!" He laughed so hard. "Maybe, I should put my clothes back on, too."

I took a deep breath and decided to drop the discussion, but I was also worried whether Zorla was watching.

"Montor, should you not be hiding it? Zorla will see."

"Trust me, if Zorla was spying on us, the video was turned off the minute he saw me like this," he said, gesturing down to his privates. "Go ahead, sweetness. You do the honors."

Ever since we started on the trip, Montor had wanted to prioritize teaching me how to block telepathic connections. We had not spent much time practicing Sotkari Ta skills because I had made a habit of retreating to my room in the evenings to avoid interacting with him. Now that our relationship was blossoming, we reverted to our original schedule of meditation and mental exercises after dinner.

In the beginning, the training process required him to place his hands on my shoulders like Kaya did when she first instructed me on telekinesis. We had a lot of false starts. The first few times, all it took was for him to touch me to make us forget about the lesson and move on to more pleasurable activities. We decided we'd focus better if we moved our meditation and Sotkari Ta practice from the evening to the early morning before our physical and sparring workouts.

That first morning, we were determined to make progress.

"Mina, I would like you to remember the time when Kaya was teaching you telekinesis. Put yourself in the same frame of mind as when you were learning to use your Sotkari Ta abilities for the first time. Close your eyes. Can you see my light in your mind?"

"Yes."

"Now, imagine covering that light with the palm of your hand. When you no longer see the light, you have closed yourself off from receiving any telepathic connection."

Of course, like telekinesis, it sounded easy but was hard to execute.

After five days of investing long hours trying, I was ecstatic to finally be able to block Montor's telepathic communication. My excitement was short-lived.

"That is good, but pretty simple, sweetness."

I crossed my arms and shot him an impatient look.

"The difficult part is when you are in a room full of people and you want to block everyone who might have telepathic abilities at once, or perhaps only one person among several telepaths."

"How am I supposed to practice when it is only you and me here?"

"Yes, until we arrive on Renna One you will not be able to.

In the meantime, what you can practice here is the speed with which you can close your mind."

For the remainder of our trip, any time we were in different stations or rooms, I immediately blocked him whenever he came into my line of sight. We played games where he tried to communicate before I had a chance to close my mind. Sometimes, he would try to creep up on me. It made for a lot of "gotcha" moments where we ended up giggling in each other's arms.

During our meals and free time, we had interesting conversations. One time, I asked him whether he knew of other people kidnapped from Earth.

"Mina, the Lostai have been taking people from your planet over two generations, but my understanding is that not many have a full set of dormant Sotkari Ta genes as you do. You and the other three are the first kidnapped under Zorla's supervision. This is why he is so fixated in demonstrating to his commanders that you are rendering benefits for the Lostai military. Since the Sotkari targeted technologically inferior planets to embed their genes, it has been similarly easy for the Lostai to kidnap people without detection. I have heard that they cause aircraft accidents and manipulate weather patterns, resulting in the death and disappearance of many people, only to be able to kidnap one person with evolved Sotkari genes. Many times, they take survivors to serve as slave labor on their mining locations. They have done the same on other planets as well."

"Montor, I never thought I would say such a thing of any group of people, but the more I learn of the Lostai, the more I hate them."

"Well, not all the Lostai are ruthless killers. Although I

would say they suffer of a superiority complex, most of the general population are decent people who are deceived by their rulers and military. They are not aware of what goes on or are fed misinformation."

"Have you met any others from Earth besides myself and the other three?"

"Yes, I know a few male Earthians, but you are the only adult female that I have met. Some of these Earthians decided to openly collaborate with Lostai rather than suffer punishment. They have become just as ruthless as myself or any other Lostai soldier. Some have even assisted in kidnapping other Earthians. You might see some on Renna One."

It stung a bit that he included himself as part of that group, but at least he was being honest.

"Montor, why did they keep me separate from the others from Earth?"

"The Lostai do not like the idea of many evolved Sotkari together. It makes them nervous. A group of properly trained people with evolved Sotkari genes would certainly be a force to be reckoned with, and as I said before, you are special. You carry a complete set of Sotkari Ta genes, just like I do. They are excited about your potential but also are intimidated by it."

As well as things were going with Montor, I realized that this was a temporary situation. I assumed this was Montor's frame of mind as well. Soon, I'd be on my own heading to another planet. The fact that Fronidia was technologically advanced made me hopeful that once there, I could possibly find a way back home to my family. I had separated in my mind the fact that I was having a steamy love affair with Montor from the longing to return to my family, as if both situations were perfectly compatible. I simply refused to worry about whether I was being an unfaithful wife, how my husband would react if he knew, or how my feelings for Montor were evolving. A few days before our scheduled arrival to Renna One, I brought up the topic.

"Montor, do you think there is any chance that on Fronidia I might find a way back to my family on Earth?"

The question annoyed him and his face reflected impatience that I had not seen in weeks.

"Mina, you need to keep in mind a few things. Although Fronidia is the safest place in this sector for you, it does not mean that you will not be in danger. Lostai are allowed to travel and reside there freely as long as they follow the local laws. There are Lostai soldiers and spies posing as civilians trying to locate any evolved Sotkari. If they find you, they will try covertly to bring you back to Xixsted. You will need to keep a low profile, so you will not be able to walk around asking Fronidians if they can take you back to Earth. Also, do you know how far you are from Earth? You are several galaxies away. It is still a mystery, even to me, how the Lostai are able to travel that far."

"I cannot just give up. I miss them, my children and my husband..."

I meant to keep it as a private thought, but it slipped out, still not having perfected the transition from musing to myself and communicating. Worse yet, I had formulated the thought in Lostai. His body language and tone completely changed, reminding me of how arrogant and offensive he was the first time we met.

"Mina, once you arrive to Fronidia, do whatever you please. I am simply giving you practical advice. For all you know, your husband has found a replacement for you already."

I knitted my eyebrows.

"I doubt that very much."

He walked up to me, pulled me close, and kissed me hard. It hurt my lips.

"I, for one, will miss you greatly but will always think of you every time I *kix* another female companion. After all, you taught me how to do it, my dear," he said with a sarcastic look and a soft, derisive laugh.

Suddenly, I was pissed off.

"Oh, *fuck you*! Why should I care who you *kix*?" I said, mocking his accent.

"That is correct. Why should you care? You are dreaming of going back to your husband. And I would appreciate if you are going to insult me, you use words I can understand."

I turned to walk away, but he grabbed my arm and pulled me back towards him.

"I am still your commanding officer on this mission. You may not walk away without my permission."

I looked down so he wouldn't see the tears streaming down my face, but a moment later, I lifted my chin to face him.

"Montor, maybe you could come with me. We could hide together there on Fronidia."

A look of confusion swept across his face. He blinked, and a minute went by before he replied.

"Mina, you must be the strangest female I have ever met. Just a moment ago, you said you miss your husband, and now you are asking me to accompany you?"

He was right. What was wrong with me? My head hurt. I rubbed my forehead.

"Montor, I know I must sound like a crazy person. The reality is that I am torn. The time we have shared has been special, and the idea of leaving you is weighing heavily on me. I miss my family, but you are right. I do need to consider that I may never be able to return to Earth...You have said you have feelings for me...I have come to care for you too."

I was so frustrated with myself.

Why am I crying? Why am I so confused?

Now, he was visibly upset as well, running his fingers through his hair and shaking his head.

"Mina, what you are asking...it is impossible. I will not leave my position on Xixsted."

Stupid, stupid. Why am I even suggesting this?

"Of course you will not, Montor. I am sure it has been so much fun for you these days, taking advantage of the situation and using me for your own pleasure."

"And what about you? Are you not using me?"

I paced around now, practically rambling on to myself, although still communicating telepathically.

"Oh, shut up! Of course you will not come with me. Why should you, what with all the females, riches, and power you have."

I gestured air quotation marks for sarcasm, which, of course, Montor didn't get the meaning of.

"If all you care about is not being forced to father children for Lostai and that is why you are helping me, I get it. I am with you on that, but why put up this act with me? I suppose to make it more fun for you. At the core, you are just a lying bastard. I preferred when you were being a jerk with me. At least you were being honest."

His voice sounded deeper and lower in my mind than ever before.

"Mina, you do not know anything about me."

"Guess what? I know you lied to me. If you really cared, you would stay with me."

Bottom line, I was having a childish temper tantrum. He banged his hand hard on a nearby counter.

"Enough! I cannot leave her alone!"

I looked up at him, and we exchanged no words for a while.

"You are referring to Kaya, right?"

He turned to look out a window.

"Yes."

He sounded defeated. Several more minutes went by before he opened up.

"Kaya is strong, but she is already very old. She worries about what will happen to her granddaughter after she dies. I have promised Kaya to ensure her granddaughter remains safe. I will not break my promise."

"I suspected something like that. Why not just come out and tell me?"

"Mina, you must swear that you will never let anyone know what I have revealed to you. I cannot appear to have any vulnerability. My influence and power come from a position of strength, where I appear not to care for anyone except myself. If anyone finds out the contrary, it will put my interests and those of Kaya in danger."

"Of course. You have my word."

"I hope I can trust your fortitude, Mina. You never know when you might be tested. I admit, I am a person of questionable morals at best, but I hold loyalty in very high regard. I hope I have earned yours."

I forgave his earlier harsh words and hugged him, the kind of a hug you might give a friend. He wasn't familiar with this display of affection, and I think he took it as an overture. His hand went up the back of my neck and grabbed a fistful of hair, gently tugging it down so that I was looking up to him. He kissed me fiercely, pressing me against the wall and slipping his other hand under my shirt to caress my breasts. I thought my knees would buckle. The extreme physical attraction was overwhelming. Finally, he stepped back.

"Mina, I did not lie when I said my feelings for you are strong, but it is hard to fight a ghost. Another male, I am confident I could easily defeat. But a memory...that is the worst rival."

We didn't touch the subject again and continued with our routine as if the discussion had not even happened. I simply decided to take it day by day, my bond with Montor growing stronger, although thoughts of my family and home were ever present. On the last day before landing on Renna One, he mentioned that he planned for us to stay at one of his vacation homes.

"You will love this place, Mina. My home is next to a sparkling river, and there are waterfalls. The bedroom windows have a full view of the cascades. It is secluded and peaceful."

"Will Zorla approve of this while we are supposed to be on an official mission?"

"I do not need Zorla's approval to stay at my own house, and he is familiar with my lifestyle. I will also take you to an exclusive night spot where only the rich and famous can afford to go."

"Montor, I have no idea what the rich and famous on Renna One wear to a place like that, but I certainly do not have anything appropriate. I only have military work out clothing."

"Do not worry, Mina. I will take care of everything. I want to spoil you a little before it is time for our farewell."

Considering I had spent the last year in what felt like a penitentiary on a desolate rocky moon, I couldn't help but smile.

10

W e landed on a satellite docking station just outside the atmosphere of Renna One and traveled to the surface on a smaller craft used for both space and air travel called a transport pod. Since it was late afternoon, our plan was to touch base with Zorla and then go directly to Montor's vacation home to settle down for the night.

I stepped out of the pod and looked around. Nearby, flowering bushes gave off a sweet fragrance. I hadn't witnessed daylight or vegetation since being taken from Earth. It hit me hard, a hollow feeling in my chest. The thick lump in my throat kept me silent.

A short walk took us through a government complex with triangular buildings of different sizes built of a smooth and shiny white material that sparkled in the sunlight. Lush landscaping and several fountains completed the serene ambiance. We entered one of the buildings where I sat in a waiting area while Montor left to meet with some government officials and to check in with Zorla. Montor returned, and we walked back to the transport pod to head to his home.

During the one-hour ride, Montor filled me in on the history of Renna One. The planet was rich in natural resources, famous for vacation spots, and frequently used as a center for major business meetings. The original natives of Renna One had maintained a simple lifestyle, focusing more on the arts, archeology, and preserving history than on technology and expansion. The Lostai entered a murky treaty with the Rennans stating they would defend the planet from other aggressive races in exchange for permission to mine certain rare minerals that were plentiful on the southern continent.

Instead, the Lostai slowly extracted control from the Rennan central government. Soon, Renna One was another territory in the Lostai Empire. Many workers were brought from other planets to work on the Rennan mines. Some of these newcomers carried diseases that the Rennan immune system could not handle, resulting in epidemic loss of life. The planet's population now was a melting pot of a small amount of native Rennans who had survived, workers from other planets who labored in the mines or serviced the recreation industry, Lostai soldiers and government officials, as well as wealthy vacationers from planets all over the sector.

Montor had not exaggerated on the natural beauty of this place. His property was in a wooded area circled by a river. The sun had already set, and I heard the typical chirps, whistles, and howls of nocturnal animals and insects. I was over-whelmed by how much the area reminded me of home. This easily could have been the Smoky Mountains or the Pacific Northwest.

"Mina, are you OK? I had hoped you would like this."

"Montor this is beautiful, and I appreciate you sharing it with me. I did not expect this place to be so similar to Earth."

He held my hand, and we walked on a stone-paved path leading to his house. The building resembled luxury cabins I had read about back home in travel magazines. It was two stories high, apparently of some type of wood construction. Sections of the house had walls of glass that allowed spectacular views of the forest and river. Many small lights and lanterns lined the roadways, illuminating the whole area. The rustic exterior contrasted with the modern and impeccably furnished interior. The floors were wood, as was the spiraling staircase that led to the second floor.

Montor was pleased with how in awe I was of his property. While I took in the lavish furniture, artwork, and sculptures, he led me to what I would have called the living room. He referred to it as the resting area.

"I think we have cause to celebrate."

He spoke out loud in Lostai, I suppose no longer concerned with the possibility of being spied on, and poured us both a glass of a light blue beverage. The taste landed somewhere in between absinthe (I tried some with Josh when we dated) and anise. I assumed it was highly intoxicating, so I sipped it slowly.

"Is this where you live most of the time?" I said.

"I have several properties on different planets. Where I stay depends on where my missions take me, but I admit, this is my favorite."

Montor grabbed the bottle and took me by the hand, leading me outside to one of the many covered porches that surrounded the house. We sat side by side on one of the sofas. A slight breeze decreased the temperature a notch, and I heard the splash of the waterfalls. He placed the bottle on a small table in front of us, took my hand in both of his, and stared up to the sky. I should have been relaxed, but the change of environment from the spaceship to Renna One provoked so many conflicting emotions: a nostalgia for Earth, a reminder that soon I would be leaving Montor and traveling alone to a place I had never been to before.

After several minutes of silence, I broke his spell and my

sentiments by asking, "Montor, tell me what will be happening in the next few days."

He was distracted, but acknowledged my question, pouring himself a second glass and replying with a sly smile.

"We should talk first regarding tonight. I will show you how comfortable my bed is."

His insinuation quickened my heartbeat and brought a smile to my face.

"Ah, that is what I like to see. Mina, you seem so stressed. What can I do to help you relax?"

As if answering his own question, he grabbed the bottle and led me upstairs to the master bath and bed area.

"There is nothing more relaxing than a soak in the tub," he said.

The bathroom on the second floor was the size of my living room back in Florida, outfitted with a huge, oval-shaped, Jacuzzi-type tub and a shower exposed to the outside. The house was built by a small waterfall, and the cascades fell around the shower area, making it appear as if you were within the waterfall. He touched the controls on a nearby console to activate jets in the tub, and the water began to agitate. A small table next to the tub had on it a glass receptacle containing what appeared to be multicolored small leaves and flowers. After dimming the lights, he grabbed a handful of the mixture and tossed it into the water. Immediately, bubbles filled the tub.

He walked over to me and, without a word, motioned for me to lift my arms so he could pull off my shirt. In a trance whenever we were in close contact, I followed his lead without resistance. Next, he quickly removed the tight sleeveless short shirt underneath that served as a bra. His eyes glowed bright yellow, his pupils went from slits to almond-shaped, and he murmured something in a language I didn't understand. Kneeling, his hands on my waist, he pressed his face against my stomach. Breathing in deeply, he traced my ribcage with his thumbs and softly massaged my abdominal area. Already aroused before he even touched the obvious erogenous zones, I leaned back, and my head hung lazily.

He had explained once to me that contrary to either of our cultures, Sotkari only use hands and fingers to show affection and passion. I supposed he was channeling his inner Sotkari, so to speak. He pulled my pants and underpants down, and I stepped out of each leg. Looking up to me, he spoke in a husky voice.

"Go in, Mina. I will join you."

I finished my drink and began to feel the effects of the alcohol. Getting into the tub, I watched intently as he peeled off his clothing, already imagining touching those hard muscles. He brought the bottle with him as he stepped into the tub. I took a few more sips straight out of the bottle.

"Montor, I am surprised. You do not strike me as the type of person who does bubble baths."

"Bubble baths?"

I giggled.

"Back on Earth, it is a girly thing."

He pretended to be annoyed.

"Really? I will show you how girly I am," he said while grabbing my hand and pulling it towards his crotch.

I shrieked in mock fear and replied, laughing, "I am not afraid of that little thing."

"Oh, you think you are funny? Now you have pushed me to my limit. Mina, for sure you will pay for that."

We horsed around, causing water to splash out to the floor. Eventually we ended up in a passionate embrace, and I kissed his chest. He groaned, led me out of the tub, and grabbed some towels neatly stacked on a side table. We each dried up and used the towels to cover up.

"Mina, are you ready to try my bed?"

I didn't answer. Exhilarated, buzzed, and a bit silly from

fooling around in the tub, I dropped my towel and ran off to his bed. I got under the covers, tucking the edges under my feet to hide from him, giggling with anticipation. He was right behind me, his towel no longer around his waist, pulling on the sheets and blankets until he finally uncovered me.

He took in the view of my nakedness and nodded with an expression of accomplishment. I now most definitely was ready to try his bed. Tossing the bed linen on the floor, he rushed in. I squealed with delight as we tussled, and I moved on top of him. This was a position we had not engaged in. He always wanted to be in charge and have me be the one to lose control. For some reason, I wanted to turn the tables on him.

He grabbed my hips trying to enter me, but I wanted to take my time.

"Wait, not yet," I said.

My fingers traced the outlines of his muscles from his pectorals to his abdominals. I slid my tongue over every hard ripple.

For the millionth time, I found myself thinking, *My God, he's such a hunk.*

I purposely ignored his impressive erection, letting it slide between my breasts as I continued downward. He grunted and groaned, thrusting his hips, while I teased his body without shame, squeezing his butt and delicately kissing him everywhere except where he really wanted me to.

"Mina, you are treading on dangerous ground. I make a point to be gentle with you."

"Shhh, Montor, just lay back."

To his credit, he did try to relax, but eventually I got what I really was striving for, his total loss of control. In a frenzy, he pulled me up and easily flipped me over so I was face down, his preferred position. He wasted no time pushing into me hard and with urgency, panting and groaning louder with each thrust. I'm sure he didn't mean to hurt me, but things took a violent turn as I felt tugs on my hair and a bit of pain in my pelvic area. Still, we both soon exploded in orgasm. The last thrust was deep and prolonged, and that's when I realized my mistake. It took a while for his breathing to return to normal, and he dozed off on top of me. My fidgeting made him aware that his dead weight was overwhelming me. He rolled to the side, pulled me towards him, and kissed the back of my head. In minutes, his deep breathing signaled that he had fallen fast asleep. It took me longer, as I worried about the possible consequences of what I had instigated.

The next morning when I woke up, Montor was not in bed. There was a robe in his spot instead. I put it on and went downstairs. I found him deep in thought studying something on his tablet.

"Good morning," I said.

"Greetings," he replied without looking up.

He was distant.

"Is everything OK?" I asked.

"Yes. I am going over some intel regarding the recent rebel activities here on Renna One. I will be leaving soon to the city to start the investigation."

He still avoided looking at me.

"Should I not be going with you? Are you upset with me or something?"

"No. I will be doing interrogations, and I do not think you will approve of some of my methods."

He put the tablet down and turned his attention to me.

"Come here."

He took my hand and with a gentle pull brought me close to him, saying nothing for a while. Finally, he stepped back and made eye contact, studying my face intently.

"How are you feeling this morning, Mina?"

"I am fine. What should I do today while you are away?" I quickly asked, feeling uncomfortable under his scrutiny.

He grabbed the tablet and pulled up images of two people who, by their features, appeared to be Arandan. He explained that the couple were among the few remaining members of his clan and had been good friends of his parents. His name was Foxor and hers, Lasarta. They lived on his property, helped him with the maintenance, and kept him comfortable while he was there. He said they spoke good Lostai, so I would have no problems communicating with them.

"They will be coming here soon to prepare your meals and help you with anything else you might need. If you like, take some time to walk around the area. There is a pool at the bottom of the cascades that I find relaxing, but if anyone other than these two people enter the premises, contact me immediately."

It struck me odd that he would be concerned about intruders.

"In the afternoon, Foxor will transport you to the city to a place where females go to purchase clothing and get beauty treatments. Here is a remuneration chip. Please feel free to purchase several pieces of different clothing, as many as you want. You should have something other than military clothing to wear in Fronidia. The shop owner's name is Colora. This evening, we will be attending a place called Zamandi's Room. Colora will help you get ready. I have already notified her, so she is expecting you. Foxor will tell you at what time he will return to pick you up and transport you to Zamandi's Room."

"So, do you mean I will be arriving there by myself? Why would you not come get me?"

"Mina, we cannot let on that we are having any relationship other than my being your commanding officer and mentor on this mission. Before I forget, there may be people in Zamandi's Room with telepathic abilities who do not share your ethics and would not think twice to 'get into your head'. Make sure you close your mind when you arrive there."

"What if I need to communicate with you telepathically?"

"When we are in close proximity, and you are extremely confident that you can close everyone off except me, then do so. If not, I would rather you err on the side of safety and avoid telepathy completely. Just cover all the lights that appear in your mind."

"How will I find you?"

"Look around. I asked Foxor to take you at a time when it should not be so busy."

"OK, understood."

Without further discussion, he walked out. I waited in the resting area for Foxor and Lasarta to arrive, not knowing what to expect of these people. They had the access codes to his home, and I jumped up in anticipation as the front door opened. Lasarta spoke first.

"Good morning. You are named Mina, correct? Montor told us to expect you here."

Foxor just nodded.

"Yes, I am Mina."

Lasarta's face brightened with a kind smile. Any of my remaining jitters evaporated.

"Well, Mina, do you have a healthy appetite? I love to cook. I hope you have not had any reproduced food for the morning meal."

"No, I have not eaten yet."

"Excellent. I hear the food on the Lostai station is not very good. Come sit here in the dining area while I prepare something for you."

Lasarta prepared for my breakfast something similar to oatmeal with dried fruits and a hot tea. She also served some for herself and Foxor. The three of us ate together at the dining table.

"Lasarta, this is wonderful. Thank you so much."

"Yes, a simple but hearty start to the day."

Other than that, we didn't talk much and when I was done, I excused myself to exercise. She told me to meet them again there for the midday meal.

Lunch was soup made of root vegetables and small pieces of some type of gamey meat. The meat was tender and the broth flavorful. Again, we ate together.

"This is truly delicious, Lasarta. Everything tastes so fresh," I said.

"Well, we grow everything right here on Montor's property. We raise cattle and fowl here also. My husband even hunts animals in these woods and fishes in the river for food. Foxor, I think we should give Mina a tour."

We took a long leisurely walk around Montor's property and visited their home, a simple but inviting cottage-like structure. Next, they showed me the large greenhouse where most of the vegetables, fruits, and herbs used for Montor's meals were grown. They also took me to the stables that housed all sorts of livestock and birds. It had been so long since I had enjoyed the warm sun on my skin that I decided that it would be great to get a complete body tan.

"Lasarta, I haven't experienced daylight in such a long time. Where can I have some privacy to lay out without any clothing?"

She and Foxor exchanged curious looks, but she quickly recovered and answered, "I think I know a good spot."

They walked me to a clearing with lounge chairs by the river and left me alone. I took off my clothes and soaked in the sun for about an hour and then returned to the house to get ready for the trip to the city.

Midafternoon, Foxor took me to Colora's shop, a combination boutique and beauty salon. I found Colora to be a personable character, who chatted nonstop. Her appearance was almost human except for two notable features. She had raven eyes, completely black with small pink pupils, and her nose was reduced to two small orifices in the center of her face. Spiky short hair matched the pink color of her pupils. She wore a short blouse that exposed her midriff and a long colorful skirt. On her stomach, a tattoo of a bird with bright red, gold, and green feathers screamed on her pale skin. She spoke in Lostai.

"So, where did Montor say you were from?"

"Earth."

She inspected me as if I were a racehorse or purebred dog getting ready for a competition.

"Come, let me take a good look at you and see what I have to work with. Now, I do not know what preferences you might have. I have customers from all over the sector, so no request surprises me. Some females love to change their whole appearance, the color of their skin, even."

"I prefer to keep my skin color and pretty much everything else the same. I like more of a natural look."

"Yes, that is fine. In fact, I love your eyes. We need to enhance that color with some accessory," she said, twirling my curls around her fingers. "I like how your hair is almost the same color as your eyes...but my goodness, do they not supply you with conditioner at that military base? Your hair needs a trim. I love the curls, though. I am sure I can make them look shiny and healthy. Now, let me see this body."

Colora stared at my breasts, gave my butt a light slap, and bent down to squeeze my thighs and calves. "OK, fit but with curves."

She said Montor had arranged not only for me to get ready for the evening but also receive any treatments that Colora and I agreed on. We decided on a full body massage, skin treatment, waxing, manicure, and pedicure. She continued to talk nonstop, asking rhetorical questions but not waiting for any replies. I spent most of the time nodding and smiling.

"Very nice of Montor to look after his charges this way. Hmmm, I wonder. Do the Lostai allow romantic liaisons between soldiers? Whether or not Montor has a handsome face, I guess is a matter of taste. But that body, no questions about that, right? I am sure he makes his females sing, if you know what I mean."

She wagged her hand for emphasis. Her wink and smile were infectious. I couldn't help but giggle.

"Yes, I do," I said, leaving to her imagination what I meant.

"I know if it were me, I would make a go at it with Montor. Shhh, I mean if I were single, of course. He tells me you are a widow. So sad for you at such a young age."

It surprised me to hear how he had described my status, but it did fit my situation in a backasswards sort of way. For sure that was easier to explain than to say I was kidnapped and my husband presumed me dead.

First, Colora helped me select some clothing for daily use. Then she went to the back of the shop and returned with what she claimed was the dress I must wear that evening.

"Mina, I have no doubt. This dress was made for you. It enhances your bronzed skin color, too. I would have picked something that exposes your back, but unfortunately, the scars would ruin the look. Such a shame."

It was the one time when Colora stopped to take a breath and I sensed her curiosity, but she asked no questions. I said a silent prayer of thanks for her discretion that saved me the embarrassment of having to explain. The sleeveless white dress highlighted my tan while concealing the scars on my back. Brilliant amber-hued stones bordered the high collar, accentuating my eye color. A tight-fitting top covered my breasts except for the cut-out in front that exposed some cleavage. The bottom, long and flowing, was sheer from mid-thigh down to give a clear view of my legs. Colora asked if I wanted any other kind of adornment or tattoos. I requested only earrings to match the stones on my collar. She added a thick white bracelet with similar stones to camouflage the wristband and burn scars. She also suggested to complete the outfit with flat white platform sandals that gave me some height but were easy to walk in, which was a blessing, considering I had worn only military boots for over a year.

Colora introduced me to two employees who assisted her. My hair had not been cut since I was taken from Earth, so she had them wash and trim it about four inches. They also applied a type of conditioning mud and rinsed it out after an hour. By then, I was really getting into the primping and pampering. I asked Colora to pile my hair up high and forward to allow the curls to fall loosely around my forehead and cheekbones.

"Yes, Mina. I love it." Referring to makeup, Colora asked, "What type of face coloring would you like?"

I only requested a bit of eyeshadow, mascara, and lipstick. When we were done with the last detail, she applied a shimmering skin lotion and stepped back to take a final look.

"Oh, Mina, I think you are going to be turning a lot of heads tonight. Oh, yes, I do."

11

B y the time Foxor dropped me off at Zamandi's Room, it was early evening and dark outside. Zamandi's Room wasn't a room at all, but a series of adjacent courtyards, bars, lounges, dance halls, and restaurants. At the main entrance, I used the chip Montor gave me to pay the cover charge. The place was happening, bustling with all different kinds of people having a good time. Some areas were lit with tiny lights, others with strobe lights, and others barely any lighting at all.

I quickly identified Montor at a bar about five yards from the entrance. He stood easily half a foot taller than most people there. Several Lostai soldiers stood by him. A quick mental exercise exposed at least three bright lights in my mind. One of them for sure would be Montor, but I wasn't skilled enough to figure out which one. The other two could be anywhere in the large area within my view, so, following his earlier advice, I blocked them all from connecting with me telepathically. Also standing close to Montor was a female who appeared to be Arandan. She was almost as tall as Montor and wore a tight one-piece pants suit. Her body was what my older son would have described as "smoking hot." It annoyed me to see her staring up at him with her hands on his chest.

Also near Montor was a man who, at least from where I stood, appeared human. He took a short step away from the group and stared in my direction. His gaze was so intense that I looked behind me to see what had caught his attention. He elbowed Montor and motioned in my direction. Montor's stare made me turn my head a second time. In a few seconds, he was next to me. He took my hand, kissed it, and looked into my eyes.

"Mina, you look stunning!"

He held on to my hand, so I tapped his, not able to contain the sarcasm in my voice.

"We do not want anyone thinking there is something going on between us, remember?"

He caught himself and let go, then motioned for me to walk ahead of him towards the bar.

"Everyone, this is Mina. She is on her first official mission as a Lostai soldier and outside of Xixsted for the first time," he introduced me.

The man was definitely human. About six feet tall with dark hair and eyes, he had an athletic build and a handsome face. The light skin, dark hair, and hooded eyes made me guess he was of Mediterranean descent. He spoke perfect Lostai.

"Nice to meet you, Mina. My name is Gio Napoletano, and I must say, you have made my night. I have not seen many females from Earth in the past twenty revolutions, and forgive me for being so forward, but you are truly beautiful."

The Arandan female leaned her head on Montor's shoulder, which made me entertain the idea of flirting with Mr. Napoletano as well as annoying Montor, so I replied in English.

"Do you speak English?"

His animated reply carried a heavy New York accent.

"Yeah, I do...I'm from Brooklyn."

"I'm thinking you're Italian."

"Yeah, that's right. And what about you? You look Spanish."

"Oh, I'm Latina on my mother's side, but I have German and Lebanese on my dad's side."

"Well, I must say, that mix turned out great, you know."

"Let me order some drinks," Montor said loudly, interrupting our English banter.

As soon as Montor stepped away, Gio went back to speaking in Lostai, I supposed out of courtesy for the Arandan female, whose name I still did not know.

"So, do you and Montor have something going on?"

He was to the point.

"Errr...Oh...no...he is my commanding officer," I answered.

"I just thought, the way his jaw dropped when you walked in..."

The Arandan female joined the conversation. She spoke slowly to add emphasis, and by the way she stared at me, I knew she was trying to intimidate.

"Yes, I noticed as well."

Secretly, Gio's observation pleased me, but I brushed it off, waving my hand as if it was no big deal.

"Oh, he probably was surprised since he has never seen me in anything other than military garb."

Montor returned with a waiter who held a tray full of drinks. He gave one first to the Arandan female, who gave me a smug look, and the second drink to me. All the males grabbed the rest of the drinks.

Montor looked at me and said, "Mina has not had dinner yet and she is not familiar with this place, so I will take her to the dining area and meet up with you later."

Gio did not miss a beat.

"Montor, as an old friend, may I ask to join you? Please, you would not deny me the opportunity to spend time with someone of my own kind, especially one so attractive."

"Uhh, sure, that will be fine."

The female Arandan quickly followed suit.

"Well, to even things out, I see fit to invite myself as well."

"Fine, my dear."

Montor shot the remaining Lostai soldiers an intimidating look so that they quickly dispersed. He led us to a dining area decorated with artwork and intricate light fixtures, where most of the tables were already occupied. The minute we arrived, the head waiter took us to what I understood to be the chef's table, a spot reserved for VIPs. Montor spoke with the head waiter.

"I have asked the head chef to prepare us several sampling plates so that Mina can have a better idea of what to order the next time she is here," Montor said.

The female Arandan rolled her eyes every time my name was mentioned. I finally figured out her name was Ar Ona. I tried to start some small talk.

"So, Gio, since when have you known Montor?"

"I first arrived to Xixsted when I was only a teenager. Montor was only a few revolutions older than me, but he was already a squadron leader. Brought up on Xixsted, he lived and breathed Lostai military. In the beginning, he was very tough with me."

Gio leaned over towards me and continued in English.

"He beat the crap out of me the first time we met."

"He needed an attitude adjustment," Montor said, guessing what Gio had shared with me.

"But over time we became great friends," Gio continued in Lostai. "We have served on many missions together. Am I right, old friend?"

"Yes, right," Montor answered.

There was irritation in Montor's tone, and they didn't appear to be such great friends to me at all. If Gio noticed it, he didn't let it show or he didn't care.

Most of the food was delicious, but a few items had extreme

flavors. After the meal, Montor ordered a beverage that I guessed was supposed to be like an after-meal expresso. It was so bitter, I gagged. Ar Ona wasted no time in making fun of me. She said something to Montor in Arandan that he thought was hilarious.

I feel so out of place. What the heck am I doing here?

I found myself crossing my leg and arching my back, my nipples suddenly sensitive against the soft dress fabric. Gio had taken my hand in his and was rubbing it reassuringly.

"No worries, Mina. I have lived here twenty revolutions and I still find it disgusting," he said, his eyebrow arched.

The laughter stopped. I wasn't even sure if Gio was referring to the drink or everything in general. Then he said something that made me freeze, as if someone had dumped a bucket of ice water on me.

"I am Sotkari Ta, like Montor, here. I suspect you, Mina, are the same, and well trained at that, since I cannot read you at all."

Montor's eyes blazed with anger. I was well aware that it was not common knowledge outside of the military that the Lostai were kidnapping people with embedded evolved Sotkari genes. For sure, it was not spoken about out loud in casual conversation.

"What is Sotkari Ta?" asked Ar Ona.

No one answered her question.

"Gio, be more careful with your words," said Montor.

Gio was irreverent and did not appear to be intimidated by Montor at all.

"If you ask me, the Sotkari Ta are a bunch of horny bastards. Imagine that something as simple as the touch of the hand could be enough to make someone want to jump into bed with you," Gio said.

I slipped my hand out of his grip. He went right on saying things he shouldn't.

"Mina, you still have the wristband, so I know life is not so fun for you right now."

My eyes must have turned into saucers. I was at a loss for words.

"What is he talking about?" Ar Ona asked again.

Montor replied to her in Arandan, but his demeanor made me guess that he told her to shut up. She pouted.

"I would like another drink," I said.

"An excellent suggestion," Gio replied.

"I agree," added Ar Ona.

Montor scowled as he motioned to the waiter to get us another round. A few minutes later, I thought I heard some kind of music.

"That sounds very interesting," I observed.

"I bet you have not heard music in a while. Let us all go so you can get a feel for it," Gio said.

"Mina and I have an early start tomorrow morning, so we should be leaving," Montor countered.

Ar Ona smiled sweetly at Gio.

"I need some private time with Montor," she said.

My jaw clenched, and I imagined wringing Ar Ona's neck.

"Well, in that case, I can take care of showing Mina the rest of Zamandi's Room," Gio offered.

"That sounds great. I am curious about the music here," I said.

Montor gave Gio a death glare.

"I expect her back at the bar in no more than one hour. Do you understand?"

"No problem. Let us go, Mina," Gio said.

I said goodbye to Ar Ona, and Gio led me out of the dining area. I did not bother to look back. Gio began chatting in English.

"So, you know, this place started out as one room. The original owner, Zamandi, was an excellent chef and mixologist. As the place became popular and he started making good money, he purchased more property and added more rooms. Now his son runs the business and is filthy rich."

As we walked further, I observed that each room or courtyard area had a specific ambiance. I was amazed at the variety of people and the fact that it was so similar to a club scene back on Earth. A giant transparent glass globe where people were floating in a gravity-free environment was particularly interesting. The bartender and cart were tethered to the top of the globe. Instead of drinks in glasses, people enjoyed their alcohol in small, colorful pods that they crushed in their mouths while flailing their limbs to the piped-in music.

"Gio, was it easy for you to get used to life here?"

"Mina, I have always been...what you could call a practical person, even as a teenager. It was tough at first, but I figured out how to make a good life for myself. I won't lie, though. I wish there were more women like you here."

"So, are you saying there aren't that many of us?"

"I just think they got us spread out across the sector."

We arrived at an area where a band on stage played instruments obviously alien to me, but the rhythm was something I could move to. It sounded like a mixture of reggae and Enya music. Gio put both his hands on my waist, and I swayed my hips. Several other couples as well as individuals danced. He was graceful and followed the cadence of the music well, twirling and dipping me with ease. Soon, we were synchronized in our movements, and I was enjoying myself. Once we got bored, we moved on to another room with what sounded almost like marching band music but with plenty of electronic noise in the background. I giggled as we tried to adapt our moves. On our way to a third room, I asked Gio the time and realized about an hour had passed since we left the dining area. I reminded him I needed to be back at the bar as Montor had requested. He was resistant at first, but I insisted. When we arrived at the bar, Montor was nowhere in sight.

"I hate to break this to you, Mina, but Montor and Ar Ona are probably doing the wild thing right now. They have had a relationship in the past, and Montor is known to be a womanizer."

What would be my next step if, in fact, Montor had forgotten all about me?

"Let's wait," I answered.

"I can take you to wherever you're staying, you know. I mean, if I were you, I wouldn't feel so safe with Montor. He has quite a reputation. I've heard he uses his mind control abilities to convince women to sleep with him, and some don't even remember what happened."

How he was portraying Montor didn't help me feel any better. We waited for a few minutes more, and Montor still did not show up.

"OK, let's listen to some more music and we'll come back to check again in a bit," I said, trying to hide my concern.

Gio took me to yet another room with dimmed lights and slow-paced music. With one hand, he took mine and placed his other hand on my waist. We started dancing separated, but at a certain point, the music became more intense, and he pulled me close. He looked down into my eyes and moved his hand up from my waist to stroke my arm. Again, I felt the familiar provocative sensation.

"Mina, I know you can't talk about it, but I understand exactly the situation you're in. Remember, I was once in the same spot. I can take you away from all this. I'm already done with my fifteen-year commitment with the Lostai army. I'm a free and successful businessman now and could take good care of you. This might sound crazy and impulsive, but if you became my wife, it would be like I died and went to heaven."

His proposal caught me off guard, but before I even began to process it, someone roughly separated us. It was Montor.

"I am sure you are having a sweet conversation, but you will have to continue it some other day," Montor said.

"Montor! We went to the bar and you were not there," I said, a tremor in my voice.

"Well, I am here now, and we are leaving," Montor said to me with a stern expression. To Gio, he added, "Maybe we will meet here again another day, but now, Mina and I must go."

I thought Gio would protest, but instead he was calm and collected. He straightened out his shirt, kissed my hand, and nodded to Montor. His final words that evening were in Lostai.

"Mina, if I do not see you here again soon, I will visit you on Xixsted. I know I will not be able to forget you."

12

M ontor and I walked out of Zamandi's room in silence. Once in the transport pod, we remained quiet for a while. Finally, I couldn't take it anymore and asked the question that was pestering me.

"So, where did you and Ar Ona go? We were at the bar at the time you specified."

"I took her home."

"Well, exactly how far does she live?"

He glared at me.

"What is the problem, Mina?"

It was my turn to glare.

"Did you have sex with her?"

He was so hard to read. One minute serious, the next laughing.

"So, you flirt all night with Gio, and now you pretend to be jealous of Ar Ona?"

He sounded incredulous.

"Well, she had her paws all over you."

"Paws?"

He laughed harder than before. I guess the expression sounded weird in Lostai.

I'm such an idiot. After all, in three days, Montor will likely be out of my life forever.

He put his arm around me and pulled me close.

"No, Mina, I did not have sex with Ar Ona or her paws. She got intoxicated and annoying, so I took her home. Mina, let me be clear. You were the most bewitching female at that place tonight."

I smiled at the compliment but wasn't about to let him off so easy.

"Gio said you and she were a couple."

"Yes, Gio was talking way too much tonight. It is true we had a brief relationship some time ago, but let us discuss something else..." His breathing got heavy, and he shook his head in disbelief. "How do you think I felt, catching you two dancing so close to each other, him touching your skin, like he owned you? I was ready to tear him apart, limb from limb, right then and there."

I crossed my arms.

No. He doesn't get to make himself the victim.

"Well, you made a point that we needed to hide our relationship. Do not pretend to be so innocent. I did not see you fighting off Ar Ona as she flirted with you. On top of that, you made a big scene about the time we should meet and then you arrive late. How do you think that made me feel? I was so worried about what I should do if you did not come back."

"Of course I was going to come back for you..."

His voice lowered as mine elevated.

"I am on this planet for the first time in my life after being stuck on that moon with no outside contact for more than a revolution. I was starting to consider I might have to trust Gio, a male who I have just met, to take me safely somewhere I could spend the night. Remember, I do not know my way around here."

He was dead serious now, chagrin in his eyes.

"I miscalculated the time. I am so sorry, Mina."

"Gio said I should not trust you, that it might not be safe to ride with you, that you have a reputation, and rumor has it you play mind games with females and convince them to go to bed with you, and some do not even remember that it happened."

A pained look swept across his face. For a moment, I thought he might cry.

"I would never do that."

"Well, you once insinuated almost as much when we first boarded the spacecraft to leave Xixsted. Remember, when you said some females did not know why they found you so irresistible."

"I was being a cocky idiot. What did you say?"

"When?" I asked, rolling my eyes.

"When he said those things about me."

I chose to believe Gio had exaggerated about Montor, and now that I had him on the verge of tears, I figured it was time to end our argument and stroke his ego a bit. I made him wait for my reply, and then I let mischief creep into my eyes.

"I said if I went to bed with you, I was sure that I would remember it in the morning."

He sighed in relief and thoroughly enjoyed my joke, laughing and kissing me on the cheek.

"Are we going home now?" I asked.

"As much as I am looking forward to that, you look much too stunning to take home so early. I should show you off a bit more. I am taking you somewhere we can be more at ease."

He explained that we were going to an establishment that supplied good food, entertainment, and lodging for those who needed utmost privacy. He said it was a private club with limited members bound by an oath of confidentiality. The penalty for anyone who breached the trust was death. It seemed extreme, but my curiosity was piqued. The name of the establishment was simply Members Only.

"For example, some of the members are being unfaithful to their spouses and do not want to be seen in public. Sounds like a perfect place for you," he said.

My brow furrowed, and I folded my hands.

"I do not see the humor in that comment."

He hugged me.

"I am sorry. Please forgive me. Just a joke, sweetness."

We went through several security checkpoints before finally entering the establishment. The two-story building was of stone construction, giving it an ancient look. There was an inside and outside dining area and a dance floor. Several couples danced to piped-in music. A vast body of water bordered the establishment. From the outside dining area, we had a view of two immense and bright full moons that hung low in the sky, highlighting the magenta tint of the water and the iridescent light-pink-colored sand. Tiny lights adorned the trees, and each table had a centerpiece with a flickering light. I counted only five tables outside, but inside, there were about three times as many. Sofas and lounge chairs tastefully placed around both indoors and outdoors further lent to a cozy and casual ambiance. The sounds of waves hitting the shoreline and the soft breeze relaxed me.

"Wow, Montor. This place is spectacular."

We sat close to each other in a reclining love seat bordered by side tables. Montor ordered some cocktails. He turned towards me and, with a mischievous smile, looked down to the cutout in the front of my dress. Glancing around for privacy, he bent over, got close, and I felt the quick slide of his tongue on my skin. It took my breath away.

"I could not help myself, Mina. I needed a quick taste."

We sat back hand-in-hand, relaxing and gazing out at the

water. The type of music changed, and Montor said, "Please dance with me."

We walked inside to where other couples were dancing. He pulled me close and pressed his body against mine. Most of the females had their arms around their partner's necks. Due to his height, I rested my hands on his chest. I followed his lead, and slowly we swayed to the rhythm. The song began with a solitary male voice singing the same phrases repeatedly, accompanied only by a few basic piano-sounding chords. It wasn't in Lostai, so I didn't understand the words, but it sounded solemn and sad. The singing stopped, followed by string instruments that pulled at my heart. Soft taps and ocean sounds whispered in the background, followed by flutes and another male voice declaiming a poem. When the poem was over, each instrument sound faded away one by one until only the flutes remained. Finally, several voices joined in like a choir and the cadence became quicker with bongo sounding drums. Our dancing became frenetic, hips gyrating and arms flailing in the air, and everything repeated again in the same order. At one point Montor gently tilted my head upward and closing his eyes he pressed his forehead against mine.

"Mina, I am so happy to be able to share my music with you."

When the song was over, Montor thanked me again and said, "Mina, there is a room in the back where males get together and play silly strength games. Would you mind if I spend some time there and you could go chat with your friend at the bar?"

"My friend?"

I looked over to the bar, and there was Colora beaming and waving at me.

"Colora and her husband are the owners of this establishment," he said.

"Oh, what a nice surprise! Sure, no problem."

"I will join you shortly."

I walked over and sat at the bar. Colora called for a waiter to take over the bartending while she sat next to me. She could not stop smiling.

"So, how do you like our place?" she asked.

"It is lovely."

"So...you and Montor? You look excellent together, and you carry yourself so well in that dress."

"Thank you, you are an expert at what you do."

"I knew Montor had a special interest in you when he requested my services. They are expensive. Watching you two dance, it appears you have a special bond."

Montor appeared to trust Colora, so I felt free to open up a bit.

"We are different, but we both have been affected by things out of our control. He was extremely moved by that song we danced to."

"Yes, the artists are an Arandan group that is putting a modern twist to old Arandan folk music."

"It makes me curious about the lyrics."

"I can tell you. I speak several Arandan languages."

"You do?"

"Yes, sure, my husband is Arandan, one of the few successful Arandans who were able to escape the planet with his wealth intact. Let me see, the beginning of the song says roughly:

Some say I am a good person doing evil things.
Others think I am an evil person doing good.
What do they know about me?

"Then the spoken poem follows. Of course, the rhythm and rhyme are off when you translate to Lostai:

There is no place like Aranda.
The rolling hills of Minterox, The Falls at Xendaro.
The magnificent red river that runs by my village,
The song of the Bendaru, the roar of the Masduro.
I fell asleep and had a nightmare.
Awoken by the thunderous sounds of war
I thought I was by the water.
But by the stench, I realized, the blood of my ancestors
    flowed.
I am alone and my soul is empty.
I sing sad songs and try to survive.
Now all I can do is walk in solitude across the ravaged
    land.
No, I can do more.
I can avenge the deaths of the innocents.
I can make good use of my rage, no matter what it takes
Yes...What do they know about me?

"Then the group chorus sings:

One day, we pray all will be resolved and you can dance
    and sing,
One day, we pray all will be resolved and you can rest in
    peace."

When she was finished, there were tears in my eyes as I recalled the enigmatic music that accompanied those tortured words and the soulful voices that sang and spoke them. I looked at her, and she was teary-eyed as well.

"The Arandans have had a tough time in recent history. War, drought, and famine have ravaged their world. The Lostai took advantage of the civil war there and are now using up any remaining resources."

"I am no fan of the Lostai," I blurted out.

"And yet you are training to be a soldier in their military," Colora said.

It didn't come across as a question, or an accusation, but as a simple fact.

"It is a complicated situation that I cannot discuss."

She put up her hands.

"Of course. I do not need to hear any details. As you know, my husband and I are in the business of being discreet."

The topic was getting too heavy, so I changed the subject.

"Everyone is so content here. I guess they feel their secrets are safe."

"Yes, that is true, but do not be confused. Our customers are not only illicit lovers. Many people come alone. For example, the last time Montor brought a female here, he was a much younger male."

I smiled, assuming she was trying to put in a good word for him.

"You do not need to say that for my benefit," I said.

"Listen, in this business, I have learned to not ask questions and not say too much, but when I do speak, it is the truth. For example, Montor comes here frequently, but he comes alone. He must really trust you. He comes here to allow himself to be vulnerable and moved by a song without worrying about appearing weak. He comes to stare at the lake that reminds him of the red oceans of his home world. He likes that we have an Arandan on the chef's staff who cooks food that is reminiscent of his childhood."

I covered my mouth with folded hands as I listened to her. There were many layers to Montor's personality that I was only beginning to unravel.

"There are others who come alone to sit at the bar and tell me their dark secrets with the assurance that no one else will ever know. Others want to be free to dance all night long to their favorite music without feeling self-conscious or perhaps get intoxicated until they fall asleep in their chairs and know someone will quietly put them to bed without being judgmental. When a member comes through those doors, we immediately take notice, put on their favorite music, and cook the meals that will make them cry. We cater to their whims as best we can while respecting their privacy."

"I see, and just curious, the female who Montor did bring, was she Arandan?"

It was none of my business, but I couldn't help myself.

"I should not be talking about it, but like I said, that was a long time ago, about ten revolutions ago. Yes, she was Arandan. He had recently become a member. I think he came with her no more than two or three times."

"Was her name Ar Ona?"

Colora grimaced.

"Oh no, no. I know Ar Ona. She does not have the tact or class to be brought to this place."

She became thoughtful.

"Mina, I would not worry about her. You know, many Arandan males end up with spouses of other races. The Arandan females are attractive. I mean their race in general, they are a good-looking people. They tend to have minimal body fat and lean muscular frames, everything in the right proportion, so pleasing to the eye..."

She spoke her last words with relish and was distracted for a moment, gazing far across the room where Montor was walking toward us. For a moment, I thought she was referring to Montor, but I discarded the idea when I saw another Arandan male, Colora's husband, I presumed, walking with him. She continued her description of Arandan females.

"Arandan females appear to have a lot of sex appeal, but they tend to be arrogant, leading their males on impossibly long chases and teasing them endlessly."

"I cannot imagine someone like Montor allowing himself to be toyed with in that way," I said.

"My point exactly, and when they finally decide they will allow the male what he wants," she made a graphic and obscene gesture, punching herself in the crotch, "they are not really into it. They only care about the chase itself. So, the sex becomes boring. When an Arandan finds himself a female of another race who enjoys intimacy as much as he does, it is a wonderful surprise for them, and they never look back. Trust me, I know."

"May I ask where you are from, Colora?"

"Sure. I am from Fronidia."

My expression must have given something away.

"Have you been there? Do you know any Fronidians?"

"Oh no, no, but Montor has talked to me about that planet."

"I love my planet. I spend a lot of time on Renna One because of our businesses here, but I make a point to visit Fronidia two or three times per revolution. We have a Members Only there as well."

She ended her explanation in time for Montor and the other Arandan to arrive at the bar. The other Arandan immediately embraced Colora and nibbled at her ear. Her smile turned demure.

"Mina, this is my wonderful husband, Jortan," Colora said, her face flushed.

Montor nodded politely to Colora. Jortan was only slightly shorter than Montor, and he looked older as I noticed some white hair and a bit of thickness around the waist. However, he still appeared distinguished and strong.

"Nice to meet you, sir," I said.

"Oh, no need to be so formal. That will make me feel old," Jortan said with a wide smile.

"So, how did it go back there?" said Colora.

Montor squeezed his biceps and rolled his shoulders back a bit.

"Very embarrassing. Ron Ton beat me two out of three times," answered Montor.

Who is strong enough to beat Montor at arm wrestling?

Colora laughed and shook her head.

"Oh, come now, Montor. Do not tell me you competed with Ron Ton. He has a mechanical arm! What were you thinking?"

Jortan laughed. "I know! And it is not like he was not aware. I think he has been hit too many times on the head, this one."

I made eye contact with each of them, exchanging looks of amusement, and gave Montor a playful shove.

"Maybe we should find a creature completely made of *lirinium* for you to fight with," I said, laughing outright by now.

According to my Lostai academic classes, *lirinium* was the hardest known metal in the sector. Montor looked around sheepishly.

"I guess I cannot resist a challenge."

"Let us order a round and cheer to Ron Ton's mechanical arm," said Jortan.

We continued to joke and laugh. Later in the evening, the four of us and two other couples participated in a traditional Arandan line dance. We formed a line and passed a small crystal ball from one dancer to the next while we skipped forwards and backwards in unison. By the second verse of the song, the music changed, and we all turned to face our partner. The dancer who at that moment had the ball in his hand led the rest of us in a series of synchronized quick steps and slides while constantly handing the ball to the next dancer. When the music changed, whoever had the ball became the leader, improvising new steps for all of us to follow. I've always loved music and dancing and learned the moves quickly.

By the end of the night, I felt as if I were among close friends. Before we left, Colora pulled me apart from the group.

"Mina, it was such a pleasure to meet and spend time with you. Do you think we will see you again?"

"Colora, this was great fun. I am so thankful for everything. You have been so kind. I would hope to be so lucky, but honestly, I am not sure."

She didn't bat an eyelash or ask for clarifications.

"Well, I know your home planet is far away, and I am sure things can get lonely. Regardless of what happens between you and Montor, I would like us to keep in touch. Here are my contact codes in case you need a friend."

She gave me a circular chip with her contact information.

"Thank you so much, Colora. I really appreciate it."

When I hugged her, she squirmed, a shocked look on her face.

"Mina, I like you, but Jortan and I are not in a polyamorous relationship."

I stepped back, my face flushed with embarrassment.

"Oh, no...sorry, sorry. On my planet, an embrace is also used as a sign of affection among friends."

She laughed and tapped my shoulder. "OK, I see...no problem, but you better be careful who you do that to around here."

Montor and I finished saying our goodbyes and headed back to the transport pod.

"I think it is time to head home, Mina. What do you think?"

"Yes, I am ready to get some rest," I said.

He flashed his typical naughty smile.

"Oh, I never said anything about resting."

I looked down and smiled.

"Montor, I want to thank you for everything. Today was such a good time. I loved Members Only. Everyone was so friendly, especially Colora. Zamandi's Room was nice too."

He pulled a face when I mentioned Zamandi's Room.

"The massage at Colora's place was excellent as well as

everything she did for me there. You did not have to do all this for me."

"It makes me happy that you enjoyed it. Members Only is my favorite establishment to go to relax. Jortan and Colora have opened two other ones in this sector. I have been a member for a long time, and I have known Jortan for even longer. He was a good friend of my older brother. They were classmates studying Advanced Business. Then my brother got it into his head to join the military and fight in the Clan Wars that destroyed our planet. He died in battle soon after."

Montor further explained that in Aranda, a clan is the equivalent of a country on Earth. When the Lostai first visited Aranda, there was no central planetary government. Each clan had its own language, culture, government, and currency. Tensions had been building among several of the stronger clans that resulted in a major planet-wide conflict similar to Earth's World Wars but with much more serious results. The wars had been going on and off for decades already, prior to when the Lostai arrived. The Lostai offered advanced weaponry that did not exist on Aranda to one of the clans in exchange for control over certain resources and a commitment to establish one planet-wide government where the Lostai would share power with that clan. Then the wars really became brutal, resulting in the obliteration of entire clans. Montor's clan was wiped out with only a few survivors. That would be like if France or Germany lost their entire population. I was beginning to understand Montor's torment.

"Montor, I do not know what to say. I am so sorry."

"No worries, Mina. My people have an unfortunate history. Right now, I want to focus on today. I so enjoyed having you by my side. You were the perfect partner."

"It was a lot of fun. Colora gave me her contact codes. She said she would like me to stay in contact. It was interesting to learn that she is Fronidian."

"Hmmm," he said, stroking his chin and taking a moment to gather his thoughts. "Mina, eventually, over time, having her as a friend could be helpful to you, but in the immediate aftermath of your disappearance, there will be search teams looking for you. You will be a fugitive. As I mentioned to you before, you need to keep a low profile even in Fronidia. I would wait for a while before making contact as you may compromise her."

"Yes, I understand what you are saying. For sure I will not contact anyone for several lunar cycles. I just think it was so nice of her. She and Jortan make a nice couple. Where did they meet?"

"I do not know if you would approve of their story. She is his second spouse. His first died of an illness."

"Well, what is the problem with that?"

"They were lovers for a long time before."

"Really?"

Montor was relieved that I wasn't scandalized, and my wide eyes showed how interested I was in the juicy gossip.

"Yes, Jortan found himself in a loveless marriage, but divorce is frowned upon in our culture, especially in his case where they both came from wealthy families. He traveled a lot to Renna One for business meetings, and that is where he met Colora. She already had her business there. The fact that they needed privacy to spend time together is what inspired them to create Members Only."

"Did Jortan have children with his first spouse?"

"He did, one female and one male. They were adults already when their mother died and did not oppose him remarrying. Jortan waited a respectable amount of time after her death and then proposed to Colora. They have been spouses for only two revolutions now, but they have been lovers for over ten already."

The ride home was pleasant as we continued to chitchat about everything that had transpired that evening. When we arrived back at Montor's house, instead of heading to the bedroom, he led me around to the back of the house to where the waterfall flowing by his upstairs shower dropped to form a pool. There was a deck with lounge chairs, an outdoor canopy daybed with pillows and folded sheets, and a bar. Tiny flickering lights and the soft splash of the cascades completed the inviting ambiance.

"Oh, I did not come by here earlier today. I love this."

I sat down on the bed and looked around, taking in the view.

"Thank you. Would you like anything to drink?"

"Oh no, I have had a bit too much tonight already."

Montor sat next to me.

"Mina, would you be up to sleeping here tonight?"

"Fine by me. I love the sound of the waterfall. I assume it is safe, right?"

"Yes. I have a force field protecting the perimeter, plus you have me here to protect you."

He brushed some of my curls behind my ear.

"I loved the way you wore your hair tonight, but is it ok if I let it down?"

"Sure."

My voice was already a whisper. He took out the pins fastening my hair in place, ran his fingers through my hair, and massaged my scalp. I closed my eyes, enjoying the relaxing sensation. Soon, his lips were on my forehead, my eyelids, my cheeks, and, finally, my mouth. Each time his lips touched my skin, a few seconds went by before the next kiss. Although my eyes remained closed, I was sure that in between each kiss, he was pulling back to look at me; nothing like the fervor of our recent intimate encounters. It struck me as tender and gentle, like young love, and I was overwhelmed with emotion. At this stage of my life, I was supposed to be in a stable, familiar relationship with my husband. Instead, here I was at the start of something foreign and intense but, at the same time, forbidden and with no future. It was too much for me, and I began to cry.

"No, no, Mina. Please, please do not cry. I promise I will not hurt you. I know I lost control last night, but that will not happen again," Montor said in an alarmed voice.

"No, Montor, that is not it. I am so sorry I cannot control my emotions, but it is not about that at all. You did nothing wrong."

He was still concerned and showed me a vial of birth control liquid that he had brought along from the transport pod.

"....and Mina, no unnecessary risks like last night, either. I know I should have been more careful, but tonight, I am prepared."

"That is good, Montor, but that was not only your fault and not what has me upset. I do not mean to spoil the evening, but this whole situation is tearing me apart. I should never have been in this position in the first place. My destiny was already set. I had a husband and a family. This was not supposed to happen to me."

My words were choppy between the sobbing. He looked away.

"And now here...here I am falling in love with you. I have never had a casual fling. This is not just about sex for me, Montor. Yet in a few days, I will be off to Fronidia and maybe will never see you again. I cannot pretend like this does not affect me."

Turning back to look at me, he wiped off my tears with his fingers and spoke in a low, grave voice.

"This is not easy for me, either."

We stared at each other for a few minutes without speaking.

"Mina, if you like, you can sleep upstairs in the bedroom. I can stay here and leave you in peace."

I cupped his face in my hands and kissed him.

"Trust me, sleeping alone will not bring me peace. I guess I needed to share my feelings."

I leaned back on the bed. He embraced me and traveled down to the cutout in the dress top to kiss my cleavage. He continued to slide down until he was able to get his hands under the full dress skirt. His hands were on my thighs, my butt, my waist. His breathing quickened.

"It would be a shame to spoil the dress," I said.

"That is true, and I have made a promise to myself. You know I cannot resist a challenge. One day, Mina, I do not know how yet, but I will make you my spouse, and you will wear this dress to our wedding."

I didn't answer, thinking it a bit presumptuous of him, but we stood, he unzipped the back of the dress, and I stepped out of it. He picked it up and carefully laid it on one of the lounge chairs.

When we made love that night, it was different from previous times. We were not trying to make each other lose control. It wasn't just about the pleasure. At one point, he took my hands and lifted my arms above my head, his palms pressing down on mine, and our hips moving in sync. His upper body was in a plank position, and fueled by raw emotion, we gazed in each other's eyes, refusing to break the connection. My eyes filled with tears again, and I saw his glisten. When we reached the climax, I finally shut my eyes as satisfaction consumed me. I heard his voice telepathically in my mind saying my name and something incomprehensible, I guessed in Arandan.

We fell asleep, but a few hours later, I awoke to Montor tracing my eyebrows, nose, and cheekbones with his finger. Drowsy, I looked around and saw it was not yet morning.

"Mina, I was thinking, perhaps we should delay your trip to Fronidia."

"What do you mean? What about Zorla and the issues I am trying to escape from?"

"We can figure out ways around them. I can convince Zorla to make you my trainee, and I could take you with me on all of my missions. I would assign you to minor duties and shelter you from having to engage in any activity you disagree with."

"I do not know, Montor. I am probably going to disagree with most every Lostai military mission. It would not be fair to you. You will eventually resent continuously covering for me. Plus, how do we get around Zorla wanting us to conceive children? He will continue to put pressure on us. I am afraid of what measures he might take."

"We could think of something, get a medic here who could attest that our DNA is not compatible, or perhaps check if they really did reverse the procedure you said you had. Maybe they did not, and you will never get pregnant. Mina, please at least give it some thought. We still have two days before the scheduled time for your trip."

"Even though the idea of leaving you is breaking my heart, my fear of returning to Xixsted and losing my chance for freedom is even worse. I am not promising anything, Montor, but I will think about it."

"That is all I ask. I will figure out how we can make it work."

13

T he next morning, Montor received communication from Zorla that flew in the face of what we had discussed the night before. Rebels had set another explosive on a Lostai government building. Initial investigations linked the incident to workers who had escaped forced labor camps in the southern continent. To make matters worse, Zorla had received word somehow that Montor and I had been out on the town partying. He gave Montor an earful, telling him that I was not sent to Renna One for a paid vacation and he expected that I be closely working with Montor on this mission. Montor summed up all his patience to put up with Zorla's reprimands and complaints and appeased him by explaining he was just getting me in the baby-making mood.

After breakfast, we did physical and mental exercises, sparred, and took some time for meditation. When we were done and showered, he said he had something to show me. My jaw dropped when I saw he had reproduced a full Lostai soldier uniform for me.

"You do not expect me to wear that, do you? I am fine with my workout clothing, thank you," I said.

"We need to make a show of you being engaged in the mission and your role in Lostai military. Apparently, Zorla has people watching over us here who are feeding him information. Mina, I know you find it unpleasant, but try to see it this way. When you put the uniform on, you can envision yourself as no longer being a hostage or a prisoner."

"And becoming what? A monster who kidnaps and tortures people?"

The moment it came out of my mouth, I regretted it. If it hurt his feelings, he didn't show it.

"Listen, I am no longer asking you. It is an order!"

I shouted back, "Fine!"

We both changed into our uniforms. When I stepped out, Montor sauntered towards me with a smile.

"Oh Mina, you look sexy."

I wasn't having any of it, stopping him with an outstretched arm and a cold stare.

"Do not even try it."

He put up his hands in surrender mode.

"No problem, Mina. Anyway, we need to leave."

Once in the transport pod, Montor explained that he had never been to this particular labor camp.

"Although I have not been to this camp, I have been to some on other planets, including my own. You need to prepare yourself mentally. It is very depressing. You may see people from Earth there. Do not get emotionally invested. We need to go there to get more information and identify the workers who escaped the camp as they are the main suspects linked to the bombings. The camp has a force field, but workers have discovered underground escape routes."

"Do they not know already who escaped?"

"Apparently, the camp is large, and they do not keep good records of who is missing. Many die on a daily basis, and they just replenish with new prisoners."

I shook my head.

"Ugh, it sounds terrible."

We didn't talk much after that even though the trip to the labor camp took two hours. As we approached the area, the landscape turned mountainous. The laborers worked in mines extracting a crystalline material that the Lostai military converted to an energy source. Cave-ins, explosions of naturally occurring gas, flash flooding, and toxic fumes made working in the mines a hazardous process. Although the Lostai could have used robots and droids for this type of work, slave labor saved them the cost of technology and maintenance.

When we arrived, the Lostai commander in charge escorted us to one of the main labor areas. What appeared to be large cardboard boxes in the distance were actually the tiny shacks where the workers lived. The camp buzzed with activity. A variety of vehicles transported material from the mines to a processing plant, and a constant flow of laborers entered and exited the caves. They were of different races, male, female, sex indeterminate, young, old, even children, all with two things in common: lifeless eyes and dirty, gaunt, undernourished bodies. I learned there were about thirty thousand workers supervised by one thousand Lostai soldiers in this particular camp. Another hundred Lostai personnel worked in the processing plant.

Montor went inside the mine to extract information from workers regarding the escapees and told me to wait outside. He was in there for a while, so I paced around to release some of my nervous energy. I heard a commotion. A woman was screaming in Spanish. I turned around and came face-to-face with a brunette woman. Her tattered clothing hung loosely from her emaciated body, and tears streamed down her hollow cheeks. Without thinking twice, I asked her what the problem was. I could only imagine her shock to see a human-looking woman in full Lostai uniform, speaking in a language she understood. She looked at me, perplexed, but quickly explained that her fifteen-year-old son had died earlier in the day and the Lostai soldier in charge of her group had decided to just throw his body in a junk pile. She begged they allow her to give him a proper burial and threw herself on me crying, asking for my help. A Lostai sergeant walked over and called for several soldiers to take the woman away.

"Please, she is only requesting to be able to bury her young son. They threw his body away like trash," I said to the sergeant.

"Mind your place, soldier. This is none of your concern," he answered.

"What is wrong with you? Are you savages?" I shouted and went to help the woman.

"You are out of line, soldier," shouted the sergeant.

He ran over and pushed me to the ground while pulling his weapon from his holster. My mental training kicked in, and I caused the weapon to fly out of his hand and into mine. I was still on the ground but now aiming his weapon at him. He put his hands in the air. The woman and other soldiers froze.

"We should all just calm down for a second," screamed the sergeant while looking around.

"What is going on here?"

I heard Montor's voice. In a split second, the weapon was out of my hand and in his. He walked over with the swagger he typically portrayed at Xixsted. His face was like stone, and I jumped to my feet, adrenaline causing my pulse to race. Montor handed the weapon back to the sergeant.

"Who is this person? She disarmed and threatened me," the sergeant asked Montor, pointing at me.

"Mina, what trouble have you gotten yourself into? Now I have no choice but to put on an act," Montor communicated to me telepathically.

"This is the piece of crap trainee that Zorla has assigned to me," Montor answered the sergeant.

"Mina, brace yourself!" Montor said to me telepathically.

Before I knew it, Montor hit me with a palm strike to the face. Restrained, but still harder than when we sparred. I fell back to the ground. My lip split, and I tasted blood.

"What is wrong with you, soldier? How dare you threaten a commanding officer?" Montor shouted out loud to me. He followed with a swift kick to the side. I doubled over in pain.

"I am sorry, Sergeant. I will make sure she gets the proper punishment. I already informed your commander that I have extracted the names of those who escaped and where they are probably hiding. My next move is to intercept them and their ringleader in the city and question them regarding the recent bombings. I will also send you a report on what I discovered regarding the escape route being used."

"Thank you, Montor, and how will you punish her?" asked the sergeant with an apparent bloodlust. Montor cracked his knuckles and looked at the sky.

"I will screw her up the ass so hard that she will forget her name."

"Ugh, Montor, do you need to be so vulgar? Now I need to get that visual out of my head."

The sergeant covered his mouth and appeared to be nauseated. Montor chuckled to himself and then turned to me.

"Get up, you piece of crap."

I stood and avoided looking at him. As I trudged back to the pod, Montor shoved me hard in the back.

"Hurry, we do not have all day!"

I stumbled forward, lost my footing, and was on the ground once again. Rage built up inside me, but I resisted the urge to turn around and show defiance because I knew it would make things worse. I understood he was putting on a show for the

Lostai soldiers and anyone who might be a Zorla informant. Once inside the pod and at a safe distance away from the camp, Montor reached out to me. My first instinct was to flinch and recoil

"Do not be silly. I am not going to hurt you. Are you all right?"

His voice sounded tormented.

I licked my swollen lip and waved my hand.

"I am fine," I answered without looking at him.

Montor erupted with anger, banging both fists hard on the console and roaring curse words in Lostai and I assumed in Arandan as well.

"I never should have brought you to that wretched place!"

I stared at my lap awkwardly as he continued to display frustration, shouting out loud, punching and kicking the side of the pod.

"Montor, I am sorry I put you in a compromising position. It was my fault."

When he finally calmed down, he reached over for the first aid kit and applied a cooling ointment for the swelling on my lip. Hugging me, he said, "Mina, you cannot imagine how hard it was for me to behave that way with you. What happened, anyway?"

"A female from Earth was crying for help because her young son had died earlier in the day and the Lostai in charge of her group threw his body in the junk pile. All she wanted was to give her son a proper burial according to her customs. I saw myself in her eyes, lost control, and tried to help her."

He looked down, burying his head in his hands.

Why do I feel sorry for him? I'm the one who got roughed up.

I decided to inject some dry sarcasm.

"So, I have one question. Are you going to screw me hard up my ass here in the pod or by the waterfall in your house?"

He was mortified.

"I only said that to make the sergeant uncomfortable."

"The sergeant? Umm...he is not the one getting screwed," I said.

"I have explained to you that Lostai are uncomfortable with anything to do with sexual relations. For them, it is like a reproductive chore. I knew just the mention of it would make him sick."

"They are so weird," I said, shaking my head. "Are you actually going to give the Lostai information on how those poor people are escaping that terrible place?"

"I must, but I will also supply some misinformation that will lead them to an area prone to cave-ins and toxic gas. Many Lostai soldiers and drones will be lost. That will be my revenge for what I had to do to you today."

I rolled my eyes.

"You are almost as weird as they are, doling out your own strange system of justice."

"How dare you compare me to them," he spat.

I knew I should be careful with my words as spurring his anger might result in permanent damage to the transport pod, but I couldn't stop myself.

"Well, now I am really confused. Why are you offended? Are you a Lostai soldier or not?"

He looked me straight in the eyes.

"I will tell you what I am not. I am not a victim. I am in charge of my own destiny."

"Really? Well, that is what I want for myself too. That is why I am going to wear this disgusting uniform one more day, and then I hope to never have to put it on again."

Those words made it clear I was rejecting his proposal that I become his trainee and delay my escape to Fronidia. He looked away, took a deep breath, and waited a while before answering.

"I see, very well." He cleared his throat, and his voice took on a flat, emotionless tone. "We need to make a stop before we go home tonight. One or more Sotkari Ta individuals are harboring the escapees somewhere in the city. It is not clear how many or whether they are original Sotkari Ta or people like you and me, with embedded genes. These same individuals are probably the coordinators of the recent string of bombings here on Renna One."

"You told me that you sometimes have dealings with rebel forces, like those who helped the three Earthians escape from Xixsted. Could the people behind these bombings be anyone you know?"

"No. The people I have worked with do not target civilians. Their focus is on causing problems directly for Lostai military."

"How will this intervention work?"

"The address I was given is in a part of the city where paid laborers live. Normally, I would not go alone to confront several Sotkari Ta in hiding as that might put me at a disadvantage. If they are Sotkari Ta, I will not be able to use my mental abilities to extract information and will have to resort to more traditional interrogation techniques that you are not going to be comfortable with. So, you can stay at the entrance of the neighborhood and wait for me. Try to stay out of trouble, please."

I hadn't considered the possibility of him being in danger and couldn't bear the idea of something bad happening to him. I grabbed his arm and looked him in the eyes.

"No. There is no way I will allow you to go into a dangerous situation alone. I will go with you and be your backup. I promise to stay in control this time, regardless of what I witness. I promise. I will defend you no matter what happens."

His expression softened, and he stroked my hair.

"I do not want to put you in danger either. We will go in the neighborhood together and find the actual dwelling that I was told about. I will go in the house alone, and you will guard the entrance. If I need your help, I will call to you, and you can come in to assist."

"OK, but please do not hesitate. The minute you sense you are outmatched or in trouble, let me know."

"I will, my little guardian. You know, we have one hour still before we arrive to the city limits. Plenty of time..."

He kissed me on the cheek and narrowed his eyes. I knew that look.

"Montor, really? It is kind of cramped in here."

"Come here," he said and motioned that I sit on his lap, straddling and facing him. "We have all the space we need."

The hour went by too fast as we barely had time to get dressed again and regain our composure before landing in the city.

We arrived in the neighborhood at dusk. Montor handed me a weapon as we stepped out of the transport pod. There were several people on the streets on the way home from their day jobs. The house in question was at the edge of the neighborhood on a less trafficked street, bordering an empty lot. It looked like a small hotel, much larger than the other houses, two stories high, and there were easily about twenty rooms on each floor.

"Montor, I will not let you go in there alone. The building is large and too easy for you to be ambushed."

"We will enter together, but when I decide that you stay back, heed my orders." He made a point to wait for me to acknowledge his instruction with a nod before approaching the building.

We knocked on the main entrance door, and a woman of Sotkari appearance greeted us. Montor spoke to her out loud in Lostai.

"What is this place, and who are you?" he asked, pointing to the large building.

She stammered as she replied out loud. Good. She definitely was not Sotkari Ta. Perhaps only Pasi or non-evolved.

"I-I am the cle-cleaning supervisor, and this pl-place is lodging for the employees who work at the jewelry factory down the block."

Montor folded his arms across his chest.

"We are Lostai law enforcement searching for individuals who have escaped prison." He gave her their names and description. She shook her head, indicating she didn't recognize them.

"Are people in there now?"

"Yes, s-s-some are already home, and others ha-have a night shift."

"I am authorized to search the place, so please give me the keys and leave."

She was obviously intimidated, or maybe he used his mind control techniques on her, because she did not hesitate to hand them over before rushing down the street.

Montor decided that I would stay in the front hall while he went knocking door to door. Some doors were answered, and others he used the keys to enter and search the rooms. Something caught his attention in a room at the end of the long hall because he remained inside for a while. I was able to identify Montor's "light" in my mind, and I quickly asked him telepathically if everything was OK. He confirmed that he had found one of the people we were looking for and was in the process of interrogation. He said he had things under control and I should wait at my post.

Alert with my hand on my holster, my eyes darted from the hallway to the building's entrance. Someone walking through the main doorway startled me. To my surprise, it was Gio Napoletano. He gave me a once-over.

"Mina, what a surprise to find you here. I must say the uniform looks good on you."

"Gio? Do you live here?"

"Oh no, I am just meeting someone."

Uneasiness and my instincts drove me to close my mind. I knew that meant I would not be able to receive any telepathic messages from Montor, but I could still communicate to him.

"Wow, you are really good at that. Montor has trained you well," Gio said.

"I like to keep my thoughts private and remain in control of my actions," I replied.

"Sure. Did you get enough sleep last night? I mean, after spending all that time at Members Only with Montor."

I knew then that something was not right.

"What?" An adrenaline rush fueled a confrontational tone into my voice. "What do you mean? Were you stalking us?"

"Stalking is such a harsh word. I happened to be in the area and noticed where you were heading. I also noticed he took you back to his place, too. I guess, no hotel vacancies? Of course, I couldn't gain access to his property, but that doesn't mean I couldn't fly over and perform a reconnaissance."

He lowered his chin and looked down at me with cold eyes.

"He was giving it to you good, huh? It was fun watching. Next best thing to doing it myself. Imagine my surprise when I informed Zorla and he was actually happy to hear it. Said it was part of the mission to make Sotkari Ta babies. I told Zorla that maybe there'd be better luck if two of the same species were engaged."

I didn't wait another second to send a telepathic message to Montor.

"Montor, Montor! Gio Napoletano is here, and I think I am in danger. Please come back. He followed us all around last night and has been talking to Zorla."

I pulled my weapon from my holster, but at that same moment, Gio sprayed something into my face, and I lost consciousness.

When I came to, I was in a transport pod, cuffed at the wrists and ankles, with Gio and two other human men. The two other men were armed, and Gio had my weapon.

"Gio, I don't know what the hell you think you're doing, but you're making a big mistake. I let Montor know that you took me. He will come after you, and then things are going to get ugly. I suggest you drop me off, and we can forget this even happened."

I spoke with bravado even though I was terrified. One of the other men became concerned.

"Yo, Gio. I don't want issues with Montor. I didn't sign up for that."

"Don't pay attention to her. She means nothing to him," said Gio.

I started to hash through my possibilities of escape. Gio tapped the weapon against my head, taunting me.

"Don't get any ideas in that locked up mind of yours, Mina. Tony, here, is Sotkari Ta also. Between the two of us, we can handle you just fine."

I thought about using mind control on the other guy who wasn't Sotkari Ta, but I had never successfully practiced it on someone. I only had the theory that Kaya and Montor had taught me. Even if I manipulated him to help me, there would still be two Sotkari Ta to contend with. I looked at the cuffs. I was adept at moving things, but I never caused anything to break apart. As I was racking my brain, the transport pod stopped.

Between Gio and the other Sotkari Ta man named Tony, they carried me into a small house. The third man was named Steve. Gio made him stay in the first room of the house while he and Tony carried me towards a bedroom in the back. I studied the sparsely furnished rooms. The tables and chairs strewn about were made of a heavy wood and not attached to anything.

Using my mind, I lifted two chairs and smashed them over each of their backs, taking advantage of their surprise to get my legs out of Tony's grasp. I kicked him hard in the chest, and he fell to the floor. I tried to maneuver out of Gio's grip, but he applied a chokehold so hard that I got dizzy and couldn't continue to concentrate on moving the furniture.

"Jesus Christ, Tony, you're such wimp. Will you get up and grab her already?" shouted Gio to Tony.

They had control of me again and brought me on to a bed with railings bolted to the floor.

"Get me the other cuffs," said Gio.

He placed the weapon against my arm.

"If you don't keep still, you're going to start losing limbs."

They cuffed each of my wrists to the railings and did the same with my ankles, so I was face-up on the bed with my arms and legs spread out wide. Gio looked at my wristband and pinched it between his fingers. The burning sensation brought tears to my eyes.

"You can be tracked by this, but if I try to take it off now, there will be a lot of blood. I don't have time for the mess, and it's not very appealing. Honestly, I don't care if they find you as long as I have enough time to take care of business."

"You are a piece of garbage, ganging up on a woman. I can't wait till Montor comes and tears all of your heads off."

"You give yourself way too much credit. Montor doesn't give a shit about you."

Gio unbuckled my belt, pulled it off, untucked my shirt, and unbuttoned it. Hysterical, I shouted obscenities and struggled, but because of how I was cuffed, there was not much I could do to defend myself. I looked around the room, trying to identify something to strike Gio with, but other than the bed, the room was bare. I focused on my belt and made it whip hard across Gio's face, but he also used his abilities to hurl it to Tony.

"Get rid of this," he said to Tony. "Once I'm done, you can have a go."

"Whatever," answered Tony, not showing much interest.

Tony threw the belt outside of the room and shut the door again. My blouse was open displaying my undershirt. He would have to take the cuffs off to remove it. Instead, he tore it in half and now, to my horror, my breasts were fully exposed. I thought it was time to use some psychology.

"Gio, I'm sure you would enjoy this more if I do this willingly. Get rid of Tony and take off the cuffs. I'll make this worth your while."

"What, do you think I'm an idiot?" Gio answered.

At that moment, there was a blood-curdling scream outside, and one second later, the bedroom door flew off its hinges, striking Tony and rendering him unconscious. Montor stood in the doorway, armed with a phaser rifle the Lostai called a *mizora*, like my knight in shining armor...I thought. Instead of tearing Gio's head off as I had expected, he strolled to the bed. Gio pointed his weapon towards Montor, but immediately it was out of his hand and smashed against the wall.

"You see, Mina, why it is important to do your workout every day? Otherwise, you get rusty like this fool," Montor said. "What is going on here?"

I was speechless at his behavior. He was showing no emotion whatsoever.

"Are you blind? He wants to rape me!"

"Montor, let me have my fun with her and you can take her. You know how sex feels with another Sotkari Ta."

"So, I suppose things are not working out between you and Tony anymore."

Montor's tone was sarcastic but still under control.

"Montor, think about it. All this time without an attractive female of my kind, and she is Sotkari Ta to boot. Cut me a break. What do you care what I do with her?"

"Not a chance. She is a Lostai soldier now and deserves respect. I will be reporting this to Zorla and the authorities. You have caused me to get distracted from an important investigation."

While they haggled over me like a couple of pork chops at the butcher's, my breasts were still fully exposed, and I was indignant.

"Montor, what is wrong with you? Get me out of these cuffs now!"

"Soldier, you and I will have a serious discussion later on how you allowed yourself to be captured this way. I guess I have wasted all those hours of training with you," Montor answered.

I understood that he was purposely acting indifferent, but he should show at least some outrage at someone being violated.

"Do not be so hard on her. Never underestimate the element of surprise," Gio said with a smirk.

How dare he be so condescending!

He leaned in towards Montor and lowered his voice as if he were sharing a secret.

"Zorla claims you dislike this baby-making assignment, but from what I saw last night, you seem to be enjoying it. Whatever the case may be, I am willing to take over for you and make as many babies with Mina as Zorla wants."

I struggled against my cuffs as I became more and more enraged.

Montor didn't reply but pointed his gun to Gio while now directing his attention to me.

"OK, soldier. Let us make this a learning moment. What can you do to free yourself?"

Montor's voice was impatient. I took a deep breath to control my outrage. Gio, my attacker, was now an observer while my commanding officer grilled me. In the meantime, my breasts were still exposed.

"I cannot think of anything," I answered.

Montor came closer and glared at me, speaking through gritted teeth.

"Examine the cuffs. How are they constructed? Which components can be manipulated?"

I took a good look at the cuffs on my ankles and thought about the tiny pins, torques, and levers. I focused my mind, rotating and moving the levers until I was able to unlock them. I turned my head to look at the cuffs on my wrists and did the same. Once I was free, I quickly buttoned my shirt.

"Good job, Mina. Now we must leave as we need to discuss what I learned regarding the bombings," Montor said.

"And what about this asshole? Does he not get any punishment for what he tried to do to me?" I shouted.

"I will not stop you if you decide to punish him."

I rushed over to Gio, who had stepped away from the bed, and aimed a jab to his face. He blocked and attempted a counterpunch. I ducked and got him in the ribs with a hard roundhouse kick. He fell to the ground and tried to grab my foot. I jumped out of the way and kicked him in the groin. He doubled over in pain. I kicked him there again, and he cried out. He was still on the ground when I kicked him in the face and drew blood. He no longer defended himself, and I got ready to kick his groin area a third time when Montor grabbed my arm to stop me.

"OK, that is enough."

I ignored Montor and kicked Gio in the groin even harder. Now Gio was grunting, writhing, and I enjoyed his pain.

"If we run into each other again, you better pray I don't have a weapon because I will kill you!"

Montor didn't understand what I said in English, but he must have had a general idea because he raised an eyebrow. Until then, I had never expected to use those words with anyone. I found my belt in the next room as I marched out of the house. Montor was behind me, and I heard him speak to Gio.

"Oh Gio, before I forget, Steve is going to need medical attention. I had to break both his legs. He did not answer quickly enough when I asked in which room you had Mina. If you follow or spy on me again, I promise to do the same to you. Do not test me."

14

Once we were in the transport pod and on our way, Montor embraced me and asked if I was hurt. Upset, I pushed him away and started punching him in chest. He didn't try to deter me or defend himself, absorbing my blows until I was exhausted. I went from shouting to sobbing, and when I stopped, he hugged me again.

"Mina, I am so sorry this happened. What can I do to help you?"

Sullen, I replied, "Nothing."

"Let us go home, then."

Amid the thick silence, I finally spoke

"I know you are constantly having to put on an act where I am concerned, but did you really need to prolong my time in cuffs there?"

"I am sorry, but some lessons are better learned under pressure."

I covered my mouth with my fist and shook my head.

"Maybe Gio was right when he said you do not give a crap about me."

For the second time that day, it appeared Montor might

cause major damage to the transport pod. He slammed both his fists on the console. The jarring sound made me jump, and my heart accelerated.

"Mina, you really do like to talk nonsense."

I couldn't believe my ears.

"I was almost raped and now you get to insult me, too?"

He took a deep breath and looked away. Still not facing me when he spoke again, I detected a tremor in his voice.

"I am sorry, but this situation is making me crazy. My self-control has never been tested to the extent it was today."

He turned back to me, his eyes blazing.

"Of course, I care about you, much more than you realize. I am glad I arrived in time to stop him. If they had touched you further or hurt you, I would have killed the three of them without a second thought."

"OK, Montor, let us not argue and make matters worse."

By the time we reached Montor's house, I had calmed down. We were both hungry, but my first priority was to shower and take off the uniform. He wanted to shower with me, but I said I'd prefer to have some time alone. He understood, and we agreed to meet for dinner.

I took off my clothes and turned the water to as hot a setting as I could bear. As I lathered, the memory of Gio ripping apart my undershirt returned. A weakness in my legs made me want to slide to the floor. Instead, I held myself up, both my palms against the wall while hot tears mixed with hot water. When I stepped out of the shower, I was done crying.

While I toweled myself dry, I looked in the mirror and said to myself, "Mina, don't dwell on this. It was horrible, but things could have been much worse. You'll be OK."

I got dressed and met Montor downstairs. He was standing looking through the glass walls to the darkness outside. He turned once he sensed I was there.

"How are you doing, Mina?"

"I am feeling better."

"You know, as terrible as what happened today with Gio was, I think some good can come of it."

"How so?" Irritation crept into my voice.

"Well, I have already filed an official report with Zorla and Renna One authorities. Guess who now will be the prime suspect when I get ambushed and you disappear? They will primarily focus on Gio in the aftermath of your escape, spending time interrogating him and searching for you on Renna One, rather than investigating possible escapes scenarios. I also believe Gio is involved with the rebel bombings here on Renna One and have given this input to Zorla. Gio is about to find himself in plenty of trouble."

"I can only hope. I never expected him to be such a despicable person. I cannot believe you are friends with him."

"He is NOT my friend!" His voice boomed. "He just served in my squadron."

"Anyway, I do not want to think about him anymore. What is the plan for tomorrow?" I asked.

"Tomorrow we are staying here all day. With the information I obtained today, I have given enough details to Zorla to capture the main organizers of the rebel group. So, we are going to take the day off. You will not have to wear the uniform that you dislike so much. We have plenty to talk about, and I want to have you all to myself without any further charades. What do you think of that?"

"Thank you, Montor. Yes, I do like that idea."

"How about you and I having dinner on the terrace tonight?" said Montor.

"I am curious, when you are here without any...company, who do you have dinner with?"

"I eat with Foxor and Lasarta. They are like family to me."

"Back home, I was not a wealthy person, and I am not used to being served to in my house. I would like to help with the preparations and then for all of us to dine together. I think it would be interesting to hear stories of your childhood."

He shot me a curious look, as if trying to figure out whether it was a good idea.

"OK, come with me to the food preparation area," he said.

Lasarta and Foxor were pleasantly surprised at my suggestion. They had almost everything ready, but I helped her chop some greens and vegetables for a salad and spoon the food onto serving platters. Foxor and Montor set the table and started taking the platters over. Montor opened a bottle of wine, and we all sat to eat. He proposed a toast.

"To good food and excellent company."

We all lifted our glasses and smiled. I was in a better mood. Dinner was delicious but quiet, so I tried to make conversation by asking about Montor's behavior as a child. Lasarta was the first to speak.

"Well, he was taken..." She hesitated and looked towards Montor, as if waiting for approval to continue.

I finished the thought for her.

"Yes, taken is the right word. I was also taken."

Montor nodded, and Lasarta continued speaking.

"Umm, he was taken from us at a very young age, but I remember he was by far the strongest and tallest child of his age in our neighborhood. Always ready to learn new sports and so competitive for such a young one. He always pushed the limits and got himself into trouble often, but even at that age, it was clear that he had a sensitive side. He was close to his older sister, who doted on him unconditionally."

"How many siblings do you have?" I asked Montor without giving it much thought.

"They are all dead."

His voice was flat.

I wanted to kick myself. I should have known better. Montor had already mentioned to me about his older brother and twin sister being dead, and Kaya had told me he had lost his family. Foxor rescued the moment by jumping in.

"...but they were five in total. Montor had a twin sister, an older sister, and two older brothers. A proud and fine Arandan family. His parents were well-respected leaders in our community, and their love for each other and their family was strong."

Lasarta changed the subject.

"What is your home world like?"

"Physically, it looks like Renna One, but we are not as technologically advanced. We have not traveled yet beyond our nearest neighboring planet called Mars and have not made contact with people from other worlds. Most people on my planet still believe that we are alone in the universe. We do not have one government for the entire planet. We have many countries, what you would call clans, each with their own language, culture, and government."

"And do your people live in peace?" asked Foxor.

"Many countries have created alliances for cooperation and peace, but many others are in constant conflict. We have many problems on my planet. There are still too many people who live in poverty, still too much hate, but there is also positivity and people working towards improving things."

"I see, sounds like Aranda before the Lostai arrived and stuck their noses in our business," said Lasarta.

Apparently, Foxor worried whether it was appropriate for Lasarta to make this open criticism of the Lostai. He glanced at Montor and shot her a stern look.

"Shhh, female. What do you know about politics?"

"No worries, Foxor. Lasarta knows she is always free to speak her mind here," Montor said while giving her a respectful nod.

Lasarta gave Foxor a smug look followed by a smile and changed the subject again.

"What about you, Mina, do you have family?"

Montor had been absentmindedly eating as we conversed, but when Lasarta asked that question, he put his utensils down and locked eyes with me for a few seconds. I recalled what he had told Colora about me and decided to lie.

"I was a widow when I was taken, and I have three children."

Lasarta covered her mouth with both hands.

"You mean your children are like orphans now? That is horrifying."

She looked around to each of us at the table.

"This is what the Lostai do. Destroy. Destroy planets, destroy families, and destroy people," she said.

Montor resumed eating with his eyes glued to his plate.

"Yes, my heart breaks every time I think of them, but I have two sisters and a very close friend. I am sure they are watching over them."

Before I became too emotional, I decided it was my turn to change the subject.

"This meal is delicious. Is this a typical Arandan recipe?"

"Yes, we usually prepare Arandan meals for Montor. I am so glad you like it," said Lasarta.

She asked me about food from Earth, and we continued on comparing everything from holidays to music to politics. I described how Thanksgiving is notorious for awkward reunions where family members with different points of view who have not seen each other for a long time start discussing touchy subjects such as religion, politics, old wounds, and gossip. I said it was especially uncomfortable for new spouses joining the family for the first time. They saw the parallels to our earlier conversation, and we all laughed.

The evening became more easygoing and enjoyable. Foxor served for dessert thin wafers sandwiched with a variety of sweet creams and jams. Lasarta brewed the same bitter beverage that I couldn't handle at Zamandi's Room, so I politely declined. Afterwards, we all helped clear the table. Lasarta and Foxor thanked us for our help but asked that we let them finish cleanup on their own. We understood they were making a point to allow Montor and me to have some time alone.

"What would you like to do now, Mina?" Montor asked.

"I guess I can have another glass of wine. And you know what? I would like to hear more music like what we danced to at Members Only."

He bounced out of his chair.

"Really?" he said, sporting the boyish grin that I had seen only a few times. "Excellent idea. We can go out back by the waterfall, and I will have the music piped in. Let me get another bottle of wine."

It was a clear night with a star-studded sky, and the two Renna One moons still appeared almost full. In addition to the flickering lights, someone had added candles to the area, which lent to a romantic ambiance. The first song was bluesy, similar to the one we heard at Members Only. We began to dance slowly.

"Thanks for lying about being a widow, Mina."

"I sensed you were stressed about that. I did not want to spoil our dinner."

"Yes, in my culture it is inappropriate to steal another male's spouse unless he has a chance to fight for her. Foxor and Lasarta must have realized already that we have a relationship. Your husband on Earth has no way to defend his position, and it would be like taking the female from a male who is disabled. Totally dishonorable."

"So, if you fight for her, it is OK to take another male's spouse?"

"Only if she wishes it."

"Wow, in my culture things are different. A married person is considered off limits. Of course, this is only theoretical. Many people engage in extramarital affairs. I thought you told me that in Arandan culture divorce is frowned upon."

"Yes, except in the case I just mentioned." He stared down at me, his eyes darkened in excitement, pupils enlarged, almost entirely covering the yellow irises. "Mina, I have to admit that I have fantasized about engaging in a duel with your Earthian husband, killing him, and then being able to be with you without any shame."

That image disturbed me, so I disregarded it and didn't reply.

He must have read my expression because he asked, "Is that so wrong of me?"

"On Earth, you cannot just go around slaughtering your rivals."

He didn't answer, and we continued to dance with no space at all between our bodies. I pressed my head against his chest. The music had me entranced.

"I like this, Montor."

"Me too. Your hair smells so nice. I enjoy spending time like this with you where I do not need to hide my feelings. We fit each other perfectly."

We couldn't have been more different, he being so much taller and of an entirely different species. Yet a part of our DNA was identical. He rubbed his head against my hair, breathing deeply.

"Our situation is so unfortunate. If only we had met under normal circumstances, I would have proposed, and if you accepted, we would have created a family and spent our lives together. I do not know why now this feels so important to me. In the past, such things did not concern me," he said.

The song was over. Montor poured us each a glass of wine, and we sat on the daybed.

"Well, maybe it is a matter of what stage of life you are in," I said.

"Are you saying I am old?"

He pretended to be offended.

"No, of course you are not, but like everyone else, your perspectives change as time goes by. Although I am flattered with what you have said, how can you be so sure that I would be the right lifelong partner for you? We have been in this relationship for less than one lunar cycle. These decisions should not be taken lightly. I can speak about this because I have experience in such matters."

He side-glanced and turned away from me.

"Yes, I know you have already lived what I described, back on Earth, with your husband, the love of your life, and the Lostai took it all away. You need not remind me."

"I did not mean to offend you. My point is that my husband and I rushed into marriage too young because I was pregnant. Things eventually worked out for us, but it was difficult in the beginning...for many revolutions."

He turned around to face me and look down into my eyes. His yellow eyes held mine captive. I dared not look away.

"I can tell you this. In the short time I have known you, I have learned that you are a female of conviction. You stand by your values. At first glance, you might appear weak and vulnerable, but in fact, you are strong, a survivor. You have shown me loyalty, and I know you have a kind heart. I can only assume you were a fine mother. You are a fun person. My favorite people, Kaya, Jortan, Colora, Foxor, and Lasarta, love you already. Let us not forget that I am very physically attracted to you and I cannot get enough of your body. Seriously, Mina, what else do I need to figure out?"

I was touched by his declaration.

"I...I do not know what to say..."

"These are just simple facts, Mina," he said, shrugging his shoulders.

I leaned in towards him and tried my best to convey with kisses the tender feelings that his words had evoked.

"You know, Montor, I question why I find myself in this situation, too. I thought my life was set. I never expected to fall in love again, but I pray that *God* helps me have the faith to see that there is a reason why all this has happened and everything will eventually turn out for the best."

"What does the word *Gohd* mean, Mina?"

"I believe Kaya calls *God*, The Farthest Light."

"Ah yes. I understand. Kaya is a very spiritual person, as is Lasarta. I respect their beliefs, but those are just fairytales for me. In Arandan culture, there is also belief in a supreme deity, but if such an entity exists, how can it allow some of the atrocities I have witnessed? No. Only I am in charge of my destiny."

"I believe that, sooner or later, we all find ourselves in situations that are out of our control and we need to reach out to something beyond our power," I said.

Another song came on. It had more of a rambunctious beat, reminding me of reggaeton. Montor showed me how to dance to it. It involved sexy and sensual moves. We had fun with it. We drank more wine.

"Montor, if you had a child, do you have any idea what you would name it?"

"I am sure I will have a son, and I will name him after my father. His name will be Josher."

My heart skipped a beat. When he pronounced Josher, it sounded like Joshua, my husband's name. I continued to drink wine and got tipsy. Soon, we found ourselves lying on the daybed. I cuddled close to Montor, and he ran his fingers through my hair. I became so sleepy that I'm sure I dozed off because I don't remember anything else until I opened my eyes in the early morning hours. It was still dark outside. I found him lying on his side, his head propped on his hand, looking at me.

"Well, *carinbo*, how are you doing? You escaped from me last night."

"What does that mean?"

"It is an Arandan word that means a sleepy child. I was ready to make love to you, but you got comfortable and fell asleep."

"Oh." I lifted my head. "I think I had a glass too many... ouch, what a headache."

"Here, sit down."

Montor asked that I sit on the edge of the bed while he got off and stood in front of me. He massaged my temples with his thumbs using a circular motion. I thought I would feel the typical arousal provoked by his touch, but instead it was more of a healing sensation. He also massaged my neck and shoulders.

"Hmm, that is great but different than when you usually touch me. Anyway, thank you. I am better already."

"Even non-evolved Sotkari transfer energy and feelings through touch, but for Sotkari Ta, it is much more powerful. To be honest, usually when I touch you, my thoughts are of a sensual or erotic nature. However, right now, my focus was on helping to reduce your headache. For example, when a Sotkari mother is touching her children, she is transmitting feelings of parental love and caring. Friends are usually focusing on companionship and loyalty, and so forth."

"I see. I do remember once Kaya transmitted strong feelings of friendship by barely touching my finger. I do not believe I have ever purposely focused on transmitting a particular emotion. What do you sense from my touch?"

"Oh Mina, you are always a jumbled mess...friendship, anger, love, fear, mistrust, desire...But that is fine. It makes you even more enticing to me. However, to intensify any particular emotion, all you need to do is focus on it, in the same way as when you are trying to move an object. Actually, now might be a good time to focus on sensual thoughts. I deserve a recompense for helping you with your hangover," he said, his smile widening.

I laughed and scrambled back on the bed, pretending to escape.

"I owe you nothing," I said.

He tackled and smothered me playfully. I thought about what he had just explained and filled my mind with lusty thoughts. He groaned, and in no time, we lost what little clothes we had left on.

"I like what you are doing, Mina."

He was in a heated rush.

"No, Montor, let us take this slow. I would love to hear some romantic music," I said.

He sighed impatiently but reached over to a side table to where the controls were. Soft, sensual music came on. Instruments only. I stroked his chest, kissed those hard abs, and took his hand in mine. Remembering his first overture on the space-craft, I brought his hand to my lips and licked his palm. He moaned as I sucked on each finger. I shifted my body around to continue the journey down his body. He grabbed me, kissing my feet, my calves, my thighs, and further. Sweat evaporated in the cool night air. Once we were face-to-face again, my body scent was on his breath and he was inside me. I shouted his name and how good a lover he was until I was hoarse. He only moaned and panted until the very end when I heard his voice in my mind.

"Mina, what have you done to me? I am lost in you."

15

Montor and I got up for breakfast around mid-morning. I helped Lasarta with the food preparation again. We made sweet dough balls that were fried and dipped in a fruity jam and a heartier version of the omelet Montor had replicated for me on the spacecraft. After breakfast and a long walk, we started our workout routine as usual.

"Mina, remember to continue your daily routine for both your physical and mental fitness as well as make time for meditation," he said.

A simple reminder, but when I looked up to nod at him, it hit me. Tomorrow at this time, I would be on my way to another planet. This might be the last time we did any of these exercises together. We locked eyes, and I covered my mouth as my heart broke into a million pieces. His jaw clenched.

"I promise, I will," I mumbled.

His hands rushed to my shoulders, and he pulled me in. We embraced in silence. Finally, he pushed me back to arm's length.

"OK, let us continue."

Once we completed our exercises, Montor took me to the front terrace, and we sat down. He wanted to explain to me what to expect regarding my trip to Fronidia.

"We will leave early tomorrow to the location where my contacts have the shuttle ready for me. The shuttle's sensors will be rigged to make it appear as if it is a drone in auto flight mode without a pilot. I chose the morning time due to the high amount of traffic landing and taking off from Renna One. The safest route to Fronidia will take sixty days. You absolutely may not communicate with anyone during the entire trip, as that will give away that there is someone on board. I programmed the shuttle to send an encoded message to my tablet once it arrives back to Renna One. This will be the only indication that your trip has been completed."

My stomach was in knots.

Montor explained that the landing destination was a major city in the Fronidian northern hemisphere near a refugee center where I would be processed and supplied with food and temporary lodging until I was settled in. He explained Zorla would probably assign him to the search force, but he would make a point to limit the search to Renna One as long as possible. He said to avoid any suspicion, it would be some time before he could secretly look to reunite with me, possibly six months or even a year.

Our mood soured by the minute as we hashed through these details. My mind wandered as I tried to come up with any scenario that would allow me to stay with Montor. He said he needed to check in with Zorla to address some work issues and suggested that I rest, but I never was a fan of napping during the day. I asked where Lasarta was, and he said she must be working on meal preparation, so I looked around and found her in the kitchen.

"Hello, Lasarta. How are you doing? May I help you?" I asked.

"Oh Mina, that is kind of you, but I am sure you have better things to do."

"I do not, and I would like a task to distract me, unless I would just be getting in your way."

"Oh no, no. I could always use a helping hand," she said, smiling.

She had what appeared to be poultry on a cutting board on one of the counters and kitchen shears nearby. It was larger than a chicken but smaller than a turkey.

"Do you want me to butcher this for you?" I asked.

She looked skeptical, so I described to her how I would do it: the drumsticks, wings, thighs, and breasts cut in smaller pieces.

"Is that how you would do it?"

"Yes, exactly. I am surprised that you would know such things," said Lasarta. "Many people these days produce their meals using machines, but Montor likes his food homecooked the old-fashioned way."

"Well, I do not claim to be an excellent cook, but I prepared the meals for my family. You know, there is a dish I used to make back on Earth with a similar bird. My family loved it."

"Well, if you like, you can prepare it today."

"Oh, but I am not familiar with your condiments, herbs, and vegetables. I do not want to delay your process...or worse, spoil everyone's dinner."

"Nonsense...We have plenty of time. Let me show you everything that we use here, and you can discover which items are like what you cooked with on Earth. Let us have fun with this!"

She went to get a bottle of wine. I told her that I'd had too much the night before, but she assured me it was not strong. She poured us each a glass. It was sweet, like a dessert wine. After I cut up the bird, she took out samples of the herbs, vegetables, and tubers she normally used for cooking. I carefully tasted and smelled each one and explained how I was planning on incorporating them. She agreed with almost everything I suggested except for one item that I thought tasted like shallots but she explained that, once cooked, would be too pungent. I found items similar in taste and smell to green peppers, onions, and garlic. She had herbs that reminded me of cilantro, parsley, and oregano and a spice mix that tasted like salt, pepper, and cumin. I also found tubers resembling potatoes. She did not have anything like canned tomato paste or sauce, but I did find a vegetable the size of a watermelon with the same color, taste, and texture as a tomato. I asked if we could puree and cook it down, and she agreed.

I carefully prepared the stew, checking with Lasarta after each step and making sure I seasoned it well, as I knew Arandans prefer savory dishes. Soon, the aromas of the different ingredients filled the kitchen. She laughed when I poured a splash of the wine in the pot and told her it was for good luck. When the stew was done, I tasted it first, and in my humble opinion, it was pretty damn good. However, I had no idea how it would taste to the Arandan palate. I asked Lasarta to try it and tell me the honest truth.

"Mina, this is exquisite. I should be careful Montor does not give you my job. I know exactly what to accompany this with."

She prepared steamed grains and fried a sweet vegetable. We finished the bottle of wine, toasting to what a good team we made. When dinnertime arrived, we were giddy with the surprise we had in store for Foxor and Montor. Before we started taking the platters to the outdoor dining area, Lasarta confided in me.

"Mina, you are the first female friend Montor has brought here who has ever prepared a meal or taken any interest in getting to know Foxor or me. They usually see us as his servants and only are looking for us to cater to them."

I couldn't resist asking whether Montor had many "friends" over.

"Well, to be honest, Mina...yes, we have seen many over the years. However, to be fair, Arandan males have a healthy... appetite and Montor, I suspect even more so. As he does not have a spouse or steady partner, it is to be expected, but I suspect that you are something different."

Instead of feeling complimented, her words saddened me, considering that after the next day, I possibly would never see her or Montor again. Once the table was set, we called Foxor and Montor over. Foxor immediately recognized that the stew was not what Lasarta had originally planned to prepare.

"Lasarta, this is...different," Foxor said, giving us a curious look.

Montor was distracted until Lasarta answered, "I cannot take any credit for the stew. Mina prepared it all herself."

Montor raised his eyes, a worried look on his face.

"Really? OK, who will have the first taste? I guess I am a brave male, so I will do the honors," said Foxor, smiling at me.

"No worries, Foxor. Your wife saved you from that terrifying task."

Montor rubbed his chin, taking in the scene. Foxor belly laughed before sampling a spoonful and exclaimed something in Arandan that I didn't understand, but by the look on his face, it was clear that he approved. He continued joking.

"Delicious! Montor, have you brought a chef here to embarrass us?"

Lasarta smiled and winked at me. Montor tasted it and beamed.

"Did I not tell you she is something special?" Montor said, his chest puffed with pride.

Both men served themselves huge portions and got seconds. Montor could not stop smiling at me. Foxor, who seemed to be the one always in charge of dessert, stepped away to prepare it while the rest of us cleared the table. Earlier in the day, he had baked small individual cakes that he was now topping with fruit and a syrupy mixture. After everyone was done eating, we all helped with the cleanup. Montor asked if I was interested in learning a popular Arandan game. Foxor and Lasarta joined us to sit at a table specifically made for this purpose. The table was ornate, and the top had drawings and etchings that were part of the game. Similar to dominoes, players take turns putting down pentagon-shaped pieces with different markings on each side to connect to other pieces with matching markings. The sides had magnetic strips so the chips could attach to each other. It took me a while to understand the other rules, but after several rounds, I got the hang of it. I even won a few rounds, which garnered me even more praise from Foxor.

At some point in the evening, we heard the rumble of thunder so Foxor and Lasarta said it was time to get to their home before the weather got worse. We said our goodbyes and I mentioned to Montor that I had not seen rain since I was taken from Earth. We walked to one of the covered porches to observe the lightning, and eventually the storm came through with strong winds and heavy rain. I was transfixed and even extended my arm out, letting it get soaked. I explained how such weather was common in Florida.

"It feels a little chilly. I think a warm bath would be nice," he said.

"OK."

He ensured everything was locked and secure, then led me upstairs to his bedroom. He turned on the tub settings. Without saying much, he carefully took off my clothing, and so, I returned the favor.

"Mina, I am trying to forget that tomorrow at this time you will not be here."

I sat on his lap in the tub, closing my eyes and abandoning

myself in his arms, giving him free rein to touch and position me any way he wanted. Our bodies gently swayed in the warm soothing water until he reminded me that we had a set wake-up time the next morning. We got out of the tub, dried each other and went to bed. After a short nap, we made love again, and then fell into a wonderful slumber. I opened my eyes next morning to find our bodies entwined, my face against his chest. When Montor awoke, he nuzzled and kissed the top of my head. I started out of bed to get ready, but he asked me to sit for a moment.

"Mina, I would like to give you something," he said.

I bit my lip and worried about becoming too emotional as we were quickly approaching our last intimate time together for a long time or, perhaps, ever. He took off one of the two cords he wore around his neck. Each had almost identical shiny, silver-toned amulets engraved with unfamiliar markings that I assumed were in Arandan. Tiny transparent crystals encrusted in the metal sparkled in the daylight as it streamed through the bedroom windows. The burning sensation in my nostrils and eyes predicted the hot tears that would soon follow.

"Mina, in my clan we have a custom where parents give these amulets to their children one revolution from their birth date. They are worn for life, save for certain circumstances when it is deemed appropriate to gift it to someone. The second one belonged to my twin sister. Normally, upon her death, she would have been cremated with it on, but my father could not bear the idea that she was gone. So, he broke with tradition and put it on me."

He hesitated, looking away for a moment before turning back to me.

"He said since I was her twin and we were conceived and formed together in the womb, a part of her was always with me.

I am keeping hers, but I would like you to have mine to remember me by until we are together again."

By the time he was done with his explanation, I was a blubbering mess. I wanted to tell him I couldn't accept it, but instead of speaking, my shaking body only produced sobbing sounds. He pulled me close, his fingers entangled in my hair, and all I heard was the beating of his heart. We finally separated, and without saying another word, he placed the cord with the amulet around my neck. I looked up to him and saw one solitary tear go down his cheek. This was as hard for him or worse as he was parting with a sentimental item. The idea that he might break down and cry was too perturbing and helped me regain control.

"Montor, I will wear this with honor until the day we see each other again. Thank you so much for this and for everything."

He rubbed my cheek with the back of his hand and looked away again, taking a deep breath before speaking.

"OK...Good...We should have the morning meal and finish getting ready."

We went downstairs, and I immediately went to the kitchen to find Lasarta. She was there, and our eyes locked. She must have noticed my swollen, red eyes. I willed myself not to cry anymore.

"Lasarta, I will be leaving today, and I am not sure when I will be back...ummm, because I...I need to continue my training on Xixsted. So...so...I wanted to thank you very much for everything you have done for me and for your friendship. I hope we will meet again soon."

She rubbed my cheek with the back of her hand, in the same way Montor did. Taking the amulet in her hand, she stared at it and looked at me again.

"Mina, I know what is going on," she said in a calm voice.

"What...what do you mean?"

"Foxor is like a father to Montor. When all his family was gone, we became his foster parents, until they took him from us. There are no secrets between them, and Foxor keeps no secrets from me."

"Oh...I see."

"Montor appears to live a life of luxury and power, but his has been a torturous path. He is not a perfect person, but he is not evil, either. I know in my heart that it is soon time for my foster son to have true happiness in his life. That is why I am confident we will meet again in due time."

I wanted to hug Lasarta, but I remembered Colora was taken a bit aback when I did that. Instead, I rubbed her cheek with the back of my fingers as she had done to me. She smiled, and when I turned around, I was face-to-face with Foxor. He nodded to me as in their culture it would not have been appropriate for him to touch me.

"I hope it will not be long before you can make us that delicious stew again. Do not forget us. We will always have you in our prayers," he said.

"Thank you, Foxor...thank you for everything."

"OK, let us have our morning meal together," said Lasarta.

We didn't speak much as we ate. Lasarta said she knew we were on a schedule and not to worry about helping with cleanup. I went upstairs to get dressed and prepare the bag I would take with me. It would only contain the clothes I had purchased at Colora's shop, my tablet, some toiletries and grooming items. Montor dressed in full soldier uniform and gear and brought me mine.

"Oh no, Montor...It is bad enough that the last time I see you will be in that uniform, do not make me put mine on."

"Unfortunately, we must. If something goes wrong, we cannot risk getting caught looking like we were on our way to a vacation. Zorla gave me another assignment, so he is expecting that is what we will be working on today."

I reluctantly grabbed the clothing and put it on. Montor put on a mask and an oversized thick cloak to conceal his uniform and physique. He handed another set to me.

"Obviously, I cannot let my contact see us in Lostai uniforms. We operate with each other on an anonymous basis. I have never met them in person or seen their face. I intend to keep it that way, and I suppose so do they."

We walked downstairs to find Lasarta and Foxor standing together by the kitchen entrance. We must have been quite the sight with masks and cloaks. They looked at each other with quizzical expressions and nodded to us. Once in the transport pod, Montor held my hand in his.

"Mina, are you sure you want to go through with this? I can call this off, and you can stay with me. We can try to find another solution."

"Montor, I am so tempted to do just that, but then I am reminded about what happened at the labor camp. I cannot become a part of the Lostai military. I will not be able to tolerate doing what they expect of a Lostai soldier or even being associated with those types of activities. If I were to try to stay under my own terms, I would become a liability to you. I will not allow that either...putting you in danger, us sneaking around, and you constantly having to hide your feelings for me. Even though my heart is breaking, my mind is made up."

I was convincing myself as much as I was answering him. He stared at our hands for a long while before speaking again.

"Then, Mina, please take care of yourself. I know you have strong opinions about certain things, but please consider that there might be times when taking the moral high ground will not serve to keep you safe. Remember to be wary of who you trust. Learn from your experience with Gio. It is possible you will run into Sotkari Ta in Fronidia. Keep your guard up. There are many that are good like Kaya and many who are not. The only thing that is stopping me from going crazy is that I know your Sotkari Ta powers will serve you well in defending yourself. Please promise you will use them to stay safe."

I moved my hands around so that now I was the one holding his hands.

"I promise."

We arrived at a desolate lot that appeared to be a junkyard or repair center. Strewn about were all kinds of spacecraft and pods in different levels of disrepair.

"This is where people with lower incomes purchase and repair their vehicles and spacecraft. It is still early. Operating hours have not started yet," Montor said.

We walked towards the main entrance of the lot. Montor brought with him a club and a *zirem*. Montor also brought his side bag and tucked a smaller-sized tablet in his back pocket. I wondered why he brought the weapons but supposed it was a precaution. Standing there was a figure also cloaked and wearing a mask.

When we reached where the person was, Montor nodded and spoke in a language I didn't understand. The person replied, opened the perimeter gate, and led us to a corner of the lot where there was a shuttle parked. I was surprised to see Montor give the person the access chip to his transport pod. This wasn't making sense to me. The person remained outside as Montor punched in a security code and motioned for me to step in. It was a small shuttle not much larger than a transport pod. Montor showed me the piloting station and the areas for sleeping, food replication, and the bathroom. He pointed out environmental, weapons, and other important controls. I saw some seats were gutted out.

"I wanted to make sure you had at least some space for your physical exercises and workout since you will be here for a while."

After Montor checked the controls, he walked to the shuttle entrance and gestured to the person outside that everything was in order. To my surprise, he closed the shuttle door, sat in one of the piloting seats and gestured for me to take the other seat. He engaged the launching sequence and we took off.

"Montor, what is going on? Are you coming with me after all?"

"I wish...but no...I decided it is best if we are alone at your launching location. We are going to a remote area now. I'll tell Zorla we were following a suspicious vehicle."

"What about your transport pod? And you mentioned you needed to appear incapacitated...I am confused."

"I exchanged this shuttle for my transport pod. A transport pod with Lostai military insignia is of utmost value for a rebel group. I am going to have you incapacitate me before you take off. I figured the fewer people involved, the better. It minimizes the risk when the Lostai begin investigating your disappearance and will appear like they stole you and the pod."

"But you said you needed to appear injured."

"Yes, like I just said, you will need to help me with this."

The shuttle landed.

He stood to take off the cloak and mask, and I did the same. Taking my hand, he pulled me towards him.

"We only have a few minutes, but I want to hold you close."

His hands were on my waist, and he slid one up to caress my neck. I looked up to him with my hands on his chest and we kissed desperately, like what it was, possibly our last time. We remained embraced in silence for a few minutes before we stepped outside.

"OK...OK...it is time," Montor said, followed by a deep sigh.

"Oh..."

I tried to say something but couldn't speak anymore as tears filled my eyes.

"Mina, I need you to pull yourself together. This is what is going to happen. You need to strike me a few times in the face. Also use the club and *zirem* on me. I have the *zirem* on the highest setting, so it will penetrate my clothing. In my bag, you will find an injectable drug. I need you to insert it in my back so that it is clear that I could not have done it myself. Then you will take the bag and the weapons with you and launch the shuttle craft on autopilot mode, and you will be off."

"I will inject you, but I am not hurting you...I cannot do it."

"Mina, this is not a negotiation! You must. Kick me in the face like you did to Gio."

"No way am I doing that!"

He shook me violently, slapped me, pulled out my shirt, and ripped it open. He stared into my eyes, squinted his, and roared, "I am Gio, and I am about to rape you. You must defend yourself!"

Filled with rage and anger, I took several steps back and jumped high and forward to land a flying kick to his face. He did not block at all. I did it a second time, and he went down. His brow bone began to swell. Skin broke open, and he bled.

"I am Zorla. I have ordered that you be beaten with this very club, and I have used the *zirem* on your back. Take revenge!" he said from the ground.

I wanted to hurt him the same way I had been hurt. I wanted him broken the same way I had been broken. I struck him hard with the club once, twice, three times and then used the *zirem* on his chest and abdomen. When I heard him finally cry out in pain, whatever spell I was under broke.

"Oh no...Montor...what have I done?" I said, horrified.

His breathing was labored.

"It is OK...you did good...hurry, get the injectable."

I found the syringe. He slowly sat up, blood trickling down his face. The smell of burnt cloth and flesh made me nauseous. I knelt next to him, caressing his face and kissing him where he bled.

"Mina, there are two more important things I must tell you

before you inject me. First, change the settings on your tablet so that you cannot be tracked by its signature."

That was an important detail not to forget, so I took a moment to make the adjustment.

"Good. Also, in my bag is a tool for removing your wrist-band and an ointment. Once removed, you can destroy the pieces with a laser gun I left for you in the weapons cabinet. When you remove the band, it will be painful. Your skin will break and bleed, but use the ointment immediately and daily for ten days and you should be fine. Do this while the shuttle is taking off to ensure you cannot be tracked. Do you understand?"

I looked in the bag and saw the items he mentioned.

"Yes...OK, I see them."

"Good, then inject me and leave...the effect is not long. I will regain consciousness in less than an hour and will use my tablet to call for help. I will be fine. Do not worry."

I hugged him, and my sobbing got worse.

"I love you, Mina...one day, you will be my bride."

I surprised myself.

"I love you too, Montor. I pray we will be together soon."

He smiled.

"Mina, those words will be my motivation for the hard days to come."

I inserted the syringe between his shoulder blades, and in about a minute, he passed out in my arms. I gently laid him down and kissed his forehead. Grabbing the bag and weapons, I ran to the shuttle and entered it. The door closed, and I launched while wailing at the top of my lungs.

16

The shuttle took off, and I knew I would have to delay any grieving for later. The most important thing I needed to attend to was removing the tracker wristband. The tool that Montor had left me was a small laser drill to cut through the wristband material. The band was pliable but resistant, and worst of all, it stuck to my skin. It was painful just to pinch or tug at it.

Drilling through small sections of the band wasn't too bad, but I knew what the hard part would be. Taking a deep breath to steady myself, I grabbed a cut end of the band and gave it a tug. I hissed in pain, and my eyes filled with tears. It was a million times worse than a bad waxing job. As I peeled the piece of band from my skin, large blots of blood appeared. Exhaling in quick, short breaths, I applied ointment to the area, which provided some relief. My hands trembled as I continued the tedious and painful process of peeling small pieces of the band off the skin. My wrist was raw and bloody when I was done, but the ointment helped with the pain. As Montor instructed, I used the laser gun to destroy the pieces. Despite the discomfort, destroying the wristband that had been a symbol of bondage was exhilarating. I celebrated by closing my eyes and saying a prayer.

"God, thank you for allowing me to be free of this. Please watch over me as I make this journey. Keep Montor safe, bless everyone who has been kind to me, and watch over my family back home, Amen."

The shuttle possessed the speed capacity of a much larger spacecraft. It cleared Rennan atmosphere in thirty seconds. After one hour, I was halfway across the star system. Seeing the dark expanse and the stars reminded me of the time Montor and I had shared on our trip from Xixsted to Renna One. By that time, Montor would have already regained consciousness. Remembering the injuries I had inflicted, I prayed that help was on the way.

I can't believe how crazy I became. He must have manipulated my mind. Damn him. He promised he would never do that to me!

As much as I disliked the idea of mind control, I knew it had been a selfless act. The thought that he had allowed himself to be hurt to help me escape brought new tears to my eyes.

After these initial thoughts, I sat in the piloting seat staring at the controls. Another hour went by, and I remained dressed in Lostai uniform with the shirt ripped open. I changed out of those clothes and used the laser gun to pulverize them, which led to another brief, joyous moment.

I checked the time. It was late morning, the time when Montor and I usually worked out, so I went through our routine as I had promised. Skipping the sparring portion over-whelmed me with loneliness, which led to skipping meditation also because I lacked focus. I decided to record in my tablet everything that had happened since the Lostai kidnapped me from my home fourteen months earlier. Once I started, I couldn't stop. It was cathartic. Already late evening, I finally got thirsty and developed a bit of an appetite. I ate something light, showered, and lay down. The bed was narrow, and I was grateful for it. I had spent the last four weeks sleeping in Montor's arms. A wider bed would have made me miss his strong embrace even more.

With no Lostai forces chasing me and the shuttle's autopilot functioning fine, still on track to Fronidia, the days went by uneventfully. My wrist healed well, albeit some ugly scarring. I prayed every day for faith and kept up the workout and meditation regimen. Journalizing experiences in my tablet distracted me, but there were still many hours of just staring into space. I had asked Montor to upload some of the Arandan music on my tablet, but I couldn't bear to listen because it made me miss him more. Other times, I wondered what was happening with my family on Earth. Since starting my affair with Montor, I had not composed any new letters. Finally, I summed up enough courage to address one to my husband.

Dear Josh,

I pray you and the kids are well. As for me, I have escaped the place where I was held prisoner and am on my way to another planet. I'm alone in a shuttle that is on autopilot. I can almost see you shaking your head thinking I have gone bananas, but the fact is, it's true.

The Lostai military that kidnapped and held me hostage are ruthless and focused on expanding their empire at all costs. Their plan was for me to join their military, which would require me to perform unspeakable acts and become as heartless as they are... things that I knew I could not bring myself to ever do. I'm so grateful that I was able to leave that place. Now each day I pray that everything continues to go per plan. I don't know what will happen to me once I reach Fronidia, the planet where I'm heading. I've been told I have a much better chance at hiding from the Lostai there.

So much time has gone by since I was taken...more than a year already. I wonder what you are up to, but I'm almost afraid to ask. I'm sure my being away has taken a toll on you and the kids, and I pray that you were able to overcome it. At the Lostai base where I was held, I endured boot camp, difficult chores, long hours, and many new things to learn. If I didn't follow orders, I was severely punished. I fell into survival mode. As bad as it was, it did serve to numb me a bit from the sadness of being separated from you. I hoped that you all were well and together. I can imagine it must be terrible for you not to know what happened to me. In the beginning, I had more hope that I might find a way back to Earth. Now I'm not sure. I'm told that Earth is galaxies away. On the other hand, the place I'm going to is technologically advanced. There may be eventually a way to get back, but unfortunately, I need to stay in hiding for a while as I'm considered a fugitive now and the Lostai will be looking for me.

I'm thankful to God that I've met a few people who have been kind to me. Now, I need to share something with you and it's difficult for me. I met someone here who has taken many risks to help me escape and have developed a relationship with him. At first, I thought he was a horrible person, and although there are things about him I don't like, I've come to learn that he can be very noble. There is more to him than meets the eye. Our time together has been short, but he already has said he loves me, and I have to admit, I have developed feelings for him too. I never thought in a million years this could happen to me...never thought I could love another man. I may never even see him again, but I feel the need to confess this to you. I realize that as time goes by, the same may happen with you. You are still a young man and might find someone else to share the rest of your life with. I'm distraught about all of this because I still love you too. As you can see, I'm very confused. I guess all I can do is pray and put all of this in God's hands.

Please take care of the kids and give them my love.

Love always, Mina

. . .

It was tough recording those words. Tears rolled down my cheeks as I ended the letter, but I felt good about putting the truth out to the universe. I decided there was no reason to delete this or any future letters I might compose.

After two weeks of monotony, I counted and double-checked. I started to panic. I would wait another day, and when it still didn't come, I counted and double-checked again. There was no doubt. I missed my period. Other than the first months after being kidnapped, my cycle had usually been regular. I knew that it was not impossible for me to be pregnant, but I convinced myself that it was highly unlikely. I told myself that all the commotion in recent weeks could have thrown my system out of whack. Even if the Lostai had reversed my tubal ligation, I was getting to that age where things were supposed to start winding down for me where reproduction was concerned. I knew the Lostai had pumped me with hormones and drugs to rejuvenate me, but I put any concern out of my mind until I started developing morning sickness. Another month went by and I started having breast tenderness and still no period. Having been pregnant three times, I knew the symptoms. I was familiar with the on-board first aid equipment, but I wasn't aware of how to run any pregnancy tests, and I still had two weeks more of travel time.

My thoughts were now flooded with all the possible ramifications of my being pregnant.

Will I be able to deliver a healthy child? How will I care for it and ensure its safety? I'm not even clear where I'll be sleeping after I land.

I scolded myself daily for my part in not insisting on proper birth control.

What the hell is wrong with me? Why have I behaved like an ignorant teenager?

I remembered the night I purposely enticed Montor to lose control, and there was at least one other time we chose to ignore the possibility of conceiving. Finally, after several days of driving myself crazy, I decided the most important thing I needed to do was keep myself as physically and mentally healthy as possible. I focused on choosing my meals more carefully to ensure proper nutrition. I continued my exercises but avoided anything too risky. I meditated and prayed more than ever.

Finally, the day came when I approached Fronidia's atmosphere. I kept my packed bag near me in the cabin, and in there, I included the laser gun in case I ran into trouble. I never received communication from Fronidian Border Control. Instead, strange environmental readings indicated a strong electromagnetic storm. The dramatic flashes of light and particle clouds startled me. As I focused on the controls, there was a strong thud, and the shuttle tilted to one side. I didn't have time to strap into my chair. With another thud, the shuttle tumbled forward, and I fell out of my seat. The communication equipment crackled with static, and the autopilot was knocked offline. The shuttle went through bouts of gliding and tumbling, free-falling to the surface. I needed to take over piloting control. The erratic movement caused me to lose balance. I was thrown several times hard against the control panel, resulting in electrical sparks and a burning sensation on my thigh. I couldn't let panic take over, so I inhaled and exhaled slowly, forcing myself to focus on everything I had learned about operating the shuttle.

A careful read of the controls revealed that I was way off course. Instead of heading towards the northern hemisphere, I was in the south and barreling towards the surface at an unsafe speed. My main concern at that point was no longer getting to the location Montor had programmed on the autopilot but just surviving a crash landing. The maps of the region showed mountainous areas and a vast sea, neither good options for landing. I was able to slow down the shuttle's descent with enough time to look for somewhere safer to land. I found a strip of shoreline that was not too rocky and manually initiated the landing sequence.

"It's OK," I told myself with a sigh of relief. "You're going to make it...you can do this."

Another thud threw off the direction again. The shuttle was heading too close to the hilly area bordering the beach. I did my best to control the descent and direction, but the shuttle hit the side of a rocky ledge, and smoke filled the cabin. I put my tablet in my bag, threw the bag over my shoulder, and went to grab a gas mask. Before I could get to the mask, a hard bump caused me to lose balance again. I tried to brace myself but twisted my ankle and fell, banging my head against a console.

When I opened my eyes, I had the sensation of having blacked out for an unknown amount of time. I shook my head to get rid of the dizzy feeling. My eyes and throat burned, and I coughed uncontrollably.

Knowing I was likely to lose consciousness again, I shouted, "Oh God, please help me!"

17

I woke up to humming, beeps, body aches, and a splitting headache. I remembered losing control of the shuttlecraft and crash landing, but nothing else. Outdoor light trickled in from somewhere ahead of me. Storage cabinets, electronic equipment panels, and what appeared to be refrigeration units obstructed my view. I sat up on the berth I was lying on to take an inventory of my injuries. Cuts and abrasions covered both arms, and a large gauze was taped on my left thigh. When I tried to stand, pain shot up my leg and my left ankle buckled. The best I'd be able to do was hop on one foot. Not a good game plan for a quick getaway. I chomped on my fingernails as heavy footsteps interrupted my thoughts.

What should I do next?

In ten seconds, he was standing in front of me, tall with a lean, athletic build. I guessed his age was close to mine. Handsome facial features, azure hair and lips contrasted with slate-colored skin. He appeared to be Sotkari and reminded me of Kaya. Perhaps that's why I remained calm, although his ultramarine eyes took my breath away. I knew most Sotkari spoke

Lostai as the language had become mandatory in Sotkar after the occupation.

"My ankle is sprained. Who are you?" I said, avoiding his gaze by looking down to rub the injured area.

He understood the language.

"My name is Kindor Grahmon, and I rescued you from the shuttle wreckage."

He did not speak out loud. His words and voice were in my mind and communicated in Lostai with an accent similar to Kaya's.

So...He is an evolved Sotkari. The question is how evolved and how powerful. He could be a Pasi, a Sotkari Ta of mixed heritage, or a pure blood Sotkari Ta.

I didn't display any sense of surprise, so it was clear to him that this was not my first telepathic experience. He nodded, an inquisitive look on his face.

"It is good that we can communicate this way," he said.

I owed him my life. We had a telepathic connection.

What next?

He gave me a quick once-over.

"I planned to take you back to my village where someone could better tend to your injuries. The trip back will take several days due to the bad weather. Where were you heading when you crashed? You do not appear to be native to this planet."

"I am not familiar with this place. I was trying to escape from the people who kidnapped me. It is a long story."

I reminded myself that as a fugitive, I was at the mercy of this stranger. Losing my initial composure, my heart accelerated, and I found myself clenching my hands into tight fists. Curiously, he appeared equally agitated and stepped away. After a few long minutes, he returned, took a deep breath, and made deliberate eye contact.

"Who kidnapped you? What is your name? Do not worry. I will not harm you."

How do I even begin to explain everything that has happened to me?

"My name is Mina," I said.

I reached out, and we squeezed each other's forearms in the typical Sotkari greeting. Pleasurable sensations coursed through me coupled with a feeling of warmth and well-being, but not as intense as when Montor touched me. I yanked my arm back.

Not this again.

He continued to lock eyes with me.

Montor said I should be careful who I trust.

I closed my mind to avoid any possibility of mind control or him learning too much about me. He definitely noticed, leaning forward and tilting his head.

Let's see what he does now that he can't communicate telepathically. Can he speak?

"Are you familiar with the Lostai?"

I waited for a response.

"Did you understand the question?" I asked again.

He gestured what I understood to mean that he was mute, so he was definitely Sotkari Ta, since Sotkari Pasi are able to speak. Depending on how well trained he was, I could be dealing with an extremely powerful being. This made me even more cautious.

"OK, you are mute, so you must be Sotkari Ta."

He nodded yes.

"I am aware of your abilities. That is why I have closed my mind. I am afraid of leaving myself vulnerable."

He gesticulated some kind of sign language that I obviously could not understand. We were at a standstill.

"I am not familiar with your sign language. We are at a crossroads now. Should I trust you or not?"

He pointed to his head and extended his hands palms up as in offering. I understood that he was giving me permission to look deep into his mind and subconscious. Having never done this before, not even with Kaya or Montor, I hesitated. Kindor vehemently gestured again as if insisting, so I summoned up my courage. I envisioned myself walking towards his "light" in my mind, reaching, and gingerly moving beyond it. This required significant mental effort. I squeezed my eyes shut to focus, catching my breath as I experienced a blinding, bright light. It only lasted a few seconds, and then he was revealed to me. He didn't have bad intentions but was curious as he realized that I was Sotkari Ta as well. I sensed no deception or ill will towards me at all, but the fact that I said I was running from kidnappers and now asked about the Lostai had put him on edge.

"Would you believe that is the first time I have done that?"

He raised his eyebrows, nodded his head, and pursed his lips as if to show he was impressed.

"OK, I am going to open my mind now, but I do not give you permission to go beyond communication. If you are a properly trained and morally sound Sotkari Ta, you will honor my request, correct?"

He nodded yes, and I unlocked my mind.

"Thank you, Mina, for trusting me. I promise I have no intention of tricking or harming you. However, I am curious, as you appear to be a well-trained Sotkari Ta. You must be the result of genetic transfer."

"Yes, I have been told the story of how Sotkari Ta scientists decided to transfer their genetic material to unsuspecting people across many planets."

"It is not just a story. My great-grandfather was one of those scientists. You asked about the Lostai. Obviously, I know about them. They are the reason I live in exile, away from my beloved planet. You said you were escaping from those who kidnapped you. Who are you running from?"

I said a silent prayer of thanks as it appeared that Kindor could become an ally. Before I could share any other information, there was something else I needed to know.

Rubbing my abdomen, I asked, "Kindor, I see you performed some first aid on me. Did you notice any evidence of...um...internal bleeding?"

"Uh, no...it has been about half a day since I rescued you. You were unconscious, a bump on your head and a burn on your thigh, and some minor abrasions, but I do not have any sophisticated medical equipment. Are you feeling any internal pain?"

"No...no... but I think, I think..." I hesitated, but the rest of the words came out in a tumble. "I may be pregnant and am concerned for the health of the baby."

His eyes widened.

"Oh...I will try my best to get us to my village doctor as soon as possible. Unfortunately, the same storm that probably affected your landing will be a factor in how fast we can get there. In the meantime, you should try to relax. Are you hungry?"

Kindor brought me something to eat and my bag, which he said I was clutching when he found me. I was happy to see my tablet was still working. My laser gun was in there as well. While we ate, I gave Kindor a short summary of my situation. I told him that I was purposely leaving out names and descriptions of the people who had helped me escape.

"I have been held prisoner for more than one revolution at a Lostai science station. It was a hard time for me, but I was lucky to find people who were willing to help me. In the interim, I became romantically involved with someone...the father of the baby."

He pressed his lips into a fine line, and his eyes took on that intense look again.

"Is there any chance the Lostai followed you here?" Kindor asked.

"No, I don't think so. The shuttle was disguised as a drone. During the whole trip, no other spacecraft approached or contacted me. My tablet is also set to ghost mode, so it cannot be traced."

He exhaled with relief.

"That is good. Who trained you in Sotkari Ta skills?"

"I prefer not to say. I need to err now on the side of caution. I am a fugitive, and most probably, the Lostai have search parties looking for me. If, by any chance, you encounter one of them, the less you know about me, the better."

"OK, I understand," Kindor replied, nodding.

"What happened to the shuttle?"

"A few minutes after I pulled you out, it exploded in flames. There is no chance of repairing it."

Kindor excused himself to tend to some maintenance issues, and I spent some time updating my journal. Later, he asked if I wanted to shower. He explained we were in an amphibious vehicle that could travel on different types of terrain as well as in water and was equipped with amenities needed for longer trips such as a bathroom and food replication. He gently put his arm around me to help me get up and limp towards the bathroom. I was able to get a better idea for the layout of the vehicle. It was only slightly smaller than the shuttle, but a lot of space was devoted to refrigeration because he was on a hunting and fishing trip. It reminded me of an oversized RV or food bus. He provided a seat that I could use in the shower, as I couldn't stand for more than a few minutes. When I was done, it was already dark. He helped me back to the berth.

"Where are you sleeping? Have I taken your only bed?" I asked, embarrassed.

"Do not worry, Mina. I can sleep anywhere. It is important for your recovery that you get proper rest, especially if you are pregnant."

Before Kindor left me to rest, he got on one knee and placed his hands on my leg.

"I think I can help with your ankle," he said, closing his eyes.

A soothing sensation radiated from my shin to the end of my toes. Before I could say "thank you," he said a quick "good night" and walked to the front of the vehicle. As I tried to get some sleep, I rubbed the amulet that Montor had gifted me. The shuttle was supposed to send a message confirming that it had landed. The malfunction had started before landing.

What message, if any, did the shuttle send back to Montor's tablet?

The next day, I woke up to find no swelling on my ankle and was able to walk again. I remembered how Montor had helped me with a headache but was amazed that Kindor had used Sotkari Ta powers to not only alleviate pain but also physically repair the torn ligaments and reduce the inflammation. I walked up to the front of the vehicle and found him eating slices of a dark bread spread with some type of cream.

"Good morning, Mina. How are you feeling?"

"Much better, thanks to how you helped me with my ankle. That is amazing."

"I am glad I could help. The burn on your thigh is severe, so although I have treated it to avoid infection, I prefer a doctor examine it to ensure there is no scarring. Would you like some bread? I also have dried fruit and crackers. Sorry, but I do not have much more to offer for the morning meal."

"Bread is fine, thank you."

He walked to a cabinet and one of the refrigeration units

before returning with a few more round rolls of dark bread and a glass container of what he called cream. I spread some on the rolls, and it tasted like butter but with the consistency of sour cream. He poured me a hot transparent beverage in a cup. I took a sip, and it was so sweet, I squinted and smacked my lips.

Once I recovered from the sugar shock, I asked, "Are we on the way to your village?"

"Yes. If you would like, you can sit up front with me and take in the view. We will be on high speed to take advantage of the good weather today and tomorrow because after that, the weather will worsen, and we will need to slow down."

After breakfast, I washed up and accepted his invitation to join him in the front. The vehicle was set on six pairs of what looked similar to tank treads and sped over the rocky shoreline and a long strip of beach. The area seemed very remote, and suddenly, I wondered if Kindor lived alone. He had been a perfect gentleman so far, but I still had my guard up.

"Kindor, you mentioned that you are living here in exile. Do you have family here?"

"Yes, I live with my mother and niece. My mother is Sotkari Ta, and my niece is Sotkari Pasi. During the time when the Lostai invaded Sotkar and started rounding up Sotkari Ta, rather than flee, most of my ancestors remained with those who were trying to defend their planet. My grandparents, aunt, uncles, cousins, and two older siblings were all captured or killed. The Sotkari Ta elders asked my great-grandfather, an expert in bioengineering and genetics, to join a group of scientists secretly working on the genetic transfer project. They begged him to leave and facilitated his escape from Sotkar. Only my parents, my sister, and I remained on the planet. The Lostai found where my sister was hiding with her husband. They killed him since he was a non-evolved Sotkari and took her."

I sensed a break in his communication, but his eyes remained focused on where he was driving.

Another family destroyed by the Lostai military.

"Her daughter, only a baby at the time, escaped capture because she was with my parents. Finally, my father decided it was time to leave and found a way to sneak my mother, my niece, and me here. I was a teenager at the time. He tried to go back to rescue my sister but was killed in the process."

"I am so sorry, Kindor."

"Yes, well, our family was only one of many who suffered loss at the hands of the Lostai. Now, my mother, niece, and I live in a small village bordered by several plantations. We operate a small restaurant that serves the people who work those farms. I come to this area twice every lunar cycle to fish and hunt for my family's meals as well as the restaurant's menu."

"Have you ever seen any Lostai in the area?"

"Oh, no, Mina. This land is separated from the other continents by violent oceans and is subject to unpredictable weather patterns like the one that caused your shuttle to crash. It is not easy to travel here. The only reason some natives come to work here is because the produce from those farms is considered a delicacy and is quite a lucrative business."

"I have been told that the Lostai can scan for evolved Sotkari brain waves."

"Yes, but the electromagnetic storms and the properties of certain metallic ores found in the nearby mountains interfere with the sensors that the Lostai use. The main risk for our family results from the few Fronidians who come in from the city to work the land on a temporary basis, who potentially could reveal our location to a Lostai soldier or spy when they return home. Usually, the same few people make these trips, and so far, they have proven to be trustworthy. No Lostai has ever visited our village or the nearby plantations."

Please, God, don't let me cause any problems for Kindor or his family.

Later that day, Kindor parked the vehicle.

"Mina, I am stopping to perform my daily exercise routine."

"May I join you for a few repetitions?"

"Of course."

His exercises were similar to calisthenics, and he used bars attached to the back of his vehicle for various types of pull-ups. He also practiced a form that was a combination of self-defense and dance that required balance and core strength but was graceful as well.

When he was done with the physical part of his workout and getting ready to transition to mental exercises, I asked, "Can I follow you on the mental portion of your workout also, unless you prefer privacy?"

"Sure. I see that you follow the main tenets of all classically trained Sotkari Ta."

"Yes, my Sotkari Ta mentors were adamant about this. Any chance you know what physical exercises are appropriate for pregnant women?" I said, more as a joke rather than a true request.

"As a matter of fact, I do. My parents instructed my older sister when she was pregnant. I will show you," he answered.

I wanted to avoid any possible arousal from skin-to-skin contact, so I tried to learn the movements by observation only. Although thankful for Kindor's help and instruction, sadness consumed me as well.

Had Zorla blamed Montor for my disappearance, or were the Lostai focusing on Gio Napoletano as a suspect? I prayed Montor was safe and thought about how he might feel about my being pregnant. It was the one thing we had both agreed shouldn't happen.

❄

Two days later, we entered a dense tropical forest, and as Kindor had anticipated, the weather became stormy with electromagnetic disturbances. Our navigation was reduced to a crawl. It wasn't safe to go outside of the vehicle, so we were limited to doing stretch exercises, squats, and lunges. Kindor kept our conversation animated as he explained everything from the flora and fauna of the area to Fronidian civics and Sotkari history. He asked many questions about Earth, as he quickly understood that I avoided discussing my time on Xixsted. I didn't even tell him that I had come from Renna One and gave him no details regarding my escape. To pass the time, Kindor began to teach me Sotkari and Fronidian sign language.

After the seventh day of travel, we left behind the tropical forest and approached a clear, wide river. He sealed all the openings, reset environmental controls to include breathable air, and drove the vehicle straight into the water. The river was calm and led into magnificent—but unnervingly pitch-black— river caves. The lights of the vehicle reflected shiny strips on the smooth cave walls. Kindor explained those were examples of ores that interfered with Lostai scanning equipment.

It took two more days to navigate the river caves. As soon as we exited the darkness, the village came into view on the mountainside. I expected modern structures made of artificial materials similar to the smooth, shiny government buildings of Renna One. Instead, natural stone buildings with dark, pyramid-shaped roofs and neat landscaping lined the narrow streets.

"Welcome to the tiny village of Zuntar. I will take you straight to the doctor," Kindor said.

"I was told Fronidia was a technologically advanced planet. This seems much more antiquated than what I expected."

"Oh, yes, the larger cities do not look like this. These are simple people who prefer a no-frills lifestyle." He pointed out the farmlands in the distance. "The owners of those lands, on the other hand, live in nearby larger towns with all the luxuries of the latest scientific inventions."

We walked into a two-story building. Kindor used sign language to communicate with the Fronidian receptionist. Over time, enough mute Sotkari had immigrated to Fronidia so that it was typical for professionals to learn sign language. I already understood many basic phrases. The receptionist's features were like Colora's except her black eyes had a brilliant lavender center, and her hair was long and blonde. Kindor explained we would need to wait a while since we had arrived without an appointment. He laughed when I said it was the same story in all doctor offices no matter what the galaxy.

Eventually, the doctor called us into his office. He was a short, bald man also with lavender centered eyes. Kindor told me the receptionist was his daughter. A look around the room revealed only basic medical equipment. The doctor observed me curiously while Kindor used signed language to explain my situation. The doctor replied out loud, but I needed Kindor to translate, as I didn't speak Fronidian.

"The doctor asks how far along you think you are," said Kindor.

"A little over two lunar cycles," I answered.

The doctor led me to an area with a cot and closed off with a curtain. He asked me to disrobe, gave me a gown, and had me lie down. My belly was much rounder than what I would have expected at two months. If I compared to my previous pregnancies, it appeared more like four months. He returned with a device about the size of personal computer but super thin and held it over my abdomen. After a physical examination, he checked the burn on my thigh and hovered over it with a hand-held device that healed the skin. He gestured that we were done, to get dressed, and to meet him back in the front of his office where Kindor was also waiting. He spoke to Kindor.

"The doctor says you are definitely pregnant, that he has

detected the heartbeat of the fetus. He asks what the normal gestation period for your species is."

"My normal gestation would be nine lunar cycles."

The doctor furrowed his brow and became pensive when Kindor relayed that information.

"The doctor says this fetus is developing at a much faster pace. He says there is no way you could carry a fetus at this rate of development for nine lunar cycles."

I turned away as I thought about whether it was safe to start sharing more information than I had until then. I sighed and answered, "The father is not of my same race. He is Arandan."

Kindor signed this information to the doctor.

"The doctor is not familiar with this species, and neither am I. He said the fetus must be following the gestation period of the father's species. He strongly suggests that you visit a clinic at one of the nearby larger towns that have more specialized doctors and equipment. However, in the meantime, he says everything is in order. Let me get you to my home, and we can plan a trip to the next town in a few days."

The doctor's comments made me worry even more about the unknowns that I was facing with this pregnancy. However, I was thankful that the baby had survived the shuttle crash and that Kindor was being so supportive. On the way out, he stopped back at the receptionist's desk to settle the bill.

"Kindor, I do not know how to thank you for your kindness."

"Mina, we both have been displaced from our homes by the Lostai. I am sympathetic to your situation. It is the least I can do."

On our way to his home, he explained that it was located near the plantations.

"Our restaurant is next door to our home. We have our own plot of land with a vegetable and herb garden. Farm laborers stop in for breakfast, lunch, and dinner on their way to and from work."

We arrived at the two-story building. The restaurant next door was only one story with countertops that extended from the windows so a person could grab something on the go or eat while standing on the sidewalk. Showy flowers adorned the countertops. Kindor parked his vehicle in an empty lot on the side of the building.

No one was home when we arrived. The entrance led to a foyer, followed by a sparsely furnished sitting and dining room. Tall windows in the dining area gave a view to the garden he had mentioned. To one side was a bedroom and to the other side was a kitchen. He pointed out a bathroom behind the stairway and explained there were other bedrooms, a second bathroom, and what he called a reading room on the second floor.

"My mother and niece should be working next door in the restaurant. Let us go to meet them. I should warn you...My mother has a strong personality. She is blunt and opinionated, but underneath the tough exterior, she has a kind heart."

We walked back outside and into the restaurant. I counted fifteen tables, some square, others round or rectangular. Candles were the only illumination. At the back of the room was a counter and, behind that, the food preparation area. Same as in his house, at the end, floor-to-ceiling windows allowed a view to the garden.

"Right now, we are in the lull between the morning and midday mealtimes. They must be in the back preparing food."

He led me to the back, and sure enough, his niece and mother were there washing and chopping vegetables. They were both much taller than me, close to Kaya's height.

I immediately heard all their voices in my mind, but I didn't understand their language. I guess he explained I did not speak Sotkari or Fronidian because they switched to Lostai.

"Grandmother, Kindor has finally brought home one of his girlfriends."

"Disregard what she says. She is young and immature," Kindor said, pressing his fingers against his temples and shaking his head.

His niece laughed mischievously. She had an attractive figure and was about twenty years old, and her skin was a much lighter grey than Kindor's and his mother's. Her eyes were cobalt blue, and her long, straight hair reminded me of the Crayola crayon color Periwinkle.

His mother washed her hands and walked over, immediately giving me a deliberate once-over. I'm sure she noticed my belly.

"Mother, this is Mina. She was traveling to Fronidia by shuttle from another planet and suffered a crash landing. I helped her as she was injured. It is a long story, but she was kidnapped, held hostage, and forced to train as a Lostai soldier. She escaped the Lostai camp and has come to Fronidia to hide from them."

Kindor resembled his mother, both with the same striking eyes. She extended her arm in greeting, and when I held hers, she glanced at me sideways and back at Kindor.

"Is it possible? Is she Sotkari Ta?"

"Yes, by way of genetic transfer. Her home world must have been one of the places where scientists spread Sotkari Ta genes."

"Interesting. I have never met a *counterfeit* Sotkari Ta," Kindor's mother said, rubbing her chin. "Pleased to meet you, Mina. My name is Kora."

Counterfeit Sotkari Ta? That doesn't sound like a warm welcome.

Kindor's niece introduced herself with a fake innocent smile. "...And my name is Karrina."

"Hello, Kora. Your son has been more than kind to me."

"Mother, Mina's initial plan was to land in the capital city in the northern continent next to the refugee center. Now, it would be dangerous for her to try to make the long trip there. The Lostai military considers her a fugitive, and they are most probably searching for her all over the sector. She does not speak Fronidian, have any funds, or know anyone here. Also, she has another situation..."

Kindor looked over to seek my approval before he continued. I nodded yes.

"...She is pregnant and needs specialized care...Doctor Semillar will not suffice—"

"What are you getting at, son?" interrupted Kora.

"I would like to offer her to stay with us for a while."

That took me by surprise, but he had summed up my precarious situation very well. Montor could not even give me a remuneration chip because it could be traced back to him, so I had no way to pay for anything. Kora's expression was one of concern. Karrina snickered and went back to chopping vegetables.

"Kindor, I am sympathetic to Mina's situation, but we are in hiding ourselves. Do you think harboring a fugitive Lostai soldier is wise? And we barely make enough income right now to cover our expenses," Kora replied.

I was mortified. She was right. I was a problem they did not need, so I quickly chimed in.

"Please, Kindor, you have done enough for me already. Perhaps I can get a loan to pay for a trip—"

No one paid any attention to me. Kindor insisted.

"So, you will have me send her on her way...in her condition?"

Kora turned her back to us with her hand on her hips, I assumed not happy to be put on the spot. After a few seconds, she turned and looked me straight in the eyes. Karrina poked her head out of the kitchen.

"Mina, can you cook...prepare food?" Kora asked.

"Yes," I answered simply.

"Our customers have been asking for a second seating in the evening and also lunch deliveries. Karrina and I cannot meet this demand. I can offer you a job here for the short term. You can sleep in the reading room, but a lodging fee will be deducted from your pay. Obviously, this is a temporary solution until you save enough money to be on your way. Also, you will pay Kindor back for any medical bills," Kora said.

Kindor beamed.

"Thank you, Mother."

I nodded reverently to Kora.

"Kora, thank you so much for your kindness. I promise to work hard and not abuse your charity."

"OK, your training starts now. Karrina, please find Mina a clean apron."

18

The reading room was the largest room in the house with two comfortable chairs, a table, a wall unit filled with books, digital files, and other reading material. A musical instrument was moved out of the room to the dining area to make space for a small bed and storage unit for my clothes and personal items. The next day, I began my new routine.

My workday started before sunrise when I joined Kora and Karrina in the restaurant kitchen to prepare morning and midday meals. The most requested breakfast item on the menu was a warm cereal made from a bitter, brownish grain sweetened with macerated fruit and honey. We also baked two different kinds of bread and a variety of muffins, in addition to preparing something similar to an egg scramble. Those without time for lunch could request that a meat patty be added to any meal. Some customers sat in the restaurant. Others ate at the counter outside, and others took their meals with them. We served about one hundred morning meals. Most of the customers were young Fronidian males on their way to work in the plantation. Before long, I learned that Karrina preferred waiting on customers, rather than preparing food in the kitchen. She was a shameless flirt. I was fine with taking over most of her kitchen chores.

After the morning rush, the restaurant was closed, and the four of us spent an hour and a half doing physical and mental exercises. I was surprised to see even Kora, whose age was the equivalent to late sixties, join in on the physical ones, albeit with some modifications. Karrina skipped the mental exercises as she, being Sotkari Pasi, possessed the ability to communicate telepathically but not other enhanced mental capabilities. When we were done with the workout, we had an hour to finalize meal preparations for the midday customers.

We began the new delivery service to the plantation workers and some of the other village businesses. Karrina wasted no time requesting delivery duty as it gave her a chance to get out of the restaurant and meet people. An early dinner seating was served at sunset and a second seating was added for two hours later. Kindor butchered the meat and cleaned the fish and seafood. He tended the garden and, during the afternoon, ran a side business of repairing machinery and other technical equipment at the plantation. He would return to the restaurant in time to have his dinner at the second seating. After the last customer left, he and I remained to clean the restaurant and leave everything in order for the next day.

The Fronidian work calendar called for four workdays and a day off. On the off days, the restaurant only opened for the late-night dinner seating, and twice every lunar cycle, the restaurant was closed to allow us a full day of rest. During the off days, Karrina taught me the Fronidian language, which she spoke like a native. The restaurant income increased significantly, and Kora was pleased with my work ethic. Our daily schedule was grueling, but I was grateful for the lack of free time. Idle time was my enemy, bringing on waves of emotion and stress. I missed Montor's touch, wondered how my family on Earth was doing, and worried about my future and that of my baby.

On my first full off day, Kindor took me in the morning to a neighboring town called Rondarium to visit another doctor. Rondarium was more populated and technologically advanced than Zuntar. The doctor's office was in a large, modern clinic. Kindor again served as my translator using sign language. The doctor had archives of data relating to many native species of the galaxy, including the Arandan. Of course, he had no data relating to humans, but he said my physiology was comparable to a Fronidian female. Using the data he had on Fronidian females conceiving children with Arandan fathers, he was able to hypothesize what I should expect of my pregnancy.

"Dr. Magon says the baby appears to be healthy and developing according to a typical Arandan four-lunar-cycle gestation period. The doctor is asking if you would like to know the sex of the baby."

"Yes, I do."

The doctor spoke, and Kindor's face lit up with a broad smile.

"Mina, it is a male!"

I wished Montor could have been there to see how his prediction had come true. Once Kindor got over his excitement, he continued translating the doctor's information.

"You are halfway through your pregnancy. He also says the baby is already trending to be on the high end of the spectrum of what is considered normal for Arandans and might not be able to safely make it through your birth canal during labor. He is recommending surgery to extract the baby by an incision to the lower abdomen. He says he has performed the procedure many times without any complications and no scarring."

A C-Section.

I let Kindor know I was familiar with what the doctor was explaining. The doctor also confirmed that I would be able to nurse the baby. I also explained that I once had a tubal ligation to avoid pregnancy and it was later reversed.

"Please ask the doctor if he can take advantage of the surgery to also re-do the tubal ligation."

Kindor frowned.

"Are you sure you want to do that, Mina? It seems an extreme approach to birth control."

"I am not in control of my life. I should not risk bringing any more children into the world."

"Do not say that, Mina. You are Sotkari Ta and should always be confident that you are in control. Of course, you cannot foresee what fate has in store for you, but you need to have faith that you possess the abilities and strength to deal with whatever comes your way. I think you should wait before making that decision. You still have two lunar cycles to think about it."

I wondered why he had such a strong opinion about my reproductive cycle, but I let him convince me to delay the decision until the time came for delivery. I was quiet during the ride back.

"Mina, you look sad...It is good news that the baby is doing well, right?"

"Of course. It is excellent news. I am so thankful for it, but his future concerns me. I not only need to provide for him, but I need to protect him from the Lostai. Kindor, his father is like me...what did your mother call me?...a counterfeit Sotkari Ta. The Lostai would love to get their hands on our son and see if he inherited our Sotkari Ta genes."

"I hope you were not offended. My mother has extreme views about the destiny of the Sotkari Ta. She does not believe the genetic transfer was a good thing for any of the parties involved."

"I tend to agree with her. I would have been with my family back on Earth living a normal life if I did not have these genes."

I stared down to my lap.

"Do not second-guess your destiny. Embrace it. You are not alone. I am here for you," Kindor said.

He took my hand in his and with the other hand lifted my chin so he could look into my eyes.

"Today is a day for smiling. Your son is doing well."

"Thank you, Kindor."

His words improved my mood, and I couldn't ignore the sensual aspect of his touch. Although not as intense as Montor's, it definitely was there. The last thing I needed was to complicate my life even more. Smiling politely, I slipped my hand out of his, turning to look out the vehicle's side window, and focused on the sights and sounds of Rondarium.

We arrived home and being an off day, there was not much to do. I went into my room, sat in one of the chairs, and pondered on what to expect during the rest of my pregnancy. I would reach full term in two months and get really big, really fast. How would it affect my ability to work? If I required a C-section, my recovery time might take longer. I did math in my head calculating my salary, my expenses, and potential savings. A knock on the door interrupted my budget exercise.

"Come in," I answered.

Kora walked in and sat in the chair across from me.

"Mina, how did it go at the doctor's office?"

"The baby is a male and, thankfully, development is on target. The gestation period is half the time what is normal for my species. He should be born in two lunar cycles. The doctor foresees the need to deliver the baby through surgery as the baby will be too large for my frame. His father is very tall."

Kora pressed her fingers against her temples as if she were trying to figure something out.

"I hope I do not come across as nosy, but I cannot help but wonder, why are you alone? Where is the father of the baby? Were you assaulted?"

Her genuine expression of concern reminded me of Kaya, and I welcomed a conversation with a mother figure. Up until then, I had avoided talking about the details of how I arrived at Fronidia, but I felt the need to unburden myself.

"No, nothing like that, but my situation is...complicated."

I explained Zorla's idea that Montor and I mate to have a Sotkari Ta child.

"So, he is Sotkari Ta...? The father?" she asked.

"Yes, but not from Sotkar. He is from the planet Aranda and has embedded Sotkari Ta genes same as me. He was kidnapped as a child, raised on the Lostai military station, and became a Lostai soldier. Neither one of us wanted to conceive a child, so we came up with a plan for me to escape. We left the station to travel to a nearby planet on an official Lostai military mission. Our commander had placed devices on the spaceship to spy on us and ensure we were carrying out his orders. We came up with a ruse where we would pretend to be mating but not actually going through with it."

"I see where this is going," said Kora nodding, her lips pursed.

"What?" I asked, surprised that she was so confident in what I would say next.

"Ah...the curse of Sotkari Ta..." she said, shaking her head.

"The curse of Sotkari Ta? What does that mean?" I asked.

"These days, every bad thing that has happened to our people is referred to as the curse of Sotkari Ta. If you ask me, it is unfair as we, Sotkari Ta, are proof that our people are destined to evolve to a higher level. The saying originated when, as part of our evolutionary process, Sotkari Ta became predisposed to prefer each other as mates, as opposed to regular Sotkari. I suppose it was nature's way to further the evolution of our race."

"Oh, yes, this was explained to me, but I never heard that expression before."

"Yes, well, some Sotkari Ta are offended by it. As I was saying, the attraction between Sotkari Ta is extreme, almost irresistible, and occurs through any skin to skin contact, especially that involving the hands. In the early days of our evolution, we did not understand what was going on in our bodies and minds. The first evolved Sotkari had not yet learned how to become disciplined with their new abilities. People became romantically involved based only on this extreme physical attraction, resulting in many failed relationships. Marriages were broken due to illicit love affairs for the same reason. As these situations became more common, people began to blame it on what they called the curse of Sotkari Ta. Later, Sotkari people coined the term to describe all of their problems in general....the divisions between our people, children born with genetic defects, the Lostai takeover of Sotkar, the persecution and exile of the Sotkari Ta..."

"Oh, I see. I guess we can say even innocent people from other planets have become victims of this curse."

"Yes, I suppose...but anyway...I still do not understand. Mina, why did the father of your baby send you alone on this trip? Does he not care about his child?"

"He does not know. I only became aware that I was pregnant after I left. Once we realized that we had feelings for each other, he asked me to stay with him, but I could not bring myself to be a part of the Lostai military. As you know, they are ruthless and cruel in their quest to grow their empire...I just could not do it...On the other hand, he could not come with me because he..."

I hesitated to continue. Should I mention Kaya? I decided

that I might as well go for the full confession. I took a deep breath.

"...On the same station there is a Sotkari Ta elderly female who trains the hostages to use their Sotkari Ta capabilities. She was my mentor. The Lostai have threatened her granddaughter, so she agrees to do the training for them. She raised and trained the father of my son as he grew up on that station. He is loyal to her and refused to leave her alone at the mercy of the Lostai. He even has pledged to protect her granddaughter when she passes on. He needs to stay on the station to fulfill this vow and could not risk the Lostai finding out that he had helped me escape."

"So, he is noble and a Lostai soldier...it seems impossible," said Kora, a skeptical look on her face.

"He is by no means a perfect person. There are things that he does as a Lostai soldier that I do not approve of, but he is truly committed to the people he cares about. His plan was for me to get help at the refugee center and keep a low profile here in Fronidia until he could come find me. He admitted it might take at least six lunar cycles or maybe a whole revolution before I was removed from the fugitive list. Instead, I ended up crash landing far from my destination, and I cannot make contact for the time being because I would compromise him and our mentor."

"I see, Mina. It is a tough situation. We are in hiding from the Lostai as well. I assume you must be troubled about your immediate future."

"Yes, truthfully, I am."

"I want to let you know that you are not a burden to us. I am paying you less than what I would normally have to pay for the amount of work you are putting in, and your lodging fee is more than enough to cover your expenses...so, it turns out we are now benefitting financially from you being here."

Kora was all about brutal honesty.

"You are going to slow down a bit towards the end of the pregnancy and the recovery after the birth of the child. Do not be troubled about this. It will not be a problem. We will be fine, and you need not be in a rush to leave us. However, I ask you only one thing."

"That is very kind of you, Kora...of course...what is it?"

"Stay away from my son, Mina."

I blushed and was about to protest, but she put up her hand, requesting that I let her finish what she had to say.

"Kindor has had plenty of relationships. After all, he is a healthy male and needs companionship, but I believe it has been a while since he has been in contact with a Sotkari Ta female. I do not want him feeling attracted to you and getting confused. Did you know that the Sotkari Ta have registered their DNA for over two hundred revolutions?"

I shook my head.

"Yes, and both my husband and I are registered as pure blood Sotkari Ta. In other words, there are no Sotkari Pasi or unevolved Sotkari among our ancestors since the records first started...not one! Our families were once considered Sotkari Ta royalty. There are not many Sotkari Ta still alive today that can make such a claim. Before Kindor reached puberty, my husband had already fully trained him in all his evolved capabilities. My son is a humble soul, so it might surprise you to hear that he is a powerful being. He must fall in love with a pure blood Sotkari Ta female and continue our family lines and our evolution. My daughter, Karrina's mother, defied me and married someone of unevolved heritage. Now, Kindor is the only child I have left, and I will not let him deviate from his destiny. Do you understand?"

I was embarrassed at her bluntness and that she believed I might be interested in having a romantic relationship with Kindor. It took me a minute to recover.

"Kora, my only focus now is to keep my baby safe. My life

has no room for any more complications. Kindor has been very kind to me, but I am not looking to share anything more than a friendship with him. I am hoping to one day be reunited with the baby's father and that we can be a family."

"Good, I am relieved to hear that. I shall leave you to rest now."

19

A month went by, and my belly grew exponentially. I appeared seven months pregnant, but other than the fast progression, nothing else was out of the ordinary. I continued my workout routine, tweaking as necessary. Kindor took me to Dr. Magon for a second visit, and thankfully, the doctor found both the baby and me in perfect health. After giving it some more thought, I stuck with my decision to re-do the tubal ligation. I had already determined once before in my life that I was already past the age of having more children. It was clear to me that under my current circumstances, this was even more so. Kindor didn't like the idea, but it was my decision, after all. Dr. Magon confirmed he could do it.

When we arrived home, we found Karrina in the sitting room. It was a rest day, and the restaurant was closed. She appeared to be ready to go out, dressed in a sexy outfit that hugged her body and showed off her toned legs and arms.

"How did the doctor visit go?" Karrina said.

"Perfectly, everything is going as it...oh!" I said, my hands rushing to my belly.

Karrina shot up from her seat, and Kindor grabbed my shoulders.

"What is wrong?" they asked in unison.

"Oh, I did not mean to alarm you. The baby is moving quite a bit. I think I should sit down."

They sat on either side of me. Karrina, not having had any close experience with a pregnant person, was mystified.

"Mina, does it hurt?" she asked, hugging herself.

"No, it is just that I do not know when the little guy is going to wake up. Here, give me your hand," I said.

She hesitated at first, but I ignored her apprehension and guided her hand under my blouse and onto my belly. The baby was super active, and Karrina pulled her hand away at first, but I grabbed it and placed it there again.

"There is nothing to be afraid of," I said.

She shrieked, and her face lit up in wonder. Seeing his niece's reaction, Kindor's eyes widened as well.

"Kindor, it is amazing," she said in a loud, excited voice. "You need to feel this."

"Uhhh, no need for that. I am familiar with it. I felt you move in the same way when your mother was pregnant."

His expression didn't match his words. He was just as curious as Karrina.

"It is OK," I said, nodding to Kindor. "Really, go ahead."

I prepared myself mentally for any strange sensations that might result from his touch. He slipped his hand under my blouse, but instead of the sensual feeling that his touch had prompted at other times, I perceived something best described as benevolence and trust.

"Get ready, Mina. It seems he will be a handful," Kindor said with a smile.

His hand was still on my belly when Kora walked into the room.

"What is the commotion?" she asked, her brows knitted.

"It is the baby. He moves so much," said Karrina.

"Hmm...yes, that is normal," said Kora, a bit of irritation in her tone.

Kindor pulled his hand out from under my blouse and stood.

"We just arrived back from Dr. Magon. He assured us that everything is going well."

Kora nodded, her lips pursed, and turned her attention to Karrina.

"Are you going somewhere?"

"Yes, and it is perfect that you are all here together so I can introduce you to my new friend. He is the son of one of the plantation owners and was away studying but has come back to help his father administrate their properties. His name is Tadium, and he is very good-looking." Karrina tapped her grandmother on the shoulder. "And he really, really likes me," she said with a mischievous smile.

Kora shook her head with a sigh.

"So, Fronidian, huh?"

"A handsome and very rich Fronidian," clarified Karrina.

Kora rolled her eyes.

"Well, we will see how long he keeps your interest."

The front door buzzer rang, and Karrina sprung again out of her seat. She rushed to the door.

"Come in, Tadium. This is great timing. I would like you to meet my family."

She led him back to the sitting area where we all stood waiting to see him.

"This is my uncle, Kindor, my grandmother, Kora, and our friend, Mina."

The fact that she introduced me as a friend warmed my soul. Karrina appeared to be uncaring, but there was a softness to her.

"Tadium understands Fronidian sign language."

He bowed and replied, "It is an honor to meet you all."

Kora and Kindor gesticulated their greetings, and I replied out loud, "Nice to meet you, Tadium. Karrina has taught me a bit of Fronidian, but you will have to excuse my mistakes and accent."

"I understood you perfectly, Mina."

His genuine smile and polite manner won me over right away. He wore a vest ornamented with small expensive opalescent stones. His clothing fit well on his athletic build. He had dark hair and light green pupils that popped against the typical dark Fronidian sclera.

"Tadium, Mina is responsible for the new stew on the menu that you like so much. It is her recipe," said Karrina.

"Oh, I am glad to hear you like it," I said, blushing.

"Not just me. All of our workers rave about it. That is why I decided to try it."

Karrina checked a device half the size of a small cell phone that dangled from a thick, bronze-toned necklace. Then she showed it off to us. I had not seen anyone in the village of Zuntar wearing anything similar.

"Tadium gifted this to me. He says all the young females in the city are wearing them. It is a mini-tablet. I can communicate across all of this sector with it, and I see it is time for us to go. We have a reservation at a fancy restaurant."

Tadium's pale skin started to turn pink around the neck, embarrassed at Karrina flaunting his wealth.

"That is very nice," signed Kora, her expression stern and clearly not impressed. "But I hope Karrina has explained to you our situation. We are hiding from Lostai military and cannot call attention to ourselves. She better be careful how she uses that device, where she goes, and who she associates with."

The pink color traveled from his neck to Tadium's whole face.

"Oh, I did not know."

Karrina rolled her eyes and grabbed his hand.

"No worries, handsome. Let us go. I will explain to you later."

Kindor signed to Tadium that he needed to talk to Karrina privately and initiated telepathic conversation in a conference mode.

"Mother is right, Karrina. Do not forget. We have known the plantation owners and their families for years now. They are sympathetic to our situation and can be trusted. However, Tadium has been away since he was an adolescent and can easily expose you unintentionally. If you continue to spend time with him, he must be made aware about what caution is needed."

"Yes, yes...OK."

"Also, I will need for you to help Mina with the evening cleanup for the next two days. I will be traveling to the city."

"Oh, is it that time again...when you go check out the females?"

Kindor glared at her, and she giggled, which made me laugh also. He shook his head, mortified, avoiding my eyes.

"You know very well I go to get updated on the latest news on what is going on in the rest of Fronidia and the sector. It is good for us to be informed on what the Lostai are up to, and we rarely get any inter-planetary news here."

"Sure, sure, Uncle," Karrina replied, her lips curled in a smirk. "Yes, I can help Mina. No problem."

Tadium, not privy to our conversation, shifted his weight from leg to leg, getting more red-faced by the minute. He let a sigh of relief escape once Karrina grabbed his hand again and, saying a quick good-bye, led him out.

❄

One day after Kindor had returned from his trip, we were working the evening cleanup, and it was clear he was distracted. During the two hours that we spent alone almost every workday cleaning up the restaurant, we always had lively exchanges on a variety of topics. On this day, he barely said anything to me. Finally, I asked him if something was troubling him.

"Yes, I am trying to think through a situation related to a female I used to date years ago. I have run into her again, and she is interested in getting back together."

"Oh, I see...do you want to talk about it?"

"Well, Mother would love for us to get together. She was disappointed when things ended the first time. This female is a pureblood Sotkari Ta, and Mother is fixated on this idea that my destiny is to continue our pure Sotkari Ta bloodline. I will have nothing to do with this thought process, but I can see why Mother thinks we would be a perfect couple. She comes from a sophisticated, wealthy family, attended one of the best Fronidian medical schools, and is very attractive."

"So, what is the problem?" I asked.

"What bothered me last time was I found her to be arrogant and to have a bit of a mean streak. Now, this was, mind you, ten revolutions ago. I was a much younger man, and she even younger than me. Maybe it was just immaturity."

"I guess you will not know unless you give it a try."

"I know, but I would hate to get our families all excited again about our possible union and have it not work out."

"Forget about your families. Kindor, the most important thing is whether you like her or not. I suppose since you both are Sotkari Ta, you must feel that strong physical attraction, no?"

"Well, yes...but I know how to keep that in check and not let it cloud my judgment."

I laughed to myself.

"I wish my mentor would have trained me on that," I said.

"You know, Mina, I do not mean to sound negative, but based on what you have explained to me, I believe your baby's father took advantage of you. Being a well-trained Sotkari Ta, he knew how to manipulate his energy to seduce you."

"Well, to be fair, at first, he was just as surprised to have those intense feelings towards me. Other than his mentor, who is elderly, I was the first Sotkari Ta female he had ever been in contact with." I looked down before continuing. "But he did admit that afterward, his energy was usually focused on sex where I was concerned."

"Mina, that is exactly my point."

"To be honest, I was not very virtuous, either."

"Yes, but he has been trained for years, and you were just recently made aware of your abilities. He had it in his power to keep those urges in check. In my view, he has no excuse."

Kindor's comments made me stop and think about my relationship with Montor, and for some reason, I was crushed and feeling stupid. I didn't reply and continued to mop the floor quietly with my back towards him. He walked over to me, put his hands on my shoulders, and gently turned me to face him.

"Mina, I am sorry. I have no right to speak badly about someone whom I have not met and whom you obviously cared for."

A surge of emotion caused tears to well up. I didn't have a chance to turn away in time. Before I knew it, he pulled me close in an embrace while I cried, not knowing exactly why. His hands rubbed my back, consoling me. He nudged my chin up and wiped my tears with his thumb, his remaining fingers slowly stroking the side of my neck.

"Those beautiful eyes should not cry, Mina."

My knees weakened and things took an intimate turn. Remembering Kora's words, "Stay away from my son, Mina," I stepped away from him and faked a smile.

"Sorry for all the drama. I am fine. It must be my hormones raging. You know, with the pregnancy and all...I am probably just overly sensitive."

His hands went to his waist, and he stared at the floor.

"Right...go ahead to bed, Mina. I think you need to rest. I can finish up here on my own."

After that day, Kindor visited the city more frequently. Kora was ecstatic because Kindor had rekindled his relationship with his old pureblood Sotkari Ta flame. When he was away, Karrina helped with the evening cleaning, but it was getting tougher as my belly got bigger. Kora said I could stop working whenever I no longer felt up to it. Of course, she would have to stop paying me, and I would still be required to cover my lodging fee from my savings or pay her later. Knowing I would not be earning a salary during my recovery, I hoped to continue working until the baby was born. Between severely swollen ankles and barely getting any sleep, my daily mantra had become, "I am ready to deliver this baby."

One evening a week away from my due date, Kindor had me sit while he did all the cleanup work. He said it was to compensate for the nights he hadn't been around to help, but I knew he was also embarrassed about his mother being so strict with my lodging fee. We chatted as usual, but soon, he got serious.

"You know, Mina, I have found out something regarding the female that I am dating that I find troubling. Something I was not aware of before. Her name is Karixta, by the way. I did some digging into her family history and found that both sets of her great-grandparents were among the Sotkari Ta who collaborated with the Lostai on the takeover of Sotkar."

"I can see why that would bother you, but can you hold her responsible for something her ancestors did? Have you talked to her about it or told your mother?"

"I have not, but I will."

"I am curious, Kindor. Why is it that your family is hiding in this remote area while Karixta lives out in the open in a big city without any fear of being found by the Lostai?"

"First of all, Karixta and her parents were born here on Fronidia. They are Fronidian citizens. If the Lostai were to kidnap or threaten them, it would cause a diplomatic issue... especially in their case, since they are wealthy and powerful. Her father holds a seat in the legislature of the province they live in. Her great-grandparents left Sotkar with their families and settled here in Fronidia early in the conflict with the Lostai. The fact that they come from a line of people who collaborated with the Lostai protects them as well. My parents and their families were among those who remained in Sotkar, struggling to keep control of our planet. My mother's side of the family were mainly warriors while my father's side were the diplomats. Neither was successful in defeating the Lostai. We lost everything for our cause."

"I see...you come from a line of patriotic and honorable people."

When he was done with cleanup, he helped me stand. Suddenly, a squirt of warm liquid rushed down my legs.

"Kindor! I need to go to Dr. Magon's clinic right now. My water broke, and I am not sure what to expect with this pregnancy."

Kindor rushed to contact the clinic to let them know we were on our way and to ask any pertinent questions. He woke up Kora and Karrina to explain that we were leaving. On the way to the clinic, the contractions kicked in. I recalled the breathing and focus techniques that I had used in my previous deliveries, but these labor pains were far more excruciating than any I had experienced before. I tried to hold back the tears, but soon, I was shouting in pain. Kindor remained calm, although his expression was one of concern.

"Mina, maybe I can help you. May I place my hands on you?"

"Sure, do whatever you want!"

He raised his eyebrows, as my tone was not at all pleasant.

"OK, we will recline the seat as far back as possible... OK...now, we will open this here...OK, that is good."

Although I heard his calm voice in my mind, he seemed to be talking himself through certain steps. Once he had me almost horizontal, he repositioned my clothing so he could discretely place his hands on the lower part of my abdomen. He closed his eyes and pressed his fingers against my skin ever so slightly. After a few seconds, a numbing sensation relieved the pain a bit.

"Thank you, Kindor...that helps."

We arrived at the clinic, and the medical personnel rushed me to a room. When Dr. Magon examined me, it was clear that he was concerned. Although I knew basic Fronidian, I was afraid I might misunderstand something, so I asked Kindor to translate.

"Mina, Dr. Magon says the baby's lungs are not completely developed, but his heart is under some kind of stress. The baby needs to be delivered right away."

I grabbed Kindor's arm, my fingers digging into his skin. Here, in this alien environment, my three previous deliveries did nothing to make me feel like an old pro.

"Kindor, please stay. I want to understand every single thing that is happening."

His eyes met mine.

"Of course. I have no plans of leaving you."

There were two other medical assistants in the room besides Dr. Magon. One assistant helped me to lay on the hospital bed. The other pressed a flat oval instrument on my lower belly. I heard a hissing noise. Kindor was alternating between signing with the doctor and translating to me as quickly as he could to keep me informed of each step. It would have been almost comical if I weren't so stressed out.

"They are anesthetizing you from the waist down, so you will be fully conscious during the whole process."

Soon, I no longer felt the contractions, but instead of calming me, I was more nervous. My heart exploded in my chest. A horizontal panel dropped from the ceiling and hovered over my abdominal area.

"This instrument opens and seals the incision," Kindor explained to me.

My mind played tricks on me. The foreign medical equipment and devices reminded me of my time on the spaceship when I was first taken from Earth and transported to Xixsted. My chest tightened, and as fast as I was breathing, I couldn't get enough air. To calm myself, I prayed out loud in English.

"Oh, God, please hear my prayer. Please watch over me and the baby. Please let everything be OK."

Dr. Magon looked at Kindor with a quizzical look on his face. Kindor shrugged his shoulders and signed that he didn't understand what I was saying.

"Our Father who art in heaven," I continued, "hallowed be thy name."

Everyone stopped what they were doing, looked at me, and back to Kindor.

"Mina, Mina...What is it? Are you feeling anything out of the ordinary? What are you doing?"

"No, Kindor. I cannot explain what I am doing. Just ignore me, please."

He frowned and signed to the doctor. The doctor nodded and shifted his attention away from me and my prayers and towards his assistants and the medical monitors. A vertical panel slid down from the ceiling, shielding my view from the waist down. Perhaps it was more to shield me from them as the assistants appeared disconcerted with my chanting. I continued to pray loudly while Kindor held my hand throughout the whole process. His calming energy helped to lessen my stress. About five minutes after the vertical panel lowered, I heard a whimper, and the doctor barked orders to his assistants.

"Kindor, please go find out what is happening," I begged.

He left to speak with the doctor. After what felt to me like long, agonizing hours, he returned. It only had been a matter of minutes.

"Mina...good news...the baby has been delivered."

"Thank you, Lord," I said out loud in English.

Kindor continued, "They have put him in an incubator and attached him to a respirator to aid with breathing, and he is being treated to complete his lung development. The next few hours will be critical. Your incision was closed with no issue, and they also took care of the other thing you requested. Stay calm, Mina. They have dealt with issues like these before. I am sure everything will be fine. I suggested the doctor give you a sedative so you can rest."

"I do not want to rest. I want to see my baby!"

"Once you have rested and are stable, I will walk you over there myself. Trust me, you need to rest. Your body has gone through a major change during a relatively short amount of time...something that is not typical for your species. If you want to be in good shape when it is time to take the baby home, you need to rest. Now."

"OK, Kindor, you are right."

He nodded to one of the assistants, who came over and pressed a small circular disc on my forehead. I didn't notice when I drifted off to sleep.

When I opened my eyes, Kindor was sitting in a chair next to me, looking ragged.

"How long have I been sleeping?"

"About twelve hours."

"Have you gone home to rest? You look exhausted."

"I am fine, Mina. I did not want you to wake up alone. How are you feeling?"

"I feel OK. How is the baby?"

"The baby is responding well to the treatment. They are doing some tests, and if the results are positive, we will be able to take him home soon."

"Kindor, I am dying to see him."

Right at that moment, a nurse came in with the baby bundled in a blanket. She helped me sit up, and I took him in my arms, overcome with love and relief. He was perfect, and my heart skipped a beat as I took in his features. I counted six fingers on each hand and six toes on each foot. Almond-shaped slanted eyes, broad, flat nose, thin lips, soft fuzz on the skin, all made it clear that my son resembled his father and his father's race. I detected nothing human about his appearance.

The nurse spoke, and I had learned enough Fronidian to understand that she said I could nurse the baby. When he latched on my breast, his eyes opened, and we made eye contact. Tears welled up in mine. He had inherited at least one thing from me.

"His eyes are like yours and the same color," Kindor said.

I smiled at Kindor. He was in awe of everything unfolding in front of him.

"What will you name him?" Kindor asked.

"Josher...his name is Josher. It is the name of his paternal grandfather and what his father would have named him."

Kindor took a deep breath and stared at his hands.

"I see."

"Do you want to hold him?"

"Errr...I do not know...I guess so."

I handed Josher over to him.

Hmm, he seems a bit unsettled. Maybe he's just nervous handling a newborn, but then again, he probably carried Karrina.

Deep in thought at first, he became mesmerized, playing with Josher's tiny fingers. I watched them, and after a few minutes, he looked back at me and smiled.

"He is beautiful."

Before I knew it, there was a lump in my throat.

"Kindor, thank you for treating me with such kindness. Thank you for caring for my child. I do not know how I will ever be able to repay you." Tears filled my eyes by the time I was done.

"Mina, stop. Remember, I told you once before, those beautiful eyes should not cry. Do not speak of repaying me. You both deserve someone to care for you."

The doctor requested both Josher and I stay at the clinic for a few more days to ensure we both had proper time to recover. Looking at my new baby reminded me of who used to be my baby, my youngest son, Robert, whom we called Bobby from the day he was born. I had told myself to enjoy Bobby's infancy since he would be my last child. Now, I had a new baby.

I hadn't written him any letters as I did to the rest of my family. It broke my heart that my youngest son, only nine at the time of my kidnapping, would live the rest of his childhood without his mom. As usual, I tried to keep my letter upbeat, but I ended up crying the whole time I recorded the short note.

Dear Bobby,

Hey, sweetie. How's it going? You know how you always hate that we call you our baby? Well, I have news for you. You are no longer the baby of the family. You are officially an older brother. Your new baby brother's name is Josher. He doesn't look much like any of us, except I think his eye color will be like Amber's and mine.

Honey, I miss you so much, and I imagine you miss me, too. If it gets very sad for you, I hope you can remember when Nana (my maternal grandmother) passed, we talked about how she watches over us from where her soul is now. Well, although not exactly in the same way, know that I'm watching over you, too... always with you....and always praying that God continues to protect you.

Love, Mom

I was bawling when Kindor walked in on me. The nurse had taken Josher for some tests.

"Mina, what is going on? Is something wrong with Josher?"

"Kindor, I just realized I am never seeing my children again...ever."

"Why do you say that?"

"Josher...He looks nothing like me. Even if I were to somehow find a way back home, I would not be able to bring him with me. We have never had contact with people from other planets. He would be considered a freak."

"Well, do not jump to conclusions. Maybe there could be a way..."

I clenched my fists and banged the mattress. Kindor was the unfortunate recipient of my anger and frustration.

"What is wrong with you? Do you not understand? I never in my life imagined having to face such an impossible choice. If I were to go back to be with my family on Earth, I would have to leave Josher behind." I shook my head and used my shirt to dry my tears and clean my nose. "He's my child, too. I love him. I cannot do that."

"Of course, you cannot. Mina, I do not have children, so I cannot even imagine what you are feeling, but you should focus on the present for now. Right now is a time for happiness. You have a beautiful, healthy son."

My sadness was like a tightening vise in my chest, but he was right. There was nothing I could do at the time to change my situation. The nurse returned with Josher and let us know his tests were looking good. We were on target to be discharged soon.

For the next three days, Kindor traveled daily between the clinic and Zuntar. He spent several hours with Josher and me each day. On the fourth day after Josher was born, Dr. Magon gave us the green light to return home.

Before we left the office, Kindor signed to Dr. Magon, "Do you have information regarding the growth, health, and development of Arandan babies?"

I pressed my fist against my lips. Kindor's sincere concern for Josher's well-being moved me to tears every time.

"Yes, I will have my assistant prepare a data package for you. Kindor, I must say, you will make an excellent father one day. Please have Mina bring Josher back in two weeks and each lunar cycle afterward."

On our way home, Kindor stopped at a large retail market. I didn't know what he needed to buy. Emotions and hormones had left me exhausted.

"I think I will stay here while you get whatever you need," I said to him.

"If you can manage, I would prefer you and Josher came with me," he answered.

He led me to a store that sold infant clothing and supplies. I had already purchased some basic items in Zuntar throughout my pregnancy. This store sold fancier items of much better quality than what was available in Zuntar.

Kindor led me to an area of the store with holographic data catalogues. Items could be viewed, selected, and, after presenting a remuneration chip, replicated. We viewed the toy section. I saw everything from rattles and bath toys similar to what I might find on Earth to sophisticated electronic devices. Kindor's face lit up as he studied the items. He selected a colorful stuffed animal and an educational toy made of a pliable plastic-like material with a screen display, levers, buttons, and lights.

"I think he might like this. What do you think, Mina?"

"Yes, yes, but I need to watch my budget."

"No, I will cover the cost. I also would like to gift him a few outfits. Do not even try to refuse. I insist."

Kindor moved on to the clothing section.

"Pick out something you like for him."

I found an adorable shirt and short outfit. Kindor saw another he wanted Josher to have also. He paid for everything, and we headed home. During the trip, I thanked God once again for putting Kindor in my path and wondered how Montor might have reacted to the birth of his son.

20

At two months, Josher had grown to the size of a four-month-old human baby. Karrina, who at first glance didn't come across as the warmest person, fell in love with Josher. Perhaps it was because Tadium had already proposed marriage to her, and she was beginning to envision starting a family of her own. She often convinced Tadium to buy Josher fancy accessories, toys, and clothes. He was financially able to cater to all her whims and truly was in love with her. I worked most of the day with Josher strapped to my back on a baby carrier. He continued to grow at a much faster pace than a human child, and Karrina helped me to care for him when I needed a break. Kindor also doted on Josher, usually using the carrier himself when we cleaned up the restaurant in the evenings. Kora remained distant and concerned about all the attention Josher was getting, especially from Kindor. He continued to visit the city a few times a month, and I assumed he was still dating Karixta, although he never mentioned her anymore.

One day when the restaurant was closed and we were having dinner together, Kora brought up the subject of Karixta.

Kora insisted at these times that we all conversed in conference telepathically as she was a stickler for no private conversations at the table.

"Kindor, how are things going with Karixta?"

"Fine," Kindor replied without looking up from his plate.

"Are you ever going to invite her over...for dinner, perhaps?"

Kindor put down his utensils, wiped his mouth, and looked at his mother with furrowed eyebrows.

"Mother, we have discussed this before. I am not sure if it is the right time yet."

"Is she still obnoxious?" asked Karrina, mustering her best fake innocent look.

"Karrina, how rude...and what do you know anyway? You were only a child when you last saw her," Kora said.

Karrina rolled her eyes but decided not to annoy her grandmother further. Of course, I did not interject as this was a private matter between Kindor and his mother. To my surprise, Kora brought me right into their conversation.

"Mina, what do you think? They have been dating for over three lunar cycles now, not counting their previous relationship. I would like for her to feel welcome to our family."

She eyed me like a cat about to pounce on a mouse as she waited for my reply. I got distracted thinking about how my husband's family never forgave me for "getting myself pregnant when we were still in college," as his father was fond of saying.

"Mina?" Kora insisted.

"If a couple is looking to form a serious, lasting relationship, it helps that they be comfortable with each other's family. We have a saying on my home planet that one does not only marry the spouse but also that person's entire family."

"So, what are you saying?" asked Karrina sarcastically.

I sighed.

"I think it is a good idea for Kindor to invite her here to dinner."

Kora nodded and smiled.

"Please, son...what is the big deal? Make it happen."

Kindor's face was expressionless when he replied.

"OK, I will see."

A few weeks later, Kindor announced that Karixta would be over for dinner the next time the restaurant was closed. Kora was beside herself getting the house ready and planning the meal. Discussion arose about how I should be introduced to Karixta. Kora suggested that they present me as an employee of the family, and to that effect, I should wait on them the night of the dinner.

"Absolutely not!" Kindor disagreed.

"And why not?" asked Kora.

"When we sit at the table together, we usually all help out with the cooking, setting the table, and cleaning up afterward. Why should we portray something different to Karixta? A good relationship should be based on truth."

"Yes, but what will we do with the baby?" asked Kora.

"To avoid any conflict and make things smoother, I can have dinner in my room that night. Josher and I can stay out of the way," I said, but no one was listening to me.

"Grandmother, what is the problem of keeping Josher near the table in his crib, like we usually do?" said Karrina, always ready to defend Josher.

"This matter is closed. We will all have dinner here as we always do, and that is final," said Kindor.

The discussion was over, but Kora was tight-lipped the rest of the night.

The day finally arrived for Karixta's visit. Kora worked Karrina and me hard to make sure the house was spotless and the several-course dinner was cooked to perfection. She also specified that we dress up for the occasion. I chose one of the outfits I had purchased from Colora's shop. It wasn't showy or flirty, but the lines and fabric were of exceptional quality. Josher was also dressed in an expensive suit that Tadium had bought for him.

When they arrived, I noticed Kindor had pulled his hair back into a tail that called more attention to his striking eyes. I was used to seeing him in work clothes, and today, he was dressed smartly, accentuating his athletic frame. There was no denying he looked very handsome. Karixta was tall and elegant with a slim frame, not curvy at all. Her short blouse displayed a tiny waist, and the wide split in her skirt revealed long, toned legs. She had shiny, royal blue hair that fell in waves below her shoulders and steel blue eyes framed by thick, dark lashes and perfectly shaped eyebrows. Her light grey skin, prominent cheekbones, and lips were flawless.

Kindor introduced me simply as Mina without much explanation of what my role was. Karixta gave me the once-over when I extended my forearm for the typical Sotkari handshake. We all communicated telepathically.

"Hello, Karixta, pleasure to meet you."

"Greetings, Mina. Kindor has spoken to me about you...the lonely pregnant traveler that he rescued. How brave of you. I can sense you are Sotkari Ta. It amazes me that you and I share the same genes, although I come from a line of pureblood Sotkari Ta that goes back for generations. It is a cruel joke, no?"

"Cruel...does not even come close to describing it," I said with a quick smile.

Her attention turned to Karrina.

"My goodness, Karrina, the last time we met, you were but a child. Now look at you. I must say I have not seen a prettier half-breed."

The tone was condescending and unpleasant.

"...and I have not met a more obnox—" Karrina started to

reply when Kora pulled her away, asking for help with getting drinks.

I felt sorry for Kindor, who clearly was already uncomfortable. Kora and Karrina were back with drinks when Karixta noticed the baby crib and walked over to take a look.

"Oh, this must be the fatherless child...Oh, my, that is... different," she said, referring to his appearance.

Karrina walked towards Karixta with quick, long strides and clenched fists. Kora discreetly caught up with her and pulled her back by the wrist.

"He is a handsome and healthy baby," said Karrina, fuming.

I was not about to let Karixta's words and behavior faze me. I kept my cool, my answers brief and with a tone of indifference.

"His father is Arandan," I said.

"Oh...so you do know who the father is?" asked Karixta.

"Of course," I said.

"Kindor tells me he was with you when the baby was delivered. I hope you do not get used to him constantly coming to your rescue," Karixta said with a laugh.

"Right," I answered.

Shaking my head, I gave Kindor a quick look of disapproval mixed with sympathy. Ready to escape the uncomfortable ambiance, I offered to start setting the table. A few minutes later, Tadium arrived. Karrina had begged Kora to allow him to join us. When Karrina introduced him as her betrothed, Karixta looked him up and down and only said a quick hello, after which, she turned around to continue talking to Kora. Tadium, who is one of the most good-natured people I have ever met, made a funny face behind Karixta's back and winked to Karrina. Apparently, she had already warned him of what to expect. Once we were done with the "unpleasantries," we moved to the table, where things went better because Karixta ignored everyone except Kindor and Kora. Tadium and

Karrina spoke softly to each other in Fronidian. Karixta bragged about her family's businesses and properties. Kora told the story of the elder priest that had blessed Kindor when he was born and prophesied that he would become a savior for his people.

"Now that we have so few pureblood Sotkari Ta left, I see the relevance of this prophecy," said Kora.

Although I wasn't supposed to take on the role of the servant, I purposely offered to bring food out and clear the plates after each course to keep myself occupied. Kindor's expression grew more annoyed with each trip I made from the kitchen to the dining room table. Finally, he decided to get up and help me.

"I think I need to stretch my legs. Let me help you with those plates, Mina."

I only nodded, but Karixta sucked her teeth as he walked behind me to the kitchen.

"Kora, how long will Mina remain here with your family?"

Instead of addressing Kora specifically, she communicated in conference mode, intentionally ensuring everyone could hear, except, of course, Tadium, who was not telepathic.

"Well, we are benefitting financially from her staying here. She is a hard worker, so I see no reason for her to leave yet," answered Kora.

"I am not typically a jealous person. However, it does bother me a bit that Kindor lives under the same roof with a single mother whose morals are probably questionable at best. What if she sneaks into his bedroom at night?"

To Kora's credit, she answered, "Karixta, you do not need to worry about that. Mina has been through a lot and is not looking for any romantic entanglements. She is focused on her son."

I was relieved Kora didn't reveal any of the details that I shared with her.

"OK, I hope that is the case. You know you have a very handsome son, and I must say, he has such a special...touch."

Karixta followed the innuendo with a soft giggle and exaggerated expression, but Kora did not laugh or reply. I'm sure she didn't approve of Karixta's last comment. She held decorum and restraint in high regard, having reprimanded Karrina for much lesser indiscretions. In the meantime, Kindor, who was still in the kitchen with me, ran his hand over his hair and shook his head. I pretended not to hear her insulting words, but he knew I had. He said nothing, but we made brief eye contact before returning to the table. Karrina and Tadium were playing with Josher, and Karrina sent me a simple telepathic message.

"I told you she was obnoxious."

As I finished clearing the table and cleaning up, the time came for Kindor to take Karixta back home. Only Kora saw them to the door.

Within a few days after Karixta's visit, Kindor informed us that they had broken up.

"What happened?" asked Kora, not able to hide her disappointment.

"I let her know I was not proud of how she behaved during our dinner. She did not like my pointing that out to her."

"Kindor, maybe you were too critical. She is just a little headstrong, is all," said Kora.

"Headstrong? Grandmother, she practically called me a mutt and was rude with Mina for no reason at all. She purposely ignored Tadium. You would not approve of me behaving that way. I was waiting for Mina to defend herself and lash out at her, so I could join in," said Karrina.

"I have to agree with Karrina," said Kindor. "You and Father taught me to treat everyone with respect. Why would I be attracted to someone who does the exact opposite, much less consider her a good candidate to be the mother of my children?"

"The mother of your children needs to be a Sotkari Ta. Do I need to remind you there are not too many of those around here to choose from?" answered Kora.

Karrina never missed the chance to be controversial.

"We have one right here," she said while gesturing towards me with an innocent look on her face.

"Do not try to be funny, Karrina. You know what I mean," said Kora.

"In my experience," I chimed in, and everyone stared at me with expectation, "people who say or behave unpleasantly sometimes are hiding pain inside."

They could not believe I would be willing to cut Karixta some slack.

"We all have suffered pain and loss. That is not an excuse," answered Kindor.

"I agree, but some of us are able to process it better than others," I said.

"Do you think it is final, or is there any chance of reconciliation?" asked Kora.

"Mother, are you listening to me? She is spoiled, arrogant, and mean-spirited. She was that way when I met her years ago. I thought perhaps now, being older, she would be different, but I find that she has become even worse. I want nothing to do with her."

Kora shook her head but said nothing more.

21

A fter the breakup with Karixta, Kindor did not go back to the city. Instead, he made more hunting trips than usual to the area where I had crash-landed. I first assumed he wanted to have time alone but later learned that his trips were due to an upcoming local holiday. He was stocking up on additional game and fish because the restaurant played a major part in the celebration.

The holiday celebrated an important event in Fronidian history and was observed with long meals, dancing, and drinking. Typically, family matriarchs were responsible for creating these feasts. Many of the villagers were young unmarried males far from their hometowns. Also, some young wives wanted to enjoy the holiday rather than work on the preparations. The restaurant offered these villagers a hassle-free option by hosting a daylong event of food, drinks, and music. Everyone who wanted to participate paid a fixed fee. It worked out well for the residents as well as being a moneymaker for Kindor's family. The activities even attracted folks from other nearby towns. Tables and chairs set in the street strategically created pockets of areas for eating and dancing.

Josher was getting more handsome by the day, the spitting image of his father except for the honey-colored eyes he inherited from me. At four months, he was the size of an eight-month-old human baby and very rambunctious. He started crawling a few weeks before. Although he already was eating mashed and bite-sized versions of adult food, I also continued to nurse him. I was back to my regular physical workout, which helped me return close to my pre-pregnancy shape. He was now too heavy for me to have him strapped onto me in the carrier all day while I worked, so Karrina cared for him while I did most of the chores. During the days leading up to the holiday, Kora and I prepped many traditional Fronidian food staples that we would be warming up or frying the day of the party. We hired extra help for serving food and drinks by offering a free-of-charge admission. The whole affair had a family feel to it.

The celebration began mid-morning. The inviting weather reminded me of a typical autumn day in the Southeastern United States. There was a crispness in the air, but it was sunny and not cold enough to require heavy clothing. By the afternoon, we had four hundred or so people in attendance. Karrina and Tadium proudly showed off Josher to everyone they met as if he were their own son. During the evening, those who remained had moved on from eating to socializing, drinking, and dancing, so I had a chance to sit and rest a bit. Every so often, Kindor checked in on me. He insisted I should try to enjoy the party now that most of the food demand had died down, but I remained focused on my chores. Smiling, I politely declined when a few young Fronidians asked me to dance. As it got into the later hours of the evening, even Kindor came by and tried to convince me. Again, I declined and began to clean up instead.

On my way to gather more trash, Kindor grabbed my hand and circled his other hand around my waist. He twirled me around, pulled me close, and stepped back so that we were at arm's length again. The music was up-tempo.

"Here, Mina, let me show you...three steps to the front, three steps back...then a quick double-step," Kindor said.

Kindor had indulged in a few drinks, so although not intoxicated, he was much looser and more unreserved than what I was used to. As our hands touched, my heart skipped a beat. The song was over, and the music became slow-paced and romantic. Kindor pulled me close and embraced me. I rested my head on his chest, closed my eyes, and allowed my body to relax, as if it were the most natural thing to do. The warmth of his breath in my hair and our bodies swaying brought on a sensation that I hadn't felt in a while. The last time I had danced this way had been with Montor.

"Mina, have you ever considered the possibility of..."

Karrina and Tadium arrived with Josher, and the spell was broken.

"OK, folks...time to wake up," said Karrina.

We laughed at her joke, and she handed Josher to Kindor, who held him overhead playfully and spun around. Josher's giggles were infectious, but then he rubbed his eyes, and I knew it wouldn't be long before he got sleepy and cranky.

"I have to put this little guy to sleep and will come back to finish cleaning up," I said.

"Mina, you have been working nonstop since sunrise. I will have the hired workers finish picking up. Go to bed," Kindor said.

"Truthfully, I am exhausted. Thank you."

I tucked Josher in, took a shower, and went to bed. Through my window, I heard the band announce their last song and the lingering people say their goodbyes. I said a prayer and closed my eyes, ready to welcome the sleep my body craved.

I must have slept a few hours when I heard a knock on my door. At first, I wasn't sure I had heard correctly. No one had ever approached my room that late at night before. In my mind, I heard, "Mina, Mina...May I come in?"

"Kindor, is everything OK?"

"Yes, but I would like to talk to you. Can I come in?"

Odd.

I had on a skimpy nightshirt, so I pulled the blanket up to my neck.

"Uhhh...OK...the door is unlocked."

He stepped in and shut the door. I trusted Kindor, so I wasn't afraid. It took him all of three seconds to reach my bed.

"Kindor, what is going on?"

To my surprise, he kicked off his shoes and got into bed, as if it were the most natural thing. He had showered, the aroma of basic soap bouncing off his skin. My jaw dropped as he turned towards me, propping his head in his hand. His expression was casual, as if we were sitting at the dining table. I inched back to keep space between us and smelled on his breath the evidence of a few more drinks.

"I never had a chance to finish my question," he answered with a boyish grin.

In my surprise and drowsiness, I struggled to remember what he was referring to.

"OK...I guess it is pretty urgent, huh?" I said, trying to keep things light, even though the situation was getting heavier by the second.

"Yes, I think it is. Mina, we spend so much time together. We eat together, work together, and exercise together. Maybe we should consider doing other things together...wait, that does not sound right...I meant, have you considered the possibility of us being more than just friends?"

He let his head slide on to the mattress so now he was completely down on his side facing me and took my hand in his. He used his thumb to do a circular massage on the palm of my hand. The sensation was calming but pleasurable as well.

My toes curled. I should have firmly asked him to leave at that moment, so I could be alone to gather my bearings about what he had proposed, but I didn't want to hurt his feelings. There had never been a cross word between us.

"Kindor, your mother would not like that at all. She specifically told me to stay away from you. I do not want to cause family problems. Besides, I am not in a position to focus on that type of relationship now."

"Mina, I am an adult. My mother cannot dictate whom I fall in love with."

He traced my mouth with his fingers.

"I like the shape of your lips...like a bow...and so full."

I started feeling giddy but still safe.

He moved from touching my mouth to sliding his fingers down my neck and towards my breasts. I went from giddy to full-on arousal, my breath quickening.

"Do you have any feelings for me, Mina?"

"Well, you have been like a guardian angel to me. We have developed a close friendship. I find you handsome, but..."

"You do?" he said with a wide-eyed look.

He tossed the blanket and rolled on top of me in a playful manner, propping himself on his elbows, and yet I still did not feel in danger.

"Mina, how do your people make love?" he said, smiling.

The weight of his body on mine brought back memories of the last time I was asked that question. He gathered my body between his arms and legs with familiarity as if we had been in this position many times before. His hands moved to the back of my neck where he continued massaging and slowly running his thumbs over the edge of my ears. Everywhere he touched me turned into an erogenous zone.

"I do not think I should..."

"Please, Mina...I am so curious..."

Those remarkable blue eyes stared deeply into mine, my resistance weakening.

"We should talk about this another time."

"Please, Mina, show me a little sample...just something..."

Our faces were so close, and before I knew it, I slid my bottom lip across his mouth. He breathed deeply. I kissed him, a few soft taps, and then a juicier version. This unleashed a tidal wave of passion. Everything was moving fast. His hands were under my nightshirt, touching me everywhere, teasing my nipples, fondling my breasts, squeezing my butt, and stroking my thighs. I continued to kiss him and was overwhelmed with a euphoric sensation, like I was high on drugs. He got up on his knees, his breathing quick and heavy, and rushed to unbutton his shirt. When he lifted his hands from my body, an unusual discomfort pained me. He grimaced as well.

"Yes, Mina, I know...the touch of a Sotkari Ta is an addictive intoxicant."

His voice sounded like a whisper in my mind. It took all my willpower not to grab his hands and place them back on me again. With his shirt now off, he grasped the edges of my nightshirt. I heard movement in Josher's crib. It had a sobering effect. I became rigid and stopped his hands.

"No, Kindor...I am sorry...this cannot happen...we cannot take this any further. I will not disrespect your mother's wishes, and I owe it to my son to wait for his father."

He tightened his lips.

"I love that child as if he were my own."

"Yes, I know...and I am so grateful...and I do care for you, but we are not doing this...I...I love his father."

He took a deep breath, his jaw clenched. A tremor shook his upper body.

"I think you have forgotten what love is. How can you be sure you love someone whom you spent so little time with?"

"So what! I do not think what is happening here is love, either."

Kindor turned away, got off the bed, put on his shoes, and grabbed his shirt. He walked out of the room before buttoning it and slammed the door. I heard his heavy footsteps going down the stairs and Kora's voice in my head.

"Kindor, what were you doing upstairs? You look a mess. Were you in Mina's room?"

"Whatever I was doing is none of your business. Do you have nothing better to do than to constantly hound me...?"

He continued with words I didn't understand but sounded angry and impolite.

"How dare you speak to me that way!"

I did not hear any reply from Kindor. I got up from bed and opened my door a crack in time to hear the front door slam.

Kindor left the house and stayed away for five days without contacting any of us. Kora refused to even look at me. Finally, by the third day, I summed up enough courage to explain to her that I had not let things take their full course, but she didn't want to hear anything I had to say.

She glared at me and said, "Kindor has never before disrespected me or left the house without telling me where he is going or keeping in touch."

Even Karrina avoided any smart remarks. I made the decision then and there that it was time for Josher and me to leave. I took inventory of what steps I needed to take to that effect. When Kindor finally returned home, it was late morning. He walked to the restaurant kitchen where Kora and I were preparing the midday meals in silence.

"Mother, I am sorry. I was upset and needed some time alone. I hope you did not worry."

Kora's answer was quick and to the point.

"After tonight's cleanup, we are having a family meeting at the dining table."

After the restaurant closed, I began my usual cleanup routine. Kindor arrived late. I couldn't look at him. I was embarrassed for the both of us. Up until then, our friendship had been so pristine. He broke the silence.

"Mina, I was out of line. I am sorry. I should not have come to your room at night and propositioned you."

"I should have stopped the conversation right away. I let things get out of hand, so this is my fault as well. I do not want our friendship to be damaged, Kindor."

He walked over to me, cupped my chin, and tilted my head up. Our eyes met.

"Neither do I...but I must be honest. My feelings for you have gone beyond friendship. It is not anyone's fault...not something we can control."

I nodded because I didn't know what else to say. We finished our tasks and headed to the dining room where we found Kora sitting at the table like a judge waiting to impose her sentence.

"Where is Karrina?"

"Does she really need to be here, Mother?

"Yes, she does."

Karrina appeared. She had been putting Josher to bed.

"I am here," she said in an exasperated tone.

"OK, obviously, we all know that I am upset about what happened the other night and the fact that Kindor behaved in a way that I have never seen before. Mina, I do not blame you for this. You have been a respectful and hard worker. Even at the holiday festivities, I saw that you were focused on your duties, although others were trying to distract you..."

She looked at Kindor and rolled her eyes before continuing.

"However, what I feared could come about as a result of your presence here has occurred. Kindor believes he has fallen in love with you. Obviously, he is confused..."

"Mother, I admit I was out of line with you and with Mina

that night...but please do not pretend to know about my feelings. I am not an adolescent."

Kora ignored his comment and cut to the chase.

"I think Mina should start planning to move out of our home and get on with her life."

"And Josher?" asked Karrina. "What about him?"

"Well, obviously, the child must go with his mother," Kora said.

"Grandmother, I do not know what the big deal is if Kindor and Mina want to have a relationship," said Karrina.

"Of course, you do not know because your pretty little head does not bother with things that are transcendental," Kora said.

"Please, Mother, you are taking things out of proportion," Kindor said, shaking his head.

"Is the survival of our people not important?"

"I am sorry, Mother, but I disagree with you. I will not be made to feel obligated to carry the weight of repopulating our species on my shoulders. It sounds ridiculous," said Kindor.

The pause that followed was a perfect moment for me to speak up.

"Excuse me. Regardless of what you are all discussing, I have already reached the conclusion that I should look for the father of my son. It has been six lunar cycles since I escaped the Lostai. Thanks to the kindness you all have shown me, I am not in the helpless position I was in when I first arrived. I can speak and sign in the Fronidian language. I have some savings. My son and I are healthy. It is a good time to venture out of this village."

Kora smiled, her chin up in victory.

Karrina tugged Kindor's sleeve, visibly concerned for Josher's welfare. I was moved by how much she cared for my son.

"No, Kindor, do not let her go. She and Josher could be in danger if the Lostai are still looking for her."

"I have made up my mind," I said firmly.

"Then I will accompany you. We can discuss the logistics tomorrow," answered Kindor, equally resolute.

"Wait...and you plan to leave your niece and me alone?" asked Kora.

"We will be fine, Kindor. We have never had any problems here, and if there is any issue, Tadium will be here. I do not like the idea of Josher leaving, but if Mina is determined to go, I think they need some protection," said Karrina.

I was impressed with her loyalty. In six months, she had matured from the cheeky young woman I met when I first arrived to Fronidia. Kora scowled, unhappy that things were taking an unexpected turn, but she already had become insignificant in the conversation.

22

I told Kindor that I was hoping to send a message to Colora using the contact codes she had given me when we met at Members Only. In a typical Fronidian city, every home or residential unit had a device used for communication across Fronidia and other planets within the same star system. People also carried around personal communication devices or tablets comparable to cell phones on Earth. Others had micro devices embedded in the brain.

The remote village of Zuntar had no such technology, so he took me to the communication center in Rondarium where people rented the use of such devices. I slid the chip in the device and punched in the personal codes Colora had given me that allowed me to send either an audio or video message. I set up my own personal codes so that, after sending the message, I could come back a few days later and access any replies. In all the time I had been in Fronidia, I had not seen a Lostai, but the fear of possible capture was ever present. I kept the message short and general in nature, audio only, in Fronidian, and purposely avoiding the use of Montor's name.

"Colora, this is Mina. Do you remember me? I am from

Earth. We met on Renna One at your shop, and I was able to spend some time at Members Only. You were nice enough to give me your contact codes. I am currently in Fronidia and need to ask you for some advice. The topic is of a delicate nature, so I prefer to discuss it in person. Please, I would appreciate if you did not mention to anyone that I have contacted you. Let me know if you intend to visit Fronidia anytime soon."

I didn't have to make a return trip because in a matter of minutes, I received a reply.

"Mina! Of course, I remember you, but I am truly surprised to hear from you after all this time. It just happens to be that I am taking some time off from work and will be staying at my home here in Fronidia for another seven days or so. Here are my home location coordinates. I am staying put at home, so feel free to arrive whenever is convenient. Looking forward to seeing you."

Hoping to take immediate advantage of the opportunity to see her before she left Fronidia, I consulted with Kindor regarding the logistics of getting to that location. He explained our options. Fronidia was a planet of many small continents separated by huge bodies of water and substantial areas of the planet subject to sudden electromagnetic storms posing certain risks for travel by air. The Fronidians had developed a form of transportation using portals where a person simply entered a tunnel within a magnetic field at one location and exited at another. This technology had been perfected, making it the quickest and safest way to travel between continents and big cities, but the fare was out of our price range. Plus, I didn't know if I was still on some Lostai wanted list, so I needed minimal exposure to the general public. The best option would be a transport pod, but we didn't own one. Kindor suggested we ask Tadium if we could borrow one of his. Using a transport pod, the trip normally would take eight hours as her location was on the opposite side of the planet.

Once back at the village, Kindor got in touch with Tadium. As we had expected, he had no problem in lending us a transport pod. Kindor also asked Tadium to keep an eye on Kora and Karrina while he was away, which, of course, he had no problem with, either. He spent most of his free time with Karrina anyway.

Kora decided to hire someone to replace me. It took her three days to find someone, and she asked me to train the person for two days. That left me two days within the seven-day window Colora had mentioned. In my free time, I packed our belongings to ensure we could leave on the sixth day in the morning and arrive in the afternoon. Now that the main steps were taken, I was filled with nervous anticipation.

Kindor and Tadium helped me load my few belongings in the transport pod. They consisted of a small bag of clothing, my tablet, the laser gun Montor had left for me in the shuttle, and the reference material related to Arandan child development Dr. Magon had supplied when Josher was born. Josher had more items to his name than I did due to the many presents Karrina and Tadium had gifted him. He had a huge trunk of clothing, another trunk full of toys, a crib and furniture, and a variety of carriers and gadgets. However, we could only fit the clothing, some toys, a carrier, and the crib. I said we would come back at some point to get the rest.

It was time for goodbyes. Karrina had Josher standing on her lap, holding him by the hands, talking to him both in Fronidian and Sotkari in the typical sing-song, high-pitched voice universally used with babies. I understood the Fronidian part.

"*Sa veranttay*...are you ready for this trip...are you? I wish you did not have to go..."

Her voice cracked. She used a term of endearment that Fronidian females use for males they care about. It meant, roughly, beloved and handsome male.

"...Yes...Aunt Karrina will miss her *Sa veranttay*...yes, she will...but you will come back to visit, right? My strong, handsome boy."

He cooed and babbled. It made me sad to think he would miss her.

"We are ready. It is time to leave," Kindor said.

Karrina enveloped Josher tightly in her arms and said something in Sotkari, her eyes glistening. Kora stepped out of the kitchen and came over to me. She looked down to me while extending her hand.

"Mina, may the Farthest Light guide your steps and keep you and Josher safe. I hope you find his father and can create a happy family."

She glanced at Kindor as she finished the last part of her blessing.

"Thank you, Kora...your kindness surely saved my life. I am very thankful."

Karrina handed Josher to Kindor. I took hold of Karrina's wrist for a Sotkari handshake, and then could not help but hug her even though I knew that gesture was foreign to her.

"Karrina, thank you so much for everything. I promise once my situation is stable, I will come back and visit."

"You better," Karrina answered, true to form. Then she added in a softer tone, "Good luck, Mina."

I also thanked Tadium for his generosity with Josher and for allowing us to use his transport pod. I looked around at what had been my home for the last six months and sighed.

The small town of Zuntar had treated me well. My situation could have been much worse. Now, I was ready to move on.

We took off, and I continued to ruminate, my mind filled with so many questions.

Where might Montor be at this time? Does he have any idea what happened to me? Is he safe? Is he thinking of me? What will be his reaction when he learns we have a son? Will he be happy or upset?

He had purposely avoided any entanglements that could make him vulnerable. A child was a fairly significant entanglement.

"What is wrong, Mina?" Kindor interrupted my train of thought.

"Nothing."

"You look worried."

"No...just thinking about what the future holds for Josher and me. Back on my planet, I sometimes thought my life was dull and uneventful. Now, I do not even know where I will be living tomorrow or if I will be able to find Josher's father."

"You do not need to worry about Josher's future while I am around, Mina."

I turned to look at him, frustrated with myself.

I should have been happy that someone kind and powerful such as Kindor cared so much for my child.

Why am I so stressed?

After a few hours, I picked up Josher from his carrier and nursed him. It was easy to see why most everyone who met him found him endearing. Never cranky unless hungry or sleepy, he always rewarded attention with a smile. Even at this early age, you could tell he would have the same strong, well-proportioned body as his father.

"I love to see you do that," said Kindor.

"What? Have you not seen other babies being nursed?"

Why am I cranky?

He brushed it off.

"Yes, but I never dared to pay as close attention to detail as I do with you and Josher."

The truth was that, in some respects, Kindor and I behaved almost as an old couple. I didn't know how it had developed, but there was so much trust and ease between us. Having accepted the fact that, especially now with an alien child, it would be unlikely that I could ever return to Earth, Kindor should have been a perfect choice for a partner. He loved my son, apparently also had feelings for me, and was upright, kind, and caring. Yet I pined for Montor, maybe only for the simple fact that I met him first, or perhaps because I found the various layers of his personality intriguing. Although I would never admit it out loud, I liked Montor's badass attitude, his sarcasm, and his larger-than-life persona.

Once I put Josher back in his carrier, I brought some food out from the provisions for us to eat.

"Mina, have you thought about how you will approach your meeting with this person. Uhhh...you said her name is Colora, right?"

"I plan to ask her how I might contact Montor with the least possible chance of outside detection."

Lately, he knitted his brows every time I mentioned the name "Montor."

"You only met this person once. Do you think you can trust her? It will be obvious why you might be looking for him once she sees the baby."

"She said she thought Montor and I made a good couple," Kindor rolled his eyes while I mused, "and was very friendly with me. I think she will be sympathetic to my situation...Oh!"

A bump and dramatic drop in altitude interrupted our conversation. Kindor checked the control panel.

"We are going through a patch of bad weather. If it continues this way, we will need to return to the surface and wait it out a bit."

A notification on the controls warned of electromagnetic storms in the area. The safe thing to do was land. We were lucky to be near a rest stop in the small city of Zalbadar.

"How long do you think we will need to wait before taking off again?" I asked, biting my nails.

"Looking at these weather projections, we should wait at least six hours before heading out."

This would put us arriving at Colora's home location later in the evening.

"Maybe we should find lodging near her home and go visit her in the morning," suggested Kindor.

"No, I do not want to take the chance of missing her. I would like to talk to her today, even if it is late."

I looked out the window and saw flashes of green, orange, and blue lights against a canvas of dark grey clouds. Strong wind gusts blew in all directions. The main risk was how these storms affected navigation controls.

What to do now for six hours?

Kindor suggested that, for the time being, we recline our seats and rest since we had woken up early. After a nap, we took advantage of a break in the weather to stretch our legs and take a look around. The rest stop had everything I would have expected but much more automated than on Earth. Everything was either self-serve or serviced by robots. There were restrooms and places to refuel and take care of any repairs for several types of spacecraft and terrain vehicles. I let my mind be distracted by the different shops selling a variety of food, drinks, and everything from clothing to gift ideas and spirits. Fronidians made up the majority of people I saw. There were people of other races that I was not familiar with but only a few Sotkari and certainly no one from Earth, so we did get a few curious looks. I began to question if it was a good idea to be walking about. It was midday, and the place was busy.

After about an hour, I was ready to sit and have a drink. We decided on a beer and ale establishment. The room was long and narrow with one wall lined with glass enclosures and control panels used to order and pay for the drinks. Against the opposite wall was a continuous counter and seats. There were hundreds of beer varieties and other beverages to pick from, some native to Fronidia and some from other planets. Customers also selected how they wanted the drink served. A person could choose a traditional metallic mug from ancient times or a modern crystalline receptacle available in various sizes and shapes. Once the selections were made and paid for, the beverage appeared within the glass enclosure, slowly taking form as if it were being painted on a canvas. Once complete, a front panel slid open to give access to the drink.

I asked Kindor to order something nonalcoholic for me as I had no idea what to pick. I held Josher in my lap and looked around, amazed at how people's behavior was similar no matter which galaxy you were in. I saw couples, business groups, families with kids, and loners. Other than the advanced technology and the variety of species, this could have easily been a typical rest stop on any U.S. state turnpike.

Someone sat next to me, and when I turned to look, my heart jumped. It was a Lostai in full military uniform. The Lostai soldier eyed me with interest and looked at Josher. I gave him a quick nod and smile to appear as natural as possible, but my heartbeat was like the wings of a tiny bird. I quickly thought through who might potentially be in more danger, Kindor or me? There were only two possibilities to explain why someone from Earth would be anywhere in this galaxy. Either I was an escaped hostage or I had already fulfilled my fifteen-year duty to the Lostai and was now a free person like Gio Napoletano. On the other hand, Sotkari were native to this galaxy but always of special interest to Lostai. I decided it was more dangerous for Kindor. I focused my mind to identify him in the crowd and send him a telepathic message.

"Kindor, stay away. There is a Lostai soldier sitting next to me."

"Do you speak Lostai?" the soldier asked.

I debated with myself on how I should react. If I said yes, I might get tripped up in a conversation trying to explain my circumstances. What were the chances that he had seen someone from Earth before? He looked young, so I took the chance that he had not, and I shook my head with an apologetic look. He nodded and gestured to someone in the crowd to indicate where he was sitting. To my dismay, another soldier, this one female, arrived with two drinks. She also gave me a curious look.

Having seen one Lostai too many, I left the establishment and walked towards a general sitting area in the center of the rest station that we had recently walked by. I let Kindor know telepathically where I was heading. Twenty minutes passed, too much time for me.

Where is he? It's only a five-minute walk.

Finally, I saw him approaching with our two drinks. When he was next to me, I quickly asked, "Did you see them?"

"Yes, there was a whole squadron, and they did spot me. I attracted some attention, but it seemed they were on leave and more focused on relaxing. I decided to walk around before returning here, just to make sure I was not being followed."

"I have to admit, they scared the crap out of me. I prefer to go back to the pod and rest."

Kindor agreed with me. After we finished our drinks, we purchased some food and brought it back with us.

Once back at the pod, I asked, "Kindor, how did you manage when you visited Karixta? That is a large city. There must have been plenty of Lostai there."

"Yes, but a Sotkari community lives there who are native-born Fronidians, such as Karixta's family, and whose families I suspect has had ties with the Lostai. So, it is easy enough for me to pretend to be one of them."

"I wonder if I will ever be able to walk around without having to constantly worry. Hopefully, Josher is protected by the fact that he is a native-born Fronidian."

As we rested, Kindor brought me up to speed on some current events he had researched in anticipation of our trip.

"There is some friction building up between Fronidia and

the Lostai government. The Lostai government is accusing Fronidia of harboring fugitives and rebel factions. Fronidia reciprocated by restricting travel from the Lostai home world and their colonized planets."

"I guess that is a good thing, right?" I asked. "Maybe if things continue to deteriorate between the Lostai and Fronidia, we will get lucky and they will kick all the Lostai out."

"Absolutely. And in the meantime, the less Lostai coming to Fronidia, the better for the Sotkari Ta and others who have taken refuge here."

"I cannot believe there is not more outrage against the detestable things that the Lostai military is doing."

I shook my head in disgust. Nothing riled me up more than talking about the Lostai.

"Well, not everything is common knowledge. Maybe the general population is not even aware that they are kidnapping people and forcing them into servitude."

I crossed my arms and huffed.

"How convenient for them. I find that hard to believe."

"I did hear from Karixta's father that the Lostai government is facing some challenges on their home world. A few newly elected younger officials are opposed to the significant amounts of funds invested in military technology, armed forces, and expansion projects. Even other officials have begun to question the morality of the Lostai expansion policy."

"That's something to be hopeful about. Not to mention, the rebel factions that are trying to fight against the Lostai."

He raised his eyebrows in surprise. I scolded myself for letting that slip. Despite all the time I had spent with Kindor and his family, this was not a topic I had shared with them.

"So, it is true? There really are rebels?" he questioned.

"Yes, but they are fractured, small pockets of rebellions easily squashed by the Lostai military. Imagine, though, if they all banded together. Then they might have a chance."

"How are you aware of this?"

"The commander on the station where I was being held sent me and Josher's father to investigate the beginnings of an insurgency on one of the planets the Lostai have added to their empire."

He nodded, intrigued. "So, what happened?"

"That is when Josher's father helped me escape, but I prefer not to discuss the details."

"I see," he answered, studying my face.

I turned away with the pretense of checking on Josher.

"Josher is sleeping. I think I will take a nap, too," I said, reclining the chair and ending our conversation.

23

As soon as our navigational controls confirmed it was safe to resume our trip, we took off. The remainder of the trip went smoothly. However, as we approached Colora's home location, the wind picked up, and I saw the lightning again. It was already evening and dark. Her home was isolated on a large plot of land at the top of a hill with a landing platform at the base and an elevator that took us to the top. By the time we were in front of her door, the weather had degraded. I bundled up Josher in a warm blanket, leaving barely his nose exposed, and held him in my arms. Kindor stood right behind me. I took a deep breath and rang the doorbell.

The next few minutes went by in slow motion. The door opened, and I found myself face-to-face with Montor.

"Mina!" he gasped, his eyes wide.

He looked at Kindor and the bundle I held against my heart. His eyes competed with the flashes of lightning around us. He seemed to be at a loss for words. Before I could greet him, I heard a female voice inside speak in Fronidian.

"*Sa veranttay,* who is at the door?"

Colora approached the entrance and slinked her arm around Montor's waist in a gesture that oozed intimacy. My heart sank, and my knees almost buckled. Kindor placed his hands under my elbows to steady me. I heard his voice in my mind.

"Mina, I am so sorry."

Colora was either unaware or indifferent to what I might be thinking or feeling. She smiled at me, and her voice was cheerful.

"Mina! It is wonderful to see you again," she said.

I looked at Montor.

"You and Colora? Where is Jortan?" I asked telepathically.

Montor ignored my question, narrowed his eyes for a few seconds, and asked another one instead, speaking out loud in Lostai in an aggressive tone.

"Mina, who is this Sotkari?"

"He is a friend."

"Friend, my ass. He desires you." Everything from his voice to his stance and expression meant to intimidate.

Colora looked at Montor. She was trying to piece together a puzzle. A mixture of anger and sadness boiled up inside of me.

"How would you know?" I said.

"It took me all of five seconds to read him," Montor answered with a smug expression.

I deflated even more, like when your teenaged boyfriend meets your family for the first time, and then says and does all the wrong things.

"How disappointing for poor Josher. This creature has no honor," I heard Kindor's voice in my mind.

Apparently, he communicated in conference mode, and Montor heard it, too. His expression was one of disbelief, his voice a roar as he lunged towards Kindor.

"How dare you mention my father's name!"

Colora was quicker and stepped between us, looking at me

curiously as something caught her attention. She touched the amulet I wore around my neck and recognized it as matching the one Montor always wore. Her eyes scanned each of us, and then she spoke in a matter-of-fact tone.

"It seems you two might have unfinished business that I was not aware of. May I see the baby, Mina? You know, I regret not having a child. Jortan and I were forced to wait too long, and when we finally were able to get married, it never happened for us."

Montor and Kindor glared at each other. I nodded to Colora, so she came closer and moved the blanket slightly from Josher's face. Her jaw dropped, and she covered her mouth.

"Oh, my..."

Montor chuckled, but it sounded more like he was choking.

"Come now, Colora...how hideous can this Sotkari's child be?"

"Ummm, well, he certainly looks exactly like his father. I think you should take a look," Colora answered.

"Me? Why should..." Montor started to say with a quizzical look on his face.

Colora ignored Montor and directed her attention to Kindor.

"I am pretty sure we will all need a stiff drink before the evening is over. Come, sir...what is your name?"

Kindor signed to her in Fronidian.

"OK, Kin...Dor...Grah...Mon...Please come and help me with the drinks. I think it is safe to assume you and I are going to be the odd ones out here. You two come inside already. We should not keep the baby out in this weather," Colora said.

Kindor looked at me, and I nodded, letting him know I agreed with Colora's suggestion. She led him off while Montor and I stepped in, and the door closed behind us. There was a sitting area right beyond the entrance. My heart was heavy, and I needed to sit and gather my thoughts. Montor remained standing, his hands on his waist, looking around and shifting his weight back and forth.

Finally, he whispered, "Mina, I thought you were dead..."

"I would have been...Kindor saved my life."

"Is that why you had his child?"

I rolled my eyes.

"Montor, look at the baby." It came across more like a command than an invitation.

He pursed his lips but reluctantly sat down next to me, leaning over as I removed Josher's blanket. His reaction was comical, eyes wide with amazement, speechless for several minutes.

"Mina...he looks like...us!"

"Well, that would make sense, considering he is our child," I said.

He sat up straight and puffed his chest to return to his typical posture.

"Actually, he looks exactly like me, right? Except for his eyes...beautiful like yours."

Discovery crept into his expression. His lips formed a fine line. Covering his mouth, he stared at his lap.

"I understand now. You honored my wish by naming him after my father."

"Yes."

He stood again, turned away from me, and ran his fingers through his hair.

"What is it, Montor?"

No answer. I stood and gave his arm a gentle tug. When he turned to face me, his eyes were watery. He covered his mouth again.

"My father would have been so happy..." His voice cracked. It took him a moment to recover.

He rubbed my cheek with the back of his hand, but I pulled back.

"Not so fast. What is going on between you and Colora?"

"Nothing important, Mina...I assure you...When I thought you were dead..." His voice broke again. "Now, I feel as if...as if I have died and come back to life."

We both sat again. I couldn't think. The pounding in my temples matched my quickening heartbeat. I didn't know what to say as I held Josher even closer. Montor's eyes met mine. A solitary tear rolled down his cheek. I bit my lip hard.

"Oh, Montor. I missed you."

He leaned over and kissed me softly on the lips. The gentleness of it brought me to tears. Although I wasn't satisfied with his reply to my question, my soul needed a balm. He gathered Josher and me in his arms, and I let his lips linger on mine, enjoying the intimate moment that I had been imagining for so long.

Colora's voice broke the spell.

"You see, Kindor? What did I tell you?"

We looked up. I pulled back, embarrassed.

"Colora, I am sorry. We should leave," I said.

"Do not be ridiculous. The weather is terrible. Kindor and I have fixed drinks. Follow me."

She led us to a spacious room with a bar and different types of seats and sofas, a library, and an entertainment system which, in Fronidia, in addition to music and telecasts, delivered holographic and virtual reality experiences. She turned on mellow music, and we sat around a table where the drinks were already set. Kindor went back outside to the pod and brought in Josher's crib. I set Josher down in the crib, so he could sleep comfortably.

"Cheers," said Colora, raising her glass. The rest of us remained stiff with awkward expressions on our faces.

"It is clear that we have all held back some truths from each other and need to clear the air. I will go first," said Colora as she placed her glass back on the table.

"Mina, I do not know what happened between you and Montor after that evening that we shared at Members Only. I remember Montor coming by alone a few days later. I asked about you out of curiosity because you two had looked so good together. He said you were transferred to another Lostai station and he did not expect to see you again. In my mind, that was the end of it. Two weeks later, my husband, Jortan, was murdered..."

I covered my face in horror. She stopped for a second and looked down to her folded hands.

"...The crime is still unresolved. I was devastated. Jortan was my best friend and soulmate. I will never fully recover from losing him, and I know this was a hard blow for Montor as well. Over time, Montor fell more and more into intense depression. Now, I can only guess that he had more on his mind besides Jortan's death..."

She looked at me specifically at that point, then continued.

"It is true that Montor and I found some strange solace in each other's company, but I can honestly say we both were clear that it was a bandage that eventually would be peeled off once our wounds were healed or at least scarred over. Mina, I hope you do not think I purposely hid this from you or tried to hurt you. When you reached out to me, I did not suspect it might have anything to do with Montor, and you told me to not speak of it to anyone, so I did not tell him, either."

She made eye contact with me. I was convinced that she wasn't hiding anything.

I turned to Montor and said, irritation clear in my voice, "Montor, you go next."

After some hesitation, he spoke.

"Mina and I were already in a relationship by the time I brought her to Members Only the evening that you met her. The Lostai were holding her against her will."

Kindor interjected, communicating telepathically and using sign language, "Aren't you a Lostai soldier?"

Montor glared at Kindor but ignored the question.

"I helped Mina escape and could not risk speaking of it to anyone. After the expected travel time to Fronidia, I received codes from the shuttle indicating a catastrophic malfunction, crash landing, and explosion."

He rolled his shoulders and continued.

"I had no idea of the actual location. I quietly investigated but found no evidence that Mina had survived."

At that point, he stood up and turned away from us. I knew he was not one to bare his soul or expose his vulnerabilities.

After a few seconds, he turned back around and said, "The important thing is that Mina and I have found each other again, and together with our son, I look forward to us forming a family. They are the most important things in my life now."

I studied Colora's face and didn't see any evidence of ill will or disappointment, only the look of someone who was listening with interest and absorbing information.

It was my turn to speak. Montor's eyes were fixed on me.

"Montor has already explained the circumstances regarding my escape from Renna One. It was during my trip to Fronidia that I discovered I was pregnant with Montor's child. That is why he was unaware of Josher's existence. When I approached the Fronidian atmosphere, I was caught up in an electromagnetic storm before I was able to make contact with the Fronidian border patrol. The shuttle was thrown off course and crash-landed in a remote area. Luckily, Kindor was hunting nearby and rescued me. His family offered me shelter and a job. He ensured my safety and that of my son."

I made eye contact with Kindor and nodded.

"I have no way to repay his kindness and consider him a special friend. Montor had warned me that I needed to keep a low profile even in Fronidia as I would be on a wanted list, but I knew that sooner or later I owed it to my son to seek out his father. After six lunar cycles had gone by, I felt in a better position to venture out of Kindor's remote village. That is when I remembered I had Colora's contact codes and reached out to her. Not knowing what my current status is with the Lostai military, Kindor insisted on accompanying me on the trip here."

I think Montor was disappointed that I didn't profess my unwavering love for him, but the situation was awkward enough already. We all turned our attention to Kindor.

He stood, folded his arms across his chest, and made a point to look at each of us before communicating in Fronidian sign language, which we all understood. The slow rise and drop of his chest signaled something simmering underneath.

"I want it to be clear. I love Mina and care for her son as if he were my own. I will respect her wishes, but I don't intend to leave her or Josher until I am sure they are safe."

Colora was impressed and, in her typical bluntness, said, "Oh, my, he is a passionate one. I do hope he sticks around."

Montor banged his fists on the armrests of his chair before standing to face Kindor, chest puffed, eyes narrowed, his typical swagger on full display.

"Look at me. Do I appear to you like someone who needs help to protect my female and son?"

Kindor didn't move, remaining cool and unimpressed as he continued signing.

"I can see you take pride in your brute force, but do you realize I can use my mind to make your heart stop beating and in two seconds swat you down like a fly?"

Montor blinked in disbelief at Kindor's quiet defiance. I had never seen this side of Kindor. It worried me, and I quickly stepped in to settle things down.

"OK, stop it, both of you! Or should I send Colora for a measuring stick to see who has the largest member?" I shouted.

Kindor raised his eyebrows while Montor could not help a tiny smile at my obscene suggestion.

"Changing the subject, Montor, what is my status? We ran into a squadron of Lostai soldiers at a rest stop apparently on leave, and I almost had a heart attack. Are the Lostai still searching for me?" I asked.

"Technically, you and the other three Earthians who escaped Xixsted are still on the fugitive list, but the Lostai military have their hands full with various rebel factions that are increasing their activities throughout the sector. Lostai law enforcement considers that there is a high probability that you are dead. Relations between Fronidia and the Lostai government are degrading significantly, and I think most Lostai soldiers and visitors will be asked to leave Fronidia within the next few lunar cycles. Things will get easier for you here, but you are still at risk in other areas of the sector," Montor said.

We finished our drinks, and there was an awkward silence.

"Kindor, we should look for lodging in the area. I am exhausted," I said.

"Under no circumstances will I allow you to leave in the middle of this storm, especially with the baby. I have three guest rooms and a master bedroom. Montor and Mina, you and Josher can have the master suite, and the rest of us can get accommodated in the other guest rooms," said Colora, eyeing Kindor with a nervous giggle.

"I appreciate your hospitality, Colora...but let me ask you this...had I not showed up at your door tonight, you and Montor would have slept together in that master suite, correct?" I asked.

Montor's face was like stone, but Colora's eyes met mine, and she did not hesitate.

"Yes, Mina, I suppose so, but now that you have more or less risen from the grave, everything has suddenly changed. I am a practical person and do not have a problem facing reality."

"I am not sleeping with anyone tonight, Colora," I said.

Kindor looked down, but I could see it was his turn to smile.

"OK, then let me take you and Josher to one of the guest rooms...and Kindor, I'll come back and show you to yours."

Montor was quick to assume his parental duties. He gingerly picked up Josher from the crib, handed him to me, and carried the crib as we followed Colora to the guest room she had designated for me. Colora left us and went to attend to Kindor. After putting Josher down to sleep, Montor sat on the bed.

"Mina, we need to talk."

"Yes, we do, but I am very tired now."

"No, Mina...this cannot wait...I know you are upset about Colora, and I do not want to be indelicate, but you need to know...I do not love her nor does she love me...we sometimes meet up, get drunk, and go to bed together to forget our sadness..."

"You do not owe me any explanations, but I am not sure what you are expecting of me."

I remained standing.

"Come sit next to me."

"No. I think I'll stay standing right here. Montor, do not think you will slip into my bed. That is not why I set out to find you."

"Mina, do you not understand? You being here changes everything. My heart is exploding...I love you! I want to marry you immediately and for Josher, you, and me to live together as a family."

"Montor, for all you know, Colora does love you. Have you thought about that? I feel embarrassed showing up here and getting in between you two."

He stood and walked towards me, and I stepped back.

He shook his head.

"Mina, you are not hearing me. That is not how things are between Colora and me."

"OK, I believe she is an honest person. I remember that I instinctively liked her when we first met. Still, you know, I always had a funny feeling that she was attracted to you. I will have a heart-to-heart talk with her tomorrow, but there is something else on my mind that I would like to share with you."

He took another step forward. This time I didn't back away. I guess it felt like a small victory to him. He put his hands on my shoulders and bent to kiss my forehead.

"Tell me, Mina."

I looked up at him with a frown.

"You owe a debt of gratitude to Kindor. Neither Josher nor I would have survived without him. He made sure I had a good doctor during my pregnancy. He was with me when Josher was born. He has grown to love our son. You were very rude to him and read his thoughts without his permission. You owe him an apology."

Montor knitted his eyebrows.

"Mina, have you slept with him?"

"Seriously, Montor, what does that have to do with what I just said? You have a lot of nerve to ask me that while you have been having sex with Colora and who knows how many other females.

He shook his head again and searched my eyes, begging for a reply.

"No, Montor. There was one evening that he came to my room and it almost happened, but I put a stop to it. I thought of our son and of you. I want my son to have a father who can teach him the culture and language of his ancestors, someone who looks like him and leads him to be proud of his roots, and someone who can be a role model and teach him to be honorable and strong. I would not have come looking for you if I did not believe you could be that person and would have considered accepting Kindor as a partner instead. Please do not prove me wrong."

Our eyes remained connected.

"Mina, there is no doubt in my mind that I can be the father Josher deserves, but I need to know...What about us...as a couple?"

His hands slid from my shoulders down my arms. He took my hands in both of his.

"I need time, Montor. If we were married tomorrow, where would you take me?"

"I have property and a home here in Fronidia. You would be safe. We could finally be together."

"You are part of the Lostai military. Will the rising tensions between Fronidia and Losta affect your ability to stay here?"

"Maybe...but for the time being, we will be OK. I am willing to change my life drastically for you and Josher. If the time comes, I will figure what to do and where to go to keep us safe."

Pressing my fingers against my temples, I felt a headache coming on.

"I need to think about all this, but I am tired now. Depending on my talk with Colora tomorrow, I will agree to be a guest at your home. We will take things slowly from there. After one lunar cycle, I will decide if I am ready to accept your marriage proposal or if we need more time. Please, leave me now. I need some rest."

He nodded, kissed my hands, and quietly left the room.

24

I was the last to get up the next morning. After nursing Josher, I walked over to the dining area. Montor and Kindor were already sipping hot tea. When I approached, they both stood up and said good morning. I nodded to them and handed Josher over to Montor. Kindor's lips pressed into a tight line, but I knew the right thing was for Montor to become acquainted with his son. I was sure that, as much as it bothered Kindor, he understood it was the natural course of things.

"I am going to see if Colora needs any help," I said.

Colora was using a food reproducer for the morning meal.

"Good morning, Colora."

"Hello, Mina. I hope you were able to rest well."

"Yes...Yes, I did."

I helped her slice the bread and cheese as well as spoon fruit into bowls. Being alone together was the perfect time to talk about the gorilla in the room. She was one step ahead of me.

"Mina, I know finding Montor here with me must be confusing and upsetting for you."

"I am embarrassed, Colora. Had I known you were together,

I would have further explained my situation when I contacted you and found a less intrusive way of introducing him to Josher."

Colora waved her hand as if shushing me, speaking in a stern voice.

"Mina...Mina...stop and listen to me carefully. Montor and I are not together. It is important you understand this. He has come in a few times to check in on me...we had drinks...we were depressed...we tried to stamp it out with sex. Honestly, it was joyless."

I avoided her eyes. I thought I could have a cool and collected conversation, but a part of me was angry with her, jealous of any time she had spent with Montor in bed. It was too much for me. I started to walk away to grab the plates.

"Colora, you do not need to explain to me."

"Yes, I do. Look at me," she demanded, walking over to obstruct my exit. "There cannot be any misunderstanding. In my line of business, I naturally gravitate to appreciating beauty and aesthetics. Let us be honest, Montor's body is a work of art. Also, I care for him as an old friend, and I am sure he feels the same for me. We were only trying to ease each other's pain, perhaps in a misguided way. I never had any ideas of any long-term, deeper relationship with him..."

She stepped closer and shook her finger at me.

"More importantly, when I observed you with him that evening at Members Only, I remember never having seen him so happy and at ease with a partner. Imagine, you had only started to know each other! I assumed it was a sign of better things to come. If you love him, do not lose him again. I promise to be your greatest fan."

She gave my arm a squeeze, and her sincere smile warmed my soul. I let go of my anger and hugged her, forgetting again that it was not a normal way to show affection among Fronidi-ans. When I explained my plan of staying with Montor and taking time to decide where things would go, she said she thought it was an excellent idea and that his house was not far from hers, so we could keep in touch.

"I hope your friend, Kindor, sticks around. I find him interesting. Maybe we can do a switch," she joked in a mischievous tone. We both laughed.

We took the food out to the dining table and found Kindor, Montor, and Josher crawling around the floor, the baby giggling hysterically. The men looked at us sheepishly, got up, and sat at the table, Montor with Josher on his lap. While we ate, I asked about the status of things at Xixsted.

"Zorla has been promoted, so he is no longer there. He is back on the Lostai home world but frequently visits the various military stations in the sector. A younger dimwit named Rewarlt has taken his place on Xixsted," said Montor.

"What about Kaya? How is she doing?" I asked.

"Some sad news with her. Her granddaughter had an accident and passed away. She requested a leave of absence to bury her granddaughter in her family's ancestral burial ground in Sotkar and, honestly, I doubt will return. Long past normal retirement age, she has more than rendered her service time to the Lostai. In addition, now that she has lost her granddaughter, they have no way to extort her services, which we all know she performed under duress. I am sorry for her loss, but I am happy she is free of the chokehold the Lostai had on her."

"I guess it frees you as well, no?" I asked.

My question did not sit well with Montor.

"I am not sure what you are referring to, Mina," he answered, and by his tone, I knew not to insist.

"I would like to see her," I said instead.

"Maybe I can make it happen," Montor said.

When we were done eating, Kindor and Montor stood up and looked out the windows. As I helped gather the plates, I heard them communicate telepathically in conference mode. Montor purposely wanted me to hear.

"Kindor, I owe you an apology. I behaved rudely and in a dishonorable way yesterday. There is no excuse, especially considering Mina and Josher owe you their lives. I have no way to repay you for this, but if I can do anything for you, please do not hesitate to let me know."

"I accept your apology, Montor, but I will be frank. I am jealous of you...that you have the upper hand with Mina...that you met her first...I am jealous that you are Josher's biological father."

Why can't Kindor keep things simple? Does he always have to be so brutally honest?

"...And you saying things like that makes me dislike you as well. I am angry that you desire Mina. I do not like the fact that you were there holding her hand as she gave birth...that you cradled my son in your arms before me, that you have seen her nursing him..." Montor was getting emotional as he placed both hands on his head, his voice deepening. "That should have been me..."

"Well, Montor, at least we are united in that we care very much for both of them, but..." Kindor turned and stared up at Montor, who was at least three or four inches taller. "I am not going anywhere for the time being. Remember, if you cannot make her happy, I will be near."

I glanced back and saw Montor take a deep breath and nod, surely trying to control his temper as he was not used to putting up with anyone challenging him. I sighed as well, feeling thankful that they were able to get through that conversation without getting aggressive. After we finished cleaning up, I let everyone know that Josher and I would be staying at Montor's nearby home for the time being.

"I will look for lodging and perhaps a temporary job in the area until Mina determines what her longer-term plans are," signed Kindor, while Montor rolled his eyes and shook his head impatiently.

"You are welcome to stay here, Kindor," offered Colora, winking at me.

"Ummm...no...thank you very much, but I can no longer abuse your hospitality."

"OK, but let me at least help by showing you around," Colora said.

By midday, it was time to part our separate ways, Josher and I to Montor's house, while Colora accompanied Kindor to get familiarized with the area. Before I left with Montor, Kindor gestured that I step a few feet away from Montor and Colora to speak with me privately. Even though Montor's stare could have drilled holes in our heads, Kindor had no qualms in putting his hands on my shoulders and looking deeply into my eyes.

"Mina, you have my contact codes. I expect you to communicate with me every few days and let me know how you and Josher are doing. Promise that you will not hesitate to contact me if you are unhappy or afraid for any reason. Do you understand?"

"Yes, of course." I hugged Kindor, forgetting for a moment that Montor was watching us intently. Kindor's body stiffened at first, but he relaxed and put his arms around me. "Thank you, Kindor. Thank you for everything."

I walked back to get Josher and bring him to Kindor, so he could also have a few minutes with him before we left. I found Montor not looking at all pleased but trying to be patient. Kindor held Josher up and looked in his eyes for a few minutes before bringing him close to his chest, his brow furrowed when he returned Josher to me. I said goodbye to Colora and made plans to meet up with her in the next few days. Montor took us to his transport pod, and we were off.

The trip to his home took about fifteen minutes. Similar to his property on Renna One, this one was comprised of several thousand acres of land bordered by a lake and surrounded by a lush forest. The building was of ancient architecture, constructed in stone, with arched entrances, vaulted ceilings, and balconies. Colorful flowered plants in large ornate pots, decorative pools, and fountains surrounded the courtyard. Montor explained that the stunning, two-story structure was a thousand years old and had been the vacation home of a famous Fronidian monarch.

As we walked in, Montor proudly announced to Josher and me, "Welcome to your new home."

The inside was equally impressive with elegant lighting and décor and handmade furniture beautifully married with modern amenities. He showed me to my room and quickly identified a second guest room that he said would be redone as Josher's room. He completed the tour of the remaining rooms, finishing with the spacious master bed and bath featuring a tub like the one in Renna One.

"I will have Foxor and Lasarta relocated here from my property in Renna One. Using a more direct flight plan than what you were on, they should arrive in fifteen days. In the meantime, with the help of domestic robots, we will have to keep the place up on our own. As you know, I do not trust many people with my privacy."

"Sure, it will keep me busy. I look forward to it."

"Once they get here, they will set up a vegetable garden and livestock for our meals like in Renna One. Foxor and I can also hunt and fish. You know how I abhor reproduced food."

"Kindor's family runs a restaurant, and he was in charge of those types of things. Maybe you could offer him a job."

Montor took one long step towards me and grabbed me by the arm.

"I do not want Kindor anywhere near us!" he shouted, glaring and pointing his finger down at me.

Taken aback by his outburst, I yanked my arm out of his

grip. He caught himself and, after a shuddered breath, lowered his voice.

"I mean...he can come visit sometimes, but I think we three need time to ourselves. Do you not agree?"

"Yes, I understand, but you better learn to control your temper. I will not put up with it," I answered in a low but firm voice.

"I am so sorry, Mina. I never thought I would find myself in this situation, but the truth is I am insanely jealous of him. For the last six lunar cycles, you and he were together almost all the time. I have a lot of catching up to do."

"OK...I get it."

I unpacked and organized our belongings in the guest rooms. Afterwards, Montor suggested we go out to dinner and bring something back for the next day's breakfast until we purchased some groceries. When I asked whether it was safe for me to be walking about, he explained we were heading to an area populated by Arandan immigrants. No Lostai, soldier or civilian, would dare walk into the enclave for fear of being lynched.

We landed the transport pod in a corner lot and from there walked to the main street. Interspersed between the small homes were picturesque shops selling everything from art, clothing, and baked items to hunting and fishing supplies, giving the neighborhood a distinct ethnic feel. We stopped in a bakery where aromas of fresh cakes and pies filled the air. An elderly Arandan female and her teenaged grandson ran the shop. Within minutes, she and Montor were engaged in a lively conversation in Arandan.

"Mina, we should get a sweet pie and a savory one for tomorrow's morning meal. Trust me, they are delicious."

While the grandson packed our pies, Montor showed off Josher to the owner. They were speaking in Arandan, but I could see she clearly was making a big deal over Josher, and

Montor looked proud. As we walked through the neighborhood, I asked Montor about it.

"I explained to her that Josher was my son. She commented
that he is such a handsome baby...friendly and so healthy and
strong. As you must know by now, Arandan children develop at
an accelerated pace until they reach puberty at around the age
of seven or eight. At that point, they continue their development and age at a slower rate, but Josher is big for his age, even
for an Arandan child."

He smiled and added, "He takes after me." After that, he
became serious. "Was his delivery difficult for you?"

"He developed at double the rate of an Earthian child. The
normal gestation period for my people is nine months, but I
gave birth at four months. I required surgery because he was
already too large for me to deliver normally."

Montor took my hand and kissed it.

"Mina, you have done such a good job bringing him into
the world and taking care of him. I am impressed how you,
being so much smaller than a typical Arandan female, have
been able to nourish him so well. I knew you would be a
wonderful mother. I must admit, it makes me even more
attracted to you."

We reached the restaurant, a small, cozy place constructed
of huge stones of various shapes and colors. Orange vines with
small green flowers climbed the walls. The four tables sat in
four individual cubicles with curtains that could be closed for
privacy or pulled to the side. Lanterns mounted on the walls lit
with real candles gave off a flickering warm light. I always felt a
tug at my heart when I came across things that reminded me of
Earth. There was a wait, and Montor put our names on the list
so they could contact him when our table was ready. In the
meantime, we continued to stroll the streets. While we walked,
I asked Montor what happened in the aftermath of my escape.

"As we had planned, once I regained consciousness, I called

local law enforcement to come get me. When Zorla found out you were gone, he was livid but believed I was attacked once he saw my wounds."

I had forgotten about that part of our farewell.

"Wounds?"

"Yes, remember? You did quite a job on me, but that was good. It was necessary." He paused before continuing. "I reported that because my attackers were masked, I could not identify anyone, but that I suspected Gio Napoletano because of the earlier incident with him. Lostai law enforcement questioned Gio and held him for investigation. They eventually let him go for lack of other evidence. Lucky for Zorla, your loss came on the heels of having uncovered the individuals behind the rebel activities on Renna One and the labor camp's escape route. He received credit for that, and it eventually earned him his promotion. He asked me whether I had succeeded in impregnating you. I said that although we had been intimate, I had no idea."

"Did they launch a search for me outside of Renna One?"

"They did, but there was no sign of you anywhere. After three lunar cycles, Zorla was promoted and the new guy inherited the problem but is inexperienced and has been busy learning his position. I have not been assisting him in the way I helped Zorla. Although your name and image are still in the fugitive database, it is not so top-of-mind anymore. There has been an uptick in rebel attacks against the Lostai army all across the sector, and the priority is to gain intelligence on these groups. Once Zorla left, I started taking different assignments away from Xixsted. Now that I have found you—or, rather, you have found me—I will take a leave of absence."

"Montor, would this not be a good time for you to leave the military for good? As I understand Lostai law, after fifteen years of service, anyone is entitled to retire from the military."

"I suppose now I should consider it, but I need to weigh the

pros and cons. Being a Lostai soldier has its advantages, especially for some of my pro-rebel activities."

At that point, Montor received notification that our table
was ready. We walked back, and the main waiter led us to our
cubicle.

"Should we close the curtain, in case Josher gets restless, so
that we do not disturb the other customers?" asked Montor.

"I do not think it is necessary. As long as we keep him entertained, he is well behaved, and now that he has begun to chew
food, he is even easier to manage. He has a curious mind, eager
to try new things."

Montor was so pleased to learn details about his son and
was intent on making up for lost time. He took him on his lap
and helped him try bite-sized versions of food, describing to
him the name of everything in Arandan. I laughed as Josher
babbled to his father.

"He will be either a linguist or very confused. Kindor's niece
always spoke to him in Fronidian, Kindor in Sotkari, myself in
the two Earth languages I speak, and now you in Arandan."

Montor's brow creased with worry.

"I am joking. Children are very receptive to learning
different languages," I said.

"In another month or so, he may start saying his first
words," said Montor.

"What is the Arandan word for father?"

"*Taristo*, but usually children say *Tari* for short."

"I wonder how it works with Sotkari Ta children...are they
immediately telepathic or does it develop at a certain age?"

"I do not know...never thought to ask Kaya that question."

"Maybe we can ask Ki...I mean, I suppose we can research
it."

He patted my hand and laughed.

"It is OK, Mina. We can ask Kindor. I am curious about this
as well."

Dinner was delicious and a pleasure for the three of us. The waiters and staff found Montor and me to be a curious couple, but he told me that they praised Josher on how well behaved he was. Besides trying the food, I showed Montor the little gadgets and toys I brought along on these occasions to keep Josher busy.

"It is obvious that you are experienced in dealing with children," Montor said.

"Yes, well, I have been through this three times already. Although, I never thought I would have to go through *potty training* again." I used the English term, so Montor was clueless, but he tried to pronounce it.

"*Pahthii trah neng?*"

"Bathroom training."

"Ah, yes...that will not happen for several months still."

"I will delegate that task to you," I said, laughing.

25

On the way to Montor's house from the restaurant, I asked Montor about Jortan. He cleared his throat and took a few minutes before answering.

"I can barely speak of it, Mina. On a business trip from Renna One to another nearby planet, his shuttle was intercepted. He was not just killed but tortured, as if they were trying to get information from him. I hate to admit this, but I have a bad feeling that it was related to your escape. As you know, Gio Napoletano followed us that evening and told Zorla that we were in Members Only. It happened when the Lostai were in the heat of investigating your disappearance. I know Zorla believed my story because I scanned his mind, but perhaps his superiors had their doubts."

My eyes filled with tears at the thought, and I reviewed in my mind everything I recalled about Jortan.

"Montor, I remember Jortan speaking full of emotion about Aranda and against the Lostai...I am not trying to make this not be about me, but is it possible he was involved in rebel activities?"

Montor remained silent for a few minutes.

"He never mentioned anything like that to me, and I considered us to be very close. Then again, he did not know about my activities, either. He always portrayed himself as being all about business and profit, but now that I think about it, in the recent months, I have noticed the Arandan rebel movement to be a bit in disarray."

I almost heard the gears of his mind turning, but he spoke nothing more on the topic. We arrived back to Montor's house, and I prepared Josher for bed. It was early evening, and the weather was calm and pleasant, considering the previous night's storms. After putting Josher to bed, I walked out to one of the covered balconies. This particular one faced away from the forest and instead had a spectacular view of the city lights in the distance. I was lost in thought pondering what my next few days would be like. For the past two years, except for the few days I had shared with Montor on Renna One, my days had been regimented, busy, and exhausting with barely any free time. I was a bit concerned because without the strict work schedule, there was nothing to keep me from worrying about a million things...about my past... about my future.

"Oh!" I shouted out loud as Montor placed his hands on my shoulders.

"Sorry, I did not mean to startle you," he said.

"No problem. I was just thinking, you have a great eye for location. What a beautiful view."

His hands slid down my arms, and my heartbeat accelerated. He kissed my shoulder and then my neck. A jumble of doubts and decisions and desire ransacked my brain. I dared not turn around to face him.

"Mina, I know you talked about taking it slow, but I do not understand why. The last thing I remember before you left to Fronidia is us pledging love to each other, so I am confused about all this hesitation."

"That was before I realized you and Colora had the hots for each other."

"Hots?"

Why do I keep translating English slang literally to Lostai?

"It is an expression on Earth meaning when you are attracted to someone."

"Not this again. I thought we had surpassed this hurdle already."

"You said you loved me, but it did not take you long to jump into another female's bed...and who knows how many more there were besides Colora. I guess I have no right to be upset. It is not your fault. That has been your lifestyle, right? What was I expecting? Our time together was too short for you to be truly committed to me."

I thought that might be enough to dissuade his advances, at least for the time being, and make it easier for me to stick to my guns. I was wrong.

"Mina, I am sure that you are the partner that I want by my side for the rest of my life. Perhaps you are unsure about your feelings towards me. That is a different story."

"Maybe I am unsure...and yet, I was faithful to you. It was hard, Montor...to resist him. His hands on my skin were like an intoxicating drug, but I was able to control myself and reject him. I hurt his—"

"I do not want to hear about Kindor's hands, Mina!" he shouted. I didn't turn around, but his footsteps were heavy as he walked away.

Tension tightened my neck and back as I continued staring out to the city lights. After a few minutes, I heard his deep voice from a few feet behind me.

"When you left, I thought I could execute the plan as we had discussed and not do anything that might cause suspicion until adequate time had passed, but I could not. I had already decided to go be with you in Fronidia regardless of the consequences. Even though the data I received indicated you probably had died in a crash, I came to Fronidia and tried to find you. There was no record of the shuttle even entering Fronidian air space. Mina, the only time I remember being so grief-ridden was when, as a child, I realized my whole family was dead."

I chewed on my lip as I heard him walking back to me.

"Mina, turn around...look at me..."

In that moment, I knew once I turned around to face him, I would, in fact, be closing a chapter in my life and starting a new one. His hands were on my shoulders again.

"Mina...please...how are we going to decide if we should marry unless we spend time together as a couple?"

I thought about my new child, said a silent prayer, and turned around. The minute I looked up to him, his lips were on mine. He embraced me, and I closed my eyes, finally relaxing. His lips traveled down my neck, and I moaned softly. My mind might have had doubts, but my soul and body were so ready.

He picked me up in his arms and carried me to his bedroom, laying me gently on the bed. Sitting on the edge, he removed his footwear. After those were off, he stood up and began to take off his clothes. He moved with too much grace for such a tall, muscular frame. I anticipated the moment when he'd remove his undershirt, ready to enjoy the view of broad shoulders and muscle definition. Instead, an ugly mess of waxy scar tissue, angry red lines, bumps, and crevices stretched across his chest and abdomen. The soft fuzz, gone in those areas. Barely breathing, I jumped off the bed to see and touch up close. My first reaction was horror.

"I did this to you!"

"Lucky you did, or I would be in prison or worse by now."

Oddly enough, I became angry.

"I did not want to. You got into my head and made me. You promised you would never do that. What is wrong with you? I guess you do not have any reservations about routinely violating people's minds!"

"Sometimes, I have to make the hard choice between being less-than-honorable and saving the day...and yes, because I am a survivor, sometimes I can be unscrupulous."

My fingers slid over the rough, scarred skin.

"Do they hurt?" I whispered.

"Do the ones on your back hurt?" he asked.

"Not anymore," I answered.

"Neither do mine," he said.

I covered his chest with soft kisses as if I could erase the scars with my lips. His heartbeat quickened, and he ran his fingers through my hair, as if encouraging me to continue, but then he pulled back.

"Wait, I need to get something," he said.

I guessed what he was referring to.

"Montor, I had the doctor who delivered Josher redo the procedure to avoid conception. There is no risk of pregnancy."

"Oh, so, Josher will be an only child?"

"Well, it could possibly be reversed again, but let us keep in mind that I am not a young female anymore."

"I suppose we can look into that later, but we have more urgent things to attend to now," he said, flashing the sly smile I had not seen in such a long time.

Small clips ran down the front of my dress. Unfastening them required patience. The clips were small and his fingers large. I attempted to help him, but he insisted I let him undo them on his own. One by one, he opened them, revealing more of my skin and underclothes. The dress skimmed my knees, so he knelt to reach the final clip. When he was done, I slipped off my shoes, pulled my arms out, and let the dress fall. He remained on his knees and pulled down my underwear. I stepped out of them, and he tossed them aside, pulling me close, his breath warm against my tummy. I moaned as he slid his hand up between my legs, stroking the inside of my thighs, his fingers, and then his mouth exploring me intimately. I leaned into him, bursting with wet desire.

"How quick you are ready for me, my honey-eyed sweetness."

"Take me to bed, Montor."

Once in bed, he asked me to lie face-down, briefly teasing my nipples with his thumbs. Without waiting any longer, he growled, thrusting into me hard and quick. My hips hardly had a chance to move, and the speediness of it all disappointed me.

"Sorry, I could not help myself. You are so enticing. It has been so long since we were last together. I will make it up to you later," he whispered as he left a trail of kisses on my back.

Within a few hours, he did, taking his time to pleasure me and allowing my hips to express themselves.

"Mina, I love your flexibility and how your body shows me it is pleased."

Soon, our shouts and moans were so loud, I was afraid we might awaken Josher, who was in the bedroom down the hall. After an explosion of ecstasy, we collapsed into a deep sleep. Josher woke us up early, ready for breakfast. I brought him to our bedroom, and Montor watched as I nursed him.

"Mina, my heart is bursting with happiness. I cannot describe it."

After Josher was done, we remained in bed, the three of us playing until Montor and I got hungry. I made hot tea, and we tried both of the pies we had bought the day before.

"Mina, I need to buy food and supplies for our meals. Also, I want to better furnish Josher's room to make it appropriate for a child. I wish you could come with me, but I still fear for your safety. I hope you do not mind trusting in my taste."

"Your taste has not failed you before."

I hugged him, and he pulled me even closer.

"You are the best proof of that."

Before he left, we discussed when would be the best time to schedule our daily exercise and meditation regimen, agreeing on midafternoon, which was when Josher typically napped. While Montor ran his errands, I took advantage of the time to get familiarized with the house, its features and appliances, as well as the robots that helped with maintenance and cleaning.

Montor arrived back after a few hours. Together, we stored the food and supplies, put Josher down for a nap, and changed into our workout clothes. He led me to a room in the house set up as a gymnasium with advanced exercise equipment. The fact that I had become accustomed to Kindor's workout style and had forgotten the routine we used to follow irritated Montor. We bickered a bit at first but got over it. When we reached the mental activities, Montor reflected on how I had not gained new capabilities.

"I would have thought the pureblood Sotkari Ta could have shown you a few new tricks...you never did grasp much of mind control."

"We barely had enough time to get through practicing the basics, and I do not like the concept of mind control, anyway. There is one area that I would love to explore. Kindor is very capable with manipulating the body and healing. Now that I have a new child, I think it is a good skill to have."

"Yes, I have some knowledge on this, but by no means is it my forte. I focused on learning to defeat my opponents rather than healing. You are right. I agree it is something we should learn."

He looked at the ceiling as if contemplating his next words.

"Let us invite Kindor to come visit once every six days to train us both in this area."

My heart leapt with surprise, then delight. I tried to mask it but couldn't help my words tumbling out quick with excitement.

"That is an excellent idea. We can also ask him questions

about the development of Sotkari Ta children and when we should start any training for Josher, and I know it would please him so much to see Josher."

"Do not look so happy, Mina, as I may get jealous and change my mind," he said, but it was in a good-natured tone.

"OK, OK. Let me keep you in a good mood by making you a nice dinner."

26

T he days that followed reminded me of the start of our love affair during the trip to Renna One. Each day, we planned a special activity. We walked to the lake and had picnics. The temperature was perfect for swimming, and Josher loved splashing in the water. Montor explained that in a few more months, Josher would be ready to learn how to swim. Other days, we visited the Arandan enclave to try the different regional eateries and browse through the arts and craft shops.

We also spent time redecorating Josher's bedroom. Montor had the room retrofitted to include an age-appropriate holographic entertainment center. He added a wall unit full of traditionally bound hard copy books that included everything from picture books to Arandan folk tales to history and science. For a society that did most of its learning through electronic and holographic devices, the books were more expensive antique collector items than instructional material. I thought it was a bit of overkill for a child who was still a baby, but he said Arandan children started learning to read and write by the time they were a year old. Montor also bought child-sized instruments. And elegant, handcrafted furniture. And several types of mechanical toys. And something that looked like a motorized bicycle that he said Josher would be able to ride in about six months. Of course, you love all your children, but everything is so new with the first one. Montor was beside himself with pride and awe with every new thing he observed about Josher.

On the third day after moving in with Montor, I called Kindor and let him know Josher and I were doing fine. When I spoke to him about Montor's idea of having him over to train us, he was incredulous but then pleased. With Colora's help, he already had secured a job repairing transport pod navigational systems. Two days later, Colora invited me for a day of shopping and pampering at a private vacation complex where we were sure not to run into Lostai. I filled her in on my status with Montor while we sat dipping our feet in a refreshing mud pool.

"I have not slept in the guest room since moving in," I said with a giggle.

"It is obvious. You are radiant. I have spent time with your friend, Kindor, but without such good luck yet," she joked with a mischievous smile.

"We have asked Kindor to train us on Sotkari Ta healing skills. He will come over tomorrow and stay for dinner. I would like for you to join us as well."

"I would love to. Maybe I can be his assistant, and he can practice on me."

We laughed out loud and ordered another drink.

Kindor arrived late afternoon after Montor and I finished our physical exercises and self-defense work out. Josher was still napping, so he would have to wait before seeing him. We went outside to one of the porches and communicated telepathically in conference mode.

"Kindor, I appreciate your help in teaching us this Sotkari Ta skill," Montor said, trying his best to appear humble.

"Sure, the pleasure is mine, but I must say, you have surprised me with this request. I never expected someone as arrogant as you to ask me for this type of assistance," Kindor answered, as usual, being ever-too-honest.

Montor rolled his eyes.

"I guess I am full of surprises."

Kindor started out explaining that one thing was the concept of a calming touch that transfers a sensation of well-being through skin-to-skin contact, and something different was the possibility of manipulating bodily functions. We learned we could control parts of the body in the same way we moved inanimate objects with our minds. He cited, as examples, the beating of a person's heart, the expanding and relaxing of the lungs, blood flow, the inflammation of muscles and nerves, the digestive process, and, with enough skill and focus, the reproduction of cells and the healing process. Part of our training would be to gain a deeper knowledge of anatomy. He was a good teacher, and I recognized in him leadership qualities that I had never paid attention to before.

Montor took the lesson seriously, but once we were done, his demeanor changed, moving with his typical swagger and showering me with exaggerated displays of affection. Kindor pretended not to take notice, but soon enough, I heard his voice in my mind.

"I thought you said you were waiting a lunar cycle to make a decision. It did not take him long to convince you to sleep with him," he said in an accusatory tone.

Our eyes met, and I was peeved that he should try to make me feel guilty.

"What is your problem? After all, he is the father of my

child, and it is my decision to make," I said way too harshly, considering how much I owed him.

In the meantime, Josher had awoken, and Montor brought him over, breaking the tension between Kindor and me. Josher recognized Kindor, and they were elated to see each other. There is a special place in a mother's heart for someone who sincerely loves her children. I regretted how I had spoken to Kindor. Even Montor smiled.

I excused myself to shower, change, and start working on dinner. As I began setting the table, Colora arrived. Soon, we all were at the table, including Josher, as Montor had purchased a child seat that allowed him to sit with us. During dinner, I asked Kindor about Sotkari Ta child development.

"As you know, original Sotkari Ta cannot speak out loud, but the children begin to display signs of sensing language tele-pathically around the age of two revolutions. The Sotkari Pasi, who are telepathic but have use of their vocal cords, develop both forms of communication simultaneously about the same age. I have not had experience with children with embedded Sotkari Ta genes. So far, Josher has been following an Arandan child development pattern, so I assume that he will begin to speak words out loud at the typical age for Arandan children. What age would that be, Montor?"

"I would expect in another month or so."

"When he starts, at that same time, I suggest you focus on communicating those same words telepathically to him. Once telepathic language is free flowing, you can begin training in other abilities, but typically, we wait for them to be old enough to have the maturity of understanding wrong from right. In the meantime, you can establish the routine of meditation to strengthen his focus and mental agility."

"Yes, what you have described makes sense. Thank you for the insight, Kindor," Montor said.

As I cleared the dinner plates from the table, Montor also

got up to help me. Colora complimented me on the meal, saying she had no idea homemade food could be so delicious.

"She is an excellent cook," Montor said, lightly slapping my butt.

It was obvious that Montor was marking his territory.

"Is that really necessary?" I asked Montor telepathically, avoiding Kindor's eyes. Montor's mischievous expression tested my patience even more. To mask my irritation, I smiled and turned to Kindor and Colora.

"Kindor will be coming every sixth day to continue our training. Let us make it a standing dinner date for us four and Josher," I said out loud.

During our next session with Kindor, a call came in for Montor. It was not typical for him to stop in the middle of a training session for anything. While he went to take the call, Kindor and I continued with the training, which involved becoming more aware of anatomy through touch and hearing. I was concerned about wasting valuable training time, since I didn't know when Kindor planned to return to his village and I was determined to learn about these skills.

Kindor opened his shirt, displaying his bare chest, and had me touch the area where I could detect his heartbeat. He asked me to place my ear there and listen while meditating. Perhaps it wasn't such a good idea, as his breathing quickened and, for a few seconds, he ran his fingers through my hair.

Montor's voice startled me. "I am back."

I took a step away from Kindor, trying hard to pretend nothing out of the ordinary had happened.

We continued the session with Montor baring his chest instead, but it was clear that he was cranky, and there was an awkward tension in the air. To make matters worse, Kindor brought up some disturbing news during dinner. He communicated to Montor and me telepathically while simultaneously using Fronidian sign language so that Colora could follow the conversation.

"This morning, I spoke with Mother and learned that Karixta has paid them a few visits. During the first visit, they told her that Mina had moved out and I was accompanying her to meet a friend. She did not like that..."

"Who is Karixta?" asked Colora.

"His ex-girlfriend," I answered.

"For some reason, she was jealous of Mina," signed Kindor.

"I wonder why," said Montor.

"Anyway...During another visit, Karixta claimed she had done some research and found out that Mina was a fugitive, wanted for escaping the Lostai military illegally. She said she hoped, for my own good, that I had dropped off Mina with plans to hurry back home because she had notified Lostai law enforcement that Mina was somewhere in Fronidia."

Montor's jaw dropped as he clenched his fist.

"This is a serious problem and comes at a bad time. I have just been asked to travel to Aranda for an important meeting and will be away for a few days."

He stood and paced around, deep in thought.

"Kindor, I have a favor to ask of you. Can you stay here with Mina and Josher while I am away?"

Kindor raised his eyebrows with just a hint of amusement.

"I must admit, you are full of surprises. I never expected to hear that from you."

Montor noticed the beginnings of that smirk, walked closer to Kindor, and glared down at him.

"Well, I worry about leaving them alone, especially now that your...ummm...friend has let the Lostai know Mina is alive and here in Fronidia. I know you desire Mina, but I figure you had six lunar cycles to convince her to be your lover without success. It took me only one day for her to move into my bedroom."

Montor's tone dripped with sarcasm and anger, his body language confrontational. Kindor's mouth tightened, and I saw a look on his face I had never seen before, one of utmost contempt. Even Colora, who usually remained unfazed no matter what she heard, shifted uncomfortably in the chair.

"You cocky bastard! What is wrong with you! Why do you have to be so unpleasant and inappropriate? No one needs to know those details...and by the way, is this how you ask for a favor?" I said, outraged.

Montor covered his mouth with his hand, looked down, and took a deep breath.

"Mina, you are right. Kindor, I am sorry. The truth is I cannot think of anyone else I would entrust with my son's safety."

Kindor's eyes, which had frozen into blue ice, melted at the mention of Josher. He gulped before replying, "Of course. I will stay and keep them safe until you return."

"Thank you, Kindor. Also, my foster parents, Foxor and Lasarta, will be arriving before I get back from my trip, so they can help to keep an eye on things."

Emotions cooled off a bit as we settled in for dessert. Afterwards, Montor and Kindor played with Josher, while Colora and I stepped out to the terrace to chat a bit.

"I tell you, Colora, sometimes Montor is so difficult to deal with. When we are alone, he can be thoughtful, tender, and caring. I know he has sincere feelings for me, and I care very much for him as well. He risked a lot to help me escape Xixsted. But when something crosses him, he becomes so unpleasant and ruthless. It scares me sometimes."

"He is not used to being provoked, and let us be honest,

Kindor sometimes is overly blunt. I think we need to cut Montor some slack after Kindor openly proclaimed his love for you. Frankly, I am surprised at the restraint he has shown. Arandan culture is old-fashioned in these matters. Normally, he would have challenged Kindor to some sort of duel."

"I know, but maybe I have let things move too fast. Montor is talking about getting married. Sometimes, I find his behavior so offensive, and at other times, my love for him is so intense, our intimacy so mind-blowing."

"Mina, are you trying to choose between him and Kindor?" asked Colora with an alarmed look on her face.

"Oh, no, no...I am thankful to Kindor for all the ways he has helped me. He has been a savior for Josher and me. We have developed a close friendship, and I am very comfortable with him, but I do not feel the same romantic attraction as I have for Montor."

"I see...are you sure?" she said, her expression skeptical.

"Yes, I am."

"Are you thinking of returning to your planet? I was shocked when you confided to me the other day that you have children there."

My stomach churned as I fought back tears.

"No, I cannot. Even if I found a way back, which is unlikely at this point, I could not bring Josher with me. My people do not have the technology for space travel and have not made contact with people from other worlds. There are those on my planet who believe we are alone in the universe. Josher would be an outcast or worse. They would try to study him, as if he were a lab rat. I love all my children...I miss them so much...but right now, Josher is the most vulnerable."

I covered my face so she wouldn't see how emotions were getting the best of me. She placed a hand on my shoulder.

"Oh, Colora, being separated from my children is worse than any punishment I suffered on Xixsted."

"I am so sorry if I have upset you. I cannot even imagine what you are feeling."

She looked almost as distressed as I felt. I patted her hand.

"No, no, it is not your fault. Those are logical questions. I know you are trying to help me think through my relationship with Montor."

"Perhaps you hesitate at the idea of remarrying because you still feel committed to your dead husband. May I ask, how did he die?"

"What?"

"Your husband, Mina...how did he pass away?"

"Oh, yes...umm...a vehicular accident."

"I see...terrible, an unexpected loss, like my Jortan."

"Yes."

"What was he like?"

"Well, as I think about it, truthfully, his personality is somewhat like Montor's and he is ex-military."

Colora cocked her head.

Damn it. Did she notice I referred to him in present tense?

"So, a soldier, like Montor, huh? I guess you have a type you prefer. I think some of the things that supposedly concern you about Montor, you secretly find attractive."

"I have to admit I like how Montor's strength and self-confidence makes me feel safe. No one messes with him."

"Exactly, and do not ask me why I say this, but I think the situation in this sector is going to get more unstable with the Lostai trying to manage rebellions across their empire. My Jortan said times are approaching where we should grab hold of our loved ones and keep them close. I do not know how long it has been since he died, but I am sure your husband would want you to be happy. Montor loves you, Mina. He is the father of your child. I have always believed in trusting my first instincts. Yours have led you back to Montor's arms. You should consider yourself lucky to have found love again. Do not fight it."

"Yes, Colora, you are probably right."

After we put Josher to bed, Kindor and Colora stayed for a drink and left. Montor had to get up early for his trip to Aranda, so we showered and went to bed. We usually cuddled before falling asleep, but I was still upset at his crude remarks during dinner. I inched away from him towards the edge of the bed with my back towards him. He ignored my gesture of rejection and pulled me back close to his torso, entwining his legs with mine, his hands playfully stroking my body.

"Mina, I am sorry for the stupid comment I made at dinner today. Hearing that the Lostai now officially know you are alive and here in Fronidia upset me. I was already angry to begin with, when earlier I saw you leaning against Kindor's chest, his hands in your hair. Seriously, Mina, what were you thinking? He is so obviously in love with you. Are you purposely trying to tease him or make me jealous?"

"What? Of course not...it frustrates me because...do not get upset...but I can be so at ease and relaxed with him and yet..."

"And yet what?"

"You are right, I should be more mindful..."

Montor sat up in bed and rolled me gently on my back so I faced him.

"Mina, I am only going to have the nerve to say this once, so listen and consider this carefully. Do not feel obligated to be with me because of Josher. I can still be a part of his life and watch over your welfare without you being my spouse. I only want to marry you if you love me. If you want to be with Kindor, let us be clear about it."

"I do not love him that way. I think I love him like a family member, like a brother," I said.

"I am sure his feelings are different. It is not fair to him or me if you send mixed messages."

I lowered my eyes.

"Yes...yes, you are right..."

"And regardless of what Kindor means to you, I need to know what you feel for me."

I looked back up to him. Here was this person I once only thought of as a strong, complicated alien being but who now had become an intricate part of my life. His eyes were troubled and sincere at the same time. I thought about Colora's words and tried my best to sort out my feelings. Taking his hands in mine, I brought them to my lips and kissed them. I said words that I had only used once before in my life. Now, it felt like someone else's life, like a book I might have read or a movie.

"I love you, Montor. I want you, Josher, and me to be a family."

He interlocked his fingers with mine, and soon, we were making love. Once our breathing returned to normal, he got off the bed and went to look for something.

"I do not see why I should delay this any longer," he said, almost talking to himself.

He came back with a small shiny container, took me by the hand, and asked me to stand in front of him, both of us completely nude. I couldn't see at first what was in the box. He took my hand and showed me a thick, solid bracelet made of silver-toned metal embedded with amber-colored stones. It had a tiny lock and key to open and close it.

"Mina, I wish you to be my spouse and partner until I breathe no more. Do you wish the same? If so, accept this bracelet, and on the day of our wedding, we will destroy the key so that you may wear it forever."

"My God, you're proposing!" I said out loud in English, overcome with emotion.

He cocked his head, obviously not understanding, but his eyes were wide with expectation. My answer came quicker than I had expected.

"Yes, Montor, I do wish it and accept this precious bracelet."

He laughed in a joyous, childish manner.

"You have made me so happy, Mina."

He kissed me, and we went back to bed, him spooning me again. Before we dozed off, I asked him about the purpose of his trip. He said it had something to do with Arandan rebel activities.

27

Kindor arrived from work the next day in the late afternoon. I set him up in one of the guest rooms, and after he rested a bit, we started our workout routine. Afterwards, he helped me prepare dinner, and as we ate, he told me he had received another call from Karrina.

"I am very concerned. Karixta realized that she put my family in danger when she told the Lostai about you. She warned Karrina that she believed the Lostai would be paying them a visit and suggested they close down the restaurant and move somewhere else. Regardless of her age, my mother being a pureblood Sotkari Ta would be a nice prize for Lostai military. Karrina said they have moved in with Tadium. As a wealthy Fronidian citizen, he does not have to answer to Lostai law enforcement, so they should be safe there. Karrina also advised me to stay away for the time being."

"This is all my fault. Your family is in danger because of me."

"No, it is Karixta's foolishness that has caused the trouble, but I give her credit for having the common sense to warn Karrina. I cancelled my contact codes and created new ones under a different name in case the Lostai can track them. You should keep Montor apprised."

After dinner, Kindor took Josher in his lap and showed him one of the picture books Montor had bought him. Soon, Josher was rubbing his eyes, so Kindor tucked him in. Once Josher was sleeping, I poured us each a glass of wine and showed Kindor the bracelet.

"Montor proposed marriage to me last night, and I accepted."

Holding my hand, he moved my wrist around to better inspect the bracelet. First, he rubbed the metal with his thumb but then touched the skin underneath, scarred from the wristband I used to wear at Xixsted. A brief energy burst ran through my fingers, causing me to pull my hand into a fist. He exhaled deeply and stared into my eyes, his thoughts a mystery to me.

"I guess you forgave his impertinence at yesterday's dinner."

"I did not like what he said, but I understand why he was upset. He apologized and was sincere about it."

"I see. You are making fast decisions. Let me ask you this. Are you happy, Mina?"

"I am. Montor can sometimes be difficult, but I know he loves me. I love him, too, and we owe it to Josher to try to be a family."

He looked down at the bracelet again and stood up, lifting his wine glass in a toast.

"Very well...then I am happy for you. It is a beautiful piece of jewelry. I guess congratulations and a blessing are in order. May the Farthest Light shine its brightest ray on your union."

I lifted my wine glass and thanked him.

"Have you set a date for your wedding?" he asked.

"Not yet...like I said, it was only last night. I suppose we will discuss it when he gets back."

The next day, Foxor and Lasarta arrived. Their effusive greetings made me feel like a long-lost family member. Lasarta grabbed my hands in each of hers and brought them to her own cheeks. It was equivalent to a hug. Foxor disposed with the protocol of not touching me and did the same.

"We were so overjoyed when Montor informed us that you had found him," said Lasarta.

Foxor noticed the bracelet right away.

"Excellent...This is more good news!" he exclaimed.

"Oh, Mina, he also told us about the baby. I cannot wait to see him," said Lasarta.

Kindor took that as a cue and went to check if Josher was up from his nap. He came back with him. The minute Lasarta saw him up close, she covered her face and began to cry.

"Lasarta, relax. This is a happy occasion," said Foxor in his typical fake-gruff tone.

"I know, I know. It is just that I cannot help but think how happy Montor's parents would have been if they could have met him. He will continue the family lineage."

"How old is he?" asked Foxor.

"Four lunar cycles," I answered.

"He is definitely his father's son...large for his age, as Montor was."

"What did you name him?" asked Foxor again.

"I named him Josher, after Montor's father."

This bit of news made Lasarta cry even louder. Foxor was embarrassed, so he turned his attention to Kindor.

"And you must be Mina and Josher's guardian spirit."

Kindor reacted with surprise at this description.

"Kindor is a Sotkari Ta, so he is mute, even though he hears perfectly well. He communicates with sign language to those who are not telepathic," I said.

They did not know sign language, so I translated for Kindor.

"He asks whether that is really how Montor referred to him."

"Oh, yes...that is exactly what he said...he speaks well of Kindor and explained that he saved your life and ensured your safety while you were in hiding and still even now."

Kindor and I looked at each other astonished. I smiled and communicated telepathically to Kindor, "You see...he is full of surprises."

"Kindor says it is a pleasure to meet you, too," I told them.

Foxor and Lasarta settled in another guest room and soon began to make lists of everything that needed to be purchased and constructed to set up a vegetable garden and raise livestock for the homecooked meals Montor preferred. Montor was scheduled to arrive back in two days.

The next day, I received a call from Colora, her voice shaky.

"Mina, I was just visited by Lostai law enforcement. I think you all need to leave right away because I am guessing Montor's house will be their next stop. They asked me many questions about you. The only reason they were not tougher with me is because I am a Fronidian citizen."

"Oh, no...Colora, where do you think we can go?"

"I suggest you go to the Member's Only location I have here in Fronidia until we figure out what to do next. I have a special permit that forbids anyone, even law enforcement, to go in without permission. That location is closed for business, but I maintain guards there that will enforce this. I will send you the location codes and the permit information and will order the guards to not answer any questions from the Lostai. Keep your tablet deactivated until you need to present the permit and turn it off again right away. I tried to contact Montor, but he did not respond...I will try again...hurry, Mina."

My heart raced, and I could barely breathe. I ran over to Kindor and Foxor and explained the situation. We grabbed what we could, and within half an hour, we were all in Kindor's rented transport pod heading to Fronidia's Member's Only. Similar to the Members Only in Renna One, this one had lodging facilities. We discussed whether we should split up in separate rooms, but Kindor decided it was safer if we all remained together. The spacious suite that we selected had two beds, a restroom, and a food reproducer. Tall windows provided a view of rolling hills and a river, perfect for lovers but not so much for us. A view of the entrance would have been preferable. I was surprised to find that Kindor carried two laser guns in the transport pod and brought them with us to the room.

We settled in and collectively caught our breath. Lasarta, who was devout in her religious beliefs, retired to a corner in the room to pray. I faced away from the men to nurse Josher while Kindor and Foxor, unable to communicate with each other, paced around nervously. Once Josher was fed, I put him to sleep and joined the men. Acting again as translator for Kindor, we discussed what options we had if we were found. The room was on the ground floor, but the building itself was on a hill. If Lostai law enforcement stormed through the front door, we could possibly use the laser guns to break the windows and make a run for it in the woods. However, the small ravine immediately behind the building would be difficult to negotiate with Josher in tow. Kindor brought up something else that hit me like a punch in the gut.

"Karixta saw Josher, and I remember Mina saying the baby's father was Arandan. I am concerned if this puts Montor in danger."

"Well, when I was in his charge on Renna One, he was under instructions to impregnate me, so it would not be so unexpected that I have an Arandan baby as a result. What the Lostai will find questionable is that I was at his home in the company of his foster parents, and he had not turned me in immediately. I suppose we can say I arrived after he left to his meeting."

"OK, that possibly protects Montor, but what about you and the baby?" said Foxor.

I took a deep breath and, for a moment, was at a loss for words. What rights might I have? I wasn't a citizen of any recognized world in the sector.

"Josher was born in Fronidia. Maybe that gives him some protection, but honestly, I do not know."

As it got late, we became hungry, so we had something to eat and decided to rest in case we were faced with problems later in the evening. Without giving it much thought, Kindor suggested Foxor sleep with his spouse, which would mean he would sleep with me. Foxor quickly made it known that this arrangement was inappropriate. Instead, Lasarta and I slept in one bed, Kindor and Foxor in the other, and Josher in his crib. Kindor, Foxor, and I established a watch, with me taking the first one.

The first watch went by uneventfully as well as the second and third. I thanked God that we had survived the night without anyone finding us. The next day was a carbon copy of our first day there, Lasarta praying while I cared for Josher and talked with the men.

The following morning as we discussed our next steps, the front door burst open. Lasarta shrieked, and Foxor, who happened to have Josher in his arms, handed him to her and stood in front of them in a protective stance. Kindor and I immediately grabbed our guns, but we stopped short of shooting as we saw Montor step in, an imposing figure suited in Lostai military uniform and flanked by two other Lostai soldiers.

In less than a second, our weapons flew out of our hands and into Montor's, but Kindor was just as capable in his tele-kinetic abilities and got his back. Montor muttered something under his breath, rolled his eyes impatiently, and pointed my gun at me. He spoke out loud in Lostai to Kindor.

"Drop the gun or she gets disintegrated! Do not test me!"

Kindor's jaw dropped and a look of utter rage swept his face.

"What game is this creature playing?" Kindor said to me telepathically. Montor took a step towards me and pressed the end of the gun against my head. Kindor let his gun fall to the ground. I heard Montor's voice in my mind.

"You two listen carefully. I only have a few seconds to pull this off. Kindor, I am going to place you in the custody of these two Lostai idiots. Can you disarm them, render them uncon-scious, and wipe their memory of the last two days?"

Kindor looked at me as if asking my opinion.

"Trust him, Kindor!" I said telepathically.

"Outside of practicing with my family, I have never done such a thing to anyone, but yes, I can do it easily," answered Kindor.

"Well then, there is a first time for everything," said Montor.

Montor addressed the two Lostai soldiers.

"The Arandan couple has nothing to do with this situation. I am sure they were misled by these two," he said, waving the gun in my and Kindor's direction. "The baby is a valuable asset to the Lostai military and at all costs must remain unharmed. You two soldiers take this Sotkari garbage into custody while I secure the Earthian fugitive and the child."

The soldiers walked over to Kindor, while Montor kept the gun pointed to my head. They handcuffed him and shoved him outside. Lasarta cried, and Foxor shouted angrily to Montor in Arandan, but Montor motioned to him with a finger over his mouth to remain silent. A few minutes went by before I heard Kindor's voice in my mind.

"OK, it is done."

Montor breathed a sigh of relief and told us all to remain inside while he went out to check. In a few seconds, he returned with Kindor no longer in cuffs.

"Is there a reproducer in this room?" asked Montor.

After reproducing several bottles of an alcoholic beverage, we carried the unconscious soldiers to the military transport pod they had traveled in, emptied all but one of the bottles, and threw them around the floor of the pod. Montor set the pod on autopilot, punched in the location codes of a distant Lostai military station, and sent them off.

"How long will they remain unconscious?" asked Montor.

"I put them to sleep until this time tomorrow," answered Kindor.

"How confident are you in being effective in erasing their memories?"

"Extremely," said Kindor.

For the briefest moment, there was a flash of admiration in Montor's eyes before he turned his attention to us. He spoke to us out loud in Lostai, the one language we all understood.

"Colora should be arriving soon in a shuttle craft. We will travel to the Fron Onta space station. On the way there, I have a lot of information to share with all of you. We have serious decisions to make."

28

We left the room carrying the few personal items we had brought with us and walked towards the landing site. Montor put his arm around Lasarta and spoke to her in Arandan using a soothing voice. I asked Foxor what they were talking about.

"He is asking for forgiveness for having upset her. I guess I should ask them both for forgiveness as well. When he had those soldiers cuff Kindor, I told him I was going to put him on my knee and spank him like a child. I also used obscene language that I regret my wife had to hear."

After making his peace with Lasarta, Montor walked next to me and took Josher in his arms. I asked him what happened.

"I arrived home from my trip and found the house empty. When I checked the security recording, I saw Lostai law enforcement trying to get in and surveying the perimeter, so I contacted Colora. She explained what happened. Since I was not sure if they were tracking your movements, I decided some trickery would be best. I contacted Lostai military and told them I had learned the location of an Earthian fugitive, so they sent the two soldiers to help me make the arrest. I asked Colora to be ready to come get us at my call."

When we arrived at the landing site, Colora was already there. We piled in the shuttle and took off. I thanked Colora for her quick thinking and hugged her, disregarding whether it was appropriate or not. She said Earthians were weird but embraced me anyway, easing my nerves and making me laugh. Montor quickly debriefed us on his meeting.

"I need to share with all of you what was discussed at the meeting I attended as it may affect you. I will speak of things here that I only can do with people who I trust with my life and that of my family," he said, nodding at Josher and me.

He made eye contact with each of us before continuing.

"My foster parents and Mina know the truth, but Kindor and Colora, I must now entrust you with a secret I have been keeping for a long time."

He hesitated, rubbing his forehead, the rest of his body rigid. Making eye contact again, he continued.

"In spite of being a Lostai soldier since adolescence, I have, for most of that time, also been involved with the Arandan insurgency that engages in rebellious activities against the Lostai military."

Kindor's eyes widened, astonished.

"He is definitely full of surprises," he communicated to me telepathically.

Colora licked her lips nervously as if trying to anticipate what else Montor had to say.

"The rebels always knew I was an Arandan, but I have worked with them undercover, and they have never seen my face. Because of the information and assets I have shared with them over time, they also inferred that I somehow had access to the Lostai military, making me a valuable partner. In the meeting, I was informed that in the past year, several of the Arandan insurgency's commanding officers were murdered. To my surprise, I learned that our old family friend, Jortan, had been their strategic leader for a long time."

In unison, everyone turned to look at Colora with questioning expressions.

"Yes...of course I knew...a secret we kept even from Montor," she said.

Montor shook his head as if still in disbelief.

"The Arandan insurgency has decided that nothing concrete is being accomplished by random assaults against the Lostai military. They have decided to take a more aggressive stance and start an all-out war against the Lostai to regain control of Aranda. Jortan helped them raise funds, and they have quietly been building a significant fleet of battle crafts and other tactical technology, as well as a militia of over ten million Arandans."

We all looked at each other, thinking through the implications of this news.

"To explain my vast military knowledge, I deceived my Arandan contacts by saying I had fought in The Clan Wars years ago in Aranda. Obviously, I could not tell them I was a Lostai soldier. They believe I am perfectly qualified for military leadership and proposed that I become one of their battalion commanders. This position would require me to lead troops into battle."

As if on cue, Josher began to babble.

"Had they made this request a few weeks ago, I would have readily accepted. I was empty and honestly did not care whether I lived or died. However, now that I have a son and am betrothed to Mina, I have a different outlook. My son needs me, and I do not think it is the right time to take on such a role."

Lasarta and Foxor exchanged a sigh of relief, and I hugged Josher closer to my chest.

"I rejected the request, explaining my situation, and they made a counteroffer. They explained to me that besides the

Arandan faction, there are currently three other groups engaged in rebellious activities against Lostai military rule... the Sotkari, the Rennans, and a relatively primitive people from a planet at the far end of this galaxy who call themselves the Namson. The Arandans are proposing to join forces with these other groups and have one united rebel army. That is why they are calling their movement the United Rebel Front and are asking I represent the Arandans in meetings and negotiations with these other groups. I would be replacing Jortan as Strategic Officer and have an additional role as Liaison."

Kindor asked me telepathically to translate for him, as Foxor and Lasarta could not follow his sign language.

"Kindor points out that this still would put you at considerable risk," I said.

"The fact is that I have always been at risk by being involved with this group, and honestly, what happened today with the Lostai is not over. We have bought some time by sending off those soldiers with their memories wiped, but sooner or later, they will regain their memories, and I will have to answer for what happened. The search for Mina is not over by any means and hiding her makes me guilty of treason. The truth is my time as a Lostai soldier has inevitably come to an end."

The moment he spoke those words, he covered his mouth with his hand and looked down. We were all quiet for a moment.

"Aranda command also spoke to me about something called the Sotkari Transportals. Apparently, the Sotkari elder scientists not only had technology to embed their genes but also to create portals that allow for traveling long distances in space in relatively short time, similar to what the Fronidians have here for their local transportation. The Arandan rebel group discovered that the Lostai found some of these portals and learned to use them. That is how they easily travel to other star systems and even across galaxies to hunt down people with embedded Sotkari genes."

He looked at me when he stated that last bit of information.

"Even I was not aware of this. I think Jortan learned of this through his influence with wealthy executives and crime leaders, many of which apparently have worked with the Lostai military to use these portals for profitable ventures. This knowledge is probably why he was killed."

The mood was getting more and more somber, as Colora's eyes brimmed with tears.

"One of the main goals for the United Rebel Front proposed by the Arandan insurgency is to find and take control of these portals away from the Lostai and learn to use them to send kidnapped people safely back home."

Everyone's eyes were now on me. My breathing became rushed, and I gulped. Montor seemed to be looking through me, and he lost track of his thoughts for a moment.

"Errr...Coordinating this effort with the different factions would also be an important part of my mission if I accept. They want to prioritize sending young children back to their families first. Also, they are looking for any adult Sotkari Ta, embedded or original, who is sympathetic to the cause to join forces with the United Rebel Front."

Montor then made a point to make eye contact with each of us again.

"So...I told the Arandan insurgency leaders that I would reply to them in one day of my decision. My reply is soon due. I am inclined to accept the position they have offered me since Mina, Josher, and I are all fugitives now anyway. I think I can be of great assistance to this worthy cause, but of course, I need Mina to give me her opinion. A spaceship is waiting for me at the Fron Onta space station and would become our new home and mode of escape if I accept. Kindor, Colora, Foxor, and Lasarta, I am concerned that the Lostai will harass you for information regarding our disappearance, but I suppose Kindor, you can quietly go back to your village and stay with your niece...and Foxor, you and Lasarta—"

Kindor shook his head, looked at me and his response was immediate.

"Kindor says if we go, he is coming as well to join this united front and help with its mission."

"Son, you know that where you go, we will follow," said Foxor.

"I am not staying behind to be harassed by Lostai soldiers," added Colora.

"Think about this carefully before you commit to coming with us. We are not talking about a short field trip. I have no idea about the timeframe, and our lives will still be in extreme danger. You will all become fugitives like Mina and me. Even if I only act as a liaison with a strategic role, we still may find ourselves in the midst of a battlefield. Mina and I will speak now in private to make up our minds. Please take this time to consider the implications of your decisions."

I had been wringing my hands while Montor spoke, my heart heavy with guilt.

"I am so sorry," I cried out. "I have put you all in danger...I should have never come here...I should have..."

I couldn't continue because of the knot in my throat. Instead, quiet sobs took over.

"Mina, do not be ridiculous. I, for one, have been in danger ever since my husband decided to become a rebel a long time ago," said Colora.

Montor put his arms around me and gently nudged my head against his chest.

"Mina, the one to blame here is Kindor's friend who exposed you. Even if you had stayed with Kindor's family, it would have been only a matter of time for her to lead Lostai law enforcement to find you there..."

Kindor stood up, his hands on his hips and an angry look on his face.

"She is not my friend, and I would have protected Mina and Josher!" said Kindor telepathically.

Only Montor and I could hear it, but everyone else got the gist of what he might be feeling from his body language. Lasarta stood up and spoke in an assertive tone.

"This is not a time for blame. First, we need to be thankful, as we have survived the day. Secondly, if we are destined to embark on a dangerous mission, I cannot think of a better team to execute it."

A proud, wide smile appeared on Foxor's face as she continued.

"I look forward to do whatever little bit I can to help my people be free from Lostai rule."

Everyone seemed to stand a little taller after Lasarta's words.

"Kindor, after I speak with Montor, I also need some time with you in private," I said while handing Josher over to Lasarta.

Montor's eyebrows furrowed a bit, but he said nothing as we walked to the back of the shuttle. We sat down next to each other, and Montor took my hands in his.

"Mina, I am so sorry you have had to go through all of this, but I am grateful we are together. You heard everything I said about the position I have been asked to fill. Please, share your thoughts regarding our next steps."

"What would be our alternative to joining this rebel initiative?"

"I suppose we could go into hiding in some remote corner of this galaxy. I will still have access to most of my properties and income, and I could find a job, or maybe we can live off the land."

"What about everyone else?"

"Well, I know for sure Foxor and Lasarta would come with us. I do not know about Colora, but would you mind if she decided to join us? Out of respect for Jortan, I feel we shouldn't abandon her."

"Of course, that is fine with me, if she wants to."

"...and Mina, what are your thoughts regarding Kindor?"

"Well, I want to reassure him that he does not need to be our guardian spirit anymore. I am going to be your wife. That is your job now. He should go back to protecting his family."

"Yes, I agree...but..." Montor ran his fingers through his hair as he stopped a moment to think before he finished his sentence. "I cannot believe I am saying this, but having someone with his abilities who cares so much for you and Josher...can come in handy."

"Montor, honestly, I saw your face when you talked about the end of your military career. You would love to be a part of this war against the Lostai, and you are already visualizing Kindor as an ally in this mission."

"Yes, truthfully, all I have ever been is a soldier...it is who I am. In some strange way that we never could have foreseen, the fact that you were taken from your family, that we met and fell in love, had a child...has resulted in my finally having the opportunity and motivation to focus all my efforts to fighting on the right side, the side of my ancestors. It has been a terrible thing what the Lostai put you through, taking you from your Earth family. We should make it count for something."

"We are risking not only our lives and future but that of our son," I reminded him.

"I would like to think that when he is a grown man, we will be able to tell him we took the risk so that he could live free in the land of his ancestors."

My head ached with the pressure of what we were about to decide. I was heading closer and closer to a life so far away from Earth and the family I had left there. Staring at my hands in Montor's, I closed my eyes and prayed for guidance. I prayed for my family on Earth to be OK. I prayed for protection for my young son. When I was done, I squeezed his hands and kissed him on the lips.

"Fate is moving us in a certain direction. Who are we to deviate? Yes, Montor, it feels right that I help in the fight for my son's people. I am in."

"Thank you, Mina...thank you so much. As usual, your courage and loyalty shine," he said with a broad smile. He stroked my cheek with the back of his hand.

"Please go tell Kindor I need to talk to him."

As Montor walked away to send Kindor over to me, I pondered what tact I should use with him. I would miss him if he left, but I was not going to be selfish. Kindor needed to move on. He walked up to me.

"Montor said you needed to discuss something with me."

"Yes, please sit down."

"Mina, I know what you are going to tell me. You are not going to change my mind."

"What? Are you now reading people's minds without permission, too?"

"Very funny...of course not."

I looked into his beautiful eyes; a person could get lost in them.

"Montor and I have decided that he will accept this offer. It is risky, but we are already in trouble with Lostai military and law enforcement. I know Montor will not be able to move to a remote area and hide."

"You mean as I have been hiding all these years."

"No, I did not mean it like that at all. It is different for you. You have been taking care of your family, and you took care of Josher and me. You have been a special person in my life and the life of my son, but I will be marrying Montor soon, and you no longer need to bear the burden of watching over us. That will be his job now."

"So, now Montor has a family, too, and yet he still is ready to put himself and his family in danger to fight for his convictions."

"He has a warrior spirit. He needs a challenge."

"Listen to me carefully, Mina. A priest told my mother that I was destined to be a savior for my people. It is time I live up to the prophecy, but not by procreating pureblood Sotkari Ta babies like my mother thought...that is ridiculous. Pulling you from that shuttle wreckage has led to an opportunity for me to help the cause of my people. I am convinced now that we were fated to meet. I am not staying because I love you. I am staying to try to make a difference and fulfill my destiny."

"Are you sure, Kindor? What about your mother and niece?"

"They are safe with Tadium. Karrina just sent me a transmission. He is going to move to administrate another of his family's plantations far away from the village. He will help to sell our restaurant for a good price so that Mother and Karrina can invest the proceeds however they see fit...I guess in some venture that will keep Mother busy. I will let Mother know what I have decided to do. She will eventually understand. Remember, she comes from a long line of Sotkari warriors... and my father's side of the family were diplomats, so he would have approved of our role as liaisons."

I shook my head and smiled. Ever the responsible and efficient one, he hadn't wasted any time ironing out the details with his family and making sure they were in good hands before he made his decision. I took his hand and kissed it.

"Well, if your mind is made up, it is going to be good having you around. Josher will be happy and so will I, and...Montor will never admit it, but I think, in a strange way, he will, too."

29

Once Montor, Kindor, and I informed the others of our decision, they did not think twice to confirm they were coming with us. Our next hurdle would be to arrive at the Fron Onta space station, board the spaceship, and take off without any intervention from Lostai military. As we discussed worst-case scenarios and how to address them, Montor received an audio transmission from Rewarlt, Zorla's replacement. Montor took the call on an open shuttle receiver so we could all hear.

"Montor, what happened with the Earthian fugitive? Did you find her?"

"Yes, we apprehended her."

"And when will you bring her back to Xixsted...where are you?"

"I am holding her for interrogation. I have a special interest in this case. This lowly Earthian was under my command when she escaped. I want to know everything about the people who assaulted me and helped her get away. I will need some time to get the information from her...then I will discipline her in my special way."

I made an exaggerated gesture of mock fear, and Montor rolled his eyes at me. I covered my mouth to not burst out laughing.

"Say no more...I have heard about your methods with the females, and I would rather not hear any details. Just make sure you do not permanently damage her for breeding. By the way, did you find the child? We were told she had an Arandan baby, which, based on what Zorla explained to me, I assume is the result of your task to impregnate her."

Montor clenched his fist and breathed deeply.

"I was not aware of the existence of the child. It was not with her. Now, with more reason, I need to conduct an in-depth questioning."

"OK, but I want her here as soon as possible. Keep me apprised of your progress. Be aware that Fronidian law enforcement will protect her, so you need to conduct your matters covertly."

"Yes, I know. That is why I decided to take care of the matter alone to avoid attracting the attention of the local authorities."

"Are the other two soldiers with you?"

"No. I sent them to their previous duties."

"I see...very well...I expect an update in one day."

"Yes."

Montor slammed his fist on the control to end the transmission and muttered under his breath, "Filthy Lostai scum."

He explained that our spaceship was state-of-the-art. Although complete with the latest weapon, shields, sensor, and communications technology, it was not a war ship and would not attract the attention of military forces. This was the kind of spacecraft a wealthy businessperson might use to take the family on a vacation trip across the galaxy. Montor purchased it under an alias on credit, which he would subsequently pay off with the sale of his estate in Renna One. This news tugged at my heartstrings because I knew how much he loved that property.

Montor was irritable the rest of the ride, but he made sure to discuss how we would approach boarding the spaceship. Although we did not expect Lostai military presence at the space station, we planned that Montor and I would walk separately from the rest of the group. If we were intercepted by the Lostai, he could simply state he was taking me into custody. Once the Lostai were out of sight, the others could board the ship.

The Fron Onta space station was one of the largest in the area, providing docking for several thousand different types of spacecraft, transport pods, and shuttles large and small and for different purposes. Luckily, there were no Lostai in sight. Montor took care of the administrative work, and soon, we boarded the craft. Before Montor set off the launching sequence, Lasarta called us together on the bridge. She had us all hold hands and said a prayer in Arandan. Compelled to do the same, I requested everyone get on their knees and clasp their hands while I prayed in English. I translated to Lostai and asked them to repeat the "Amen" at the end.

"Thank you for protecting us today and for hearing our prayers. We ask that you bless our travels and our mission. Keep each and every one of us out of harm's way. Help us help each other. Amen."

Montor had told me once before that he was not a believer, but he went along with us, anyway. After the prayers and completing takeoff, he gave us a tour of the vessel and showed us to our living quarters. As I organized the few items I had brought with me, Montor sat on the bed with Josher on his lap. He spoke to him in Arandan in a soft, sad voice. I sat next to them and stroked Montor's cheek.

"What are you telling him?" I asked.

"Oh, nothing..." Montor answered.

"Come on, I know it is something."

"I was telling him that I am sorry he will not be enjoying the room we set up for him in Fronidia, but I will get him a few toys as soon as I can."

"Do not worry about that. What he lacks in toys, he makes up in people who love and protect him. We will find plenty of ways to teach him new things and keep him entertained."

"Yes, I suppose that is true."

Montor took a deep breath, handed Josher to me, and stood.

"Mina, I want you to know I have started the process to put my financial affairs in order so that you and Josher are protected in case something happens to me," he said while pacing the room.

I didn't like his ominous suggestion and shook my head.

"Do not say such things. Nothing is going to happen…"

He stopped pacing and looked me straight in the eyes.

"Let me finish. I want you to know the Lostai will not be able to seize my assets, and we will have a continuous stream of income. I will keep one property, a small home in the Arandan neighborhood in Fronidia where I took you for dinner. Eventually, when all the Lostai are forced to leave Fronidia, it will be the safest place for you."

"Come. Sit down, please."

He returned to sit next to me. I ran my fingers through his hair and kissed his cheek.

"Thank you for worrying about our future, but I am sure we are going to be stuck with you for a long while."

He smiled at my joke and tilted his head, kissing me on the lips.

"I hardly can wait until we have some time in bed, my sweetness…hmmm…but now duty calls."

He announced over the communication system that we would all meet in the dining area where he would inform us of our next stop. On our way over there, he received his first transmission from Arandan insurgency command. He took the call in his captain's private office, and we assembled in the dining area. I handed Josher to Colora as Lasarta and I used the food reproducer to put together a meal for the group. Montor joined us after his call. We engaged in small talk and jokes as we ate. Montor praised Lasarta and me for making the reproduced food edible. It was a complaint disguised as a compliment, and he was grumpy. As we finished our meal, we waited in expectation for Montor's news. He stood before us, shoulders back, chin up, for the first time as our leader.

"Inspired by our strategy of different groups working together, I have decided to name our spacecraft the *Barinta,* which means 'collaboration' in Arandan. We are heading to Aranda, to the rebel command center located on the remote island of Penstarox, where we will pick up three more passengers. They are two of the three Earthians who were held on Xixsted at the same time that Mina was there, and the third is a female Arandan who will be the closest thing we will have to a medical officer."

"What happened to the third Earthian?" I asked.

As he answered, I thought about the female Arandan medic he mentioned. Would she be unpleasant like Ar Ona or kind and wise like Lasarta?

"The group of three was an elderly male, a young male and a female child. They never made it to Fronidia as the team that freed them from Xixsted ran into trouble with Lostai military and had to retreat to Aranda. The elderly male became ill, and the Arandan medical team was not familiar enough with his physiology to be able to treat him. He has died, and the female child has fallen into a depressive state. She grew close to him as he reminded her of a beloved grandparent. Eventually, if we are able to find and take control of a transportal, she will be one of the first candidates for return to Earth. Mina, I suggested that perhaps, in the meantime, you might be able to help the young girl."

"Of course," I said in a quiet voice.

The news of a possible pathway to Earth and a human child under my care left my stomach knotted up.

"One more thing..."

I detected irritation in Montor's voice, his words clipped. He rubbed the back of his neck as he paced around.

"Just to let you know, as there is no going back to my old life, I confessed to Arandan rebel command that I was a Lostai soldier all along. I explained everything to both the High General and the Commander of Operations. It was only fair to let them know that Lostai military would soon be searching for Mina and me. This is all I have to inform for now. Are there any questions?"

No one had anything else to add. In fact, it was all too solemn. We all knew it must have been difficult for Montor to admit to the Arandan rebel leaders that he had been a Lostai soldier. No wonder he was so cranky.

"OK, our trip to Aranda should take one day, and I expect that we are not being pursued by Lostai military yet, so it should be a smooth trip. You all need some time to relax, digest all that has happened in the last few days, and get your minds set for what is to come. We will divide the night shift in two four-hour watches. I will take the first night watch shift, and Mina will take the second. Thanks so much for your attention."

We all said good night to each other, and I remained alone with Josher and Montor. He sat with his arms hanging from the armrests, bent over, staring at the floor, as if energy had been sucked out of him, a complete opposite of the confident stance he had shown while addressing the group.

"Well, sweetness, I guess I will see you later. Get some rest as you will be relieving me later this evening."

"Yes, I heard."

He straightened his posture and cocked an eyebrow.

"Do you have a problem with that? I chose us first because besides Foxor, you and I are the only ones with formal military training."

I knew he felt the weight of the world on his shoulders, now responsible for our crew and leading the strategy of the United Rebel Front.

"No, of course not. But I will miss giving you a squeeze in our new bed," I said, caressing his cheek.

His mood shifted, and with a mischievous smile, he glanced at his tablet.

"Hmm...my night watch does not officially start for two hours. Let us put Josher to sleep and get some alone time."

Back in our room, I nursed Josher, changed, and rocked him until he was sleeping soundly. As soon as I placed him in his crib, Montor took me in his arms and kissed me with urgency, bruising my lips. He led me to bed and, once we were lying down, continued his sensuous assault. After discarding my clothing with ease, his mouth and hands waged war against my skin, claiming more and more of my body as I surrendered. Soon, our bodies joined, hips locked, separating and reuniting in perfect cadence. He was determined to fully use the time we had, savoring every thrust with relish.

"Shhhhh," he said, as I couldn't stifle my moans.

I pressed my face against his chest and bit hard.

"Go ahead and devour me, sweetness...I like it," he said in the deepest bass tone.

His name escaped my lips as my body clenched in climax. We rolled on our sides, still joined until our heartbeats returned to normal. He kissed my forehead delicately, a stark opposite of how he had earlier.

"Mina, what do you think of us being married on Penstarox?"

"I feel I should defer to you regarding the details of our marriage. I mean, after all, this is your first."

His brow furrowed. I had said the wrong thing.

"My first? What are you talking about, Mina?" he asked.

"Well, you told me you have never been married before."

"This would not be my first marriage, Mina. It will be my only marriage. I am clear on this. Are you not?"

I stroked his chest gently to pacify him, at the same time remembering how I also once never imagined being married to someone other than Josh.

"Of course, I am clear...but again, this is your one and only marriage, and we are in your part of the universe. I am not familiar with your customs, and I want it to be perfect for you. If you are happy to marry on Penstarox, then so am I."

"I suppose it will not be so special for you, since you have been through this before," he said.

I cuddled up to him, hooking my legs with his and nesting my head against his chest.

"Actually, I never had a real wedding. Josh and I had a quick civil marriage, so this will be special and exciting for me, too. I look forward to learning your traditions, Montor. I want to be a perfect bride for you."

He pulled me closer so there was no space between us.

"You will be. I kept the white dress you wore that evening on Renna One."

"You did?"

"Yes, and when I learned from Colora that you all had to leave and hide, I knew it was likely we would have to leave Fronidia in a rush. I made quick arrangements to purchase this craft, and I was able to have the dress sent over. You see...I kept my promise. You will be my bride in that dress."

Sudden tears rolled down my cheeks.

"Oh," I said in a tremulous voice.

"What?" Montor asked, his expression a mix of curiosity and concern.

"I cannot believe you made a point to keep the dress...and while figuring out how to rescue us, you remembered to bring it along...that was so romantic and sweet."

I wiped my sniffles and kissed his chest.

He smiled and rolled his eyes, pretending like I was making a big deal over nothing.

"Well, I try to keep my promises."

"I hope I still fit in it after the pregnancy."

"I do not mind if it is a little tight, so everyone can see your sexy curves."

He slid his hands down my back and over my hips. We kissed, and he groaned.

"Mina, unfortunately, it is time for my watch. I am ready to have you again, but we will have to wait."

He got out of bed, and I enjoyed watching him get dressed. As he left, I walked to Josher's crib, leaning over to observe him sleeping, a peaceful smile on his adorable face. I smiled, too. Despite everything I had been through, the family I had lost, fate was giving me a second chance at happiness.

THE END of Book One

Book Two now available. Find it here:
https://mybook.to/BrokenBondsTCOST

Mina, Montor, and Kindor become key players in the rebellion against the Lostai Empire. Will these new challenges bring them closer, or break the bonds that unite them?

A NOTE FROM THE AUTHOR

Thank you for reading *The Curse of Sotkari Ta*. Please consider taking a moment to write a review on BookBub, Goodreads, and your favorite online bookstore. This means a lot to self-published authors such as me. I hope you enjoyed the first book in the series and will continue on to read the rest of the trilogy.

I would love to connect.
Find all my website, book, and social media links at the following site:
https://direct.me/mariaaperezauthor

ACKNOWLEDGMENTS

This book represents a milestone in my life that has been long in the making. First and foremost, I am thankful that God has given me the opportunity to achieve my dream of becoming a published author. Next, I need to recognize the many people who helped me take the stories in my head and share them with readers.

Big hugs of gratitude to my husband, who supported me when I decided to take an early retirement, giving me the time and space to devote to my writing. He works hard so I can stay at home and follow my dream. He's always steadfast by my side. I love you, honey!

My sons were patient when I demanded the TV be turned down and understanding of my other quirks during all the days, weeks, months, and, yes, years that I've devoted to this series. They also offered objective opinions on the cover art and back cover blurb. My love for you is beyond all galaxies and star systems.

My friend, Joanna, is a space opera fan, just like me. Yet, I was a bit hesitant when I approached her about reading an early draft of my manuscript. I'm so thankful she accepted. In addition to being my very first alpha reader, she has been a great cheerleader and advisor along the way. I am very grateful to my sisters, Sylvia and Wilma, and my best friend, TP, who also alpha read my book. Their different perspectives helped me mold the early versions of my story into something beta readers could work with. I can't thank them enough for the motivation they offered along the way. Thanks also to my beta readers, Alex at **https://bit.ly/3g4j7nP** and Gail (@gail-doeswords), for their valuable feedback, helping me flesh out my characters and inspiring me to make the story better. Thank you to my nieces, Alondra, for helping me proofread, and Erika, for her input on the cover and back cover blurb. You're both awesome. Many thanks to my ARC readers, especially Kelley, who was exceptionally thorough and expeditious.

I am deeply thankful to my editor, Stephanie Hoogstad, for her beta reading, her excellent editorial guidance and for taking the time to review other pieces of the puzzle. I couldn't have done this without her.

Thank you to my cover designer, Christian Bentulan. You patiently held my hand each step of the way and brought my main character and theme to life.

I must give a shout-out to my #WritingCommunity and #vss365 tweeps for welcoming me into their Twitter groups and for their advice and encouragement. A very special thanks to Migs (@OminousHallways), who wrote the beautiful introductory poem and gave me input on the cover artwork. He earned my trust early on, and I consider him a friend.

I am lucky to have been blessed with two sets of parents: my biological parents and my aunt and uncle. I am grateful for their love and for teaching me the meaning of family, hard work, perseverance and generosity.

Last, but not least, I thank the readers, current and future. I hope you enjoy my stories for many years to come.

AUTHOR'S BIO

Maria A. Perez was born in Yonkers, NY, and grew up in New York City. She also lived in Puerto Rico and now resides in Boca Raton, Florida. She holds a Bachelor's in Business and has spent a successful career in Corporate America working in Accounting and Finance. Early retirement has allowed Maria to focus on her dream of writing and becoming a published author. She is married with two young adult sons and a labradoodle daughter. Maria enjoys reading all genres, although she's partial to dystopian, space opera and romance series such as *The Hunger Games*, *The Expanse* and *Outlander*. A diehard "Trekkie" and *Star Wars* fan, she is fascinated with the possibility of what is out there in unexplored space and the potential of the human race.

www.ingramcontent.com/pod-product-compliance
Lightning Source LLC
Chambersburg PA
CBHW020919110726
47900CB00001B/214